# NOT THEIR DAUGHTER

## BOOKS BY LAURA ELLIOT

*Fragile Lies*

*Stolen Child*

*The Prodigal Sister*

*The Betrayal*

*Sleep Sister*

*Guilty*

*The Wife Before Me*

*The Thorn Girl*

*The Silent House*

*After the Wedding*

*The Marriage Retreat*

LAURA ELLIOT

# NOT THEIR DAUGHTER

bookouture

Published by Bookouture in 2024

An imprint of Storyfire Ltd.
Carmelite House
50 Victoria Embankment
London EC4Y 0DZ

www.bookouture.com



Paperback ISBN: 978-1-83525-996-2
eBook ISBN: 978-1-83525-995-5

*This book is dedicated to the memory of a dear friend. To Geraldine Rogerson, whose hospitality was renowned, as was her love of music and song. Thank you, Ger, for the summers and the Christmases past, and all the hoolies in between.*

# PART 1

# ONE

## GABRIELLE

'I stole you.'

My father's voice is barely audible. He's dying, slipping away from us on a cloud of morphine. His eyes open. They should be dulled and uncomprehending, not fixed on me with such blue, glistening clarity.

I grasp his hand and will him to speak again. To say it properly this time... *I love you...* but his gaze is already dimming, his eyelids sinking.

*I stole you.* Are those to be his last words to me? His fingers twitch as if he appreciates my distress but has gone beyond such worldly considerations. He's managed until now to hold it together, despite the pain and the loss of dignity that morphine tries to control. He was lost to its effects in the end. How else am I to understand what he just said?

How long have I been sitting by his bedside? Fifteen, sixteen hours? Time has become irrelevant. One hour is the same as the next until, suddenly it's not, and with one last shuddering breath he's gone from us.

His suffering has come to an end. This knowledge brings a certain relief but I'm aware that it will be a short-lived reprieve.

A hole has opened in my world, and it will take time before I can appreciate the depths of my loss.

My mother nursed him at home. A palliative care bed was moved into the living room, along with the necessary hospice aids, yet he was still surrounded by everything that was familiar to him. Now, Cassie's face is taut with grief. Ramrod-straight in the chair beside his bed, she lays her hand on his forehead then pulls it back to cover her mouth. She seems uncertain as to how she should react in these first moments as his widow.

Free from pain, the muscles on his face are already relaxing. We nod in agreement when she says he looks peaceful. His struggle is over. Ours is just beginning.

My sisters weep and hug each other. Twins and inseparable, Jessica and Susanne are grieving because he did not hang around long enough to meet his first grandchildren. One more month, that was all they asked from him. But Dominick Grace cut corners, as he always did, when the odds were stacked against him.

*I stole you... I love you...* of course he was muddled. He'd even mixed up my sisters' names, something he never did, even when they were new-born, so wizened and ugly that even Cassie had difficulty telling them apart. The ugliness slipped easily from them, as did the wrinkles, but even when they became beauties, they remained identical yet identifiable to him.

I hold his hand. No longer twitching, it's still warm and soft.

I left home when I was eighteen. He begged me to stay but, back then, my father's love was not enough to keep me in Ireland. I exchanged the fuchsia hedgerows of Trabawn for the shaded avenues of New York and never looked back. I came home to celebrate Christmas and his birthdays. The previous year I'd flown back for the twins' double wedding. I'd watched him walk them up the aisle, one on each arm, his face flushed with pride and, probably, some embarrassment. He was a private man, and at his most relaxed when he was out on the Atlantic trawling for fish. But he coped on that occasion and his father-of-the bride speech, though short, rang with sincerity.

He loved us all equally, but I was his favourite. My mother told me this often enough, a statement with a punch. It used to bother me that it bothered Cassie so much but in New York, free from her resentment and antagonism, it was easy to forget that she was the reason I decided to leave.

She looks at me now, and I see it again. That flash in her eyes, a spark flamed by what? I'm reminded of a bird, brittle and broken, its wings clipped. I used to believe I had the most beautiful mother in Trabawn. I have childhood memories of her wide smile and the swing of her dark brown hair. Before I left for New York, only the remnants of that beauty remained, and her skin had developed the reddened sheen of a heavy drinker. After my departure, she entered rehab and has remained sober on and off since then. Does she have the strength to carry us through this awful time?

She seems shattered as she moves away from him and breaks the chain we'd formed around his deathbed. Her steps falter as she walks backwards and Jessica, probably fearing she would fall, catches her in the breadth of her arms. My sister turns her around and nestles her face into her shoulder. Cassie's muffled sobs are audible and gut-wrenching. I want to be able to hold her as effortlessly as Jessica does. If I do so, she will stiffen against me and pull away with a feigned, awkward sigh, as she did when I arrived home in time to watch my father die. Not that I have any desire to embrace her. Her drinking drove me away. It deprived me of the years I could have spent with him... but this is not the time for bitterness. I made my own decisions, and a new life for myself in New York. One as far removed from gutting fish on Dad's beloved boat, the *Sheila Rua,* as it is possible to be.

Susanne stands and presses her palms against her spine.

The arch of her back emphasises her stomach. She and Jessica are both expecting boys. How could it be otherwise? Who will go first? Or will they labour together? Even their husbands, waiting at a discreet distance by the window, look alike – sturdy-framed and square-jawed, with thick, curly hair. Eddie is blond, and Nicholas's rust-red shade reminds me of sandstone. These distinctive features help me to separate the twins into individual units for the first time since they were born.

I remain where I am by his side as Susanne joins Jessica in the mother hug. I envy their relationship with Cassie with its uncomplicated loving. Even on her worst days, they calmed her down and placated her with well-worn platitudes that eventually brought her back to us. They hated her outbursts but never feared them.

I had to leave that smouldering atmosphere to understand that they knew her rages had nothing to do with them and everything to do with me. I didn't come to this conclusion in a blinding flash. Three years of therapy bubbled it to the surface and, by then, I was ready to handle it.

*I stole you.* His voice is an echo in my head. I imagine his mind drifting towards oblivion, aided by the relief that morphine would have given him from pain. That's what confused him during those final moments. Muddled words... *I stole you* when he meant to say... *I love you.* Three simple words that he'd said to me so often. Did the others hear? My sisters' attention is on Cassie, their concern obvious as they comfort her. They are grieving, not shocked, as they would be if they believed he'd made such a crazed admission.

Freida, the hospice nurse, gives a discreet cough. I understand the language of coughs. It's time to allow her to take over. I nod to Freida in acknowledgement of the procedures she needs to follow and move away from my father's side. When I see him again, he will be stiff and remote, his hardened lips casting an unfamiliar sternness to his mouth.

'Go on downstairs.' The nurse speaks softly to us. 'I need some time alone with Dominick.'

The twins and my mother separate. Cassie nods and leads us from the living room to the kitchen.

Earlier in the evening, Noreen Ferguson, our nearest neighbour, called with a platter of sandwiches and home-baked scones. They are on the kitchen table, sealed with cling film. My father's death was anticipated. Word will already be spreading through the community that he has passed away. More food will arrive tomorrow for his wake, quietly delivered by our neighbours, whose urge to feed the grieving and stock their larders with plenty never changes.

The urge to ring Lucas is growing. It has the persistence of a wound that appears to have healed until the scab breaks open once again. Such a picked-over scab. Why can't I leave it alone? Seven months should be long enough for healing to begin but the need to seek comfort overrides the limits time imposes. I'm not going to think about him. He's not worthy of my pain and yet... and yet... I yearn for the closeness we once shared, the sense of being indivisible, like Susanne, who is showing a text to Eddie, their heads together, his arm across her shoulder. He's more demonstrative than Nicholas but even he is standing beside Jessica and piling sandwiches on a plate for her.

'Eating for two,' he says, when he catches me staring. Nicholas speaks with pride, his eyes darting to her stomach, which Jessica cradles constantly. Irritating but understandable. I guess I'd do the same if my stomach had developed such drum-like proportions. Mine is flat and hard from gym workouts and the runs that bring me down to earth after my early morning radio show.

Freida leaves, refusing tea and food. She has children waiting for her and bedtime stories to tell them.

My father asked Cassie to hold his wake at Headwind, our family home. No funeral parlour or chemical fillers, he said.

Freida has made him ready to be seen by the neighbours and friends who will come to our house to bid him goodbye. On the morning following his wake, his coffin will be carried to the church on the shoulders of the fishermen who crewed his trawler and treated him as one of their own.

I walk with Freida to her car. We were in the same class in primary school but lost touch when she was sent to boarding school and I attended the local secondary. I remember her kindness from those younger days. Now, it is overlaid with a soothing professionalism that holds families upright when death comes calling.

'Thank you for everything you did for my father,' I say. 'Cassie told me she would have been lost without you.'

'It was my privilege to look after Dominick,' she replies. 'He was a lovely man and such a vital part of our community. I'm so sorry for your loss.'

'I wish I'd had more time with him, Freida. His condition deteriorated so quickly in the end.'

She draws back a little. It's dark outside and her face is a pale orb, featureless, yet I sense her surprise.

'Not that quickly,' she says. 'He lasted a little longer than the six months he was given.'

'*Six* months? I thought...' The front door opens, interrupting me, and spilling light across the driveway.

The twins are departing with their husbands and Cassie, in the centre of the group, is being hugged by everyone. Their voices reach us as they assure her that they will be with her first thing in the morning.

'I'd better move my car or they won't be able to leave.' Freida presses her key fob and opens the door. 'At least you made it, Gaby,' she says. 'He was holding out until he could say goodbye to you.'

I wait until the cars have disappeared into the night before returning to the house. In the kitchen, my mother is rinsing dishes and stacking them on the draining board. The dishwasher is used sparingly. It's a waste of electricity, she believes, when she has the hands that God gave her to wash a few cups.

Have we ever been together in Headwind without the twins or my father to distract us? My anger hums too loudly for me to feel sympathy for her loss. She gave no indication that his illness was terminal when she phoned me in New York to tell me he had cancer. His prostate, she said, but it was curable. The outlook was positive.

'Explain something to me.' I pick up a dishtowel and begin to dry the dishes. 'Freida just told me that the oncologist gave Dad six months to live.' I try to control my emotions, for, surely, she has a rational explanation. 'That's not what you told me when you rang and said he was ill.'

She stiffens at my tone and turns around, a dripping cup clutched in her hand. 'I said his prognosis was uncertain—'

'No, you *didn't*. You specifically said he was expected to survive.'

I remember every word of our conversation. How she insisted that there was no need for me to come home. My sudden arrival would only alarm him. The twins could help her to manage his illness if things became 'difficult,' not that she expected that to happen. His sixtieth birthday would be the appropriate time for me to see him.

He'd visited me unexpectedly in New York shortly before her phone call and made no mention of feeling unwell. Surely, he would have told me if he'd received such a deadly prognosis. We'd spent three busy days together and the image of him striding through New York was the one that stayed with me in the weeks following Cassie's disturbing phone call.

'Are you accusing me of lying to you?' Her voice rises a fraction.

'No... I—'

'I *didn't* lie, Gabrielle. I did what your father asked me to do.'

'And what was that, may I ask?' My question twangs with tension.

'Not to worry you. Your career was going so well. He didn't want you taking time off to nurse him. He knew that's what you'd do, and he was looking out for your interests.'

What she says makes sense, but I know how sincerely she can lie. Right now, the atmosphere between us is too raw for confrontation.

'Take care of Cassie when I'm gone,' he said to me in one of his moments of lucidity when she was out of the room. 'She's fragile and just about able to hold herself together. That will change when I'm no longer there to care for her. She needs *your* love...' His voice trailed away, as if the energy needed to ponder an imponderable problem was beyond him.

'I'll give her all the support she needs.' That was all I could promise this shrunken man, who was no longer recognisable as my strong-willed father with his sturdy shoulders and muscular chest.

'I would have come home sooner if I'd known how serious his illness had become.' My comment isn't meant to sound like an accusation, yet it hangs there between us.

'I did what your father asked... *as always*,' she replies.

I ignore the emphasis and rub a side plate until it shines.

'What could you have done, Gabrielle?' She takes the plate from me and flings it back into the water.

'Spent more time with him,' I reply.

'He wouldn't have had the energy for you. I was told by his oncologist that he was to avoid stressful situations.'

The unfairness of her comment rushes tears to my eyes. 'If anyone created stress...' I stop myself, aware that she is on the defensive because she knows I'm right. 'He wasn't remotely stressed when he visited me in New York. We'd a wonderful time together.'

'That visit shortened his life.' The accusation adds to the high wire pressure between us. 'I begged him not to go but he believed you were beside yourself after that man walked out on you.'

'His name is Lucas... *and* he didn't walk out on me. We came to a mutual agreement to separate.'

'If you say so.' She folds the tea towel and hangs it neatly from a rail. 'I'm going to say goodnight to my husband,' she says. 'Tomorrow, he'll belong to everyone. I need time alone with him tonight.'

She doesn't sound annoyed now, just exhausted, which is hardly surprising considering how little sleep she's had over the past few nights.

When the living room door closes behind her, I climb the stairs and enter the bedroom of my childhood. I thought one of the twins would have taken it over when I left for New York, but they shared the same bedroom until they married. My room has a musty smell, as if it's seldom aired and never used. The entire house, apart from this room, was painted before their weddings, and the pane of glass above my door is splattered with paint drops from the landing ceiling. Posters on the walls – Arcade Fire, Mumford and Sons, Florence and the Machine – speak of an arrested development. I approve my teenage preferences and still listen to their albums.

In bed, I burrow into a pillow but I'm unable to sleep. Why did Cassie lie to me...? But did Dad not do the same when he turned up unexpectedly at my apartment five months ago, armed with the knowledge that his life was measured in months.

*I stole you... I love you... I stole you... He meant it... No, he didn't.* Morphine talking... but that last look he gave me just before he died – so clear, so filled with conviction – like something weighty had finally been laid aside. What exactly was he trying to tell me... and how am I ever going to find out?

# TWO

Neighbours arrive in the late afternoon to pay their respects to my father. Over the following hours, they cram the kitchen, the front room and the conservatory at the side of Headwind. Whiskey and Guinness are poured, along with countless cups of tea. Will Cassie cope? She seems composed, sipping occasionally from a glass of sparkling water with a slice of lime, and ice. Susanne warned me not to leave out the lime and only use three ice cubes. Do these little rituals keep the longing at bay? My sisters don't seem worried about her. They are texting friends, who are driving from Dingle and even from as far as Tralee, laden with condolences and bottles of wine.

I have no friends to text. Like me, they have scattered. Australia, Canada and London have claimed them. Muriel, mother of two, and the only one to remain in Trabawn, has developed preeclampsia on her third pregnancy and is under supervision at University Hospital Kerry.

'So sorry, pet.' Noreen Ferguson arrives with two of her grandsons. 'Dominick was such a gentleman. Always ready with a kind word. His suffering is over at last and now he's at peace in the arms of the Lord.' She speaks with the same absolute conviction as everyone else who has made a similar comment. 'So, how are you doing, Gaby?' She stands back to survey me. 'You look amazing. I didn't think you could get any skinnier but there you go. Wish I had your metabolism.' Her midriff wobbles alarmingly when she slaps it. A mother of five boys, and ten grandchildren, her weight gives her the buoyancy to cope, she says. She laughs before turning to Susanne and laying her hands on my sister's stomach.

No boundaries – Noreen was always thus, and nothing has changed there. But here in Headwind, will anything ever be the same again?

'Well, guess who's after arriving.' She moves a step closer and lowers her voice to a conspiratorial whisper. 'Don't look around but it's Killian Osmond.'

I resist the urge to turn my head. In doing so, I'm giving way to her belief that his arrival is important to me.

'He must have driven down from Dublin to pay his respects,' she continues. 'He was right fond of your da. And you, too, Gaby. Poor lad. He was wild for a while after you left him with a broken heart. I thought there'd be a reason for me to buy a new fascinator with lots of feathers, but you hightailed it to New York instead.'

There is an edge to her teasing that adds to my discomfort. I need an excuse to walk away from her. Jessica provides it when she enters the room with a platter of sandwiches. 'Excuse me, Noreen.' I pat her arm and step away from her scrutiny. 'I'm needed in the kitchen.'

At last, I have a chance to glimpse the man whose heart I've been accused of breaking. He stands with his side to me, and, from this vantage point, he appears to be in remarkably good shape. He's talking to Cassie, holding both her hands, and she, as if aware that I'm watching, says something that makes him turn. Unable to look away in time, I'm caught staring.

He crosses the room without hesitation and hugs me. 'This

is such a shock, Gaby,' he says. 'I can't believe he went so quickly in the end.'

'It's still unreal.' I hold him closely, aware but uncaring that Noreen, and probably others, are watching us. 'Thank you for coming.'

'I'm glad you arrived home in time to say goodbye to him,' he says.

'I was lucky with flights.' We move away from each other. If he feels as awkward as I do, he's not showing it. But then, he never did. It's ten years since I broke off our engagement without explanation, or, at least, a reason he could understand, and he's refused to hold a grudge. His friendliness when we met again on my first visit home from New York steered us into a new relationship. One that was platonic and safe from misunderstandings. Occasionally, we meet in Dublin when I'm returning to New York. We enjoy a meal together and catch up on gossip about mutual friends and neighbours from Trabawn.

'I've paid my respects to Dominick,' he says. 'He looks so—'

'Please don't tell me he looks at peace,' I whisper, before he can finish the sentence.

'Okay, then.' He smiles and tilts his head sideways. 'Let me just say that he looks as though he's reached a safe harbour.'

'He was fond of you, Killian. Proud, too.'

'That's nice to hear. I'd no idea he was so ill. I drove down this morning when my mother rang with the news.'

'I'm glad you're here.'

'It's the least I could do. He gave me my first job. You could say that, indirectly, he kick-started my career in journalism.'

He's right. Dad put money in Killian's pocket throughout his teens. He taught him to read the sky and smell danger in the wind. We worked together on the *Sheila Rua* from the age of thirteen; cleaning jobs, at first, when the trawler was anchored. As we grew older, he took us out with him on short fishing trips and eventually made us part of the crew during our school holidays. We battled seasickness together and learned to brace ourselves against the swell of the ocean.

After we'd returned to shore one time, bedraggled from a storm that blew up with such sudden ferocity that it took my father unawares, Killian wrote his first newspaper feature. He described the struggle with the waves and how it seemed as if the Atlantic was making space for us. Such excitement when it was published in *Bayview Dispatch*, a daily newspaper where he was later to work.

'I remember that article,' I say. 'Cassie framed it. It's still hanging in the hallway.'

'I noticed it on the way in, which was gratifying,' he nods. 'Not that I'm ever likely to forget that experience.' He grimaces at the memory. 'We've both moved on a bit since then. Congratulations on building up your radio listenership. You've really nailed it.'

'I didn't realise you listen to me.' I'm flattered and rather surprised that he accesses NY Eyz.

Eyes on New York for twenty-four hours—that's what the broadcast channel offers. The thought of him listening to *Gaby's Good Morning Wake-up* is oddly satisfying.

'I catch up with you on playback when I go to bed,' he says. 'How are you managing that early morning slot?'

'With difficulty,' I admit. 'But I've adjusted. After all, I live in the city that never sleeps and, like you said, my listenership is growing. Does it not disturb Shauna's beauty sleep when you listen to me?'

I'm furious with myself for asking the question. He laughs and shrugs in a way that suggests he and his partner have it all worked out. 'Shauna brings her laptop to bed with her. There's always another press release that needs tweaking, so she's quite happy once I have my earphones on.'

He paints a picture with those words. Pillows piled behind them, a ruffled duvet, her documents scattered over it as she taps on her keyboard, and he, earbuds in place, half listening to me and my argumentative callers before he silences us and turns into her arms. I blink the image away and accept his comment that *Gaby's Good Morning Wake-up* gives him a perspective on life in New York as a compliment.

Two of Noreen Ferguson's sons arrive and cut short our conversation. They descend on us, boisterously slapping Killian's shoulder and bear-hugging me. I take the opportunity to slip away and check on Cassie.

She has a faraway look on her face. I recognise that expression. The longing for a drink is understandable when everyone around her, apart from the twins and a few non-drinkers, are lifting a glass of something alcoholic to their lips. In true traditional form, my father's wake has turned into a party. It's exactly what he would have wanted. His fiddle hangs in its usual place by the side of the hearth. He should be in the middle of this gathering, tuning up, tapping his foot and winking across at me. Instead, tomorrow he will be in the ground. The thought is unbearable.

The twins are the centre of attention, as they always are. Everyone loves them. It's impossible not to do so. I'm sorry I missed the last ten years of their flowering into womanhood. Did they miss me? I know the answer. Headwind was calmer after I left. Jessica made this comment once. No malice intended. It was simply a statement of fact. I don't doubt my mother's love for me, but it is a thorny, knotted emotion that neither of us have been able to untangle.

Finally, we are alone again. Cassie looks alarmingly fragile as we face each other in the quiet kitchen. We gather up the glasses and, on this occasion, she stacks the dishwasher.

'Dad would have loved his send-off.' I rinse out glasses before handing them to her.

She shrugs and doesn't reply.

'Did you hear what he said to me just before he died?' I ask her.

'It was difficult to understand him in his final hours, so, no, I didn't hear him.' The atmosphere is static, as if our breath has chilled on the lies that she's told.

'I heard him. He said he stole me.'

'*Stole* you?' She throws her head back and laughs. 'Don't be ridiculous, Gabrielle. Why on earth would he say something so daft?'

'I've no idea,' I reply. 'But he spoke with such feeling.'

'That's because he was telling you he loved you. You either misheard him or his mind was too confused to know what he was saying.'

'I guess…' My voice trails away. Her explanation makes sense. To think otherwise… what would that imply?

'What do you mean, you *guess*?' she snaps. 'Are you suggesting your father was a thief?' She is flushed and frowning, hardly able to contain her anger. It runs over me, causing my skin to prickle, an almost forgotten sensation and yet, feeling it again, it has an immediate familiarity.

'Of course not.'

'Then why are we talking about it?'

'It was just the way he looked at me. So intent as he said it.'

'We've no idea where his poor, demented mind was,' she replies. 'At least he's at peace now.'

There's something odd about her gaze. She's not seeing me, even though our eyes are locked. She slams two glasses so hard against each other in the dishwasher that one of them cracks. She lifts it out and flings it into the bin before walking from the kitchen.

As I finish loading the dishwasher, sounds reach me from the front room. Doors opening and being slammed closed again. She is rummaging in the drinks cabinet. This can't be happening. Not on the night before his funeral. I hurry after her and find her on her knees, dragging out the contents from the cabinet. The twins took all the bottles with them when they left. They did so discreetly when she was sitting in the conservatory drinking tea with Noreen Ferguson.

'Just in case she finds it all too much for her,' Susanne whispered, as she handed a half empty bottle of whiskey to her husband. I suspected there'd been occasional episodes of this nature and their sleight-of-hand smoothness proved it.

'Where did you hide the bottle of vodka Paddy Boyle gave me?' Cassie, half rising when she sees me, points her finger at me.

'I never touched it. And neither should you. What are you thinking... tonight of all nights.'

'*Exactly*. Tonight of all nights is the reason I need a drink but it's not here.' Her voice has a recognisable impetuousness. 'Who gave you permission to hide it?'

'I swear I didn't hide anything.'

'Liar.' She bangs the cabinet door in frustration. 'Liar... *liar*... how dare you decide what's best for me.'

I want to scream at her, as I used to do in my teens when she acted the same way. Sometimes, it was my father who triggered her rages but, just as often, I was responsible for reasons I could never anticipate or understand. He asked me to watch over her and I'm falling at the first fence.

She rises fully to her feet. For an instant I think she's going to strike me. Instead, she rushes back to the kitchen and drags a chair across to one of the high presses. She climbs up on it, her movements becoming more agitated as she searches in vain for the bottle. Foodstuffs fall out. A packet of pasta, insecurely sealed, bursts open and penne spills over the floor.

'Get down, Cassie,' I shout. 'You're going to fall.' As if adding credence to my warning, the chair wobbles. One of the legs is loose and could easily separate from the seat. Pasta snaps under my feet as I grab both her arms and help her down.

She pushes me away and pours water, drinks it quickly and shudders. Her gaze narrows, her eyes pinpoints of accusation. 'How is it that you always distress me?'

I grab the sweeping brush and clear up the penne. 'I'm sorry if that's how you feel about me. It's never my intention. You should go to bed now. Tomorrow will be a demanding day.'

When her bedroom door closes, I sit for a while with my father. I press my lips to his forehead, cold and stiff with rigor mortis. Now that he has gone beyond the veil, where is he? What is he? Stardust? Energy? Harps, hymns and halos?

Annihilation?

In the small hours, her voice awakens me. I sit bolt upright, hands to my chest, my ears straining against the silence that has now fallen. The room is dark, illuminated only by the neon numbers of the bedside clock. 3.36 a.m. Had I been dreaming? I'm hot, sweaty. I open the window and breathe in the cold air. Her voice rises then falls and becomes inaudible.

Outside on the landing the trapdoor is open, the folding stairs hanging down. She must have been in the attic. She is downstairs again and in the living room. I hear her more clearly as I walk through the hall. Her words are slurred. It's clear that she found a bottle of something in the attic.

'Damn you... damn you... damn you.' This is a chant, vicious yet dully repetitive.

I ease open the door. The light shines down on my father's body. She is bent over him, her grey hair that she had earlier twisted into a topknot, now loose and falling over her cheeks. 'Damn you... damn you... damn you... she heard you. Why... why...? What have you left me with...? Tell me... damn you... damn you...'

Now that I know what she is saying, her words have an eerie resonance. My heart drums with the memory of another occasion when she made those same whimpering sounds.

I move back into the hall and lean against the wall. I must calm down. If she sees me here it will further unhinge her. When I reach the top of the stairs I call her name.

'Cassie!' I shout it again and stamp my feet loudly on the stairs as I descend them once again.

I hear a crash, then her voice crying out for me. She is on the floor, sprawled the length of the coffin. My father lies in icy detachment, but she is scrabbling, trying to rise to her feet but unable to keep her balance. Accidentally, I kick an empty bottle that lies in my path. It rolls noisily under the coffin supports. She shivers and moans when she hears the clink.

I half carry her up the stairs and into my bedroom. The risk of her vomiting is too great to leave her on her own. Her eyes are bloodshot and there is a slackness to her features that suggests much alcohol has been consumed. How had Jessica managed to miss this one? Or it could be old stock, hidden by Cassie in the attic, lying in wait for such an occasion.

I watch over her as she sinks into a fitful sleep. She seems unharmed by her fall. How will the twins react? Will they blame me, as she will undoubtedly do, when she recovers?

'*How is it that you always distress me?*' What made her say that to me? She moans as she tries to turn over. I coax her back on her side again and run downstairs for a bowl. Not having had to do this for ten years does nothing to alleviate my disgust. At such moments, I'd hated her. That emotion is as intense as it ever was. But it's tempered with something else. Suspicion. Something I'm unable to grasp even though I can already feel its tremendous weight. *Damn you... she heard you... What have you left me with...? Tell me... tell me...*

What am I to read into her words? Random ravings, or something more meaningful?

I lie beside her on top of the duvet and watch over her. She is fast asleep, her mouth slack and open. I'm filled with a sudden desire to lift her in my arms and shake her like a rag doll. What will spill from her if I do so? *Damn you...* why curse a man who is beyond all caring? She loved him. I never doubted it, even when she was at her wildest, yelling at him about being trapped, yet, later, holding on to him with such passion that I'd have to look away. And he loved her. This, also, I never doubted. That was how I understood marriage. The tender and the tempestuous forever colliding.

Now, watching her sleep, her face looks defenceless, forlorn.

I don't believe I'll be able to sleep but I drift off on the purr of her breathing.

In the morning, I'm alone in the bed. The sound of the power shower from her ensuite reaches me. This is followed by the whirr of her electric toothbrush. She is still in her dressing gown but made up, her hair gleaming, when I enter the kitchen.

'Thank you for looking after me last night.' She flashes a guilty smile in my direction. 'I don't want you to worry. It's not going to happen again. I promise.'

Confronting her is not a solution. The twins will be here soon, followed by the undertaker and his team. They will close the coffin on my father and prepare him for his final journey. I can't even frame the questions surrounding her behaviour last night, let alone ask her what it means. I'm watchful for triggers that will upset her. Not knowing what they are under such difficult and changed circumstances is a problem. All I know is that my presence always distresses her. Is it such a deep-rooted aberration that she needs to drink to oblivion to cope with it?

When the doorbell rings she's dressed in black, her hair piled high in its customary top knot. Only her sunken eyes with their terrified glaze give her away. That impression is soon hidden behind tinted glasses as she follows the fishermen on her husband's final journey.

My sisters walk on either side of her, a fluid movement of tenderness and concern as they link her arms. I walk behind them in an empty space that is loud with voices, angry and demanding as hers was last night when she berated the man she's supposed to be mourning. And his voice is louder still. Free from morphine and filled with clarity, it has turned into a haunting refrain. *I stole you...* niggling, itching, scrabbling claws – how can I describe what those three words are doing to me as I struggle to believe they are meaningless?

# THREE

We walk away from my father's flower-decked grave and celebrate his life in the Trabawn Lights Hotel. People hug the microphone, telling anecdote after anecdote about his life on the waves. The muted atmosphere is beginning to relax and become raucous with laughter. Even Cassie is smiling as Nicholas recounts his first days on the *Sheila Rua* and how my father had produced a life-like rubber pollock that he used to slip into the catch when the nets were winched ashore. It would writhe unnoticed among the fish until it began to sing the chorus of 'Octopus's Garden'.

It's impossible to remain sad when such stories are being remembered with hilarity. He played the same prank on me and Killian when we first worked on the *Sheila Rua* during our school holidays, only in that instance, the pollock sang, 'What Shall We Do with the Drunken Sailor?' I meet Killian's gaze and can tell by his smile that he's also remembering that same instant. He'd wiped tears of laughter from my eyes, and I'd been conscious of his nearness. The trace of his fingers against my skin had caused my stomach to lurch with a sensation that was unfamiliar yet held an instinctive awareness of all that would follow between us.

The funeral reception draws to a close. People stop on their way out to bid us goodbye. Normal life is resuming, and Dominick Grace is becoming a memory that will bring a smile to people's lips when his name comes up in conversation.

'The waves are good.' Killian stops at our family table to shake Cassie's hand. She hugs him to her and says that Dominick thought of him as the son he never had. Is this a dig at me? Is she suggesting I deprived my father of the perfect son-in-law? I search her face for signs of reproach. She is smiling blandly as she releases Killian from her arms.

He turns to me, speaking softly. 'I'm going surfing before the tide changes. Want to join me?'

Cassie barely glances at me when I tell her I'm heading to the beach. She sits between the twins, a large pot of tea in front of her. I imagine her with restraints, always fighting demons with her hands tied, her life as tepid as the tea Susanne is pouring for her.

My surfboard is lodged between a sheet of plywood and the bikes the twins used to ride to school. I brush away the cobwebs before securing it to the roof rack of my hired car. Killian is waiting by the old boathouse as arranged. He surfs regularly when he comes home for weekends but I'm unsteady, so out of practice that it takes five attempts before I'm able to stand upright.

The tide is high and restless, the waves' curves perfect for surfing. Unused muscles scream warnings but soon it's as if I've never left the waves. The sheer exhilaration. This must be the nearest thing to bird flight, the swift ascent and crucial descent.

The beach is almost empty, apart from a man on a rock who

is photographing us. We're the only surfers. An ocean to ourselves.

When we come back to shore, even the photographer has left. Killian has brought beers and I unwrap the sandwiches left over from yesterday's wake.

We slither out of our wetsuits, backs turned modestly to each other. We'd undressed so often together in the past, tossing off our clothes behind skimpy towels that barely covered us, before diving into the waves. We'd wrestled in the ocean, sliding like seals from each other's clutch, or tumbled together to lie like sprawled starfish at the bottom of sand dunes. As we grew older, I knew his body intimately. First love is hot and fast. But that was a long time ago. I shiver, unsure if it's from the cold or memory. Surfing makes thoughts of anything other than balance impossible but I'm on dry land again, and the brief elation I experienced as I surfed the waves fades.

Everything seems sharper since I returned home. The sea looks wilder than ever but, perhaps, I'm projecting my own anger onto the slant of those frothing white horses.

Warmed in a fleece blanket, I sit with my back against the cliff wall that encircles the cove.

'How is Lucas?' Killian asks, as he searches for his favourite sandwich: chicken and homemade stuffing.

'Past tense,' I reply. 'Next question.'

'I'm sorry.' He lifts his head in surprise. 'Last time we met, you told me he was the love of your life.'

'I'm quite sure I never said that—?'

'Words to that effect, certainly.'

'Well, I guess I'm not as perceptive as I claimed to be.' If only I felt as indifferent as I sound.

Lucas Walker is impossible to banish – at a mental level, that is. Even during my radio phone-ins when I need my wits about me, he'll distract me with a memory, holding it up, taunting me for being so addled by love that I never suspected what was taking place *almost* before my eyes.

'Do you want to tell me what changed your mind?' Killian asks. My blanket has slipped a little and he reaches across to pull it over my shoulder. He does it casually, without thinking, as he used to do when his touch weakened me with longing. Is he remembering...? No... I won't go there... I need to keep a tight rein on our history.

He never mentions our engagement or how I ended it so suddenly. Perhaps, because he was the wounded one, he's been able to move on. I've never managed to shake off the guilt I carry over hurting him. Also, there's the fear that I made the wrong decision. Since Lucas, that fear has become more persistent. Too late now for regrets. I haven't met his partner Shauna yet but, according to the twins, she's stunning.

Killian is waiting for my response. It's so embarrassing to have to admit that the man I loved was unfaithful to me with a laptop.

'Let it out, Gaby.' He nudges me with his elbow. 'You were never one for holding back on your emotions.'

Once I begin to talk and he settles into a listening silence, I can't stop. I tell him about the dating sites Lucas accessed. So many women contacted. He never met them. Never even arranged a date. It was all virtual: cybersex and steamy texts, the short videos with their inevitable conclusions. Was this supposed to make a difference? Could it be called infidelity? How had I allowed myself to be so deluded? So oblivious of his addiction to his phone, the casual way he would close his laptop if I came near him when he was 'working'.

How much longer would it have taken me to discover the truth if I hadn't started to feel nauseous on my way to work one morning. By the time I reached NY Eyz, I realised I was suffering from a stomach bug. The effects made it impossible to present *Gaby's Good Morning Wake-up*. Zac Pérez, a close friend and one of the station's presenters, stood in for me.

I took a taxi back to my apartment, where I discovered Lucas naked and active online with a woman who must have paid a fortune for breast enhancement. By the next evening I'd moved from the East Village to Brooklyn and was renting an apartment in Zac's brownstone.

'What about you, Killian?' I want to end this confession cleanly. 'How's Shauna?'

'We'll talk about her another time,' he says. 'Today belongs to you. Did your father know about what happened between you and Lucas?'

'Only that we'd broken up. Infidelity of the flesh is easier to understand than what Lucas did. So many women... unbelievable. And he never had to set foot outside the door of our apartment. How could I have fallen in love with such a *lazy* man?'

For some reason, I start laughing. After a startled pause, Killian joins in. We laugh until tears run down my face and become a stream.

'Do you know the last thing Dad said to me before he died?' My voice is muffled and teary.

'Knowing Dominick, he told you he loved you.'

'I think that's what he wanted to say. But it came out as "I stole you."'

'He was on morphine—' Killian begins to explain what the obvious reason must be.

'I know... I know.' I nod in agreement. 'He was unconscious for so much of the time during his final hours. But he seemed to know exactly what he was saying. And the look he gave me... it was so cognisant. I know it's ridiculous to think he meant anything by it. I wouldn't even be talking about it except for something that happened last night. Cassie started drinking again—'

'Oh, fuck—' he begins before I rush on.

'*Exactly*. I found her in the living room leaning over his coffin. At first, I thought she was crying but she was *actually* giving out to him. Raving about how he left her to clear up his mess... or something along those lines. It was hard to make her out, but I can't help wondering if she was talking about what he said to me before he died.'

'That he *stole* you.'

'Do you think I'm crazy?'

Why would he not? What I'm telling him must sound outrageous.

'You're anything but.' He gives my hand a quick squeeze. 'If he stole you then he chose the right basket. You're the image of each other.'

I've never seen it myself, though people often remark on it. I guess it's the shape of our faces – long and slim – and our dark blue eyes. The twins take after Cassie: sallow skin that tans to golden in the summer and piercing brown eyes. Their features are smooth and flawless, unlike my angular cheekbones and too-wide mouth.

'Shaped to be kissed,' Lucas used to say, before he discovered that the cyber world is full of virtual replacements.

'I honestly don't know what I'm talking about,' I admit. 'I obviously misheard Dad, or he was too confused to know what he was saying.'

'Watching him go like that must have been very emotional. It's more likely you misheard him.'

He's right, of course. How could I be anything other than my father's daughter? I settle into this thought yet can't stop thinking about Cassie's behaviour last night. Today, at his funeral, she was dignified and grieving. The twins gave his eulogy. I hadn't protested when Cassie told me it was her wish that they should eulogise their father. I lost that right when I turned my back on him and left Trabawn. I must admit, they did well. Fluent as ever, they read their eulogy in sequence, and their genuine sorrow when they finished speaking evoked a round of applause from the congregation.

The flare of the setting sun settles on the waves. The smell of brine is sharp enough to remind me of the *Sheila Rua*. My father's trawler was his pride and joy. It's anchored at Trabawn Harbour, at rest until after his funeral. We reminisce about the boat, remembering incidents that make us laugh. Laughter is part of grieving. All those memories coursing through us.

'How did you end up becoming a shock jock?' Killian asks. 'Did you have to train with boxing gloves, or did it come naturally to you?'

'A shock jock... is that what you think I am?' I'm amused by his description. *Gaby's Good Morning Wake-up* is tame compared to some of the talk radio that rivals mine. 'I'll have you know I present a respectable early morning phone-in show.'

'*Sure* it is.' His laughter teases me. 'Some of those phone calls you take are mad. But to be fair, you give back as good as you get.'

The evening is cold but dry. No rain for a week, which is unusual for February. Twilight settles early and easily, a short sunset smelting the waves. A purple hue darkens the sand as the coil of a new moon becomes visible. Killian takes my hand and pulls me to my feet.

We climb the steps to the pier. Words no longer seem necessary. We've always had the ability to be comfortable in each other's company. The only sound to break the silence between us is the raucous call of gannets as they swirl above the rocks.

Did I make a mistake in sharing my father's final words with Killian? I've an uncomfortable feeling that I've given them a momentum that wasn't there until I uttered them aloud to him.

My anger with Cassie builds as I drive back to Headwind. I'm also angry with myself. I should have come home for Christmas.

The break-up with Lucas was still too raw for me to pretend it was the season to be jolly. Instead, I covered for the presenters who had children. I organised a video call with my family when we were opening the presents that we'd sent to each other.

I'd noticed the weight Dad had lost since he visited me. When I commented on it, he'd joked about giving up chips and Cassie's lemon drizzle cake.

The New Year had just passed when she rang to tell me about his cancer diagnosis. Everything was under control, she'd insisted. As I'd arranged to come home in March for his birthday, there was no need to change my plans. The shock I received when a frantic phone call from Susanne informed me that he was sinking fast still reverberates through me.

I was terrified on the flight home that he'd be dead before I could say goodbye to him. Time was on my side but all it allowed us was sixteen measly hours together. I should have had weeks, even months, if Cassie had been honest with me. Instead, she lied. Was it to prevent me from organising a leave of absence from NY Eyz? It's the only reason that makes any sense.

She's in bed when I enter the house. The twins, whose husbands are still drinking with friends in the Trabawn Lights, are trawling through a box of photographs that Cassie always intends to organise into albums.

I sit down between them on the sofa and am immediately drawn back to the past. The box is mainly filled with family photographs. I'm only in a few that cover the last decade and they are searching hard to find ones that include Dad. His shyness in front of the camera had always been a family joke. Even when he could be persuaded to stand in beside us, he usually turned away from the camera or raised his hand just enough to hide parts of his face. He was also missing from the photographs I'd taken of the crew at work during my summers on the *Sheila Rua*. I stare at a shot of Killian, so lanky then, sunglasses shoved into his hair. He'd worn it in a ponytail, flaxen strands that gleamed like gold in the sunlight. I'd no idea I'd taken so many photographs, especially when the crew were on land and relaxing in pubs, their frothing glasses held high, yet Dad was not visible in any of them.

Why have I never been conscious of this particular trait? One that was so out of kilter with his sociable personality. Like so much in life, normality is found in the familiar and seldom questioned.

'Why did he never want us to take his photograph?' I ask when Jessica puts the lid back on the box.

'It was his scopophobia,' she replies in a matter-of-fact tone that suggests I should know the answer.

'His *what*?'

'His camera shyness,' say Susanne. 'It's an obsessive fear of being watched.'

'What do you mean? I've never heard of sucaphopia or whatever it's called.'

'*Scopophobia*.' Jessica's emphasis only adds to my confusion. 'He discussed it with us before the wedding. That's why he's only in a couple of shots and wouldn't allow The Trabawn Herald to use any that included him.'

'Why didn't I know about that?'

'He was kind of ashamed about it,' Susanne chimes in. 'Not that it was a big deal. We all have our phobias. Ours is haptodysphoria—'

'Stop talking about *phobias*.' My chest feels constricted, a darting pain with questions attached to it. 'It's his cancer that concerns me. How *could* you both have kept such important information from me?'

'We were as surprised as you,' Susanne replies. 'He was so strong for months and never gave us any indication that he wasn't going to pull through.'

'That can't be possible.' I don't want an argument with my

sisters, yet I refuse to believe that they, unlike me, had been kept in the dark. 'You must have suspected how seriously ill he was.'

'Mum didn't want to worry us—' Susanne begins before I cut her off.

'That's *nonsense.*' I speak so harshly that she places her hands protectively over her stomach. 'What right had Cassie to keep the truth from any of us.'

'It's nothing to do with "rights",' Susanne continues. 'She was only doing what Dad wanted.'

'And you believe her?'

'Why would she lie?' Jessica is still holding the box on her lap. Her tears fall in splotches on the cardboard cover. 'He looked so well until the last few weeks and even then, he believed he'd see you for his birthday. That's when he planned to tell you the truth. He wanted you beside him when you heard the news, not hearing it on a phone call.'

'Did he *actually* say that to you?' I take the box from her and bend to slide it under the sofa. The twins, I suspect, are exchanging puzzled glances behind my back. They inhabit an interior sphere that attunes them to each other's thoughts and moods. Cassie said they slid easily into the world, but I was a struggle. A "hellish" delivery. That was the adjective she chose to use during one of our arguments. I've never forgotten it.

'Mum became his voice in the end,' says Susanne. 'It was a struggle for him to express himself and she did everything he asked of her. How she managed without resorting...' she hesitates, reluctant to bring up our mother's propensity to drink her way through a family crisis.

'She did good.' Jessica speaks with such firmness that I know we'll head onto thin ice if I continue probing.

'Not good enough, though.' I can't let it go. 'She knew I'd have returned home on the next flight if I'd known. She didn't want me around. That's the hard truth, no matter how you pretend otherwise.'

'Come here... come here... don't cry... it's going to be all right...' I'm unsure which twin is speaking in the mollifying tone that mothers use on distraught children. Nor can I distinguish the tangle of arms that hold me close and make it impossible to be angry with them.

In bed, I Google the meaning of haptodysphoria. A disagreeable sensation when handling velvet and various fuzzy surfaces. Perhaps that explains why my skin feels as if it's being rubbed the wrong way. A tingle that's becoming impossible to ignore.

# FOUR

It's past 8 a.m. in New York and *Gaby's Good Morning Wake-up* has ended when I video call with Emily, my producer. Libby Wolfe, my stand-in presenter, has had a good response from my listeners, according to Emily. The phone lines have been busy, the callers as outrageous as ever.

'Libby's feet are too comfortable under your desk so the sooner you're back, the better.' My producer always cuts straight to the chase. I feel a stab of anxiety, which is exactly what Emily wants. Libby Wolfe is an outdoor broadcaster who has made no secret of her determination to present her own show ever since she joined NY Eyz.

I understand her ambition and her single-mindedness. I bring both of those qualities to *Gaby's Good Morning Wake-up* and it would be a mistake to take the success I've achieved for granted.

Cassie drives away, heading to the supermarket in the town. The fridge is full, so are the kitchen presses. I offered to accompany her. She refused and said she needed an opportunity to wind down on her own.

We both know it's a threadbare excuse to avoid spending time with me.

Nicholas rings shortly afterwards.

'Will you give me a hand to remove Dominick's possessions from the trawler?' he asks. 'Jessica's offered to do it but there's no way I'd consider that in her condition.'

He took control of the *Sheila Rua* when my father became too ill to work and will now become her captain.

'That's not a problem,' I reply. 'I'm glad to have something useful to do for the afternoon.'

'Thanks, Gaby. I'll meet you on the harbour in an hour.'

He'll supply Eddie, who owns Trabawn Fisheries Enterprise, with the catch. Unlike me, the twins and their husbands belong to the roots of Trabawn. They'll rear their children here and care for Cassie as she ages. She's looking forward to helping them when the babies arrive. They create a neat family circle. I've no idea where I fit into this new reality, nor have I any desire to do so. In another two days, I'll be back at NY Eyz arguing the toss with my unruly listeners.

The wind is sharp as I park on Trabawn Harbour and meet Nicholas at the *Sheila Rua*.

Once aboard, he unlocks the door to my father's cabin. It was always spartan, used only for his office work and sleeping. Otherwise, he ate and relaxed with the crew in their day quarters.

His mother's name was Sheila. This scant piece of information was given to Dad by a nurse who worked in the institution where he was reared. She described his mother as a wild, sinful woman, who used her long, red hair to lure innocent men to her bed. He named his boat after this red-haired siren, whose voice he only ever heard when the sea heaved in the lap of a storm. Unlike the myth, her enticing song always guided him safely back to shore. On the few occasions he mentioned his red Sheila to us, he spoke kindly, and with understanding, about the decision she took to abandon him.

In my mind's eye, I see her now with her foxy hair, her hands trembling as she hands him over to others and decides her future. She gave him away. He stole me away... Stop... stop... this is ludicrous... mad... dangerous. I need to shake my head until such outrageous thoughts are scattered far and wide.

His visit to me shortly after my break-up with Lucas had been unexpected. I'd cycled home from my show and found him sitting on the stoop outside Zac's brownstone. For an instant, as he rose to his feet, I thought he was a homeless man about to reach out his hand to me. My shock when I recognised him must have shown on my face as he hesitated, his smile uncertain until I rushed into his arms.

My apartment is on the top floor of Zac's brownstone. No elevator. Despite my father's insistence that he was grand... *grand...* I took his overnight case from him when his breathing became heavy on the stairs.

I wondered how I could have thought he was homeless. He was well-dressed in a casual jacket and trousers, an open-necked check shirt, and black shoes polished to a sheen. It was his posture that had created that brief illusion, plus the greyness of his complexion and a slope that was new to his shoulders.

Throughout the three days we spent together, I sensed he was worried about something. I waited for him to confide in me. Instead, our conversations were about the twins and their pregnancies, the *Sheila Rua* and the refitting she needed, and Cassie's progress since she left the Ashford Clinic. I hadn't realised she'd been in rehab again. He sounded proud of her and, as always, tolerant of her lapses.

It was his first time to visit me in the ten years since I'd left

Trabawn, yet he seemed unfazed by the city. Nothing wide-eyed about his gaze as he surveyed the towering, star-flecked skyscrapers and the neon-lit signs dazzling the night. We took a helicopter trip over Manhattan and cruised past the Statue of Liberty.

He asked to see where I worked. I took him to NY Eyz Broadcasting House. That was the only time he looked impressed. Emily greeted him effusively. He was surprised to discover she was Irish, Dublin-born and bred. In typical fashion, she quizzed him about his background. The Irish diaspora has honed the theory of six degrees of separation into an art form, and Emily is always on the lookout for that common link. She'd recognised the lingering inflections in his accent that marked him out as a Dubliner. She asked where he'd lived and seemed lost for words when he told her he'd been brought up in a children's home. Emily likes to reminisce about Dublin bars and nightclubs, trendy restaurants, and shopping in Brown Thomas. Mother and baby homes, and the history that goes with them, are not normally part of her conversation and she asked no further questions.

When we returned to my apartment, I asked him about his childhood. I never considered it important enough when I lived at home. On that visit, he created images that brought a lump to my throat, especially when I discovered he'd left the institution when he was sixteen.

'I was an adult then, in the view of the Christian Brothers who ran the orphanage,' he said. 'That's the way it was in those days. I had a pair of strong boots, a small sum of money, and my wits. Truthfully, it was the latter that helped me to survive.'

'Did you become a fisherman immediately?' I asked.

'That came much later...' I sensed his hesitancy when he paused. Words yet unspoken were creating a fission between us. His tongue slid over his lips, as if they were dry, and the pallor on his face seemed more pronounced. I waited for him to continue. Instead, he spoke about Cassie and how much he owed her for the happiness she'd brought into his life.

Their marriage seemed like an unsolvable conundrum to me, one of mutual dependency and unassailable loyalty.

He left the following day. I walked him to the subway. We were going in different directions, and I again wondered at his ability to manoeuvre his way through the flow of subway commuters. He would have to get connections to JFK, but he assured me he was perfectly capable of finding his way to the airport. Remembering my own confusion when I first came to New York, how disorientating it was compared to the quietness of Trabawn, I marvelled at his confidence. I guessed if someone has been navigating an ocean for most of their working life, dry land is an easy course to traverse.

He must have planned to tell me he was dying. What stopped him? It had to be Cassie. She rang him regularly every day. Her neediness seemed more pronounced than ever. So many phone calls. They slumped his shoulders even further and, though I was unable to hear what they said to each other, our own conversations always seemed more stunted after those calls. He raised his voice to her once. The sound reached me from the bedroom. I was startled by the uncharacteristic sharpness of his tone. Afterwards, we visited Ground Zero where he cried and hid those tears in his handkerchief.

That was five months ago. He'd given no indication that an oncologist had passed a six-month death sentence on him, and he'd already served the first month.

Nicholas has stamped his presence on this compact cabin. A sweater hangs from the back of a chair and his deck shoes lie where he'd kicked them off the last time he was here. Photos of Jessica are stuck to the wall beside his bunk and a novel, open and face downward, lies on the pillow. *Moby Dick* – not ideal reading for someone about to head out into the Atlantic. I keep that thought to myself.

Dad preferred crime novels, mainly detective series, and Nicholas has already stacked them into a large box. Two plastic containers have been placed on top of it. That's all it takes to hold the possessions he'd acquired from all his years at sea.

I sit on the side of his bunk and run my hand over the wooden frame. What direction would my life have taken if I'd had an easy relationship with Cassie? Probably working on the boat with Dad, as I did as soon as I was old enough to gut fish.

Nicholas carries the two containers to my car. I follow with the books. I'll leave everything in the garage and let Cassie decide what she wants to do with them.

Back at home, her car is not in the driveway. She must have visited one of the twins on her way home from the supermarket. I bring the containers into the garage and leave them beside my father's tools. The books are heavy and the bottom of the box breaks. Books spill to the garage floor, the covers flapping like the wings of startled birds.

The first one I pick up has fallen face down. I recognise my father's handwriting, the graceful flourishes that made it so distinctive. As usual, he had underlined sections of text and scribbled notations in the margins. *Rubbish! That's not how it works, idiot! Call yourself a crime writer!* I used to think books relaxed him, but he was intolerant of what he called 'inadequate research'. Plots needed to be watertight and characters well-fleshed. Sometimes he praised the author but more often he was critical of how an investigation was handled by the police or the forensic team.

His handwriting blurs. Waves of sorrow come suddenly, and this one is savage. Tears and more tears. How many more will I shed before they ease? What is their purpose? No matter how violently I cry, or for how long, all I feel afterwards is a dulled headache and a fluttering in my chest that is new to me.

This almost painful tightening that shortens my breath is alarming. My heart is sound, yet it feels unstable, incapable of coping with the loss of my father. Am I responding to guilt over our years of separation, grief over his passing, fury with Cassie, or panic each time I repeat to myself his last hoarse whisper.

I'm finally able to rise to my feet and find some stacked storage containers in the utility room.

I notice a cut-out section from a newspaper on the floor. It must have fallen when the box with the books broke. I scoop it up and study it. It's a photograph, slightly yellowed with age, and without a caption to identify the people in it. Four men stand in a semi-circle around a fifth one, but my attention is caught by another figure in the background. This man is outside the semi-circle and is standing to attention, as if on guard duty.

I've only ever seen one photograph of Dad as a youth. I was working on the *Sheila Rua* during my school holidays and found it stuck at the back of a filing cabinet. At first, I wasn't sure it was him. He looked to be in his mid-teens, his black hair cropped, his arms crossed awkwardly over his chest. The stark building in the background with its many windows and crucifix above the doorway had to be the institution where he was reared. Knowing how reluctant he was to speak about those days, I'd slipped the photograph into a pocket in my shorts and never mentioned it to him.

Now, looking at this newspaper clipping, I'm struck by the similarity between the man in the background and the youth in the old photograph. It's years since I've seen the latter. I return to my bedroom and check every drawer before locating it tucked inside a tin box once used for sweets and then for mementoes. It contains a locket with two heart-shaped photographs of myself and Killian, a bracelet my father bought me for my eighteenth birthday and other pieces of jewellery, each one marking a special occasion.

I remove the photograph and compare the two. The older

man's face is fuller, more defined, but my teenage father's chin already has the same firmness – a thrust that speaks of determination and toughness. Apart from his alert gaze, nothing about either photograph bears any resemblance to the father I knew with his grey, shaggy ponytail and the wispy tendrils that framed his weather-beaten face.

The older man's hair is cut with military precision whereas my youthful father's hair is stubbled, as though it had been hacked off. Both images reveal lean, muscular bodies, so unlike the ample belly Dominick Grace carried so majestically until cancer robbed it from him.

I photograph the two images with my camera phone and transfer them to my laptop. Blown up, I know I'm not mistaken in identifying this background figure as my father. What other reason would he have for keeping the clipping for all those years? His stance is clearer now and suggests he is alert to everything going on around him. I recognise such purposefulness. Senators and celebrities who come to be interviewed at NY Eyz always bring their security with them, those keen-eyed, silent types who stand guard over their clients.

I have a suspicion that he was not meant to be included in the group and was captured when he stepped, probably by accident, into the frame.

I email Killian and attach the two photographs.

> Killian, can you check the archives at *Bayview Dispatch* and see if you can find the original of this photo. It looks old but there's no date on it. I'm convinced the man in the background is Dad. The second photo is him in his teens. Don't you think the resemblance is uncanny? Let me know what you find out.

Why am I doing this? What do I hope to achieve? Unable to answer this question, I change into running gear and drive towards Burly's Head. I park the car on the lookout platform and run towards the summit. The headland with its twining road is a challenge for even the most experienced runner. I keep to the grassy verge at the edge of it, knowing from past experiences, how dangerously some drivers take the bends. I'm not noted for speed or stamina, and though its steepness soon begins to tell on my heart and lungs, it has no impact on the mutterings of my mind.

I should have overcome Dad's reluctance to talk about the institution. Apart from the story about his mother, and occasional, brief mentions of the brutality he experienced there, I know nothing of his past.

Slowing down when I reach the summit, I stare over the ocean as it foams against the tooth-gapped rocks. I can't explain my need to find out the history of the newspaper photograph. All I know, with maddening certainty, is that I won't rest until I find out why he hid it among the books he loved.

# FIVE

It's evening time and Killian is still at work when we link in by Zoom. His office looks spacious compared to my NY Eyz studio which I've nicknamed 'the hen-coop.'

'Where did you find the newspaper photo?' he asks.

'I took Dad's stuff from the *Sheila Rua*. It must have fallen from one of his books.'

'What makes you think the guy in the background is Dominick?'

'Because of the resemblance to him in that other photo.'

'How can you be so certain?'

'I'm not *that* certain...'

'But obviously certain enough to email them to me.' Killian's glance is keen, the lines on his forehead deepening. 'Have you ever heard of a politician named Aloysius Russell?'

'No. Should I have?'

'Probably not, considering you've been away for so long. I suspect politicians didn't feature much in your consciousness before you left.'

'Nor in my father's life,' I reply. 'He hated them all.'

'I remember his rants about "the political classes and their shenanigans."' His face relaxes into a smile. 'I did some digging last night after you contacted me. It took time, but I finally located the original.'

He shares his screen to show me the image.

'The man in the centre is Aloysius Russell,' he says.

For the first time since I found the clipping, I pay attention to this dominant figure. His protuberant eyes stare directly into the camera and his hair—still black yet silver-streaked—is swept back from his face to reveal a broad, unlined forehead.

His name means nothing to me. I can tell by the formal suits worn by the men in the semi-circle, and their rapt expressions as they form a so-called 'doughnut' effect around him, that they are also politicians, and probably subservient to him. He is being interviewed. Microphones are thrust towards him, but the journalists are not visible.

'What about him?' I ask.

'He was the minister for justice at the time and had just returned from an EU summit in Brussels,' says Killian. 'He obviously needed protection and that man you believe to be your father was a plain clothes detective called Cormac Gallagher.'

'*Really*... are you sure?'

'Yes.' He's quietly emphatic.

'Then I'm obviously mistaken.'

'It's easy to do,' he says. 'Especially when all you had to make the comparison was a photo taken when your father was barely out of childhood.'

I lean closer to the screen to examine the newspaper photograph again. Cormac Gallagher's eyes are steadfast as he watches Aloysius Russell. A police officer doing his job – yet there's something about his expression, a hardness especially around his mouth, that suggests he dislikes the man he's guarding.

'What's Aloysius Russell doing now?' I ask.

'He's the current Minister for Provincial Growth,' Killian replies. 'He made a bid for the leadership of the party on two occasions but never achieved it. His son, Douglas, is also a politician.' He hesitates for a beat. 'Actually, Shauna is his press officer.'

'Oh, really.' I was aware that his girlfriend worked in communications but hadn't realised it was in the political arena. I've never asked him what she does. I'd prefer not to examine the reason why, especially now when my only concern is finding out about this stranger who bears such a remarkable resemblance to my father in his teens.

'Is Cormac Gallagher still around?' I ask.

'There's no mention of him anywhere in the archives,' says Killian. 'I checked with a friend who's in the police. Cormac Gallagher was dismissed many years ago from the *Garda Síochána* over his association with known drug dealers.'

'Can I see the reports of his arrest?'

'There's no information on him. According to my friend, his dismissal was handled quietly by the force to avoid any bad publicity.'

'No trial then? Don't you think that's strange?'

'Who knows what goes on behind the scenes in garda headquarters.' Killian straightens in his chair. 'Are you okay, Gaby? You're not upset, I hope.'

'No, of course not. I was just curious, that's all. I'd better go. Cassie should be back soon.'

'How're things?'

'No dramas. So far, all quiet on the Western Kerry Front.'

He laughs obligingly and says goodbye.

I switch off my laptop and try to analyse my feelings. Am I disappointed or relieved? Overall, I think it's mainly relief that flows through me but why I should care one way or the other about Cormac Gallagher escapes me.

Cassie returns. As I figured, she spent the rest of the afternoon with Susanne. Tomorrow, I'll join her and the twins in Dad's solicitor's office for the reading of his will.

In bed, I'm unable to sleep. I prop an extra pillow behind me to support my back and open my laptop. Links, so many of them, appear as soon as I key in the name Aloysius Russell. Killian said the newspaper that published the photograph was thirty years old. Aloysius was already an experienced politician then. The amount of information on him should not surprise me. Most of the feature and news reports were written in the last twenty years or thereabouts. It's confusing to know where to begin.

A headline seems to jump out at me. The feeling of being assaulted is so intense that I instinctively draw back from the screen.

*Minister Commemorates Tenth Anniversary of Baby's Disappearance*

The photograph accompanying the feature is captioned with the names Aloysius Russell and his wife, Maria.

This is a coincidence. One of those freakish instances where a personal situation suddenly aligns with another unrelated but similar occurrence. To think otherwise is to enter the realms of madness. I examine the two photographs of my young father and his even younger self again. The similarities that seemed so glaring when I sent them to Killian are merely superficial, tight haircuts, their taut expressions suggesting that they are displeased with their surroundings. Killian must have been amazed when I sent them to him. The urge to ring him must be resisted. Apart from intruding on his time with Shauna, it's three o'clock in the morning.

Finally, I'm able to sleep. I dream about a boy with an urchin haircut who keeps running in front of me. The more I try to catch him, the heavier my footsteps become.

. . .

This morning, Cassie cut winter roses in the garden. Her mood seems more relaxed, and she nods in agreement when I ask if she'd like me to drive her to the cemetery.

The flowers on Dad's grave are beginning to wilt. The largest wreath came from the team of NY Eyz. A nice gesture, and one he would have appreciated.

Now, we're attending the reading of his will. No surprises. Cassie inherits his estate which, in turn, will be divided between myself and the twins when she dies.

I drive from the solicitor's office to Susanne's house where she's prepared a farewell lunch for me. Eddie and Nicholas arrive in time to join us. After we've eaten, an uneasy silence settles over the table.

Cassie clears her throat before she begins to speak. 'This may seem sudden, Gabrielle, but I've had time to think about my future during Dominick's illness. I'm not used to living on my own. Headwind is too isolated. I don't think I can cope by myself.' She is sober and brisk as she outlines her future. 'So, I've decided to sell the house. Susanne and Eddie are having an extension built and their garden is large enough to add a granny flat for me. I presume you'll have no objections to my decision?' Her gaze challenges me to disagree with her.

'It's your home, Cassie. Why should I object?'

'You'll always have a room with us, Gaby,' Jessica says.

'We'll be fighting over which of us you'll stay with,' Susanne adds.

They're anxious not to exclude me from these new arrangements, yet their well-meant heartiness adds to my sense of loss.

'Well, that all sounds very well organised.' Eddie breaks the silence that has settled over us again.

Now that she has revealed her plans, Cassie's earlier animation has left her.

'You look exhausted, Mum,' says Susanne. 'You should go upstairs and take a nap.'

Cassie nods and stumbles when she rises. Susanne is on her feet immediately to assist her.

Eddie and Nicholas are discussing the *Sheila Rua* and the weather conditions. Jessica has arranged to meet a friend in the town. Susanne will drive Cassie home when she awakens. I return to Headwind, aware that not one of them will miss me in any meaningful way.

Before Cassie lay down to rest, she told me I could use the plastic containers in the utility room to pack the possessions I would need to remove from my bedroom.

I clear out my wardrobe, pack the books and albums, the CDs and the accumulation of teenage dross I acquired in my first eighteen years. I've no inclination to sort them into order. The clothes can go to the charity shop in the town and the rest will go into storage until I'm ready to decide what to do with them.

I breathe in dust and memories as I turn the pages of a maths copybook. All those equations... how terrifying they once seemed, and how irrelevant they are to the life I now lead.

What does it matter, all this clutter? A bonfire is probably the best solution. Pile it high and let the wind take the smoke where it will. But I can't bear the thought of seeing my past go up in flames.

Cassie's bruising, cold silences and sudden rages are memories from my teenage years. Yet, when I think back to my childhood, I remember it as being a happy and uncomplicated time.

'Come into my ring of love,' she would say when we finished our homework, and the evening meal was cleared away. She would gather us into her arms and tell us stories, sing songs, dance across the kitchen floor, her hair flying. When did unconditional love turn to hate...? No... I don't want to use that word. It's too unflinching. What then? The twins always assured me it had nothing to do with me personally when she experienced another 'episode' after I came home for a visit. She remained sober for their weddings. Mother of the brides, sparkling water, slice of lime, three ice cubes. Not a foot wrong over two days of celebration. But as soon as the twins had flown to Thailand with their husbands for a double honeymoon, she was drinking again, and continued to do so until I returned to New York.

Cassie still isn't home when I carry the containers to the garage. My last day here and she can't be bothered to spend it with me. Everything will be different when I come back again. Despite Jessica and Susanne's assurances that I'll always be welcome to stay with them, we all know that an era has come to an end.

Susanne rings with an apology. Cassie is not feeling well and will stay overnight with her.

'Is she drinking?' I ask.

Susanne's pause tells me what I need to know. 'She's had a few too many,' she admits. 'But she'll be fine in the morning. We'll all be over to say goodbye to you.'

I awaken suddenly, instantly alert, my body tingling. I feel the side of my bed sink, as if someone has sat down on the other side of me.

'Dad... Dad...' My voice is groggy as I search for the switch on the bedside lamp. The room is empty and I, blinking in the light, am trembling.

I lie still for a few moments before rising. The silence when I open the bedroom door has an oppressive quality, as if years of secrets have filtered free from the walls. I enter Cassie's bedroom. Her bed is neatly made. How will she adjust to sleeping alone? She shared this bed with my father until his illness made it impossible for them to sleep together.

I remember the empty space beside me on my first night without Lucas. The chilliness of its width and how I knew I'd never be able to warm it. When Zac offered me accommodation, he warned me that the apartment was small. I told him that sleeping in a single bed – or 'twin', as he called it – wasn't an issue.

My reflection stares back at me from the dressing table mirror as I lift my father's hairbrush and carefully gather the hairs from it, checking that the essential root is attached to some of the strands. After sealing them in an envelope and writing his name on it – the name I knew him by – I do the same with Cassie's hairbrush.

What am I doing? What am I thinking? Nothing sane, that's for sure.

I spoke to Killian earlier. We've arranged to meet tomorrow in his office. Perhaps he'll help me to understand the rage that's driving me and provide me with the antidote to control it. Otherwise, how can I break this spell that has transfixed me?

# SIX

Killian laughs when I tell him that the brash, multi-storied edifice of glass and steel where *Bayview Dispatch* is produced reminds me of a New York baby skyscraper. Everything looks so small here, yet Dublin is moving upward, in every sense of the word.

He introduces me to the staff in the news department before leading me into his office. The view from his window overlooks the old docks with their renovated apartment blocks and restaurants. Compared to my 'hen-coop' in NY Eyz, this is a cathedral. It even has a view of a tall ship currently moored on the Liffey.

'What do you think?' He stands beside me at the window.

'What's not to envy?' I stare down at the river as it flows through the centre of the city. 'This is an amazing space.'

'The political editor is retiring soon.' He pulls out a second chair behind his desk for me and taps the keyboard of his computer. 'Between you, me and the wall, I'm going to apply for his job.'

'Then I wish you the best of luck. I've no doubt you'll get it.'

'Thanks for the confidence but the competition will be

fierce. You must be hungry after driving from Trabawn. I'm about to break for lunch. There's a great deli just up the square—'

'Can I check your archives first?'

'Whatever for?' His glance is sharp rather than surprised.

'I'm curious about a news report I've discovered.'

'Can you elaborate?'

'Certainly. It's about a kidnapping. Why didn't you tell me Aloysius Russell's child was stolen?'

'It wasn't relevant—'

'So, why not mention it when we were talking about him?'

'What exactly are you asking me, Gaby?'

'I'm asking you if you were thinking of my father's last words to me.'

'I-stole-you.' He enunciates them deliberately. 'Is that what you mean?'

'Yes.'

'From what I remember you telling me, Dominick was heavily sedated. He was obviously raving yet what he said troubled you. I could tell from our conversation on the beach. Speculating about that baby could have upset you even more. You're vulnerable right now—'

'Can I see the archives,' I interrupt him deliberately. We've always been wired to each other's moods, and I suspect that the two photographs have also unnerved him. 'I'd like to go back twenty-eight years and read about that kidnapping for one reason only.'

'Dare I ask what that is?'

'To clear my mind. It's swinging one way then the other. I know for sure that Dad would never have committed such a brutal crime yet finding that clipping, which must have fallen from one of his books keeps niggling me. Why would he carry it around with him—?'

'Gaby, he *didn't* carry it around with him. You found it

purely by accident. You're attaching far too much importance to it. I told you that Shauna works for Douglas Russell. I asked her—'

'Oh my *god*, Killian.' The thought of our conversation on the beach being repeated back to his girlfriend inflames me. 'Don't tell me you discussed Dad's last words with Shauna.'

'Of course not.' He dismisses my question with a firm shake of his head. 'You know I'd never discuss anything personal like that with *anyone*. All I did was ask her if Douglas ever mentions the kidnapping. Very seldom, she said, and usually only around the time of the anniversary. His family are convinced she died shortly after she was taken. They don't admit it publicly, but Douglas says his father received confidential information shortly after the kidnapping that confirmed it.'

'I'd still like to read about how it happened.'

'There you go,' he says as headlines regarding the disappearance of the baby appear on the screen.

The reports I read are twenty-eight years old. A stolen baby. Isabelle Russell. My hairline is wet, and beads of perspiration begin a slow roll down the sides of my cheeks. Her name stirs childhood memories. I've a vague recollection of baby photographs appearing occasionally on the television, probably on her anniversary. The brief flurry of publicity never held my attention for long but now, I can't take my eyes off the screen.

In the photographs I see the bland features of a new-born, but Maria Russell has the dazed smile of someone who has suffered to bring a child into the world and is still unable to believe the fight is over. Later photographs show a more wide-awake baby. She was three weeks old when the last one was taken. Her hair is black and, though sparce, it still defines her skull. Otherwise, there is nothing distinguishable about her.

Her mother awakened in the small hours to feed her baby and found an empty cot. The search for Isabelle stayed in the headlines for weeks before giving way to more up-to-date tragedies and scandals.

The earlier anniversaries of her disappearance were marked by candle-lit processions from her home in Dublin to the local church. Masses were celebrated and prayers offered in the hope that the coming year would end the family's torment. I continue reading. As a couple, their reaction to the tragedy of their lost baby appears to have fascinated the print media. I wade through a trove of information that follows their progress over those early years.

Douglas Russell was only three years old when his sister was taken. A second son was born two years after her disappearance.

I need fresh air. This bubble of glass will suffocate me. I turn away from the screen, unable to read any more.

'I must go, Killian. I'll be late for my flight if I don't leave now.'

'Have lunch first.'

'No. I'm late already.'

'Gaby, what's wrong?'

'Nothing. Stop fussing over me.'

'Look, I'm sorry... you asked to see the archives. I didn't mean to upset you.'

'I'm not upset. Not in the least. Thanks for all your help, Killian. I'm satisfied now. Grief is strange, don't you think? I'm heart sore that I'm never going to see my father again but rather than face that truth, I'm doing everything I can to avoid it.'

'Are you sure you're okay?' His concern adds to my need to escape.

'Absolutely. I'm going to forget about Cormac Gallagher and this unfortunate baby.'

'Do me a favour when you reach New York,' he says. 'Text me and let me know you're okay.'

'I promise. I'm sorry for being such a drama queen.'

Out on the street, the weather has changed. The wind gusts and the clouds are heavy with rain that has yet to fall. The Liffey is moving from a sluggish pace towards something more ominous, and the lines on the tall ship tap agitatedly.

Once my flight takes off, I open my laptop and go online to read about Aloysius Russell. Killian has given me the password to the *Bayview Dispatch* archives and I continue the search that began in his office. I need to sleep but every time I close my eyes, I can't keep pace with my thoughts.

Aloysius was young when he entered politics and ambitious from the beginning. As well as being a minister for justice, he served as a minister for finance, health and foreign affairs. I find a photograph of him and Maria on their wedding day. They were married a year after his first wife died. He was thirty-five then and she was his twenty-three-year-old personal assistant.

In the photographs I study, his son Douglas has the sheen of a politician being groomed for leadership. Jonathan, their younger son, has an engaging smile but doesn't project the self-assurance of his brother and father. He is smaller and more slightly built, auburn-haired like his mother, but without her glow. In younger family photographs, he is easy to overlook. That changes later when he fills out, grows his hair into an untamed bush and starts wearing biker jackets. I get the feeling he's under duress in these family gatherings, especially the annual ball that marks his sister's disappearance. He would never have known her, yet she must have cast a dark shadow over his life.

The man sitting beside me on the flight wants to talk. I sense his sideways glance, his brisk apology when his elbow touches mine. I stare resolutely at the screen, too tired to even turn towards him.

When food is served, and I've put my laptop away, he seizes the opportunity.

'First time visiting the Big Apple?' he asks.

'No. I live there.'

'Charles Whitmore.' He thrusts his hand towards me and almost knocks over my bottle of water.

'Gabrielle Grace.' I steady the bottle and shake his hand. We're going to be together for at least another four hours so there's no sense creating bad vibes.

'How do you like the Big Apple?' he asks.

I hate that term. It reminds me of the Garden of Eden or Snow White, and the danger of apples falling into the wrong hands.

'I love it.' For a country girl, I adapted quickly to life in New York. I rode the high-rise elevators as easily as I'd ridden the waves on Trabawn strand, and, after only a week, the night-time glitter of the city no longer caught against my breath.

'New York is passé.' He dismisses my adopted city with a wave of his hand. 'For the real buzz you need to go to Singapore.' He looks as if he's dressed for a business meeting, pinstripe suit and pristine white shirt, gold cufflinks that flash when he moves his hands. 'I hope you don't mind, but I couldn't help noticing you were reading about Aloysius Russell on your laptop.'

'I'm doing research on Irish politicians,' I reply.

'Gangsters, most of them.' He nods with the certainty of someone whose opinion is the only one that matters.

'That's a broad generalisation,' I say, knowing that my father would have agreed with him.

I can never remember Dad voting. Often, when there was an election, he'd be on the sea. Even when he was ashore, he refused to talk to politicians when they called to Headwind, no matter what party they represented.

'But Russell is the exception to the rule,' Charles continues.

'Tough on crime and strong on family values, that's his modus operandi. He's the best leader we *never* had.'

He's a sizable man with a meaty neck and a voice that grates. I don't want to listen to him yet I'm hanging on to his words.

'Do you know Aloysius Russell?'

'Not personally,' he admits. 'His last leadership bid was robbed from him on some trumped-up charge. His son is just a pale imitation. Far too woke for my liking.'

'What about their baby who went missing?' I ask. 'Stole' is not the word I want to use. 'That must have devastated Aloysius.'

'I remember it well.' He nods vigorously and stabs his fork into a tub of coleslaw. 'The family had a rough time of it. The publicity... I'd never seen anything like it. She was killed, of course. Aloysius made enemies, no doubt about that.'

'I've read nothing about the baby being killed.'

'It was never proved but that's the general view. Shit happens and it's essential to move on before you're covered in it.'

'Move on?' I glance across at him and resist the urge to tell him that Cajan sauce has stained his shirt. I hope he doesn't notice the blob until after his meeting. 'Surely that's not possible when a body was never found.'

'Not much of a body at three weeks. Easy enough to dispose of the little mite.'

Is it possible to endure the flight with him beside me? The chicken is tasteless, the salad wilting. I hand my plate over to the steward and open my laptop with a decisive swing. 'You'll have to excuse me, Charles. I've enjoyed our conversation but, if you'll forgive me for cutting it short, I must finish my research project.' Before he can reply, I've put on my ear buds and continue to open the many links relating to the Russell family.

My appetite for information is voracious. I can't control this overwhelming need to discover more details of their lives. Am I becoming a fantasist, like Lucas? Look where that brought him. It's time to straighten up and allow my father to rest in peace.

The plane judders and swoops. Just an air pocket, the pilot gives his verdict cheerfully. Nothing to worry about.

I welcome the turbulence, my mind in harmony with the disruption of currents that can buffer us every which way they choose.

# SEVEN

The twins have given birth. Jessica went first and delivered Josh. Two days later, it was Susanne's turn after a frantic, midnight rush to the hospital. Josh and Michael, my two nephews, born to be adored by their aunt. I watch them on video – a new one arrives every day. I love seeing their puckering faces and tiny, kicking feet. I think of Isabelle Russell swaddled in a blanket, and how she gradually emerged from its folds in those few short weeks before her disappearance.

Such thoughts are becoming less frequent. Handling my callers in the mornings doesn't allow for too many distractions. The shock of my father's death has dulled and is allowing me to think more clearly about my obsession with this lost baby. Her story provided me with a focus. It redirected my anger with Cassie. All those wasted hours when I could have been with him. Bitterness curdles my stomach whenever I think of her deliberate lies.

Rain or shine, I run through Brooklyn Bridge Park after *Gaby's Good Morning Wake-up*. It clears my head and allows me to forget the more disturbing phone calls. The number of conspiracy theorists contacting the show has grown. This morning, a woman, who claimed to be an observer of the deep state, did her utmost to convince me and my listeners that the squirrels in Central Park have been fitted with spy cameras by the CIA and trained to kill with a bite. She was followed by two other women, a Republican and a Democrat, who squared up to each other about book censorship in libraries. Silence was *not* observed.

Emily claims that handling these calls requires the skills of a seasoned lion tamer, which is why she's glad I'm back. This morning, my hand on the whip could have been firmer, but it made good radio listening.

The ratings are growing, and Libby Wolfe has returned to the streets of New York with her microphone.

My life changed after I met Emily Mason in an Irish restaurant-bar where I was working tables. She has been living so long in New York that her Irish accent is only just discernible. She, on the other hand, had no difficulty recognising mine.

'Kerry,' she said. 'Am I right or am I *right*?'

I nodded and laughed with her. She was a regular, a serious drinker when it came to shots, yet always able to walk in a straight line towards the door. I drove her home in her own car on a few occasions and rode the elevator to her apartment. Once, I stayed the night, watching over her as I used to do with Cassie. After being warned by her doctor that she was walking another straight line and this one would lead her towards alcoholism, she came less frequently to the bar. Usually, she arrived with her team from NY Eyz when they were celebrating favourable poll ratings or a particularly successful show. She stayed resolutely sober, ordering San Pellegrino with a dash of freshly squeezed lime.

She was producing Zac Pérez's early morning show at the

time. Mexican by birth, Zac was tall, dark-haired, handsome, and had a smile that could embrace the entire bar. It would have been easy for me to define him as eye-candy or a heartthrob super-cliché. That would have been a silly mistake. Zac was one of the warmest, friendliest people I'd met since I moved to New York.

I avoided falling in love with him after meeting his girlfriend, Rosa Flores. She was a dancer who sparked with an inexhaustible energy that could turn her from an angel into a she-devil in an instant. It made sense to withdraw before the first round. Her arguments with Zac occasionally erupted in the bar and caused Rosa to storm out through the door with a well-choreographed flounce. This inevitably led to Zac leaning into my ear for succour. No amount of advice was going to change his mind about her. I kept my opinions to myself and concentrated on our friendship, which would later turn out to be invaluable after Lucas proved that infidelity has more than one face.

When a vacancy arose at NY Eyz for a researcher on Zac's early morning show, Emily offered it to me. Five years in New York had subdued the more rolling resonances of my Kerry accent and I'd developed what she called 'a radio voice'.

I began my broadcasting career by doing vox pops outside office blocks and department stores, asking pedestrians for their views on new traffic regulations, the muzzling of brute-sized dogs or whatever subject was trending in the local news that day.

I might still be there pretending to be fascinated by people's opinions on crumbling walkways or graffiti on derelict buildings if Zac hadn't developed appendicitis and needed emergency surgery. His hospitalisation coincided with the summer season when regular presenters were on holidays. Emily gave me his slot while he was recovering.

The skills I'd honed while waiting tables in bars and restaurants stood me in good stead when listeners called to rant about garbage non-collections, and the survival instincts of cockroaches. Not much different to the vox pops, but I was in a warm studio and had some control over the content I wanted to discuss. After Zac recovered, his schedule was changed to mid-afternoon, much to his delight, and I began to present *Gaby's Good Morning Wake-up* from five until eight on weekday mornings.

My life seemed complete when I met Lucas in the bar where I used to work. I'd gone there with the team to celebrate an award we'd won for the best early morning show. The happiness I felt then seems inconceivable now. A memory that could belong to a stranger with whom I have nothing in common.

I sit for a while on the shoreline. The sun hits the East River and reminds me of that day in Killian's office, the view of the Liffey from the window.

My phone bleeps. Another baby video. This time Cassie is holding Josh and Michael, one on each arm as she did when the twins were babies. I have a three-year-old memory of her happiness at that time and of my own sense of self-importance as their big sister, handing her baby creams and nappies, reciting nursery rhymes to my baby sisters when they cried.

'Mammy's little helper,' she called me. 'I'd be lost without you.' She's not lost now. She's happy, not drinking, basking in grandmotherhood.

She'll be okay for as long as I stay away.

My thoughts move from Cassie to Killian. I contacted him on my return to New York. He wished me well in his response, a friendly text that said absolutely nothing to encourage a reply. We haven't been in touch since. That's not surprising. We often went for many months between calls or emails, then picked up where we left off. Somehow, this feels different. The panic I experienced in his office is under control but there is a rippling uneasiness in its stillness. An awareness that it can rear up and veer into the past when I least expect it to do so.

Does Killian ever suffer those flashbacks or have his memories of our time together been laid to rest in Shauna's arms?

Three months, that's how long our engagement lasted. Such a short time, but its impact was a slow burn that took years before I was able to put it behind me.

We were far too young yet eager for commitment, and he was anxious to bind us even closer while he was doing a media studies course in Dublin. The transition from friendship to love had been slow yet purposeful. Something that neither of us acknowledged until we kissed on his eighteenth birthday and discovered we didn't want to stop.

The engagement ring he offered me belonged to his grandmother. She was his confidante and was willing to 'lend' it until Killian could afford to buy his own. At eighteen, that prospect was something that belonged to his future. On our last night together before Killian returned to college after the Christmas break, I accepted his grandmother's ring.

On a wet and dreary February afternoon, I came home early from school. The weather matched my mood. My stomach was cramping, my back had a low-down ache and I'd started a period. Despite the pain, I was relieved.

The old boathouse had become our secret place, a dark, dank ruin that offered us shelter and privacy. The diamond on my finger was the only chink of brightness on our last night there. We didn't need light. By then, we understood pleasure, how to give and take, and bring each other to a breathless, shattering climax. We weren't aware until our blood cooled, and the chilly night penetrated our warm bodies that the condom Killian used had slipped. This fact barely registered with us but after he left for Dublin, and my period was late arriving, it turned into a nagging worry.

My mother was drunk on the day my period came. She'd remained sober for two years and traces of the old, carefree Cassie had returned to us. But the vibrations that hummed between us were always capable of sparking an argument. Initially, I thought it was Killian's absence, and my dread that I could be a mother by the time I was eighteen, that impacted my mood. I couldn't stop contradicting her or finding something trivial to disagree over. I should have known she was secretly drinking. In later years, I'd realise that it triggered something in me and that, somehow, I felt the blame for her unhappiness was on me.

She was lying on her bed and barely coherent when I entered her room. She started crying when she saw me and attempted to sit up. She kept repeating the name 'Paddy' and demanding that he stop talking to her. 'Leave me alone... stop your talking... oh, my head... my poor head... leave me the *fuck* alone.'

Drunk or sober, Cassie never cursed. Who was the butt of her anger? Paddy Ferguson, Noreen's husband? Or their eldest son, named after his father? Paddy Boyle, who ran the local garage, or Paddy Brogan, one of the *Sheila Rua* crew? I couldn't make sense of anything she said, and I was too sick to care.

The menstrual cramps were worse than usual. I locked my bedroom door in case she came in. I heard the twins arriving home from school. Their voices were audible, yet I was detached from the sound, indifferent to their knocks on my door when it was time to eat.

I rang Killian when the clotting started. By then I'd realised this late period was something more than the usual bleed. I left a message on his phone.

He never called back.

I used a towel to try and stem the bleeding. The pain was too severe to bear on my own. The twins were sleeping when I woke up Cassie. She sat up, bleary-eyed yet alert as soon as she saw my nightdress.

'What is it, Gabrielle? Dear God, what's going on?'

'You must take me to hospital right now. I can't lose my baby. Get up... get up and drive me to hospital.'

She was gentle with me that night as she explained that early miscarriages happened regularly and, sometimes, like now, for good reason.

'You've plenty more years ahead of you to be a mother,' she said. 'To have a baby when you're so young changes everything, but nature has stepped in and given you a second chance.'

'It's not too late to save her. I need to see a doctor. Please... please... please...'

She dried my tears and seemed unmoved by my pleas. No need to involve doctors or hospitals, she insisted. My miscarriage was clean and would follow its natural course. I'd be 'grand' in a few days. She'd contact the school principal with an excuse to explain my absence.

Cassie was right, of course. I was way beyond help by that stage. Barely two months in gestation, my daughter came away easily. I was convinced she was a girl, though I would later discover that it takes at least fourteen weeks and more to tell the gender. It made no difference. To this day I believe that those precious morsels of tissue that drained from me was my daughter.

It was late on the following afternoon when Killian rang. College Rag Week was his excuse for not contacting me. He'd been drinking with friends that night and his phone battery died. His hangover was woeful, he explained, and he'd only just charged his phone.

'Is anything wrong, Gaby?' He was rueful, hoarse, apologetic. 'You sounded upset.'

'I'm okay now. It was nothing important.' How dare he be drunk on the night the consequences of his carelessness in the boathouse became clear? My mother, too, became part of my rage. I must have looked washed out, haunted, yet she never commented on my appearance. The twins were too preoccupied studying for their Junior Mocks to notice, and I – who should have been equally concerned about my Leaving Mocks – was unable to think about exams.

Trabawn closed in on me. It insisted on remaining the same. I couldn't define how I'd changed yet I understood it to be profound.

I relived that night constantly over the weeks that followed as my body slowly regained its normal rhythm. Killian rang regularly but I was indifferent to his new world. I'd no interest in hearing about it or in talking to him about mine. I didn't tell him about my miscarriage. I suffered it on my own and that was how I'd carry the memory. I felt the width between us widening with every phone call. All I wanted to do was to leave Trabawn and everyone associated with it.

School was no longer an option for me. Cassie ranted about the importance of sitting my 'Leaving'. I no longer cared about an examination that had once been my greatest ambition. I dropped the familiar 'Mum' and began to address her as 'Cassie'. She knew the reason, but never attempted to discuss what happened that night.

The weeks passed before I felt strong enough to ask her which of the many men in Trabawn called Paddy had upset her so much.

'I've no idea what you're talking about,' she said. She was probably telling the truth. Blackouts sever memories that could otherwise become torturous. Something flickered in her brown gaze, as if my words had stirred a frightening vision.

'You know me,' she added. 'A friend to all.'

*To all but me*, I wanted to say, but she would have twisted my meaning, and I was in no mood for another argument.

When he came to Trabawn after reading my letter, Killian looked wild and unshaven, his hair uncombed. I'd written to him – how quaint that seems now – but I figured it was a less hurtful way of breaking off our engagement than sending a text. I told him we were too young to make such a commitment.

I gave him back his grandmother's ring and told him I was moving to New York. We used to talk about doing so together when we finished university. We'd live in a renovated warehouse with arched-shaped windows and a roller shutter door, edgy yet comfortable and perfect for our creative personalities. Now, lost in my own misery, New York offered distance, nothing else, and I went for it at full tilt, explaining to Killian that I needed to 'find myself' first before settling down. I *actually* used that cliché, having come across it in a self-help teenage magazine, repeating it back to him parrot-fashion, without having the slightest idea what it meant.

In the park, women are doing tai chi on the grass, their arms extended then turning inwards. Joggers run along the path, and a woman dogwalker with six dogs on leads strolls past me. Parents with babies in buggies or slings are everywhere or so it seems. Were they always around in such numbers and was I simply oblivious of their presence? I see their protective arms, their watchful eyes.

One day, a toddler strayed too far from the playground. His mother shrieked his name again and again. Her voice splintered my mind and in the slivers that were released I heard my father's confession, heard Cassie's terrified fury as she leaned over his coffin, heard the thud of books falling and releasing a yellowed newspaper clipping that revealed a face I instantly recognised.

I was shaking when the child was found and reunited with his mother. That afternoon, I sent my parents' hair samples to a DNA clinic for testing.

I check the mail when I return to my apartment. The information from the clinic has arrived. I carry the envelope, along with my takeaway coffee, up the stairs to the kitchen. The envelope lies on the table as I toast a bagel for breakfast.

I open the envelope. The result is positive. Dominick Grace is my father. Tears come without warning. A river of relief streaming down my cheeks. I'd allowed Aloysius and Maria Russell to grow tentacles that had enveloped me. As I read the details again, I feel those tentacles loosening and falling away. A note at the foot of the letter apologises for an administrative glitch that has caused a delay with my mother's test. The result will be sent to me shortly.

I'm breathing easier, as I gather up all the information I'd printed out about the Russell's. A biography of their lives, it reveals a family whose only remarkable trait was the disappearance of their baby. Otherwise, they are as flawed and normal as anyone else, apart from Aloysius, whose career has seen him through power heaves and scandals that would have destroyed a less ruthless politician.

I open the browsing history on my laptop and delete the entire cache. I gather up the photographs and news reports, the cut-out social pages of glossy magazines, and twist them into kindling. I add the features that chart the successes – and sometimes failures – of Isabelle's Quest, the foundation Maria established after her baby's disappearance, along with the massive amounts of print space used by political journalists – Killian amongst them – as to whether Aloysius would survive another term in office.

I strike a match and burn everything in the kitchen sink. Maria Russell stares back at me until the paper curls and the flames reach out to devour her.

As soon as the flames die down, I remove the ash from the sink and email Killian.

Hi Killian,

I'm sure you remember that conversation we had about my father's last words to me and my even dafter reaction in your office when I forced you to tell me about the Russell baby kidnapping. I'm sorry for being so emotional. Grief, I've discovered, can do strange things to the imagination and, with that in mind, I've checked my father's DNA. I know, I know, it was a foolish thing to do but, thankfully, the results have now arrived and, of course, Dominick is my father. I don't know how I could have doubted it for an instant.

As you were the beneficiary of my craziness, I'm letting you know the results and hope that this never goes beyond the two of us.

Thanks, Killian, for being my friend at a very difficult time.

Cheers,

Gaby

He responds immediately.

Hi Gaby,

It's good to hear from you, as always. Truthfully, I've been worried about you.

Obviously, I'm not surprised that the DNA results are positive. I'm glad you can put Dominick's words out of your head now and only remember how much he loved you.

I may be in New York soon. Will keep you up to date on developments.

Bye for now,

Killian

# EIGHT

In Trabawn, during spring and early summer, it's possible to see vast swathes of flame sweeping across the hills when farmers light fires to clear their land of gorse and bracken. Under environmental regulations it's forbidden, of course, but it still happens, and this ritual burning has a pagan-like ferocity as the fires tremble on the edge of containment. Everyone who sets the spark knows that if the weather conditions suddenly change, this controlled ritual can turn into an inferno.

I think often of those farmers, in the week that follows the burning of the Russell research. My mind, cleared of pernicious weeds and prickly gorse, is free to cultivate new thoughts that should bring relief. Instead, I find myself thinking about Killian and checking too often to see if he's been in touch.

I battle against checking Shauna Ross's social media. She doesn't feature in any of Killian's posts and, when I finally give in, I regret doing so as soon as I see the tumbling pile of her blonde hair and the perfect dimensions of her heart-shaped face. Her leisure activities on the squash and tennis courts prove she has stamina as well as beauty. I don't see Killian in her photographs. They must have decided to keep their relationship private. I close her down and try not to visualise them in bed together. When that becomes impossible, I visualise him listening to my playback as Shauna hammers the keyboard on her laptop but, inevitably, all I can see is her abundant hair falling over his upturned face as she bends to kiss him.

His email, when it finally arrives at the end of the week, adds to my confusion, and brings with it the worry that my ritual cleansing of the Russell family has simply made room for a new seed to root.

Hi Gaby,

I'll be in New York next Tuesday. Are you free to meet up and have a bite?

If so, I'll look forward to seeing you.

Killian

I reply immediately.

I'd love to meet up. Do you have somewhere to stay? I have a sofa bed you can use if you need it.

Cheers,

Gaby

My phone bleeps again.

Thanks for the offer, Gaby, but I've been booked into a hotel in Manhattan. I'll be interviewing Ted O'Mahoney. Have you heard of him? Irish roots and self-made. He's setting up a pharmaceutical production plant in Ireland. Nothing is official yet but I'm doing a profile on him to run in tandem with the government announcement.

I'd also like to visit the NY Eyz studio and interview you and your producer. If I remember rightly, you told me she's Irish. The pair of you would make an interesting story. What do you think? If you agree, ask her to email me if she'd like to be involved.

Bye for now, Gaby.

Killian

Emily is unimpressed when I mention Killian's proposal. 'Sounds suspiciously like a puff piece,' she says. 'Two successful Irishwomen abroad. That type of feature is so parochial. Who is this guy, anyway?'

'Killian Osmond. He works with *Bayview Dispatch*. Politics is his thing, but he also likes to write the occasional feature about life outside government headquarters.'

'I remember that rag.' Emily dismisses *Bayview Dispatch* with a shrug. 'Sensational headlines that always outshone the content.'

'He's an excellent journalist,' I argue, perhaps too vehemently, in his defence. 'Look him up.'

'I intend to do so,' she replies. 'I'll come back to you with an answer tomorrow.'

Another text from Killian helps her to make up her mind: Ted O'Mahoney, on discovering that Killian hoped to interview us, has invited us for a meal with him and Killian in Mithaecus, one of the poshest, most expensive restaurants in Manhattan.

. . .

'I thought you were exaggerating when you said your space was small.' In an exaggerated nod to the size of my studio, Killian ducks his head when he comes through the door. 'What do they think you are? A leprechaun?'

'Better not let Emily hear you.' I nudge him with my elbow, and, in that gesture, the years we lost seem to fall away. 'This is where she reigns supreme. She'll put you to the sword if you dare to cast aspersions on her kingdom.'

As it happens, they hit it off immediately and spend the first fifteen minutes after I've introduced them finding acquaintances they have in common. Emily, having satisfied herself that none have achieved more success than she has, finally allows him to interview her about her career in broadcasting. Highs and lows, successes and failures, she talks frankly about the crutches she used when the path was too challenging. I'm surprised by her openness, her willingness to admit that she's a recovering alcoholic.

'That's how we met.' She nods towards me. 'Gaby picked me up when I fell. She gave me her shoulder when I was told I'd need to join the queue for a liver transplant before I reached my fortieth birthday.'

My own path to *Gaby's Good Morning Wake-up* sounds so effortless when I'm interviewed by Killian. His thoughtful questions may have penetrated Emily's veneer, but I'm steeled and ready for them. Nothing in my tone betrays that drag on my heart every time I think about my reasons for leaving home. He photographs us, Emily at the controls, and me in my studio with headphones. The feature should appear in next week's *Bayview Dispatch*'s Sunday supplement.

When our interviews are over, I introduce him to Zac, who has just arrived at NY Eyz for his afternoon show.

'Is he your boyfriend?' Killian asks when we reach my apartment. I've prepared lunch and have wine cooling in the fridge.

'You must be joking?' I think of Rosa and her flounces, and how I sometimes hear their passionate moans as I pass his rooms on my way to work in the dawning hours.

'How's Shauna?' I'm brisk and braced for his reply.

'She's good.' He answers readily. 'And busy as ever. Her boss is a workaholic and she's as driven as he is.'

'Is she still working for Douglas Russell?' His name slips smoothly from my tongue.

'She is indeed.'

'I hope she leaves enough time over for you.' I relax my grip on the wine glass. 'Emily gave you a vivid enough description of how the fast lane can turn into a roundabout with no exit sign.'

Tonight, she sparkles in a silver-blue dress that must have cost a month's salary to buy. She's acquired that New York chic that depends on a personal trainer combined with a rigorous diet. Her sleek figure proves that the combination works magnificently. She has cast aside her reservations about calories and is enjoying lobster thermidor. I've ordered sole on the bone, as has Killian, and Ted O'Mahoney is making his way through a tomahawk steak. He's a big man, probably six and a half feet tall, and carries just enough weight to stop him being lanky.

I'm familiar with his name. First generation Irish American, self-made and owner of EOM Analgesics, he runs a pharmaceutical empire. He has a gregarious personality and an easy-going manner that soon banishes any nervousness I feel about meeting him. His knowledge of Irish politics reveals him to be much more informed than either Emily or me. We're relieved that Killian can hide our ignorance by carrying on an informed conversation with him.

The discovery that he enjoys listening to *Gaby 's Good Morning Wake-up* on his way to work surprises me. Emily smiles and raises her glass to acknowledge his compliments. He asks how I deal with the cranks and the crazies, the conspiracy theorists, and those whose hearts have been broken.

'The callers are no different to the people I met when I worked in bars,' I say. 'That's where I served my apprenticeship.'

'No better place.' He laughs and refills our glasses, wine for me, sparkling elderflower juice for Emily. 'I worked my own shifts in bars when I was a lad and I'll encourage my children to do the same.'

Emily flickers her eyelashes at the mention of children. No wedding ring on his finger so I suspect she is eyeing his potential, which is plentiful. Soon, he will employ a staff of five hundred at his Irish plant and expects the numbers to rise swiftly. The government is supportive of his plan and is offering him every incentive to open as soon as possible.

'I can't fault them on anything,' he says. 'Particularly Aloysius Russell, your minister for provincial growth. He's on the ball, as is his son, Douglas. A smart lad, who's going places, if his father has anything to do with it.'

It shouldn't matter, hearing their names tossed casually into our midst, yet my hand shakes suddenly. I put down my wine glass before anyone notices. The relief I experienced when I opened the letter from the DNA clinic has evaporated and been replaced by a gnawing sensation in my chest. 'Gnawing' is such an appropriate word: nibbling teeth constantly at work for reasons I don't understand. Killian's knee presses against mine, and his touch, the awareness of his closeness, steadies me enough to change the subject and ask about Ted's family. Three daughters, all teenagers – he rolls his eyes and gives an exaggerated sigh.

Manhattan winks and glistens when we step out from the restaurant. A chauffeured car arrives for Ted, and Emily waves for a cab. Before stepping into it she reminds me that we both need to be in work by 4 a.m. She suspects I'm going back to

Killian's hotel room. I've described our relationship as platonic, but she denies the existence of such friendships.

I walk with him to his hotel, which is only a block away from the restaurant. The night-time city charm is magical yet I'm unable to enjoy it. I shake my head when he suggests a nightcap. That gnawing sensation is back. Maybe it never went away and was just lying dormant until it was triggered again. All it took was the mention of a name. *Aloysius Russell.*

'Are you sure you're okay?' I see the concern in Killian's eyes.

'Too much wine. I need sleep if I'm to manage the show tomorrow. I really enjoyed tonight.'

'Me, too,' he agrees. 'I admit I was nervous about meeting Ted. Thankfully, he was easy to interview, a straight talker. No bullshit. His wife died two years ago. Make sure you tell Emily.'

'So, you noticed it, too.'

'Hard not to.' He smiles and leans forward to kiss my cheek. 'Any plans to visit the family, now that you're an auntie?'

'Not in the immediate. I have a daily virtual relationship with my nephews. That will do for the time being.'

Cabs pass, the drivers ignoring my signals. The awkward silence of a prolonged goodbye falls between us.

A group of men carrying sports bags walks towards us. Lucas is among them. He must be returning from the squash courts. I'd almost forgotten the slant of his profile, the hank of hair that falls across his forehead. He's wearing the navy turtle-neck sweater I bought him on our last Christmas together.

I move closer to Killian, as if somehow, he can shield me from the shock of seeing him again. Nine months since we broke up yet, instantly, I'm swept back to that morning when I entered our bedroom and understood that the direction of my life was about to be profoundly altered. I've never compared that awareness to the feeling I experienced on the night I bled and waited in vain for Killian to call me. How strange to be in the company of the two men who marked the new directions I took.

Lucas and his friends are parallel to us. Killian's closeness has a warmth I remember and he, as if also conscious of that shared memory, moves his face closer to mine then draws back when he hears my name being called.

Lucas has detached from the group and is coming towards us.

'Gaby, what a surprise to see you here.'

'You too, Lucas.' We sound civilised, polite. Nothing in our voices betrays the venom and bitterness that drove us apart.

I introduce him to Killian and recognise that stag-like instant when two men sum up each other's strengths and weaknesses. They've nothing to rattle horns over. Lucas is my past. Killian is my friend.

'I'm delighted to see the stats rising for your show,' says Lucas. 'Congratulations.'

He's a statistician who collects data and forecasts trends. If only he'd applied the same analytical discipline to our relationship.

'Thank you, Lucas. I hope you enjoyed your game.'

'Winning is always a pleasure.' To my relief, a cab comes into view and slows down. Lucas returns to his friends.

'Are you okay, Gaby?' Killian asks. 'Seeing an ex can be difficult, even if he is a pillock.' I suspect he has another word in mind if his expression is anything to go by.

'A virtual reality pillock,' I agree. 'And a thickhead.'

'Is that supposed to rhyme with something?' Killian asks.

'Absolutely.' We're still laughing as the driver pulls into the curb.

The light is still on in the hall when I return. It's three days since I checked my mailbox. I riffle through the usual junk mail, discount vouchers and charity appeals. I'm about to dump the unwanted envelopes in the bin provided for that purpose when I notice a white envelope from the DNA testing centre.

In the relief of discovering I was my father's daughter; I hadn't been worried about Cassie's test. I assumed the administrative glitch was the reason for the delay and the result when it arrived would simply confirm what I knew to be true.

I tear open the envelope and give the letter a cursory glance before the full impact of the words sinks me to the stairs. The document flutters from my hand to the floor.

I'm stricken by the realisation that a fire, no matter how it's contained, still has the power to rage far beyond my control.

# NINE

The letter begins with an apology for not sending the result back at the allotted time. The next line reveals that our DNA is not a match. No evidence had been found that could link me and Cassie into a maternal relationship.

This can't be true. Whatever administrative glitch occurred must have affected the result. I need to ring them first thing in the morning and send another DNA sample.

Davin, a cab driver who lives in the apartment next to mine, stops on his way to work a night shift.

'You good, Gaby?' He sounds concerned.

'Yeah, I'm okay.' I bend forward and pick up the letter.

'What's up?' He sits on the stairs beside me.

'Just some news from home. Nothing that can't be sorted.'

'You sure?'

'Yes, I'm sure.'

The climb to my apartment seems interminable. I can't believe my legs will support me but, somehow, they do. I search for the envelope with Cassie's hair. I only sent a few strands to be tested. This time, I'll use every single one. I could sue the lab for causing me such distress. Two weeks, at least, before they'll send back the correct result. How am I going to endure it? The thought of being buried once again under all that suspicion horrifies me.

My anxiety grows as I wait for the second result. Spring is exploding with a green fervour in the park. The shimmy-shimmering dance of new leaves barely registers as I run beneath the overhanging boughs. Even my callers with their complaints and opinions fail to distract me from the thought uppermost in my mind.

The shock when I open the envelope is less severe this time. I can no longer convince myself that an administrative mistake had been made. There it is in black and white. Cassie Grace is not my mother. It explains so much. Her hostility and distance, her drinking, her fury at her dead husband. His dying words opened a Pandora's Box. What has escaped? I'm dizzy from the lack of answers. My curiosity nudged the box open. What have I let loose?

My gut feeling has taken over and banished all rationality. The detective who guards Aloysius Russell so grimly, and answers to the name Cormac Gallagher, is the man I knew as Dominic Grace. I must find out why. Otherwise, I'll crumple and be unable to rise again.

I can only do so in Trabawn, face to face with this woman who claims to be my mother.

Emily understands my need to grieve for my father but is puzzled as to why it has taken until April for me to seek a leave of absence on compassionate grounds. She waits for me to elaborate on the suddenness of my decision. When it's not forthcoming, her voice has a distinct frostiness as she signs me off for a week.

Libby Wolfe will once again step into my shoes while I'm absent.

'Don't stay away too long,' Zac warns me before my departure. 'Compassionate leave is not a familiar concept among the NY Eyz hierarchy and Libby Wolfe is well equipped with the three D's necessary for replacing you.'

'The three D's?' I'm puzzled by the alphabetical reference.

He nods. 'She's determined, dangerous and devious. She's already tried to usurp me twice and will see this as a gilt-edged opportunity to take over your show.'

Such considerations don't seem important anymore. My focus has narrowed to one question. Cassie must provide me with the answer.

Who is my birth mother?

On the flight home, I don't open my laptop or go online. I don't engage in conversation with the passenger beside me. I try to sleep but it has eluded me ever since that document arrived.

*Torment* is a word Cassie often used when we were arguing. 'You're my torment,' she would screech. 'You were sent into this world to plague me.'

She must have that knowledge. I won't leave her side until she tells me.

# TEN

Cassie is alone in Headwind when I arrive. I enter quietly and find her in the conservatory doing the *Irish Independent* crossword, a cup of tea on a small table at her elbow. Her hand freezes on the newspaper when she sees me.

'Gabrielle...' She half rises then sinks back into the armchair. 'What are you doing here?'

'I came to see you. I was worried as to how you're coping.'

'Oh...' She tries to smile but her shock is still obvious. 'That's very kind of you. As you can see, I'm managing. There was absolutely no need to worry.'

'You're my mother, Cassie. Why shouldn't I have concerns?'

'Jessica and Susanne are only a short distance away.' This time she rises and comes towards me. Her hug is as stiff as always. 'Nevertheless, I'm glad to see you. You look exhausted. Have you had breakfast?'

'Not yet.'

'Then it's time to eat.'

I follow her to the kitchen where she scrambles eggs and makes toast. A line she uses for airing clothes stretches above the Aga. Only a few items are pegged to it, mainly blouses and underwear. My father's shirts used to hang there, the colours faded from salt spray and the sea winds. Outside, in the front garden, a *For Sale* sign has been erected.

I make myself eat. The question I must ask seems monstrous. She pours tea into mugs and clasps one between her hands before she sits down.

'What ails you, Gabrielle?' she asks. 'Don't tell me I'm the reason you're here.'

'You are, actually.'

'But I'm managing on my own, which is not strange considering that I spent most of my married life coping by myself while Dominick was at sea. Loneliness is not a new experience for me.'

I'd never thought of her as being lonely but, of course, it makes sense. My father came and went. He created excitement and joy and happiness during his time ashore, but our real life was lived in-between his homecomings.

'You're right about the reason I came home.' I push my plate aside and take a long gulp of tea. I should walk away now and forget I ever opened that box... but I can't. 'I need to know the truth about my birth.'

Her pupils dilate. This is something she can't control. The sensation of sinking into those widening eyes is powerful and must be resisted.

'What on earth do you mean?' She sounds calm. 'You know everything about your birth. I had a difficult labour. Very long and drawn out.' She grimaces, as she always does when recalling that night and day, and into the night again. Such a 'hellish' struggle to deliver me, unlike the twins, tiny sylphs, sliding gracefully into the light.

Lies, all lies, every word, every last grimace. 'My father was right.' I speak coldly, deliberately enunciating my truth. 'He stole me from my birth mother. And you've participated in his crime.'

The mug falls from her hands, splashing tea over the floor, along with the broken shards. She sits motionless, seemingly unaware of the tea pooling around her shoes. Her hands are still coiled in a half-circle. I notice how thin her hair has become. The hair that revealed her lies.

I take the documents from the DNA lab and lay them before her. Her stricken gaze moves from them and back to me. Her hands uncoil and rest on the table. I should feel hate right now. Hatred for the man who stole me and the woman who colluded with him, yet, as I stare at her weathered hands, and her heartbroken expression, my heart melts with tenderness for her. It's a momentary aberration that passes as swiftly as it came.

'I need you to tell me what happened, Cassie.'

She bends down without replying and begins to pick up the shards. I crouch beside her and do the same. Her movements grow faster, clumsier. Her hand is bleeding. She seems unaware of the cut. The blood flowing from her palm covers her fingers. She had heart issues some years ago and is on Warfarin tablets.

I find the first aid kit in its usual place in a bottom drawer. She reminds me of a child who has suddenly become aware that she is hurt. Her hand trembles as I clean the wound and clear the blood away. The cut is deep but I'm able to bring the edges together and bandage it. She still hasn't spoken. Her eyes have never seemed so brown and yet they are sunk in shadows, her eyelids quivering. Which of us will break first?

I gather up the rest of the shards and drop them into the refuse. The clinking sound they make reverberates through our silence.

'You have to tell me the truth.' I speak softly now, but insistently, and she, hearing my determination, shudders. Her body folds over, as if her spine has caved in.

'What do you know?' she asks. Her voice is hoarse, a rasp

that longs to be softened with a drink, and another. This is what I believe, but she makes no effort to move.

'I know that you and I are not related. I know that Dad was my birth father. That's fact, Cassie. I had your DNA tested twice because I refused to believe the result.'

'Testing us... what made you do such a cruel thing?'

'*Cruel*? Since when did seeking the truth become a cruelty? Deception is cruel! Stealing is not only cruel, it's criminal. Dad came to New York to tell me what he did. What you *both* did. You never left him alone. All those phone calls. You persuaded him that I was better off without that vital information.'

I expect her to interrupt and claim that I'm lying but she makes no attempt to do so.

'That's why you were so angry with him on the night of his wake.'

Gnawing... gnawing... the sensation in my chest is so intense that I can hardly keep still. 'I heard you talking to him. You blamed him for his deathbed confession. That's what it was. A *confession*. And you did your utmost to deny him that right.'

Blood is seeping through the bandage. Cassie is drained of colour when she speaks, her face glistening with perspiration. 'You've no idea what I've had to endure on your behalf. The agonies you've put me through year after year... waiting for that knock on the door. Waking up in the morning and wondering if this would be the day you were discovered.' She holds out her hand with the blood-stained bandage and brings it close to her face. 'You didn't come from my womb,' she says. 'But you entered my heart, and blood became irrelevant.'

'Am I Isabelle Russell?' This is the most important question I will ask in my lifetime. I already know the answer. I need to hear her admit it. My fury is red and sightless, a shade that blankets me from her pain and the terror that has frozen her mouth into a rictus.

'Yes.' The power of this admission closes her eyes. She holds herself rigid for an instant before keeling forward. I catch her before she hits the floor and lay her down gently. She will look like this when she is dead, her expression clenched with a dreadful secret. But she is not dead, and she revives quickly when I elevate her legs with cushions. I'm on the edge of a momentous discovery yet my concern for her forces me to be patient.

'Your hand needs stitching.' I help her to her feet. 'Everything else can wait.'

Wait for what? Twenty-eight years of deception... I can't even begin to comprehend what she will tell me.

# PART 2

# ELEVEN

## CASSANDRA

*Everything else can wait.* That's what you say. But it's not what you mean. My hand throbs. I cut deeply into it this time. How many years since I stopped doing that? Long enough to have forgotten how exquisite and all-consuming pain can be. It stills the brain, silences its thunder. After the last time, I promised Dominick I'd stop. Noreen Ferguson took the children while he rushed me to hospital. A midnight drive there, an hour and more on the road, and the blood seeping from the bandages he'd wrapped around my wrists.

After that night, I kept my promise to him. Admittedly, the bottle helped – and created its own problems. But that's a horse of a different colour, and that early vow I made with such earnestness is no longer valid.

He voided it with his last words.

Silence was the only way to go. That was what we both agreed. To do otherwise was to slide into a fathomless pit.

Eleven months old, that's what you were when we met for the first time. You were walking then. Matchstick legs, so thin it was amazing they supported you. I hunkered down to speak to you, and you immediately flung your arms around my neck. I still remember your touch. The clutch of you. Our first hug. The first of many. Love at first sight for both of us.

I'd arrived in London the previous year. I waitressed, made beds, served in bars. I didn't belong to the new breed who go over there with their master's degrees, their sights set on law and high finance. Dominick found me in a café famous for its home-baked pastries and pies. You were strapped in your buggy, and restless. A sign of things to come, but at the time I was unaware that I would have a future with this bushy-bearded man with his mass of unkempt curls. I wondered if he was homeless. He smelled clean and his clothes, though creased and damp from the rain outside, were spotless. You were struggling with your straps and crying. He asked permission to unstrap you and I nodded agreement, though allowing toddlers the freedom of the café was strictly forbidden by my manager, a waspish woman with a discontented mouth. She was on a break and the café was almost empty when he set you free and you walked straight into my heart.

Dominick looked surprised when you hugged me. 'She normally makes strange with people,' he said. 'You must have the gift.'

'She's a dote.' I held you close, such an easy thing to do. 'What's her name?'

'Gabrielle,' he said.

'What a lovely name.'

'She's my angel,' he said. I was drawn to the warmth in his eyes. You took off across the floor towards the statue of a black dog that was used as a money collection point for an association for the blind.

'Straight guess,' he said. 'You're Irish.'

'West Kerry born and bred. Where are you from?'

'Dublin,' he replied. 'I've been to West Kerry. Only once, but I've never forgotten how beautiful it is. This must be quite a change for you.' He inclined his head towards the traffic outside the window.

'I'm trying to get used to it.' He'd touched a chord. I was lonely, heart sick for Trabawn and my mother.

'You must miss your family,' he said.

'Just my mother. My father died when I was five.'

'How very sad. I'm so sorry.'

I was growing nervous. You were attempting to climb on the back of the dog and looked to be in danger of falling. I scooped you up in my arms and returned you to Dominick.

'Your wife would never forgive you if she arrived home with a bump on her forehead,' I said.

He closed his eyes and swallowed. I heard him gulp and wondered how I'd upset him. My manager had returned and was staring over at me. Chatting to the customers prolonged their stay and was not allowed.

'Gabrielle's mother died giving birth to her.' His eyes pooled with tears. I'd never seen a man cry. Memories of my father were of smiles and laughter. This man looked lost and desperate. It was impossible to move away. I sat down opposite him and touched his hand.

'Cassie, a moment.' The manager called me over to the counter. 'Fraternising with customers is forbidden, as you've been told on more than a few occasions.'

'He's upset,' I whispered. 'He's lost his wife.'

'Then let him leave and look for her.'

'She's dead.'

'I see. Well, that's not your concern.' I can't remember her name, just her face with her pursed lips and stony indifference. 'Bring him his order and tell him to put his child back into her buggy.'

'She's not doing any harm.'

'This is not an argument, Cassie. It's an order.'

I walked back to his table. 'There are rats in the kitchen.' I spoke loudly enough for her to overhear. 'And also, outside it. I can suggest an excellent café just a short distance from here. I'd be happy to show you the way.' I took off my apron and folded it carefully before laying it on the table.

We left together and remained that way until he died.

We married when I was pregnant with our twins. They were a year old when my mother developed dementia. She'd lived all her life in Trabawn and had always dreaded the thought of ending her days in a nursing home. We moved into her home at Headwind so that I could care for her.

After she died, and I inherited Headwind, we decided to settle down in Trabawn. Dominick found work on a deep-sea trawler. This meant long periods away from us. The excitement of his homecomings, the presents he bought you and the twins, the brief honeymoon whirl before he had to leave again. Happy years, these are the memories I want to cherish.

We decided not to tell you about your mother. By then, I knew all about Mary Carter. A brief fling, Dominick said. One that ended two months after it began. She contacted him when she discovered she was pregnant and planned on having their baby adopted. Dominick begged her to marry him. Having been abandoned at birth, he dreaded the thought of a similar fate for you. Mary refused to listen. She had a life plan that didn't include marriage and motherhood.

Fate had other ideas. A postpartum haemorrhage shortly after delivering you caused her death and you belonged to Dominick from then on.

I believed him when he said it was important that you never found out how easily he could have lost you. He didn't want you grieving for a mother you never knew. Why would I have disagreed? I never thought of you as anything but my kin. My love was as pure and unconditional as the love I felt for my daughters. It was easy to invent a birth story. After a while, I forgot it wasn't true. I refused to shorten your name. Let everyone else call you Gaby but I held firm. I'd always loved my own name – Cassandra – yet it had been truncated before I could even pronounce it. Later, when I heard that the original Cassandra had been gifted with the power of prophesy but cursed by never being believed, I resigned myself to always answering to Cassie.

I thought our lives were balanced, on an even keel. There were moments that darkened and caused me to imagine horrors, but those terrifying instances always passed. On such occasions, the sun shone with a particular brilliance because I'd considered what its eclipse could be like. That's the reason for talismans, rituals, spells and lucky charms. We believe they can protect our families, but their energy is useless when chaos intervenes.

Why has this happened now? I knew I'd grieve for Dominick but there was also a slick, almost sickening relief that he would take his secret to his grave. *I stole you...* what possessed him to whisper his confession in that final moment and shatter my peace of mind? Why has he left me alone to face his daughter, who is determined to walk into a storm of his own making?

# TWELVE

## GABRIELLE

Cassie bears the pain without flinching as her wound is stitched. For the first time I notice her wrists: the criss-crossed scars that can mean only one thing. Her shoulders arch forward as she realises I've seen those telltale marks. I don't want this new knowledge of her volatility and vulnerability.

The doctor attending her has also made his own judgement. I can tell this by the gentle way he holds her hand. He looks over her bent shoulders towards me and the crease between his eyebrows deepens.

Are there other scars hidden under the long sleeves she wears, even in summer? But not always, if childhood memories serve me right. In those days, we spent our summers on the beach, building sandcastles, digging channels, collecting shells, and she was there with us in her skimpy T-shirts and shorts. When did that change? Was I even aware that she was covering her arms and, now that I look back, her legs? We were locked in combat by then and I, a rebellious and sullen teenager, was only conscious of her anger.

'Would you like to wait outside for your mother?' the doctor asks. Despite his quiet tone, I recognise the authority behind it.

I find a chair in the waiting room. It's crowded with casualties, who slump in their seats and stare at an inaudible television.

Cassie is pale and delicate-looking when she finally emerges, her hand paw-like in its bandage. She turns away from me when I try to link arms with her. I want to ask about the scars. The right words won't come. What right words are possible? *When did you start self-harming? Were you planning to take your own life? Did you deliberately slash your hand with that broken shard of crockery to avoid my accusations?*

She switches on the radio when we reach the car and closes her eyes. 'No talking until we're home,' she says, and remains silent for the journey back to Headwind.

Once inside the house, I switch on the kettle. I'm afraid Susanne or Jessica will arrive with their babies and soak up the tension between us. I need this conversation without intrusions.

Cassie takes the tea I brew and holds the mug clumsily with her left hand.

'When did you know the truth about me?' I ask.

'You were thirteen.' No more pretence, then.

'How did you find out?'

'Dominick was forced to tell me.' Her hand trembles so much she is unable to hold the mug steady. Tea sloshes over her fingers but she seems unaware of the burn.

'Why? If he carried his secret for thirteen years, what made him confess?' I feel pressure in my ears, as if I'm rejecting the information I've demanded.

'It wasn't a confession,' she says. 'He was always convinced he did the right thing. You were his daughter. You belonged to him.'

'And to Maria Russell.'

She starts to shake her head, then stops, as if she knows by my expression that we're beyond pretence.

'Your father was in love with her.' The unreality of our

conversation has no boundaries. What will I hear next? Justification? Contextualisation?

'She was married to Aloysius Russell,' Cassie continues. 'Dominick couldn't bear the thought of you being reared by another man who would damage you.'

Yes, justification.

'How could he damage me? He's spent the last twenty-eight years searching for me. Did you ever give him a thought when you saw him make another appeal for information?'

'I trusted Dominick—'

'You trusted a man who married you under false pretences and then involved you in his crime. I never took you for a fool, Cassie.'

'You have to understand—'

'I don't have to do anything except demand the truth.'

'It's a truth that must never come out.' She is still shaking but is sitting straighter.

'You *can't* be serious.' How dare she think she can deny me my birthright? 'I've lived a lie from the time I was three weeks old. Do you really want this atrocious subterfuge to continue?'

'Yes, I do.' She speaks flatly. 'Your sisters—'

'Half-sisters.' The word sounds unreal, heartbreakingly so, yet I repeat it with even more emphasis. 'They are my *half*-sisters.'

She nods in acknowledgement. 'Does that make a difference?' she asks. 'Do you love them any the less?'

'Love has nothing to do with this.'

'Love has everything to do with it,' she insists. 'Aloysius Russell is ruthless and powerful. Dominick witnessed the man behind the public image and hated what he saw.'

'Considering that my father was having an affair with his wife, I don't think he was in a position to make such a judgement.'

She shrinks back from my accusation but makes no effort to interrupt.

'You should have gone to the police as soon as you discovered the truth. Why didn't you, Cassie? Tell me, *why*?' My voice is a shrill accusation. 'You're as guilty as he was. You deserve to go to jail for your part in his crime.'

Is there any way back from this conversation? It's plunging us into unfathomable depths. I'm not sure we'll ever be able to surface.

'And that's exactly what will happen.' She brings her wounded hand to her mouth and seems astonished to see the bandage. Is she as immune to pain as she is to my feelings? 'Do you want me to end my days in prison?' Her fear is stark and etched on her face.

'I'll tell the police you didn't know what Dad did.'

'They won't believe you.' How many times has she imagined this scenario? 'I'll break under their interrogations. I *know* I will. What about Jessica and Susanne? They'll be questioned, so will their husbands. Their business partnership will collapse from the scandal. As for the media, they'll be crawling all over this story, not just from here, but they'll come from abroad. Trabawn will never be the same again. It'll always be associated in the public mind with your story.'

I can tell by the impassioned way she speaks that this is not the first time she has considered how our lives would implode if the news broke. How often had she discussed it with my father, the two of them together, plotting, planning, deceiving me?

'Am I supposed to care what happens to you?' I understand, now, why my life was divided between the years she was ignorant of his crime, and the years that followed the revelation. 'You turned against me when he told you. I thought I was to blame for your alcoholism and your violent outbursts. You hated me, I could tell. I just couldn't understand why.'

'You're so wrong.' She reaches across the table. I think, for an instant, that she is about to touch me. I tighten my hands around the mug. New York mugs, skyscrapers and traffic, brought home one Christmas as a present. I want to be back there, headphones on, listening to someone complaining about rude cab drivers.

'I still loved you, but knowing what happened had to make a difference,' she says. 'You sensed it. All that conflict and dread mixed up inside me. I could see how confused you were at first, and then your own anger sparked off mine. In the end, it was easier to drive you away rather than face reality.' She draws in her breath and releases it on a shudder. 'Don't do this to us, Gabrielle. I'm begging you. Think about the lives you'll destroy. Think about Maria Russell.'

'You mean my *mother*?'

She draws back slightly, as if the term offends her; an obscenity that intrudes on the façade she'd constructed so successfully.

'The truth will come out about her and Dominick.' She states this with a quiet emphasis. 'How can it not? She and her husband will have their DNA tested. What is that going to do to their marriage? Dominick told me that Aloysius Russell's first wife died by her own hand. It was all hushed up. No one in the media got wind of it... but Dominick knew.'

'You mean *Cormac* knew.'

The stress I add to his name is also a question. Did she know how he earned his living before meeting her? An upright member of the Garda Síochána with a brief to guard Aloysius Russell from attack. The irony of it.

'I'll *never* call him by that name.' Her flinty tone says it all: he shared his secrets with her and, even now, battered as she is by my questions, I believe she's still hiding information from me.

She glances towards the kitchen window and visibly relaxes when Susanne, followed by Jessica, pass by on their way to the back door. They're wearing identical baby slings with my nephews cocooned inside them. This is our first meeting since they became mothers, apart from the virtual world I share with them.

'Oh my god, Gaby, what are you doing here?' Susanne flings open the kitchen door and runs towards me, her arms outstretched. Michael gives a startled yelp when he is squashed between us. She releases me and lifts him from his sling. 'Meet your Aunty Gaby, Michael,' she says in a sing-song voice as she holds him aloft for my inspection. 'Do you want to hold your nephew?'

Her smile suggests there is only one answer to that question. I hold him so gingerly he immediately begins to cry.

Cassie believes that babies live in a spirit world in their early months. Their psychic awareness is awesome, apparently, as is their ability to see angels. What does Michael see in my face that reduces him to tears? Is he reacting to my trembling arms? My ravaged expression? The dust of this implosion has sucked the air from the kitchen, but the twins are utterly unaware that their parents savaged what should have been my past.

They breathe evenly and contentedly as they cover the table with nappy bags, changing mats and breast pumps.

'My god! What happened, Mum?' Jessica balances Josh on her hip as she inspects the bandage.

'It's nothing.' Somehow, Cassie manages to smile. If her daughters notice the strain behind it, they will put it down to pain. 'I broke a cup and cut myself when I was picking up the pieces.'

'Why didn't you ring us?' Susanne says.

'Gabrielle was here. She drove me to the hospital.'

Michael has stopped crying. Perhaps he senses my heart softening as he lifts his tiny fingers to touch my hair. His mouth reminds me of a rosebud that is about to open. I take Josh in my other arm as Susanne and Jessica fuss over Cassie.

Tears run down her face. She makes no effort to wipe them away. I don't want to feel sorry for her. *You were a difficult labour*, she used to say when we demanded our birth stories. *So many hours of suffering. Hellish.* How could she have lied so convincingly for all those years? Now that I think of it, those stories about my 'difficult' birth only began to emerge when I was a teenager.

And him, the man who loved me enough to steal me. What am I to make of him?

'Why are you home?' Susanne takes her son from me and sits down to breastfeed him. I watch his cheeks move in and out, his earnest eyes staring up at her. Cassie's gaze is equally intent as she waits for me to reply. I see a new purpose in her. She is determined to protect those she loves and I, who also love just as deeply, struggle to control my rage.

'I wanted to see Headwind for the last time.' I'm shocked at how convincing I sound.

'Gaby... Gaby... your home is with us now,' says Jessica. 'We'll sort out a bedroom for you in each house and no one else will *ever* use them.' She sits opposite Susanne and brings Josh to her breast. Two Madonnas, they are blissfully unaware of how close I am to ruining their lives.

'Thank you... both of you.'

'When are you going back to New York?' Susanne asks.

'Tomorrow.' My decision is sudden. I can't wait to leave this house where a terrible deceit has been played out, and will still continue to resonate long after I leave here.

'So soon,' Jessica protests. 'It was hardly worth your while getting off the plane.'

'Believe me, it was worth the journey.'

Cassie looks down at her wounded hand and remains quiet.

Her lips are chapped from the salt of her tears, but her eyes are dry.

'Come to dinner tonight,' says Susanne. 'We've invited the Osmond's. Killian's here for the weekend. Did you know his brother has a new girlfriend. Her name is Alicja and she's Polish.'

'Jamie says she's the real deal,' Jessica adds. 'He's never said that about any of the others, so we think he's serious this time. We're dying to meet her.'

'Okay, that sounds like a plan.' The burn in my chest is easing but my mind is in turmoil. It will remain so until I find a way to unravel this momentous discovery.

Susanne's signature dish, Moroccan lamb tagine, tastes as delicious as it always does. Initially, all attention is focused on Alicja, who has perfect English and works as a translator for a multinational finance company. She has been seeing Jamie, Killian's brother, for six months and it's obvious they're crazy about each other. Inevitably, as the meal progresses, the chat turns to local issues and gossip.

'Will we take our coffee outside?' Killian whispers after dessert. A heated discussion about a local council election has erupted around the table. No one, even Alicja, who is just as involved in the conversation, shows any interest in joining us.

'Why didn't you tell me you were coming home?' he asks, when we're seated on the terrace. We're bathed in the soft glow of an overhead lantern. Spring is well underway. The night is warm, the breeze balmy. Twilight took time to fall and now, as darkness settles over the garden, solar lights glimmer among the trees. 'I could have driven you here and saved you the cost of a rental.'

'It was a sudden decision. Cassie told me she'd a potential buyer for Headwind. I wanted to see the house one last time.'

'Things have moved fast since Dominick died,' he says.

'She doesn't want to be alone,' I reply. 'I understand how she feels. It's isolating living so close to the headland. She'll be better off with Susanne.'

'I guess. How are you doing?'

'Good. All is well. Emily was impressed with the feature you wrote about us. So was I... *actually*.'

'You sound surprised.'

'Not surprised. But it was strange to see myself from a different perspective.' I swallow with difficulty. Being close to him again is risky when I'm feeling so defenceless. 'I thought I'd see Shauna here tonight.'

'She considered coming with me. Work won out in the end, unfortunately.'

'Doesn't she believe in weekends?'

'Saturday is when Douglas holds his clinic,' he replies. 'She helps him out and is learning the ropes of politics in the same way as he did from his father.'

'Do you ever worry about them working so closely together?'

'It's *not* an issue.' He speaks with certainty and raises an eyebrow. 'You seem tense. Is everything okay with *Gaby's Good Morning*?' His stare can be disconcertingly direct.

'I feel as if talons are only inches from my back, and they belong to Libby Wolfe. She's had an eye on my show for months.'

'You're a professional. I'm sure you can deflect the talons.'

'What about you? Any word on that promotion?'

'Nothing yet,' he admits. 'But I've some good news.' He nods emphatically. 'I'm not allowed to share it yet so keep this to yourself. Ted O'Mahoney is setting up the Irish division of EOM Analgesics in Trabawn.'

'You're *kidding*.'

The news *almost* breaks my self-absorption. 'The interview

I did with him will run in the Sunday edition,' Killian says. 'He intends taking over the tech factory that closed last year. The announcement will be made officially on Tuesday with a press conference.'

'That'll be a fantastic boost for the community.'

'Absolutely,' he agrees. 'Alicja will be working for him. She speaks four languages or maybe five – I've lost count, to be honest. There'll be lots of different nationalities, as well as locals, employed.'

'Did you have anything to do with his decision?'

He laughs, shrugs. 'I may have mentioned the town once or twice. But, believe me, Ted wouldn't make such a decision unless he was sure it was viable to locate here.'

'It's a wonder you were able to keep the news to yourself during the meal.'

'Like I said, I'm breaking confidentiality by telling you in advance.'

'Why am I so honoured?' I'm picking up vibes, uneasy ones, and they're radiating from him.

'Aloysius Russel and his son are coming here for the press conference.' He pauses and rubs the back of his head. 'I didn't want you to see the coverage in the paper and wonder why I didn't mention it.'

'Why should that bother me?' It's difficult to stay still.

'No reason... except... well... you were upset that day in my office.'

'I believed for one mad instant that I could be that stolen baby so why should it surprise you?'

I sound convincing yet every fibre of my being longs to confide in him. Is he my friend first, or does being a journalist usurp our friendship? The Isabelle Russell revelation would shoot his career into the stratosphere. Could he resist the temptation not to frame my past in a sensational headline? His relationship with Shauna Ross worries me. What if he forgets his promise to me and decides to tell her about our conversation in Trabawn, and my insistence on checking the *Bayview Dispatch* archives? What if she feels duty-bound to repeat this information to Douglas Russell? Cassie's voice is inside my head, her dread echoing. I'm unable to brush her fears aside.

'The shock of Dad's death impacted me more than I realised,' I say. 'Thankfully the DNA result brought me back to reality. You need have no worries about my sanity.'

Laughter drifts through the open window. I wonder how Cassie is coping. Unlike me, she's had fifteen years of hiding the secret, so it shouldn't be difficult.

'I'd be interested in attending that conference on Tuesday.' My decision is unexpected yet definite.

'You'll be back in New York by then.' Killian sounds surprised.

'I can prolong my stay. I'd like to see Ted again. Bring a report back to Emily.' I laugh, artlessly, I hope, but he's frowning.

'What about Libby Wolfe?' he asks. 'Aren't you worried about her talons?'

'I'll take my chances.'

The back door opens, and the diners emerge. Some light cigarettes, others go to the end of the garden and sit down under the pergola.

When Cassie joins us and hears that I've changed my mind about returning to New York tomorrow, she closes her eyes, as if she is unable to bear the sight of me.

# THIRTEEN

## GABRIELLE

I stay out of Cassie's way as much as I can over the weekend. She lies on in the mornings so I can research my biological family without interruption. I check Douglas Russell's social media and try to see myself reflected in the face of my half-brother. It's the same with Maria. Now that I know for definite that she gave birth to me, I wait to be consumed by... what? What am I supposed to feel? A tug at my heart or the leap of recognition I must have felt each time she lifted me in her arms?

Cassie's despair and fear have numbed all normal emotions. I'm trapped in a cage called love. I wait for her to start drinking again. When that doesn't happen, I wonder if she is doing so in secret. Her eyes are clear, her complexion so pale that the red veins on her cheeks stand out in stark contrast.

Killian's article about Ted O'Mahoney's venture in *Bayview Dispatch*'s business section in the Sunday supplement sets Trabawn alight with excitement. Almost immediately, Cassie's mobile phone starts bleeping. She's on a community WhatsApp group and the messages come fast.

'I understand why you decided to stay over.' She looks up

from her phone and studies me. 'You want to meet that man and his son.'

'*You* are my family.' I don't attempt to deny it. 'That bond will never break. But it's hard... so hard.' I cross the room and kneel in front of her. 'Douglas Russell is my half-brother. All I need is one meeting. Then I'll go back to New York.'

'No, you won't.' She speaks with certainty. 'One meeting will never be enough. You're signing my death warrant.'

'Stop it, Cassie. Why would you make such a dreadful threat? It's emotional blackmail.'

'I can't handle it. I *can't*.' She sounded the same on the night she berated my dead father. Out of her depth, only this time she's sober. She grabs my shoulders, her fingers digging deep. 'Do you remember when you first started calling me "Cassie"?'

'Not exactly.' Her question startles me. 'It just happened as I grew older.'

'It *didn't* just happen. You screamed my name and called me a murderer because I refused to take you to the hospital when you miscarried.'

After all those years she's finally acknowledging what occurred. I'm ashamed that I was so harsh with her. I'm about to apologise when her voice hardens with conviction.

'And now you have the power to destroy me,' she says. 'I carried Dominick's secret at great cost to my sanity. I've not been the same since. You're going to send me back to that place again.'

'What place, Cassie? What are you talking about?'

'Hell.' Her bottom lip is split. Blood glistens when she bites down on it. I know she's going to tell me something and know, also, the instant she changes her mind.

'Blood is thicker than water,' she says. 'It's never been any other way.' I see her deadening gaze, hear her defeated sigh. 'You'll do what you want to do, as you always have.'

'I'll go back to New York as soon as the press conference is over.' I stand and stamp pins and needles from my feet. 'I'm not even going to speak to Douglas Russell. I just want to see him, no more than that. You've nothing to fear from me.'

Does she appreciate, as I do, that keeping such a promise will test the love I feel for my family to the hilt?

On Tuesday morning, Cassie is still in bed when I leave Headwind. It's a relief not to be subjected to her reproachful glances and scarcely controlled dread.

The press conference is taking place at the Trabawn Lights Hotel. Journalists arrive and crowd the foyer. Rain was predicted on the weather forecast. It arrives in a torrential downpour that splashes off the flagstones and bends the flowers. Word is out that the ministerial car is nearing the town.

Killian introduces me to a reporter, who carries an RTE microphone. The television station obviously thought this announcement was important enough to send a team to record it. Other TV logos are visible on microphones. This is a big business story.

Photographers surge from the warmth of the foyer as the ministerial car is driven through the gates. I watch from the window as Aloysius Russell steps from the back of a black BMW. The years have been kind to him. He remains an imposing figure with his puffed-up silver hair and sturdy chin. He looks younger in real life than in his photographs. The back doors open. Shauna Ross is the first to emerge. A leather tote bag hangs from one shoulder. Her black trouser suit is a perfect foil for her shoulder-length blonde hair. The twins are right. She is stunning, but I only have eyes for the man who is straightening and following his father. Douglas Russell ignores the umbrella held up by an assistant as he strides towards the waiting photographers. Shauna, conscious no doubt of her hair, takes shelter under the umbrella as she hurries behind him into the hotel.

Douglas is cut from a sleeker mould than his father and carries himself with an assurance born of wealth. Such a sheen is instantly recognisable. He is relaxed and informal, on first name terms with everyone. He pats Killian's shoulder, a comradely gesture that suggests they've crossed paths before now.

I fix my gaze on the window as the raindrops trace a filigree on the glass, forming and collapsing, reforming in new shapes that I will never be able to follow.

Another car, a sleek Mercedes, has pulled up outside the hotel. Ted O'Mahoney emerges and enters the foyer. The two men shake hands. Ted looks so bulky and rugged beside Douglas's elegance. They seem oblivious to the photographers as they walk towards Aloysius, who is surrounded by local councillors and businesspeople.

Under Douglas and Shauna's guidance, the attendees move into the room where the announcement that EOM Analgesics is coming to Trabawn will be officially declared. Killian has reserved a front seat for me.

Aloysius and Ted join my brother-in-law, Eddie, chairperson of the Chamber of Commerce, on the stage. Maeve Dooley, one of my ex-teachers, is overshadowed by her large mayoral chain as she joins them at the table.

The conference is short. This is a good news day and even the pickiest journalist cannot find anything controversial to challenge. After the speeches end, the noise rises as the media and public mingle. Killian is standing with Shauna by the side of the stage. They speak briefly. Nothing in their demeanour suggests they are in a relationship, or that she will lie beside him tonight and whisper political secrets into his ear... though I doubt that's true. Everything about Shauna Ross speaks of professionalism. I suspect that what happens in Russell land stays in Russell land. How do she and Killian manoeuvre their way through those delicate boundaries?

Finally, we make our way to the restaurant. It has been reserved for the afternoon and is soon filled with a hungry media.

Douglas is on the move, going from table to table, shaking hands, slapping shoulders, bending attentively over a female journalist who is recording their conversation on her phone. He stops at my table and holds out his hand.

'I recognise you,' he says.

My heart lurches and Killian, who had stopped to speak to me, becomes motionless in the seat beside me.

'Gabrielle Grace, if I'm not mistaken,' says Douglas. 'The terror of the New York airwaves.' His voice is deep and has an intimacy that excludes those around us. 'I read about your success in *Bayview Dispatch*, courtesy of our friend here.'

My mouth opens but I'm unable to reply. Do I look like a goldfish gasping for air? Killian stirs. I hear him swallow before he speaks. 'Gaby and I go back a long way,' he says. 'I couldn't pass up the opportunity to interview her, as well as Ted, when I was in New York.'

'An interesting feature.' Douglas is still holding my hand. 'I enjoyed reading it. It's not easy to forge your own path in New York. I must congratulate you.'

Flesh on flesh, how am I supposed to feel? His touch weakens me. Can he sense my panic? Does he mistake it for embarrassment or, perhaps, adulation? He's handsome enough to be used to the latter. His handshake is lasting longer than is deemed appropriate.

'We must meet when I'm next in New York.' He smiles as he loosens his grip and nods.

'I'll look forward to it.' My voice is calm as I rummage in my wallet and hand him my business card.

'I look forward to meeting you again.' He moves smoothly on to the next table.

'That was an interesting exchange,' Killian says, after a pause. 'Will you meet him when he goes to New York?'

'I'm sure it won't come to anything.' I push my plate away, too dazed to eat.

'He seemed willing enough. Word is that he'll do anything for a photo op.'

Douglas has returned to the main table and is deep in conversation with Ted O'Mahoney. He was three years old when I disappeared. Has he any memory of me? Did he carry me in his arms? Did I ever grip his finger, squeezing tight, as Josh and Michael do when I hold them? I must have shadowed his childhood, a ghost whose presence he was never allowed to forget.

'Are you okay, Gaby?' Killian is watching me closely. 'You look as though you're miles away.'

'I'm fine, honestly.' Cassie has turned me into a liar and made me the guardian of her secret. 'Are you going to introduce me to Shauna?'

His partner's handshake is cool and brisk. We don't rattle imaginary horns but there is a speculative glance that sums up my position in Killian's life. What has he told her about me? Not a lot, if the professional gloss of her smile is any indication.

Soon, the media will depart from Trabawn, and the town will settle back to its drowsy-afternoon self. Killian is returning to Dublin, then flying on to Geneva. I promise to contact him next time I'm home. He kisses my cheek and tells me to travel safely. Does he suspect that a new road is opening before me? One that shimmers and dulls, cracks and is renewed, as my mind swings between the family I've found and the one I'm in danger of losing.

# FOURTEEN

## GABRIELLE

Usually, when I leave NY Eyz, I stop off at the Lucky Black Cat for coffee and breakfast. This morning, I ignored the need for a caffeine rush and went directly home to change into my running gear. I run for an hour and try to shake off the unpleasantness of this morning's programme. I've always believed I can control raw encounters between callers, but an argument between two women with opposing views about racially charged police brutality was so heated and ugly that I was forced to use the mute button.

I finish my run and am warming down with stretch exercises when my phone rings.

'Gabrielle, it's Douglas Russell,' a voice says. 'Remember me?'

I'd planned what I would say to him if, perchance, he did ring, but the words are swept aside from the shock of hearing him. A lump lodges in my throat. It strangles my voice and he, probably thinking I've forgotten him, reminds me that we met last month at a press conference in the Trabawn Lights Hotel.

'Yes, I remember you.' Finally, I can speak.

'Is this a bad time to ring? Sounds like you're out of doors.'

'I'm in a park but I can hear you okay.'

'And I heard *you* earlier.' He laughs, as if amused by the battle of words that had taken place earlier. 'That's some show you present. Very lively.'

'How come you're on my time zone?' I reach a bench and sit down before my legs give way. 'Surely you should be dealing with affairs of state rather than tuning into my bear pit.' I sound chirpy, like the twittering birdsong in the background of our conversation.

'I'm in New York with a delegation of Irish designers who are exhibiting at the Hibiscus Gallery.'

'Oh... that sounds exciting.'

'The opening is tonight. It's an amazing exhibition. I hope you'll come along and cover it. An Irish presenter interviewing Irish designers in New York, what could be more perfect?'

'As you listened to my show this morning, you must know it's purely a phone-in.'

'Yes, I noticed. You're quite the shock jock... of the female variety, I mean.' He's still amused. Is his laughter indulgent? Patronising? Being annoyed with him will give me focus.

'I'm a listener, Douglas, not an interrogator. I don't do interviews. Zac Pérez does a magazine slot in the afternoon. If you're looking for publicity, which I'm sure you are, Zac has a much better time slot and a wider audience. And I can also give you other media contacts—'

'That won't be necessary. Shauna, my comms officer, has an excellent press list. Would Zac agree to you doing the interviews and using it on his show?'

Cassie's chilly gaze is on the back of my neck. Hairs lifting, cold shivers, and the sun, as if unable to cope with my heartbeat, hides behind a lowering cloud. Rain will come soon. I remember the raindrops in his hair, the sheen of his face as he faced the journalists. The image had stayed with me, battling constantly with Cassie's grip. She holds me down even though we're a continent apart. Her terror has become mine, an inner monologue that taunts, questions and torments me in equal measure.

I press my feet into the ground, but my legs continue to shake. 'I'm not sure... I'll ask Zac but no guarantees. Email me the press release and I'll make sure he reads it.' I'm pleased by my professional attitude, which is extraordinary considering the conflicting emotions running through me.

'I hope to see you at the opening,' he says. 'Are you familiar with the gallery?'

'Yes, I am.'

'Shauna will introduce you to the designers and I hope to speak with you after the exhibition ends.'

I haven't agreed to his request or checked with Zac but, already, Douglas Russell believes it's organised. What's surprising about that? Political clout breeds arrogance and, remembering the tilt of his chin, I suspect he's inherited his father's authority.

The Hibiscus Gallery is crowded when I arrive. Zac has agreed to my proposal. We've collaborated in the past and he's happy to feature my interview with the designers. I make my way to the reception and ask for Shauna Ross. After a short wait, she weaves through the attendees and extends her hand.

'I'm delighted to meet you again, Gaby. Douglas is just about to give his opening speech. Please follow me. I've organised a seat for you.' Her hair is a sleek swirl as she walks ahead of me to the area reserved for the press.

Douglas is just beginning to speak when I slip into the end of the row. He praises Irish design, its innovation and state-of-the-art creativity. His manner when he introduces each designer is personal without being cloying. What would Cassie think if she could see me now? Instinctively, I press my hands to my stomach and Douglas, as if conscious of my gaze, glances in my direction and recognises me. He gives a slight nod, barely perceptible, and I can't look away, even though his eyes have locked with mine. Locked so intensely that the wrench I feel when he averts his gaze feels physical, almost sickening. He hasn't missed a beat in his speech and that shared instant could have been imagined... and probably was... What reason would Douglas Russell have to single me out in a crowd and bestow on me more than a fleeting flicker of acknowledgement?

This thought is still turning over in my mind when his speech ends. The applause is enthusiastic, and he is soon surrounded by people as he makes his way through the exhibition of jewellery, pottery, woodwork, fashion and lace.

Shauna has chosen the designers to be interviewed and provides me with photographs of their designs. The designers are easy to record and happy to talk about their careers. By the time I've finished, Douglas is still busy. Shauna's promises that he will soon be free are repeatedly broken.

'I'm afraid I can't wait any longer.' Fate is intervening and opening an escape hatch for me. 'I need to edit the interviews for Zac's show tomorrow and I've a very early start in the morning. Give my apologies to Douglas.'

Outside, on the pavement, I lean against the gallery wall. Now that I've removed myself from Douglas Russell's steady gaze, I feel bereft. Tears come without warning.

I made a mistake coming here. It won't happen again.

The following day, Zac interviews me about the exhibition. Later, that evening, Shauna rings.

'Douglas hoped to thank you personally,' she says. 'Unfortunately, he has back-to-back appointments until late tonight. We're delighted with the coverage.'

'Thank you.'

'It was good to meet you personally again, Gaby.' Her voice changes from its professional pitch and becomes softer. 'Killian told me you grew up together in Trabawn.'

'Our mothers are friends and neighbours,' I reply. I guess he must have mentioned me after all. 'Trabawn is a close-knit community.'

'So I believe. He gave me a guided tour of the town after the EOM reception. What was he like as a boy?'

'Same as any boy – a tease and a torment.' I'm not going to give her my memories. She has him, that's more than enough. I end the call and wonder if he brought her to the places that were once special to us.

My mind hurtles towards the boathouse and instantly regrets doing so. A pigeonhole – that was where I lodged that memory; allowing it to slowly erode until it became nothing other than an occasional pinprick.

Not so these days. I didn't deal with it then, and I don't want to rake over it now when I'm consumed by the reality of the present. And, yet, the loss I suffered that night keeps stopping me in my tracks and forcing me to acknowledge it.

I don't expect to hear from Douglas again yet, when he contacts me four days later, I feel as if a long-anticipated moment has arrived.

'My sincerest apologies for not being in touch with you sooner, Gabrielle,' he says. 'I've tried to ring many times and been interrupted before reaching my phone. The week has been frenetic. Not that I'm complaining. The exhibition has been an astonishing success. Your interview created a very positive reaction. I'd hoped to have a coffee with you before leaving but I'm heading shortly to the airport. All I can do is thank you again.'

That's it, then. The exhibition is over. I no longer have to breathe the same air as my half-brother. I feel lighter already.

*Good girl, Gabrielle. I knew I could depend on you to put your own family first. I trust that the bonds we share, stronger than blood and bone, will never be betrayed.*

Cassie's voice has colonised my head, whimpering and whispering, warning me not to falter. Does she understand that the ground is shifting, and my footsteps falter a little more every day...?

# FIFTEEN

## GABRIELLE

'How are you doing?' Emily raises her voice. We're relaxing on a bench outside the Lucky Black Cat café. Brooklyn seems to be in a permanent state of disrepair and the roar of pneumatic drills makes it difficult to hear each other.

'I'm good... good.'

'How can you be "good" when you're still grieving for your father?'

I'm surprised by the personal nature of her question. Usually, our conversations are brain stormers about the show and which topics will draw the most heat. Even when I split with Lucas, she merely said, 'Crap happens. And it's better to happen this way rather than waiting for it to hit the fan.'

'I miss my father dreadfully,' I reply, 'but he'd want my life to return to normal as soon as possible.'

'And has it?'

'Yes. Why are you asking?'

'I think you're finding it difficult to hold it together,' she replies. Her tone is kind rather than judgemental, but it still alarms me.

'That's not what the ratings say.' I'm immediately on the defensive. 'My listenership continues to grow, according to the stats.'

'I sense things before the listeners do.' She prides herself on knowing in advance when it's time to restructure a show before it wanes in popularity. 'I'm not worried about your show. *You*'re my concern. I was afraid you'd lose it on the phone-in this morning.'

'Emily, those stories were harrowing. I'm not made of steel.'

'Adoption is always an emotional issue to explore,' she replies. 'But it's no more harrowing than some of the topics you've handled. I know when a presenter is in distress, no matter how hard they try to hide it. There's something...'

I brace myself against her pause.

'I really liked your father,' she says. 'I can understand that it will take time to adjust to losing him. But it's more than grief that's causing you problems. Do you want to tell me what's going on?'

'Honestly, Emily, there's nothing else going on.' I'm alarmed by her observations. 'I'm sorry if I was less than professional—'

'I never said you weren't professional. Just keep me in mind if you feel things are getting outside your control, even a little. We can work on it together. Do you hear me?'

'I appreciate your offer—'

'Then heed it.' She drains her coffee and checks her watch. 'I'd better activate my antennae. I've a meeting with management in half an hour. You never know what those assassins have in mind to axe.'

I unlock a rental bike and cycle through Dumbo into downtown Brooklyn. I abandon it at a terminal and shop for groceries. I need to pay attention to what Emily said. A meeting with management means only one thing. Changes are afoot in the schedules and Libby Wolfe will be waiting to pounce at the slightest sign of weakness on my part.

Someone is sitting on the stoop outside my apartment. My father sat on the same step, a bowed figure who was unrecognisable to me for an instant. Not in this case, however. Lucas's shoulders are straight and set with purpose as he rises to his feet. He's wearing jeans and a sleeveless top that shows off his chest and newly developed pecs. He's changed his hair and gone for a Caesar cut, shaved close at the sides with his springy curls bunched on top. Not a good look, and one that reveals a shiftiness in his expression. Was it always there, hidden by my rose-tinted glasses or am I projecting a veneer of deceit over a face I loved for two years?

'What do you want, Lucas?'

'Just to talk.' He winces at my tone.

'I was under the impression we'd nothing left to say to each other.'

'You can't believe that, Gaby. Just hear me out, that's all I'm asking.'

People passing by nudge against him as he stands awkwardly before me. 'Invite me in, please. I won't stay long, but I need to apologise properly and explain what went wrong with us.'

The newspaper clippings I burned have been replaced by others. They cover the walls of my living room. I can follow every step taken in the search that followed my abduction. The leads that promised much and delivered nothing, the false arrests and those who gave themselves up, claiming to be my kidnapper. Their moments of fame, the focus of attention, no matter how negative.

'I'm not going to invite you into my apartment, Lucas. It's my space and I don't want it contaminated.'

'Then let's go somewhere else.' He's decided to ignore the insult. 'Please, Gaby. For old time's sake, if nothing else.'

I choose an Irish pub. It has a small snug that will give us privacy. Dim lighting filters through stained glass panels above our heads. The outside sounds from the main bar are muted. Lucas orders two beers and admits to being heartbroken. His body and mind have been cleansed through therapy and gym workouts, and he's anxious to settle down.

Since our break-up, I've discovered that love can die suddenly or slowly. That's if we're allowed a choice in such matters. I chose the latter. Now, looking at him sitting beside me, I realise I no longer have any feelings for him. What I'd believed would be an enduring heartache has come to an end. His virtual infidelity is insignificant when balanced against the new direction my life has taken.

'I made a mistake. *One* stupid mistake that I'll regret for the rest of my life,' he says. 'We had – and can still have – an amazing relationship if you'll give me another chance. I've changed so fundamentally that I hardly recognise myself anymore.'

*Welcome to my world, Lucas.*

'I miss you, Gaby. I love you. I want to marry you.' He speaks with the zeal of someone discovering the value of monogamy. 'You have to find it in your heart to forgive me.'

Is this a request or a command? He has an irritating habit of running his palms along his arms when he's agitated and the sound of skin on skin adds to the urge to run as far as possible from him.

'If my decision had anything to do with forgiveness, there wouldn't be a problem,' I reply. 'I've also changed since we split up. I've other needs now and resuming our relationship is not one of them.'

I'm sorry I chose the snug. It's claustrophobic. His voice is too loud when he describes his transformation from online sex addict to repentant lover and future husband.

'I hurt you deeply, I can see that.' He takes a swig of beer before continuing. 'But you, also, should accept some responsibility for our break-up. Not that I'm excusing my behaviour. Not for *one* minute, but you were so preoccupied with your work. Even when you weren't on air, you were thinking about the next morning's show or mulling over some insult you'd received. Have you any idea how lonely I was when you were continually on your laptop—'

'*Stop.*' I cut across his analysis of our mutual blame. 'With your history, you're not exactly in a position to accuse me of being preoccupied with my laptop.'

'Gaby... listen to me. I'm trying to have a reasonable discussion about our break-up.'

'But I don't have the time for such a discussion. I've made other plans and have no intention of allowing you to derail them.'

'What plans?'

'I've decided to move back to Ireland. I no longer want to live in New York.' My conviction grows with each word I utter.

'You're not serious.' I understand his disbelief. He knows about my troubled past with Cassie. 'You swore you'd never go back. Your mother—'

'Regardless of what I said, that's where I'm going.'

'What about your show? The stats—'

'Contrary to what you think, NY Eyz was never the centre of my world.' Once again, I interrupt him.

I can't believe that I've just made such a profound decision seemingly off the top of my head, yet I know it's the right one. I'm consumed by a mystery that has taken me over. My mind churns like a millwheel, driven by a river of speculation, confusion, and an incessant longing for answers.

'I've been thinking of quitting the show for some time now,'

I tell him. 'After a while, you realise you're just regurgitating the same issues.' What am I saying? I'm shocked by the way words keep bubbling to the surface. 'Nothing really changes, no matter how often people phone in to grumble and nit-pick,' I continue. 'I might as well be working in a supermarket complaints department.'

'You love your show,' he says. 'Twenty-four-seven, like I said.' He pushes out his bottom lip, a piscine pout that reminds me of a fish. 'Is that guy you were with in Manhattan the reason you're going home?'

'Why should he have anything to do with my decision?'

'I saw the way you were looking at him.'

'You're *so* wrong.'

'I doubt that very much,' he says. 'I should have known you wouldn't hang about before finding my replacement.' He's sulking now. How could I have forgotten his tendency to do so when contradicted?

'Are you suggesting that the reason why I no longer love, or even like you, is because I've found a replacement?' It's not worth my while being annoyed with him yet I'm unable to stop. 'I always worried about your arrogance. Now, I realise it was just a disguise for stupidity. Don't contact me again, especially if you're lonely and in need of some virtual relief.'

It's a cheap shot but it allows me to walk away with the last word. I return to my apartment and spend the rest of the afternoon online. I need to read up on the issues I intend to introduce tomorrow. Instead, I browse the web and print out another feature about Isabelle's Quest.

My family turned my name into a brand, with Isabelle's Charity Auction, Isabelle's Memorial Mass, Isabelle's Gala Ball.

The hours pass. I'm stiff when I stand. I need to put some order on the information I've found before it overwhelms me.

. . .

I'm aware of tension as soon as I enter NY Eyz. Emily's expression when she calls me into her office suggests that complaints from listeners have exceeded what she believes is tolerable. She wants me to be opinionated and stir up debate, which often leads to a surfeit of calls to the station from disgruntled listeners.

'I presume you know why you're here.' She leaves me standing when she sits down behind her desk.

'I've no idea, Emily. Yesterday's show wasn't *that* controversial—'

'This has nothing to do with the show. Am I to assume from your blank expression that you haven't checked your social media yet?'

Something big has occurred. I'm in the centre of it without any idea why. I usually check my phone as soon as I wake up. Last night, feverish with longing and unable to stop probing... probing... I forgot to charge it. After fitful hours of sleep and wakefulness, I was late rising. My phone, still dead, is in my backpack. I intended charging it as soon as I reached the studio.

Emily waves aside my explanation and turns her laptop towards me.

I haven't opened Lucas's blog since our break-up and its sudden appearance on Emily's screen fills me with apprehension. He blogs about statistics. It should be a boring subject, but he uses graphics and videos to entertain, and occasionally writes stories aligned to the statistics he's presenting. In this instance he's charted the success of my morning show, alongside information that revealed my listenership approval, their age profile and social media interaction, their buying habits, and all the data NY Eyz had compiled.

I read the headline – *Female Shock Jock's Explosive Claim.* In his blog, he elaborates on my impending departure from NY Eyz, particularly my claim that *Gaby's Good Morning Wake-up* is akin to working in a supermarket complaints department.

'Did you compare your show to a supermarket complaints department?' Emily asks. 'We can issue a statement denying his claim. To do so, I need to know the truth.'

'I love my show. What I said has been taken—'

'Do you admit to saying it?'

'But not like that... not the way it looks on his blog.'

'Let me repeat myself. Did you tell Lucas Walker that *Gaby's Good Morning Wake-up* is the same as working in the complaints department of a supermarket?' Emily enunciates each word with slow deliberation.

'Yes. I can explain—'

'No, let *me* explain what that means,' she brusquely interrupts me. 'We cannot demand a retraction. Our phones have been ringing non-stop since that post went up, with calls from listeners who will no longer be tuning into *Gaby's Good Morning Wake-up*. Any hope of changing their minds has disappeared because of your unprofessionalism.'

'It was a throwaway remark, Emily. This is just petty revenge. There *must* be a way to make amends.'

'It's out of my hands, Gaby. The order came from above. Your contract specifically states that if you tarnish NY Eyz's reputation by either word or deed, it immediately terminates your contract. However, as you intend to leave us, that's hardly going to be a problem for you.'

Emily's efforts to look impassive almost succeeds. She's probably regretting breaking her golden rule to keep a professional distance from her team, especially the presenters, who, she claims, have XXL egos. I wouldn't describe our friendship as close, yet I sensed that behind her hauteur she liked me.

This forlorn thought brings no comfort as I pack my rubber plant and family photographs into a box and walk away from a job I'd self-destructed. Libby Wolfe is already in my seat and howling as the doors of NY Eyz swing closed behind me.

. . .

Two weeks have passed since I was fired. I stopped crying after the second day and had given up on the idea of murdering Lucas by the third. A decision has been forced on me. Not only does it leave me jobless, but it also allows me space to try and analyse this sudden urge to return home. Under the layers of uncertainty and conflict I've suffered since my father's death is the need to understand how I came to be born.

# SIXTEEN

## GABRIELLE

The apartment I've rented in Dublin's Liberties is a utilitarian building where people pass like ships in the night. Unlike Zac's brownstone, it's anonymous and silent enough for me to lose myself behind its walls. Holding back tears is an ongoing struggle. I'm sick of them: their slithery roll down my cheeks when I'm least expecting them, their choking hold on my throat.

I've told Cassie and the twins I'll visit soon. I sound as if I'm lying, which I am, but the twins take what I've said at face value. Sleep deprivation has killed their curiosity gene. Cassie, however, is fretting. I'm too close for comfort once again.

Killian arrives unannounced one evening on his way home from work, or so he claims. His apartment is in the opposite direction, but I let it go. He'd spent the weekend in Trabawn for his father's sixtieth birthday and heard from Jessica that I was living in Dublin.

'I can't believe you didn't tell me,' he says. 'I knew you'd left the morning show. I assumed you'd taken another time slot. What happened?'

'A difference of opinion.'

'Want to talk about it?'

'Not really.'

'Aren't you going to offer me a beer, at least?'

'Let me check the fridge. You take a seat in there.' I gesture towards the living room, which is fully furnished with a stranger's taste.

'How's everyone in Trabawn?' I ask when I enter with two beers.

'All good. Apart from my father, who can't believe he's now a sixty-year-old.'

'Was it a good party?'

'It ended at six in the morning so form your own opinion. If you'd bothered to contact me, I'd have invited you.'

'I hope Shauna enjoyed it.'

He tilts the bottle and doesn't reply until he sets it back on the coffee table. 'I believe you met her in New York?'

'I did. She was very helpful in organising interviews with an Irish delegation.'

'A delegation led by Douglas Russell, I believe,' he says.

'Yes. He phoned and asked for my help. I was able to oblige.'

'Has he anything to do with your decision to come back?' This direct question startles me.

'Why on earth would you think that?'

'I'm just concerned that you're still dwelling on what Dominick said—'

'*Oh*... for God's sake, Killian, what are you going on about?' I allow him to hear my exasperation. 'I told you about the DNA results. Why are you bringing my crazed fantasy up again?'

'I'm sorry that you think I'm interfering.' He doesn't look sorry, just concerned, and proves it with his next words. 'I noticed how focused you were on him when you met at the EOM press conference.'

'*Focused*?'

'Yes.'

Was I so transparent? If so, that's hardly surprising yet it's disquieting to realise Killian was aware of it.

'Are you suggesting I'm interested in him... *romantically*?' My laughter is a pale imitation of mirth, and it falls flat between us.

'I hope you're not,' Killian replies. 'Douglas is... how shall I put it?' He pauses, shrugs. 'He's already taken.'

'One way or the other, I don't care,' I reply. You're exaggerating and, yes, you are interfering, and so far off the mark that it's not even funny. If you must know, Lucas went online again. Only this time he used his wits rather than...' I stop myself in time. This is not a joke. His viciousness does not deserve laughter.

Killian's disgust is palpable as I describe how I lost my job.

'But surely you could have fought your corner with Emily?' he says. 'You don't usually give in without a fight.'

'I'm tired of fighting.'

'That's most unlike you.' He sighs. 'What are you hoping to do here? It can be tough to break into broadcasting. I'll give you a few contacts that might help.'

'I'm not looking for work. I can support myself for a few months while I establish myself as a podcaster.'

'Podcasting?' His eyebrows lift. 'That's certainly a change of direction.'

'It's the only way to go. Print is dying and listeners are tired of hearing the same old guff from opposing sides on television. Podcasts allow for nuance, and the time to delve deeper into issues. But who am I telling? Yours is excellent.'

He nods, knowing I'm right about his podcast, *Clearing Smoke from Mirrors*. I've learned much from listening to his interviews. His ability to sail close to the political wind is something I admire.

I want to ask him about Shauna. Why is he here instead of going straight home to her? She's probably working late for the very man we've been discussing and he's killing time until she's free. Does he appreciate this irony? And what does it matter? Their life together is their business, yet he seems determined to meddle in mine.

The longing to confide in him grows more acute. I brace myself against it. He is a newshound, one of the best. How could he possibly keep the information I'd spill into his ear under wraps? I cannot demand that from him. My way forward means moving in shadows, as has been the case since I was three weeks old.

I've bought a new phone and transferred my numbers, deleting Lucas's as I did so. Douglas Russell's number remains. It's acquired the power of a detonator. Contacting him is a temptation that never eases. I ring Cassie whenever the urge becomes too strong. She's alone in the house yet she whispers into the phone, as if she's afraid her warnings could take flight beyond the walls and expose her family to the effects of a heinous crime.

Equilibrium is no longer the master of my days. I swing from deciding to reveal my identity to a chilling acceptance that I'll never take that step. My skin feels raw, as if it has been sandblasted. New furies grab me without warning. I've heard from Susanne that Cassie is drinking again. Headwind has been sold. Nicholas has refitted the *Sheila Rua*. Libby Wolfe is a rising star on *Wolfe's Morning Howl*.

Tonight, I drink wine for courage and ring Douglas. His answering service comes on. Hearing his voice again, its engaging inflections, as if he is genuinely sorry to have missed my call, is a relief and a regret. These opposing emotions are a constant struggle. I leave a brief message and end up sitting on the floor, sobbing from too much wine and a longing I'm unable to resist.

. . .

'Douglas Russell returning your call,' he says. Two hours have passed since I phoned him and, despite the lateness of the hour, he has made contact. 'What a pleasant surprise to hear your voice, and such a coincidence. I've tried to contact you. Your old number was no longer accessible. This new number tells me you're in Ireland.'

'I'm living in Dublin now.'

'That's a surprise. When did you return?'

'Just over three weeks now. It's a long story. I won't bore you with the details.'

'Details always interest me and it's often the seemingly boring ones that prove to be the most interesting. What can I do for you, Gabrielle?'

'Please call me Gaby. I don't respond to any other whistle.' Adding this touch of levity helps to control my nervousness.'

'Gaby, then.' Is he smiling? His voice sounds lighter and suggests he is.

'I won't take up much of your time but I've an idea I'd like to discuss with you.' I sound in control, which is extraordinary considering that the trepidation I feel is both stomach-turning and exhilarating.

'Sounds intriguing,' he replies. 'If memory serves me, I owe you a coffee... at the very least. We could meet in Buswells Hotel.'

The hotel is only a short walk from Dáil Éireann, the house of representatives, and a favourite meeting place for plotting politicians. I'll be in like-minded company.

Douglas cancels at the last minute. Shauna rings to apologise. A political upheaval has suddenly erupted. Frantic meetings are underway, and he needs to enter the voting lobby later tonight.

As usual, I can't decide if I'm relieved or devastated. The evening news comes on. An issue about neutrality has arisen and the Dáil is in late-night session. That explains Douglas's cancellation. It was a crazy idea to contact him in the first place. I've been granted a reprieve. I must use it wisely and stay away from him.

I spend the weekend in Trabawn. The young couple who moved from Dublin to work in EOM Analgesics, and bought Headwind, are gutting the interior and wrapping the exterior in external insulation. No more drafts and cold showers, no more huddles around the fire, toasting bread and roasting marshmallows. All those childhood memories dispersed in the rubble.

Susanne's house is in an equal state of renovation. Cassie is sleeping in the guest bedroom until the extension is complete. Hammering and sawing compete for attention against Michael's teething wails. Eddie is tense about the cost overruns to the granny flat and Susanne bursts into tears as soon as I arrive. We hug and whisper so as not to awaken Michael, who has finally settled down. Cassie has driven into town, supposedly to shop for groceries. Susanne fears she'll call into O'Meara's off-licence for a bottle of vodka. She's drinking slyly, hiding bottles in her car and at the back of the wardrobe.

I order Susanne to bed. She looks as though she has forgotten how to close her eyes for longer than five minutes. I change Michael, clumsily I admit, and am shocked by the amount of detritus a small body can eject. I smooth cream over his little bottom and fasten his nappy. Was this what Dad did in those early months before he met Cassie and handed me into her care?

Michael is sleeping contentedly when I wheel him in his buggy to Jessica's house. Here, there is silence – another sleeping baby and Jessica, in a leotard, is doing yoga in the conservatory. The babies continue to sleep as she fills me in on what she believes is Cassie's depression.

'Her doctor has prescribed anti-depressants, but she won't take them,' she says. 'She's clammed up and become very secretive, so there's no talking to her. I used to believe you were the catalyst...' She stops abruptly and presses her fingers to her mouth. 'Oh, my god, that sounds appalling. I didn't mean to imply—'

'It's true. I was the trigger. She told me so often enough.'

'That's *just* an excuse, Gaby. If she wasn't blaming you, she'd find something else to hang her alcoholism on.' Jessica is flushed, her anger barely under control.

'You don't think it's because I'm back in Ireland?'

'No, she started drinking before you came home. We didn't notice it for a while. Then she let Michael fall from her arms. God knows what would have happened if Eddie hadn't been there to catch him. Honestly, I don't know how Susanne copes.'

Jessica has been offered a job in marketing with EOM Analgesics and will begin working there as soon as her maternity leave ends. Susanne will work in human resources. Cassie has promised to mind the boys. Now, they're afraid she'll be the one who needs minding. The tolerance they've always shown towards her has dwindled to barely concealed resentment.

Susanne phones, terse and anxious, as I'm returning with Michael. 'I've left a key for you under the red flowerpot,' she says. 'I've to collect Mum from town. It's as I suspected. She's in no condition to drive.'

Back in her house, I feed Michael, who transfers most of his food to my hair. He barfs over my favourite sweater and rewards me with beatific, gummy smiles. We're standing at the window admiring a flight of birds when Susanne returns.

The speed with which she enters the driveway and slams on the brakes jerks Cassie from her slumped position in the front seat. She straightens and glances towards the window. Razor-sharp eyes rake over me but she is too drunk to focus for long.

Susanne helps her, none too gently, into the house. The guest bedroom door slams. Michael, having caught sight of his mother in the driveway, starts to wail when she doesn't reappear. I can't pacify him. His screams bring Susanne running.

'I was putting her to bed,' she says, as she whips Michael from my arms to her breast. 'You'd better finish undressing her. She was drinking in the park. That's a new low. I'm telling you, Gaby, I can't take it anymore... I simply *can't*.'

Cassie has fallen asleep on the bed. She lies like a becalmed starfish and remains just as limp when I move her onto her side. She moans and shudders. The swell of anger I felt when Susanne told me she was drinking again has drained away. I'm the reason for her internal misery. What I'd judged to be resentment and disinterest in me was always a deep-rooted dread of discovery. I try to imagine that fear: waiting, always waiting for the knock on the door, the click of handcuffs on her wrists.

I cover her with the duvet and leave her to sleep it off.

I'll spend tonight with Jessica. The relief of escaping the tension radiating from Susanne is a guilty pleasure. Josh is sleeping soundly when Jessica slices a pizza and opens a bottle of wine. She's still breastfeeding so she pours a thimbleful for herself and hands the bottle over to me.

I make my way through two glasses while she rants about Cassie. Finally, she clasps her hands to her face and exclaims, 'Oh, for God's sake, let's stop talking about her,' which I'd happily do if I'd managed to get a word in edgeways.

'Did you know that Killian Osmond was instrumental in bringing EOM Analgesics to Trabawn?' She grabs the wine bottle and pours what looks like another thimbleful until the level rises.

I nod. 'I knew he interviewed Ted O'Mahoney but, having met Ted, I doubt if he would have made the decision based on one person's opinion.'

'Probably not. But Killian put the word in his ear. He's the local hero. How is he doing?'

'As far as I know, he's good.'

'Have you *not* been in touch with him?' Jessica has a way of turning a question into an accusation.

'Why should I? You are *aware* he's in a relationship?'

'Whatever.' She dismisses Shauna with an airy wave. 'I always thought the two of you would get it together again.'

'Don't go there,' I warn. 'You sound like Noreen Ferguson.'

'She thinks he's the reason you decided to come back. Actually... we *all* do.'

'Well, you're *all* wrong,' I retort.

'What happened between you and Lucas?' she asks. We both know that as soon as I bare my heart, she'll be on the phone to her sister, so I give her the same answer that had to satisfy Susanne.

'We were no longer a fit for each other.'

'That tells me absolutely nothing.' She tops up my wine glass. 'Come on... confess all into my sympathetic ear.'

I've no intention of revealing the details of my embarrassing break-up. That story would travel, despite any oath of secrecy she'd make. Killian is the only person I've trusted with it. I should ring him tomorrow and apologise for the calls I haven't returned.

'Lucas met someone else,' I reply. 'I'm still too raw and upset to talk about him.'

'Ah... sorry for probing, sis.' She pats my arm and nods. 'Plenty more fish in the sea, as Dad used to say...' Her lips pucker. 'God, I miss him so much. He'd have adored the boys.'

'I agree. It's just... so sad.' I've had too much wine and am developing a headache.

Jessica, after dabbing away her tears, explains in graphic detail about an attack of mastitis she suffered on her right breast. The pain in my head intensifies.

'It sounds horrendous,' I manage to say, when she pauses for breath. 'Would you mind if I go to bed?'

'Perfect timing,' she replies, as Josh's cries become audible on the baby monitor.

'Go up to him, Jessica. I'll tidy up.'

Out in the kitchen, I rinse dishes and recork what's left of the wine. This must be a migraine. I've never had one before and must assume the sensations I feel – the tilting floor, as well as the pressure on my ears and eyes – are related. I lurch to one side when I move, and the zigzagging flashes seem real enough to pierce my head. I collapse into a chair, afraid I'm going to fall.

Jessica helps me up the stairs to the guest bedroom. She brings a glass of water and headache tablets from the bathroom, as puzzled as I am by the suddenness of the attack.

After she leaves me, I lie perfectly still in the darkness. The pressure of a secret. How much longer can my head contain it? I understand why Cassie took to the bottle. She knows why I decided to come home. Family blood, thicker than water.

Killian will ease this pain. The longing to hear his voice surprises me. It must have been the comment Jessica made about my reason for coming home. They've mistaken our friendship for something more intimate. My phone is missing. After a quick search, I remember charging it in Susanne's house. My forehead tightens even further. I moan into the pillow and will myself to fall asleep.

I awaken to Josh's laughter. Nicholas has arrived home and is holding him aloft when I enter the kitchen. My headache has become a throb rather than a pound, and I'm anxious to return to Susanne's house to retrieve my phone.

The morning is bright, the sky clear. Workmen have already arrived. The grating pitch of an angle grinder fuels my headache. Susanne greets me on the doorstep, Michael snug against her hip. Cassie is missing again.

'She ate her breakfast and showed no signs of a hangover,' Susanne shouts above the din. 'I was upstairs feeding Michael when she left. I only discovered she was missing when Eleanor Osmond rang to warn me that she'd just driven erratically past her house.'

'Could she have gone to Noreen's?' I ask.

'No, I've already phoned her. Mum's hiding somewhere with a bottle. I know she is. When I find her...' Words aren't necessary to decipher Susanne's anger.

'You take your car and I'll take mine.' I rummage in my pockets for my keys. 'Why don't you go towards the strand? I'll check the headland. Let me get my phone. I left it charging in your kitchen.'

'It's on the table.' Susanne is already walking towards her car. 'That politician who was at the EOM reception rang you earlier. Douglas something... I can't remember his surname. He left a message to contact him.'

'Douglas Russell?'

'That's the one.'

'When exactly did he ring?'

'Sometime during breakfast. Mum took the call.' She straps Michael into his car seat. 'I'm ringing Ashford Clinic as soon as I return. If she doesn't go into rehab, she can visit *me* in a psychiatric hospital.'

One missed call. One missing woman. No coincidence, just hard facts. Douglas rang. Cassie answered his call. She's distraught. It's imperative that I find her and convince her that she has not been betrayed. Will she believe me or see through the smoke screen that I've erected between us?

. . .

I drive towards Burly's Head. The trees are stunted here and twisted from Atlantic gales. Today, the holiday season is in full swing. The headland with its magnificent views is busy with cars, and sightseers with walking poles and binoculars. Far below us, the waves have an unhindered ferocity as they race ashore and the sun shining from a cloudless sky fills the ocean with radiance.

Cassie's car is parked on the look-out promontory where tourists stop to gaze at the view through a telescope.

The wind almost knocks me off my feet when I step outside. Her car is empty. I can't see her anywhere as I continue climbing towards the summit.

When I call her name, it's swept aside like spume yet, instinctively, I know this is where I'll find her.

# SEVENTEEN

## CASSANDRA

Do you remember the picnics? The sighs and moans as you and the twins trudged behind me to the summit, your backpacks filled with sandwiches, crisps, apples and orange juice. I coaxed you forward with songs and I Spy games when you all declared you were unable to walk another step. All complains were forgotten when I spread the picnic before us, and there was always unanimous agreement when we returned home that that was the best one *ever*.

You discovered this spot the first time we came here and recognised it as a natural shelter from a wind that never dies on this wild outcrop. A crown of rocks forming an enchanted circle. That was before Paddy Murdock came into my life. As I drove past Burly's Bend with its wicked twists, I felt his presence in the car. His intentions seemed as clear as they'd been on the night he came to my door.

After years of crewing on trawlers, Dominick had saved enough to buy the *Sheila Rua* and form his own crew. He was fishing for cod when Paddy Murdock came calling. Not that I knew his name then. He was simply a motorist who'd driven too far along Burly's Head and was lost. His car was damaged. He'd taken a bend too narrowly coming down the headland and scraped the wing against a protruding rock. The damage affected the fuel tank and petrol had leaked out. He described where the accident occurred: Burly's Bend, a mile from Headwind, so dangerous with its curves and steep slopes.

He was drenched and shivering. You probably can't remember how difficult it was in those days to use a mobile phone in Trabawn. Unable to get a signal, he'd made his way to Headwind. The only house with a light in the window, that's what he told me. I'd stayed up late to make your costume for the school Christmas pantomime. As Pierrette, in ruffles and lace, a swirl of petticoats – you looked a dream in it as you danced with Pierrot.

But by then, I'd lost sight of you, and all I saw flitting across the stage was a lie that could destroy me.

Unaware of how our lives were about to change, I offered this stranger shelter. What else could I do? The possibility of anyone coming to his assistance at such an hour and in such a remote location was nil. I'd no reason to be suspicious of him when he sat down at my kitchen table to drink tea and eat the remains of the stew I'd cooked that day. I gave him dry clothes and hung what he had been wearing on a clothes horse in front of the fire. I made up the sofa in the living room for him and had no thought of danger when I lay down to sleep in my own bed.

I awoke in the small hours, three in the morning to be exact. I remember checking the time and wondering if one of you had cried out. I thought it could be you. Those night terrors you'd experienced when you were younger had passed but they left occasional traces.

The house was silent as I walked towards your bedroom. I could see from the glass pane above your door that the room was in darkness. I was reluctant to disturb you by switching on the landing light. You probably don't remember that I always left it on during those night terror years so that its glow would shine through the glass and comfort you.

I was about to go back to bed when a light blazed from behind the glass. Almost instantaneously, the room darkened again. I could have put that flash down to imagination, but it was repeated a number of times in quick succession. It seemed as if you were switching your bedside lamp on and off.

The room was dark again when I opened the door. I could just make out the shape of a tall figure standing beside your bed. I knew it had to be him.

He was photographing you. That much became clear when his camera flashed again. I could tell by your stillness that you were sleeping and he, as if aware that I'd entered, turned around. His face was a white blur as he came towards me. He must have set his camera down as his two hands were free. I'd no time to react before he grabbed my arm and pushed me back to the landing. He was brutal, one hand covering my mouth, his other hand twisting my arm behind my back. I couldn't call for help, not that I would have done so: protecting you and the twins was all that mattered in those moments.

He dragged me towards my open bedroom door. I believed he was going to rape me. If he did so, I knew I would endure it silently rather than expose you and your sisters to the horror he would inflict. My terror, I can't even begin to describe it. I was screaming silently. Is that possible? To hear my horror reverberating through my head yet knowing my mouth was clamped tight, my voice inaudible?

He pushed me down on the side of the bed and threatened to kill me if I moved. I'd left the bedside lamp on and I could finally see his face. This quiet stranger whom I'd fed only a few hours earlier had turned into a brute.

'Do you promise to stay quiet?' he asked.

When I nodded, he slowly loosened his hand on my mouth. I tried to speak, to plead with him not to harm us but I couldn't get the words out. He pulled over the chair from in front of the dressing table and sat down opposite me.

'I'm not going to hurt you,' he said. 'Nor am I going to harm your twins unless you give me reason to do so. My only interest is the girl.'

'What girl... what do you mean?' I was finally able to speak.

'Isabelle Russell,' he said. 'Don't bother pretending you've no idea who she is.'

I thought he was raving. Either that, or he'd made a dreadful mistake and had confused you with someone else. But these were just fleeting thoughts that scarcely penetrated my terror. 'I don't know anyone by that name. My daughter's name is Gabrielle Grace.'

'Gabrielle Grace doesn't exist.' He laughed, a sharp bark without humour. 'She's a figment of you and your husband's imagination.'

'You're mistaken. She's my daughter—'

'You're either a liar or a fool.' His contempt for me was clear. Time will never erase his face. The assured way he smiled, as if he knew exactly what he was doing. What was even more frightening was that the name Isabelle Russell sounded familiar. I'd no idea where I'd heard it or how it was recognisable until he spoke again.

'You've been harbouring a stolen child for thirteen years,' he said.

Of course, it came to me then, the reason why the name had a haunting resonance. I'd been living in London when Isabelle Russell disappeared, yet it was impossible to miss the headlines and news reports. Her story had spread beyond Ireland, mainly because she was the daughter of an important government minister. The fact that her father was Aloysius Russell kept the story alive for longer than normal. Such publicity, day after day, along with the pleas and rewards offered, her mother's tears glistening on her cheeks as she appealed to the public for information about her missing baby.

I would have laughed at him if I hadn't been so frightened.

'I'm neither a liar nor a fool.' I found the courage to snap back at him. 'It's ludicrous to believe that my husband and I could have anything to do with that baby's disappearance. We were both living in London when she was taken.'

'Correction. *You* were living in London. He was in Dublin at the time.'

'No, he wasn't. And even if he *was*, why in God's name would he steal a baby?'

'God has had very little to do with my life and his.' Paddy Murdock took from his pocket a photograph that had been cut from a newspaper and passed it to me.

A ring of men, that was all I saw at first. I recognised Aloysius Russell. No mistaking his imposing forehead and direct gaze.

The gaze of the man sitting opposite me was shifty. Why hadn't I noticed it earlier? Mean, shifty and dangerous. I couldn't relax my guard for an instant.

That was why I didn't notice the figure in the background of the photograph until he leaned forward and pointed to him. 'There's your husband. Cormac Gallagher is his real name. Not that you need me to tell you that.' His voice had a grating nastiness, so unlike the apologetic and grateful tones he'd used earlier.

'You're delusional.' I was convinced by that stage that he was mad. It made him no less threatening but, perhaps, I could reason him out of his fantasy. 'My husband's name is—'

'Cormac Gallagher.' He cut across me and jabbed his finger at my face. 'The only thing that isn't a lie is that he married you. Whether a marriage is valid under an assumed name is another matter altogether and not my concern. Look at him and tell me you can't recognise him.'

I stared at a stranger. No beard, and his hair clipped so short I could see the outline of his skull. How could he be the hairy man I loved, with a beard wild enough for birds to nest, and tangled hair that he seldom combed? But the more I looked at him, the more recognisable he became. It was his stance that convinced me. He was protecting the politician in the same way as he stood guard over the crew who worked his trawler. He watched over us with the same concentration when he was on dry land. It was never obvious, yet I was always conscious that there was something watchful about him. I believed it was part of the baggage he carried from his childhood; the feeling that danger always lurked behind his shoulders and what was precious to him could easily be stolen.

I refused to believe that a familiar posture should endanger my world. The longing to shred the photograph and fling the pieces back at this home-wrecking stranger had to be resisted.

'This man is not my husband.' I had to stay strong and convince him he was delusional. 'I can show you his birth certificate, where his name Dominick Grace is clearly stated.'

The man glowered at me. His mouth was ugly with hate. 'Maybe you're as ignorant as you claim to be, so listen carefully. Me and Cormac Gallagher go back a long way. We were kids together at St Alexis or, to be more accurate, at the fuck-end of nowhere.'

I presumed he meant the orphanage. Dominick never gave it a name, but he spoke occasionally about the indifference and the cruelty. Sometimes, he cried out in his sleep, his body jerking spasmodically from those memories.

I stared at this stranger's shoes while he told me about the life they shared in the orphanage. They were friends, he said. Two lost boys, who ran away on three occasions and were dragged back by the local gardaí. They had one highlight from that time. That was a visit to Beech Park, where George Blake lived. He was a patron of the orphanage and would sometimes invite a select few boys to visit Beech Park. He had one child, a daughter. Paddy made her sound like a whirlwind. Maria Blake didn't know the meaning of fear when it came to climbing trees and outrunning the two boys on those special days. When he spoke about her, I could see where his heart was.

By the time they were sixteen and free to leave the orphanage, they had visited Beech Park often and both boys had been in love with her.

But I was wrong about his heart. Whatever memories Paddy had of those idyllic days had hardened into irrelevance. All that concerned him was the link in the photograph of my husband to Aloysius Russell. As I stalled for time, I kept denying his accusations.

My phone was under the pillow. A dead thing that needed a signal to save us. But there was an extension landline phone on the bedside table, if only I could reach it. He must have guessed my thoughts. In that instant, he reached for the wire and wrenched it from the wall.

I tried to stand but he pushed me back onto the bed. 'Cormac stole her baby.' He spoke flatly yet emphatically. 'I've always known it.'

'Then why didn't you go to the police?'

'They wouldn't have been able to find him. You learned how to hide at St Alexis. Besides, I was in lodgings, courtesy of the state.'

'You were in jail.'

He nodded when I stated this fact. 'Thirteen years for grievous bodily harm resulting in death.' Understanding the power of fear, he smiled again. 'She was eighteen and going nowhere with her life. A junkie who didn't believe in paying her debts. I did her a favour. Then, after my release, who did I see strutting along the harbour in Killybegs?' He nodded, as if I'd already answered him. 'The man himself. Cormac

Gallagher, one-time garda, who answered to the name of Dominick Grace. Who'd have believed it?'

I lurched forward with such ferocity that he was taken by surprise. In those moments, as we struggled, I felt as if I was possessed of super-human strength. But then he took me with him when he fell backwards, bringing the chair with him. Rising to his feet before I could, he kicked me in my stomach and my head, then knelt to straddle me.

'Listen well,' he said. 'I'm not going to repeat myself. I have photographs of Isabelle Russell. She's the image of her mother, so Maria won't need any convincing. Not that I give a fuck whether they're reunited, or not. But I'll expose your sordid little secret unless Cormac silences me. Fifty thousand will do it. Delay and I'll add another ten. You've a week to get the money together.'

His spittle was on my face, his eyes boring into mine. 'Do you understand what I'm saying, bitch?'

I was petrified that you or the twins had heard the crash when the chair fell but your bedroom doors remained closed. The room was spinning, everything blurring. I thought I was going to pass out. Would you have been taken from us when I came to? This thought steadied my nerves. I managed to ease one of my arms free. The telephone had fallen from the bedside table when he broke the connection. You remember the old-fashioned, heavy one we used to have? That was the one I managed to grip and lift. I slammed it into his head. He fell sideways towards the fireplace. It seemed to happen in slow motion. I remember his startled expression, his efforts to hold on to me as he toppled and crashed his skull against the black iron surround. He didn't bleed, apart from a trickle that came from his mouth. I was still pinned between his legs, only now they had become a dead weight, and I was able to ease free.

All I experienced was relief as I stared down at him. I

thought of running to Noreen's house to safety with you and the twins and ringing an ambulance from there.

But what would he do when he recovered? What if the police came to Headwind with questions Dominick would be unable to answer? He'd never mentioned Paddy Murdock when he spoke about his years in the institution. Nor had he told me about George Blake and his tomboy daughter. He'd given me the impression he was a loner who was homeless for a year before he pulled himself together and found work in a warehouse. It would be easy to believe this unconscious man was deranged, but that would be foolish.

He was lying on his side, his eyes still closed, and breathing heavily. The colour had drained from his face, and the stiffness of his expression, trapped between fury and shock, added to my terror.

I could have saved him... or maybe not. It may already have been too late to stem the internal haemorrhage that must have killed him. I was caught in a time warp during those hours I spent watching over him. I visualised my future without you. The Russell family would claim you as their own, as they had every right to do. Dominick would be in jail. The shame and the disgrace, the frantic publicity, the impact on the twins, and on you, as you were pulled away from what you believed to be your roots.

His ragged breathing dragged me back to the present. I believed he was acting alone. He would not want, or need, a partner to share in the spoils.

I've no idea how long it took him to die. Can doing nothing be defined as a deadly weapon? That was what I wondered when I heard him draw a final, shuddering breath. I witnessed his expression change and sink into the stillness that comes with death. An unknown woman saw him into the world. I was the woman who saw him out of it.

I heard that sound again when my husband stopped breathing. At that moment, the scene from my encounter with Paddy Murdock came back with such forcefulness that I almost bent under its weight.

Dawn was breaking when I pushed his body under the bed and draped a cover over it. I locked the bedroom door and there he lay until Dominick returned that night.

Since that night I've learned to keep my back straight. Pain, and the release of blood, gives me a brief respite, as does vodka, which helps in the same way as a false friend who deceives. But any port in a storm will do when the memory of that terrible night overwhelms me.

When the children were small, I called these rocks with their upright backs and pot-bellied curves an enchanted circle. The stories I invented remain with me. I loved their rapt attention, their innocent acceptance that elves mined for gold in the crevices and fairies danced within the circle on the night of a full moon.

Gabrielle begged me to write my stories down and make a book. The story I should have written has nothing to do with magic. Violence lies at its heart, and regret, also, yet when I look back on that encounter, and all the pain that followed, I know with chilling sureness that under similar circumstances, I'd do exactly the same again.

# EIGHTEEN

## GABRIELLE

Cassie called this natural wind break 'the enchanted circle'. It should be easy to find but the rocks with their precarious angles all look identical in this monochromatic landscape. I'm about to return to my car when I recognise the familiar configuration.

The wind's howl silences my approach. I find her kneeling within the circle, her face buried in her hands. The shock of my arrival jolts her from her reverie. She is startled, also confused, her arm lifting as if to push me away. I kneel before her and draw her to me. She is stiff and resistant in my arms, but I hold on to her.

'You betrayed me.' Her body loosens as she begins to cry.

'No... no. That's *not* true. I haven't told anyone. You have to believe me. No one *knows*.'

'Liar.' The word is as harsh as a slap. 'I *spoke* to him on the phone.'

'He doesn't know anything. I swear on Dad's grave. Douglas...'

She moans and pulls away from me. 'Don't mention his name... *don't*.'

'Okay. All he knows about me is that I'm in the media. He's looking for publicity. That's his only reason for ringing me.'

'You're sacrificing me...' She stops, unable to continue.

'*Cassie*... have you any idea how I'm feeling? You keep thinking of yourself yet I'm the one who's been robbed of my family... my *other* family.'

She staggers as she rises to her feet and would have overbalanced if I hadn't steadied her.

'I killed a man.'

Her face crumples as she speaks yet there is no inflection in her voice, just words that sound as if they have been threshed of all emotions. 'He came to Headwind one night when Dominick was at sea. He threatened you... all of us. He was going to destroy our world. When I pushed him away, he fell and died.'

Is she crazy? Hallucinating, her mind poisoned by alcohol? Her eyes are slitted as she looks towards the sun with its merciless glare. She is ravaged by guilt and secrecy. 'Dominick buried him at sea... I think. I never asked.'

'What was his name?' It's important to give him an identity. Everybody is entitled to a name, even those who demean it.

'Paddy Murdock. He was in the orphanage with your father.'

'I don't believe you. You're making up this ridiculous story to frighten me.' But I know she is speaking the truth. *Leave me alone... stop your talking... oh, my head... my poor head... leave me the fuck alone.*' I recall the haunted words she moaned on the day I returned early from school, unaware that my life would change irrevocably that night.

'I never frightened you, Gabrielle,' she cries. 'Angered you, yes. Filled you with resentment, yes. Drove you away... absolutely. I needed space to save my sanity. But you were never afraid of me, just angry and confused by the change in me.'

'Tell me you're lying, Cassie. Don't do this to me.' I'm crying with her, begging her to retract that wretched confession, but it's true, every word she utters, and keeps repeating when she can speak clearly between sobs.

I've no memory of that night. It could have stayed buried forever but she is flickering it into reality. Waking to a light that flashed and threw shapes on a wall. I remember seeing two legs beside my bed. Cargo pants, pocket flaps and zips, crumpled khaki. I could see between the legs to the door where Cassie stood. I thought my father had arrived home early, but this man did not smell of the sea. I caught a whiff of something rank yet sweet, like flowers rotting in water. Cassie came into the room, and they left... no, not left... she was pushed from me and dragged away. I listened for sounds. All was silent. I was still half asleep. So easy to believe I'd been dreaming. A nightmare, over in an instant, and forgotten.

The following morning, she'd handed me the costume she had made for the school pantomime. Pierrette, so perfect in every ruffled detail.

I dry her tears and mine. We walk carefully over the uneven terrain, back to my car. Is there a word for my state of mind? That ripping apart of norms and the realisation that my entire existence has been a façade, apart from those first three weeks. And even that brief period in Maria Russell's arms was steeped in deceit.

Did Aloysius ever suspect he was not my father? Everything I've read convinces me that he never experienced such doubts. He may have believed I was dead, as Killian said, yet, on the off chance that I was still alive, he took every opportunity to highlight the circumstances leading to my disappearance. Could any father have been more devoted to my memory?

Cassie stumbles and grips my arm. The wind is strengthening. Grey clouds, suddenly visible, flit across the sun. I refuse to allow her to drive. One of the twins can collect her car later. She slumps into the passenger seat in my car and wraps her arms around her chest.

She looks vulnerable and shrunken, yet appearances can be deceptive. To bear such a secret requires strength of will. Even drunk, she has held her silence... until now. The bequeathing of her secret will bind me even closer to her.

'I can't prevent you from contacting Douglas Russell,' she says. 'But just be minded of those who are innocent. Your sisters are unaware that you can bring their worlds crashing down around them.'

I turn on the engine and don't reply. We've had this conversation already. She is forcing me to choose between my heart and my head.

'If this scandal breaks loose, I won't hang around.' She states this dully but with a ruthless certainty. 'I've no fear of dying. In fact, it would be a welcome relief from the voices.'

'This is emotional blackmail.' My anger causes the car to swerve towards the edge of the road. 'I won't tolerate it.' I slow down as I approach Burly's Bend.

Paddy Murdock lied about a car abandoned on this spot. I'll never be able to drive past without remembering him.

Cassie's warning plays on repeat in my head as I drive back to Dublin. Her safety and peace of mind must overrule my crazed quest for answers.

# NINETEEN

## GABRIELLE

A week after I return to Dublin, Douglas rings again.

'Firstly, let me apologise for cancelling our last meeting,' he says. 'It was one of those situations—'

'No need to apologise.' I interrupt him, anxious not to prolong the call.

'I'd like to make amends,' he says. 'We can discuss your idea over a meal.'

'That's not necessary. Honestly, you don't have to go to the trouble—'

'This is simply a thank-you gesture for your coverage in New York.' His laughter is as relaxed as his tone. 'I'm free tomorrow night, if you are. After that, I'll be on a state visit to Japan for a week. What do you think? Yes? No?'

Such a persuasive lilt to his voice.

For Cassie's sake, I must refuse him. He asks if I like Italian and names his favourite restaurant. I'm allowing him to talk for too long. Every word he speaks lessens my resistance and increases my curiosity. Cassie need never know. I think of her scarred wrists. How much blood has she spilled in her efforts to remain silent? How much more blood was spilled on the night she fought to save me from Paddy Murdock's grasp?

I owe it to her to end this conversation. Douglas Russell means nothing to me. What familial links could possibly have been formed between us in those three early weeks? None, is the short answer, and, yet, in the pause that hangs between us, I send Cassie to the dark side of my mind and agree a time and a place to meet my half-brother.

Garlic, tomatoes and herbs, bread, freshly baking – the air is redolent with aromas when I enter Bisallo's Bistro. His handshake is warm, practised – he has acquired a politician's touch. He remains standing as the waiter pulls out my chair, and only sits down when I'm seated. I'd forgotten his height and the smile that has been trained to charm. In his pale blue blazer, dark trousers, and a casual open-necked shirt, he looks younger than he did in the Hibiscus Gallery, and more handsome.

'I'm so sorry to have kept you waiting.' I'm fifteen minutes late and my excuse about the non-arrival of a bus sounds so fake I'm surprised he accepts it. How would he react if I told him that I'd walked away from the restaurant entrance and jumped on a bus, only to descend at the next stop and run all the way back to Bisallo's? I'd poured cold water over my wrists in the Ladies until my colour faded and my breathing slowed.

He must eat here often if the familiarity of the waiters towards him is anything to go by, and the lengths they take to screen us as much as possible from public view.

'Thank you for making time to see me tonight,' he says. 'I'm sure you have a busy social life.'

'Actually, I've become quite unsocial since I returned to Ireland.'

'I'd welcome some unsocial downtime,' he says. 'Excluding tonight, my social and working life are inseparable.'

'Does that bother you?'

'Having learned the trade at my father's knee, so to speak, I was well seasoned before I was elected to Dáil Éireann. Politics was the only subject we discussed at our dining table when I was growing up.'

'That sounds stimulating.'

Did they ever discuss me? I can't imagine being a subject batted back and forth over roast beef and two veg. Far easier to fire salvos at the opposition and plan strategies to win the next election. In Trabawn, our dining table conversations seldom strayed beyond the boundaries of our community and the price of fish on the open market. If an outside note was introduced, it was usually to blame the government for the hardships of the fishing fleet, and the Spaniards for invading our waters.

He laughs. 'Stimulating is one way of putting it. Boredom is another, especially when you're a teenager and the *very* last thing on your wish list is to be involved in politics. But, talking about stimulation, you certainly stirred the early risers with *Gaby's Good Morning Wake-up*. I listened to you on a few mornings while I was in New York.'

'New Yorkers love a good brawl, regardless of the time of day,' I say.

'I was surprised by your decision to give up your show. You'd established quite a loyal listenership.'

'The media is a transient industry. Here today, gone tomorrow.' I'm surprised by how glib I sound. Being with him in an intimate nook is wrong on so many levels. The dream-like state I entered when I agreed to meet him still persists. It feels possible that, at any moment, I'll wake up and wonder at the strangeness of my fantasy.

'You didn't shy away from tackling the controversial subjects,' he says. 'Gun control, for instance. That was a fairly incendiary conversation. How did you cope with the insults?'

'Insults are grist to the mill of talk radio. I developed a tough skin very quickly.' I'm acutely conscious of his scent. Bergamot, I think, light and not too intrusive.

'The same applies to politicians,' he agrees. 'Otherwise, they go under. I thought my father would do so on a few occasions but he's a street fighter who knows how to survive *our* particular bear pit.'

'What about you?' I ask, pleased that he remembers the reference I made to my own show when he phoned me in New York.

He laughs. 'Time will tell if it's me or the bears who survive.'

Our food has arrived. He ordered tagliarini with white truffles. I settled on veal scallops marsala.

'What's your father's line of work?' he asks.

'He was a fisherman. Sadly, he died in February. Cancer.' I cut into the veal with a steady hand.

'I'm sorry.' I sense his embarrassment as he lays his cutlery down. 'This must be such a difficult time for you.'

'It's been tough, yes. I miss him very much.'

'I can imagine. Is he the reason you returned to Ireland?'

'One of the reasons. I've also recently become an aunt to two adorable nephews. I'm wary of virtual relationships so I'd prefer to know them face to face.'

He tilts his head to one side, his expression quizzical. 'Can I ask you a personal question?'

'How personal?'

'Did we ever meet before the EOM press conference?'

'Not that I remember.' The truth can be told in ways that is not always recognisable as such.

'You're positive our paths never crossed?'

'Who can be positive about anything?' I'm surprised by his persistence. 'We could have met in another life.'

'Reincarnation, you mean?'

'Or the cracks in between the two,' I say. 'We may have had a chance encounter that neither of us can recall.'

'That sounds too esoteric for me,' he admits. 'I'm usually good with faces.'

He begins to eat again. I try to follow his example, but I don't trust myself to hold my knife and fork steady.

'Tell me about yourself,' I say. 'Are you in a relationship?'

'Not at the moment,' he replies.

A spasm crosses his face. Attuned as I am to his expression, searching for similarities between us, I notice the pain that appears then vanishes just as quickly.

Killian said he was 'taken' yet there is no wedding band on his finger, nor are there any references to a wife or partner in the articles I've read.

'I thought a spouse was a necessary appendage for a politician?' I'm embarrassed by my glibness, but it seems to be the only way I can handle this conversation.

'My mother is anything but an appendage of my father's,' he replies. 'She's very much her own woman.'

'She sounds interesting, and strong.'

He nods in agreement. 'Strong yet fragile, that sums her up. She holds us together with her love, yet there are times I think she's as far removed from us as it is possible to be.' He pauses, as if taken aback by his frankness. 'Are you close to your own mother?'

'She's also complex,' I reply. 'I used to think I knew her. However, I've come to the conclusion that I was simply scratching the surface.'

Our conversation is filled with clichés. Strong yet fragile. Simply scratching the surface. Are either of us any wiser about the two women we're discussing?

'Do you have a photograph of your mother?' I ask.

I've studied many photographs of Maria Russell. If I close

my eyes, her face will swim before me... but I'm insatiable for more information.

'Of course.' He appears surprised by my question. 'I took this one on her last birthday.' He stretches across the table to show me his phone.

It's a classic birthday image: a cake with candles, a family surrounding her. It should be a close circle yet there is a space between Douglas and his brother. I visualise myself standing there, the same smile, the same confident stance that tells me I know exactly where I belong.

'She's lovely, Douglas.'

He refills our wine glasses. 'Swipe to the left. There should be more.'

I see her addressing a group of women at a conference. She is jogging in another photograph, slim and tanned, her sweat-band the same shade as her dark-green eyes. In the last photograph she has paused to look back and smile just before she steps into a white Porsche. What secrets is she hiding behind that feline gaze?

'She looks super-efficient and glamorous at the same time.' I pass the phone back to him. 'That meeting you had to cancel—'

'Apologies, again.'

'No need. I understand. This seems like the right moment to bring up the proposal I'd hoped to discuss with you. It actually concerns your mother.'

'I see... or, rather, I don't. What interests you about her?'

'Isabelle's Quest.'

'Ah, the foundation.' He adds parmesan to the truffles and stirs the tagliarini with his fork. 'Go on.'

'I plan to make a series of podcasts about women who have managed through personal tragedies to better the lives of others. Your mother founded Isabelle's Quest after the disappearance of your sister. She's inspirational. That will be the theme of my podcast.'

'My mother doesn't do interviews.' His tone suggests I've touched a nerve. He nods at me to continue.

'I understand that she's had some bad experiences with the media—'

'That's the understatement of the night.'

'Please hear me out, Douglas. I've read everything that has been written about your sister. I can't even begin to imagine what you and your parents have been through. Yet, despite her own personal sorrow, Maria Russell has reunited so many missing children with their loved ones. It's such a powerful story, yet it's never been properly highlighted.' My food goes cold while I elaborate on the podcast I'd make.

'If I could talk to her in person, I'd be able to show her the outline I've prepared. I've no interest in exploiting her in any way, but I believe her experience could be of enormous help to others. Will you speak to her on my behalf?'

He looks upwards, as if seeking inspiration from the mural on the ceiling. 'Yes. But I can foresee her answer. Don't be too disappointed if she refuses.' He glances at my plate. 'Your food is cold. Can I order something else for you?'

'Not at all. The veal was lovely but very filling.'

He holds up the empty bottle. 'More wine?'

'Just coffee to finish.'

A party of diners arrive, pushing into the restaurant and sending a draught of fresh air through the heated atmosphere. Their voices reach us, men and women who must have come directly from a bar, if their animated laughter is any indication. Douglas's attention is fixed on the group. One of the men, as if aware that they are being scrutinised, makes his way towards our table. He is slightly built yet has a sturdiness to his body that suggests he works out regularly. His engaging smile is vaguely familiar yet I've no idea who he is. As soon as Douglas introduces me to Oisín O'Sullivan, I recognise his name. He featured in last weekend's edition of *Bayview on Sunday* where he described his struggle to become a published and successful author.

His handshake is firm, but it is to Douglas that his attention strays. Glances are exchanged between them. Discreet glances that I notice only because everything about my half-brother interests me. I now understand why his face reflected such pain when I asked if he was in a relationship.

'Congratulations on your new novel,' I say. 'I read about you in *Bayview on Sunday*.'

'Thank you,' Oisín replies. 'It's good to get some recognition at last.'

'Gaby ran her own radio show in New York,' says Douglas. 'Now, she's turning her attention to podcasting.'

'I enjoy podcasts.' Oisín sounds interested. 'Does yours have a specific theme?'

'I'm working on it. Early days yet.'

He nods. 'Nice meeting you, Gaby.' His friends are beckoning him to their table where menus are being handed around.

'I'd love to interview you when my podcast is up and running?'

'Most definitely,' he replies. 'Give her my number, Douglas. I'd better get back to the mob. It's my mother's birthday and she's finally managed to herd all our family together.'

He speaks directly to me and I can tell by Douglas's smile as he waves towards the family gathering that he's already aware of that fact.

The waiter removes our plates and returns with coffee. Soon it'll be time to leave.

'Do you remember Isabelle?' I ask.

'We always call her Belle.' He bites down on the name and releases it on a harsh exhalation. 'It gives us, not the media, ownership of her.' He finishes his coffee and waits until the table is cleared before speaking again. 'She's the dominant person in our lives. No closure. Hope, sparse that it is, prevents us from laying her to rest. We honour her once a year and that's how we've survived as a family. I seldom talk about her. It takes time to recover when I do. Do you mind if we leave it at that?'

*I do mind... I want words, torrents of words that will make me whole again... please tell me who I am... tell me... tell me.*

'I didn't mean to intrude, Douglas. I'm sorry.'

'You haven't intruded,' he says. 'I'll speak to my mother. She claims I can wind her around my little finger. That's not true, of course. My father...' He stops and checks his watch as well as his words. 'I can't believe how fast the night has flown. Thank you for making it so enjoyable.'

'Likewise. It was nice to meet you again, Douglas.'

He orders a taxi for me. It's waiting outside when we emerge. I refuse to allow him to see me home. It's not because he might suggest a late-night drink in my apartment. A niggling feeling of recognition does not create a spark and I suspect that Oisín O'Sullivan has already 'taken' his heart. No wonder Killian doesn't worry about Shauna's close working relationship with her boss. Douglas's interest in me is something he does not understand. We're both aware it's not driven by passion, but only I can recognise the vibrations flowing between us. The longing he has unleashed in me is barely controllable, yet he is oblivious of its effects. The lure of family, the voraciousness of familial blood. Only someone like Cassie can understand its demands.

Days pass as I wait to hear from him. I can't settle to anything. My heart jerks every time my phone rings. He doesn't make contact until the fifth day.

'I've spoken to my mother.' The noise in the background suggests he's driving and using his car phone. 'She's invited you to the charity event we organise every year to raise funds for

Isabelle's Quest. We're holding it on Sunday week. Would you be interested in attending it as my guest?'

This is more than I could have imagined. I struggle to breathe. Is the room moving in a dizzying swirl, objects shifting of their own accord? The silence between us is lengthening.

'I understand if the date is not suitable,' he says. 'My mother has expressed an interest in the podcast so we can organise another time to meet.'

He sounds impatient. That's not surprising. He's probably busy and I'm dithering. I focus on a spot in front of me and exhale slowly.

'Please thank her for her kind invitation. I'd love to attend.' I'm giddy and reckless, perched on the edge of a precipice. One more step will send me over the edge. The headlong plunge will be heady and exhilarating. What will happen when I hit the rocks?

# PART 3

# TWENTY

## MARIA

Another anniversary. The length of time between them appears to quicken with each year that passes. Next year will be her thirtieth. That will make it extra-important. Why decades should matter in the grand scheme of loss, yet for reasons I don't understand they are marked as significant. Does the yearning decrease during the in-between years? If it does, I haven't noticed.

I lift Belle's photograph from the dressing table and study it. The clarity of her image has not faded. She has become the barometer of my moods. Sometimes, she appears to be smiling which would be impossible at three weeks, but, at other times, her expression is melancholic, as if she senses that her time with me will not be long.

She was stolen on the twenty-ninth of July. It's possible that the crime occurred after midnight so it could have been the thirtieth when Belle was removed from the cradle by the side of my bed. I slept deeply that night. That's a fact, not an excuse. I remind myself of it whenever my guilt feels softer, less challenging. I must never forgive myself for not waking on the instant she was lifted in a stranger's arms and taken from me. What kind of mother would sleep through such an abominable act? I long for the day to come when I can answer that question.

Aloysius should have lost patience with me a long time ago. An ever-understanding husband can be as annoying as the one who tells you to stiffen your spine and deal with it. I wanted to suffer the lash of his fury. To endure a whip on my back that was strong enough to bury grief under its cut. Instead, he gave me his arms for comfort and his voice to ease my conscience. *It wasn't your fault... it wasn't your fault...*

Twenty-nine years later, it's time again to remember her. Not that she is ever forgotten, but the passage of time has allowed her to meld into my heart and become its beat. An anniversary enforces the feelings of loss even more sharply. The ritual has changed, of course. The candlelight vigils ended after three years and were replaced by a charity auction and ball. The funds are donated to my foundation. Isabelle's Quest, constantly in search of funds and constantly in search of missing children. As a result, the anniversary of Belle's disappearance has grown into a gala event.

I suspect that most of the people attending have no idea of its origins. It's simply an occasion to be seen and photographed with the Russell family.

This morning, the Calderwell Children's Choir sang magnificently during the anniversary mass. Aloysius usually speaks from the altar about Isabelle's Quest. This year, he handed the responsibility to Douglas. I listened to our son's flawless delivery, conscious of Aloysius's rigid shoulders. He dislikes being removed from the frame of public events, but the time has come to allow our son to emerge from his father's shade.

I pay lip service to a god I no longer worship. If such a deity exists, one flowing with love and compassion, Belle would be back with her family. Aloysius has no idea I harbour such thoughts. He insists it was his faith that brought him through our tragedy and beyond it. When he declares this publicly, he's showered with mass cards afterwards from those who share his view that God moves in mysterious ways, and we minions will only understand his mercy when we come into his glory.

I followed him to the altar this morning. I held out my hands to receive the eucharist and placed the wafer on my tongue. How much longer can I continue to do so? On such days, I long to throw back my head and wail. Those women of old, who tore their hair and keened their sorrow, they knew what they were doing. What has dignity got to do with loss?

Tonight, I'll dress in black and wear pearls at my neck, as I always do on the eve of Belle's anniversary. Douglas will conduct the auction and exhort everyone to spend, spend, spend. Aloysius's speech will remember her but still manage to be upbeat and forward-looking in case a pall should descend over the attendees.

We have found missing children, those who have been abducted by warring parents. My foundation has covered the costs of court hearings and journeys to faraway places to recover the ones who have been taken. I'm happy for those who've been reunited with their children, and, with the passing of time, Isabelle's Quest has buffed away the sharper angles of my rage. Time will eventually erode even the greatest sorrows.

I'm not sure when I stopped hoping. It was such a slow corrosion of my spirit that it took me by surprise to discover I no longer believed we would see Belle again. That belief has now crystalised. It is finally over.

Aloysius believes she died shortly after she was abducted. He hasn't declared his view publicly. Death is closure and he never wants this mystery to end. Am I cruel in thinking that? Or, simply, realistic? Being the father of a stolen child created a platform for him, one built on sympathy and the relief of knowing that even the most powerful father can be brought to his knees...

Except that he is not her father.

On a day like today, it's impossible to ignore this reality. It rattles cages in the deepest recesses of my mind and allows me to think about Cormac. Just for a moment I remember the wildness he aroused in me. It will never be tamed, only corralled. Our time together was brief, but all that streamed from it has left me stranded in remorse.

Aloysius lays his hands on my shoulders and leans down to kiss my ear. Our reflections in the dressing table mirror have the stilted elegance of a portrait. He's even more striking than when we first met. In those days, he was a bare-knuckle fighter, figuratively speaking, and had yet to learn the value of velvet gloves. But velvet can also be rubbed the wrong way and his enemies, so many when he listed them to the police, struck at his heart when Belle was taken.

'As always, you look spectacular, my dear,' he says. 'Stand up and let me admire the full effect.'

I do as he requests.

Most men, and particularly sons, would be unable to distinguish one black dress from another.

'Widow's weeds again. Honestly, Mum, it's *so* Victorian,' Jonathan scoffed, when I removed this year's dress from its wrappings.

But Aloysius knows that this dress is cut on a bias and will cling like a sheath to my body. The designer followed his instructions to the letter, as she always does.

The owner of the Flamingo Hotel, Beatrice Grattan, greets us in the foyer. Isabelle's Auction will run like clockwork, she says, as she escorts us into the ballroom. She remains composed while Aloysius checks that everything is arranged to his satisfaction.

His standards are exacting and Bea's signs of anxiety – the slight swaying movement she makes and her quickening voice when she answers his questions – are too subtle to be noticed by anyone except me. Conscious as I am of such signals, I resist the urge to fidget with the pearls around my neck.

The ballroom quickly fills. Jonathan arrives with his latest girlfriend, a stranger to me, yet she looks startlingly like his previous girlfriend, and the one before then. She is tiny, despite her gravity-defying heels. An elf with blonde spiky hair and a challenging stance, she would look more comfortable in leather on the back of his motorbike. For this occasion, she has dressed in yellow ruffles. His lopsided grin and effusive welcome are signs that he's been drinking. He doesn't want to be here. Changing his leather trousers for a tux ruins his street cred. He never knew his sister. How can I expect him to understand what this anniversary means to me? Douglas endures it for the publicity it creates. The good, the great and the lovely, bantering and bartering with them as he auctions off fine prints and silk scarves, antique jewellery, champagne and whiskey of a particular vintage, golf outings, flying lessons and sunshine holidays.

Aloysius greets a party from one of the banking sectors and Shauna, rushing as usual but still looking composed, stops when she sees me to say hello. She's a dash of red against my black, a flame angel who guards my son against unwelcome publicity.

'Has Douglas arrived yet?' she asks.

'He should be here shortly,' I reply. 'He's picking up his companion for tonight. Have you met Gabrielle Grace?'

Her eyelashes flutter. It's the only indication Shauna ever gives that she's perturbed. The mention of this woman has unsettled her. 'We met in New York when Douglas headed the delegation of designers,' she says. 'She was very helpful then.'

'What's she like?'

'Hard to say. Having listened to her on radio she comes

across as tough but she's quite friendly when you meet her. She has a reputation as a shock jock.'

'I thought only men were shock jocks.'

Shauna smiles and raises her voice above the hubbub. 'She's one of those successful women who take whatever their listeners dish out and give it back to them in equal measure. I was surprised when I heard she was back in Ireland.'

'She sounds fearsome. Do you know—' My question is cut short by a young couple who want details of the menu's vegan options. Shauna wriggles her fingers in farewell and hurries off to greet Douglas, who has just arrived.

I'm curious to see this woman who wants to interview me about Isabelle's Quest. The pitch she wrote was excellent. Despite my fear of the media, it could be worth considering.

Douglas is coming over to introduce her. With her upswept dark hair and long neck, she is almost as tall as my son, and willowy without being too thin. They look well together, like they were made to fit into each other in a way I can't define. Douglas likes her. That much was obvious when he spoke about the podcast she hopes to make.

'Mum, this is Gabrielle Grace.' As if suspecting my thoughts, he offers her like a package to me. 'Gaby, meet my mother, Maria.'

'It's a pleasure to meet you.' She looks confident, even slightly aloof, yet a tremor in her handshake betrays a certain nervousness. Her eyes bathe me in blue yet there is nothing sharp or challenging about her gaze.

'The pleasure is mine, Gabrielle.' I prefer the softer sounding vowels in her unabbreviated name. 'I hope you have an enjoyable night.'

'I'm sure I will, Mrs Russell.'

'Please call me Maria.'

'Thank you, Maria.' Her face lights up when she smiles.

A female shock jock, Shauna said. I'd expected someone

more bracing and belligerent, or, possibly, a Goth with a defiant mouth. Instead, her voice is low and slightly husky, pleasantly polite yet, obviously, capable of trash talking should that be necessary. Her accent is hard to place – traces of Kerry, I think, overlaid with the elongated vowel cadences she must have picked up since she moved to New York.

Aloysius joins us. 'You're most welcome, Gabrielle.' He clasps her hands between his own and switches on his smile. On, off, it has many degrees of warmth and frost. 'I hope we have an opportunity to talk to you later when we've time to draw breath.'

Nothing in his expression reveals that Gabrielle Grace has been thoroughly checked and is here purely because she passed the sensors. Not that Aloysius relayed such information to me but I'm acutely aware of how cautious he is about outsiders, especially those in the media.

Her dress, dark green and strapless, swirls around her ankles when she moves towards her seat at the main table. The fabric has a shimmer that reminds me of stardust. A sylph in lace and sequins. My impressions of people tend to be other-worldly, living as I do in fantasyland. She sits directly opposite me but at too much of a distance to speak to her directly. Douglas sits between her and Shauna. A woman on each side – that should be sufficient to keep Aloysius content.

Conversation flows around the table. I speak to the people who are seated beside me and try to stretch my voice to those beyond.

As soon as the meal ends, the auction begins. A slow response at first, but it quickly speeds up under Douglas's encouragement. The bidding remains high as people try to outbid each other for an opportunity to play golf with the legendary golfer, Earl Brandon.

When he brings the proceedings to an end, Aloysius stands and approaches the podium. His speech is different every year, yet it's still the same. He speaks about the impact of Belle's disappearance on our lives but ends on a positive note when he recounts the cases Isabelle's Quest has successfully undertaken. The applause is enthusiastic. Spirits are lifted by the knowledge that their generosity is being used so commendably.

His words have moved Gabrielle Grace. She lifts an index finger to the rim of one glistening eye and holds it there. Is she stemming tears? Mine dried a long time ago but now, watching her reaction, they threaten to surface again. Like a dried-up riverbed, they are always waiting in the shallows for release.

When Douglas speaks to her, she smiles. She has a wide mouth, strong, white teeth. Have I imagined her sorrow? Did I project my own unresolved grief onto this stranger? I haven't done that for a long time. Why would I lay such a cross on anyone's back?

I'm primed and ready for Aloysius's announcement. Once again, he is using Belle to highlight his ambitions. The unsolved crime that refuses to lie down. A past master at manipulating the truth, he knows how to pummel it like dough and reshape it.

A quick glance around the tables that orbit us like satellites show an attentive audience, apart from Jonathan, who is whispering into the ear of his elfish clone. She snuggles closer to him and laughs out loud. 'Catching my eye, he straightens and nods to reassure me he'll behave. An expectant silence falls as Aloysius begins to speak again. Can I bear to listen to him one more time?

Or will tonight be the moment I break all the rules and scream?

# TWENTY-ONE

## GABRIELLE

Am I the only one to notice how she blenches as she listens to her husband? She touches her pearls then drops her hand to the table, as if she's afraid this gesture will be mistaken for agitation. She doesn't have to worry. All attention, except mine, is fixed on him.

This morning, I sat at the back of a church and watched my family pray for me. What were they asking as they bowed their heads? My body to be discovered? My safe return? Amnesia from the constant waiting? I would have prayed for the latter. The bliss of a mind devoid of torment. Leaving the church, they filed past me. No one glanced in my direction. If they had, they would have seen a figure in a hoodie, head bent, hands pressed together so tightly my shoulders ached.

What had I expected to happen when I saw her? Shoots of electricity tingling through my body? My mind exploding in a blast of recognition? My heart pumping blood so furiously she would sense it pulsing and know who I was?

Nothing like that occurred then, or tonight, when we were introduced in this vast, tightly packed ballroom. Her handshake had the practised ease of a professional hostess. The words we spoke were banal yet, hearing her voice, I found it impossible to control a shiver of recognition. An echo from the past sealed in baby memories.

'Tonight, I'd like to make an announcement.' I force myself to listen to Aloysius. 'I chose this special occasion, when Maria and my sons are amongst those who have given us their love and support throughout the most difficult time of our lives. Only you appreciate why this occasion is so important to us. For this reason, I decided it is the appropriate event to announce my intention of retiring from my ministerial role and leaving government.'

The gasp from the crowd is collective, a gush of excitement and, from the sound of it, also surprise. He allows a moment for a buzz of conversation to break out, then silences it with his raised hand.

'I've served my country for four decades with dedication, humility and the conviction that it was the finest honour ever bestowed on me. But it's time to give way to a younger generation. My son, Douglas, is continuing in my footsteps, which makes it easier for me to make such a challenging decision.' His voice soars. 'He's benefitted at first hand from the knowledge I've gained through my many ministerial positions. I'm confident he will ensure that our family name remains solidly at the centre of Irish politics.'

On and on he goes. Maria smiles throughout. He ends by acknowledging her unwavering support. When he finishes his speech, she stands with him to accept the applause. The woman behind the powerful man. Camera phones flash and heads are bent, fingers busy on social media.

Douglas and Shauna speak quietly to each other before he stands to thank his father for his vote of confidence and to wish him well in the future. Jonathan is leaving with his girlfriend. He makes no attempt to speak to his family. They were not sitting at the centre table, so I didn't have an opportunity to meet him. What would I have said? Meaningless words about the wonderful night and how impressed I was by the work undertaken by Isabelle's Quest. His girlfriend in her daffodil dress looks back wishfully as they depart but he walks purposefully towards the exit.

Crowds gather around our table. Aloysius's smile is broad and contagious as he poses for selfies. The hype is adding to my nervousness. Cassie must never find out where I've been. I made it clear to Douglas that I must avoid being photographed with him and claimed to have a boyfriend with a jealous personality, who is unaware I'm attending the event. So far, Douglas has steered photographers away from me, but this event has become a scrum.

Maria remains by her husband's side, laughing, talking, entirely at ease in her milieu. I'm not in her line of vision and it's possible to watch her. Although *watch* sounds wrong. I'm soaking her in. Every gesture, every smile, her every feature, absorbing all of her. Is it possible to compress twenty-nine years into a glance? All that wasted time when we could have been together.

I haven't hated my father until now. When it comes, that molten rush, it smelts my very being.

Douglas is apologetic when he returns to my side.

'No need to be sorry,' I say. 'I can appreciate how busy you are. I've already phoned for a taxi. Please thank your parents for the invitation. It's been a very interesting and enjoyable evening.'

I leave before he can notice my distress. So far, it's controlled. I don't know how much longer I can assume a politeness I don't feel, and hold back a secret that will shatter the comfortable world Maria and Aloysius Russell have constructed from their loss.

. . .

This is what I've learned about my other family: Jonathan dislikes his father. Douglas has been groomed to step smoothly into his father's shoes, but the fit doesn't seem quite right. Aloysius is ambitious, probably ruthless – the world has not seen the last of him. Maria... what about her? What is she like behind the sophisticated image she projects? Does her mask fit so perfectly she can no longer remember what it's like to exist without it?

Is that a leap too far? What can I possibly know about my mother? My only certainty is that I came from her womb. How can those nine months and the three weeks that followed possibly equate with the years we've spent apart? This distance between us is strewn with obstacles. I've no idea how they can be hurdled.

# TWENTY-TWO

## MARIA

Jonathan cuts it fine for Sunday lunch and arrives just as the meal is about to be served. He has an excuse, as always, and Aloysius, after his initial annoyance, accepts it. He'll be the first to leave with another finely tuned apology. My younger son is an accomplished liar when it comes to avoiding confrontation with his father. His phone bleeps during the meal. He knows the rules and leaves it unchecked. It bleeps again. Aloysius frowns and stretches out his hand.

At first, I think Jonathan will refuse to pass over his phone. The silence between them is taut yet controllable. He's no longer a sullen teenager, but ingrained rules still have an impact. Someday he'll find the will to defy his father, but that time is not yet here. He takes his phone from his jacket pocket and hands it to Aloysius, who switches it off before placing it on one of the bookshelves. How do we manage to keep a normal conversation going every Sunday? Jonathan endures these lunches for my sake, but his tolerance is on borrowed time.

In the week following Aloysius's announcement, the media focused on who would be appointed as the new minister for provincial growth. The Sunday newspapers are regurgitating the news of his retirement. Magazine supplements highlight the people who attended the gala auction. Aloysius is pleased to see a photograph in the *Bayview On Sunday* magazine of Douglas and Gabrielle Grace. Perception is his golden rule and he made sure they'd be photographed together.

Jonathan clears his plate and refuses dessert. He plans to visit a friend in hospital. A fall from a motorbike during a rally, he explains. It's possible he's telling the truth. We all know the dangers of an out-of-control motorbike.

I walk with my youngest son to the hall door. 'I don't understand why Dad's retiring without a fight.' He keeps his voice low. 'He's got something else up his sleeve. Any idea what it is?'

'Do you think he's likely to tell me?'

'I've no idea what goes on between the two of you but, in this instance, yes, I think you do know.'

'Jonathan—'

'Forget it.' His interruption is brusque. 'I'll find out sooner rather than later, I guess. What about Douglas? This woman... the podcaster. What is she to him?'

'A friend.'

'But she's media.'

'He seems to trust her. He's good at assessing people and he was relaxed with her.'

'I noticed.'

'How did Amy enjoy the occasion?' I hope I've correctly remembered the name of his latest elf.

'We're still together, if that's what you're asking.'

I hug my son and watch him ride away, his bright red motorcycle helmet winking in the sun. Douglas follows shortly afterwards. Sunday lunch is merely a brief interlude in their lives.

I clear the table and stack the dishwasher. I lied to Jonathan about his father's intentions. To discuss his latest ambition at this stage would be to give it substance. When he revealed his plan to me, I promised him my full support. Isn't that what an obedient wife is supposed to do? To argue with him or laugh aloud would only have entrenched his decision.

I study the photograph of Douglas and Gabrielle in *Bayview on Sunday*. Unlike the other posed images, the naturalness in the way they are standing together suggests they were unaware of being in the lens of a camera.

I'm curious about Douglas's interest in her. When I saw them together, I sensed a fusion that connected them in a way I found hard to understand. The photograph reflects that togetherness, yet her appearance at the ball unsettled me. I've asked Douglas about her.

She makes him feel at ease, he said, which is not something that happens often.

I'm not going to participate in her podcast. Aloysius insists it's the wrong time to highlight the foundation. The focus needs to be on him right now. Change is happening and distractions are not allowed.

Next week the new minister for provincial growth will be appointed. Aloysius has worked hard behind the scenes to ensure it will be Douglas who succeeds him. He is confident of success.

He has yet to ask his son if that is also his wish.

If he did so, would Douglas answer truthfully? Or has he been so groomed in the fellowship of politics that he has forgotten to listen to his inner self?

# TWENTY-THREE
## GABRIELLE

Douglas has not been in touch. A week has passed since the ball and politics has taken precedence over my efforts to infiltrate the Russell family. I need to get up. Staying in bed won't change anything and is another form of evasion. The sun has a merciless sheen as it streams through my bedroom window.

Jessica sends me the latest video of Josh and Michael. How they've grown. Is it possible for them to become even more endearing? Cassie is laughing as she plays with them on the floor of Susanne's chaotic house. When did I last hear her laughing? It's an echo from the past, and yet it's instantly rememberable.

I need to run to calm my mind. It always worked after *Gaby's Good Morning Wake-up* but this morning I can't switch off.

Phoenix Park is busy with joggers, dogwalkers and families. From the main road through the park, it's possible to see the tilly lamp that shines in the window of the presidential residence, Áras an Uachtaráin. This beacon of light is symbolic, a welcome home to the Irish diaspora. Do I miss being an emigrant? Yes, I miss New York and the adrenaline rush of my show. I even miss my alarm going off in the small, dark hours.

I run until I'm exhausted and stop to admire the deer before heading back to my apartment.

On the way, I buy a takeaway hot chocolate and a copy of *Bayview on Sunday*. The afternoon stretches before me as I flick through the pages of the magazine supplement. Photographs from Isabelle's Auction fill the centrefold. The most prominent one leaps from the page. I've no memory of it being taken. I'm smiling at something Douglas said – our heads, so close together, suggest we're sharing an intimate joke.

I mustn't give in to panic. *Bayview On Sunday* is not a paper Cassie reads. Her preference has always been *The Sunday Independent*. I rush to the newsagent and flick through all the Sunday newspapers. *Bayview on Sunday* is the only one with that photograph.

My phone rings as I leave the newsagents. Susanne's name comes up on the screen.

'*Wow!*' she says. This one word weakens my knees. 'Since when did you start moving in high society?' She hoots with laughter and waits for my answer.

'What do you mean?'

'Don't tell me you haven't seen your photo in the magazine.'

'Oh, *that*. Yeah, I saw it. I look awful. Please don't let Cassie see it.'

'It's a gorgeous photo. Anyway, it's too late. She's already seen it.'

'Is she with you? Can you put her on to me?' I knew the risk I was taking when I agreed to accompany Douglas. Greed and need drove me to that auction, and now I must deal with the consequences.

'She's gone to mass,' says Susanne.

'Ask her to ring me as soon as she comes home. I need to talk to her about something important.'

'What about? Is something wrong? You sound... *off*.'

'Everything's fine. I'd like her to stay with me for a while. Give you a break.'

'Actually, she's in good form. No drinking. The thought of rehab scared her off, I think. And the extension is finally taking shape. That's helped bring down my stress levels.'

'I'm glad to hear it. Be sure to tell her to ring me. It's important.'

'When are you bringing Douglas Russell back to Trabawn to meet the family?'

'Never.' I load that one word with all the firmness I can muster. 'The reason I was at the auction was work related. I just happened to bump into him there.'

'I believe you. Thousands wouldn't.' She giggles. 'The whole town will be talking about you by now.'

As I wait for Cassie to call me, I visualise her opening the magazine and seeing that photograph. She suffered my father's lies and now she must endure his daughter's betrayal. She'll never forgive me.

My phone rings. Killian, not Cassie, is the caller. He's in Trabawn for the weekend.

'You're quite a celebrity down here,' he says. 'The general opinion is that you make a handsome couple.'

His sarcasm adds to the anger I've been trying to control since seeing the magazine. 'Are you responsible for that photo being used?'

'I've nothing to do with the magazine, as you well know. Why? Is there a problem?'

'No... no problem.' I need to stay calm and be in control when I talk to Cassie. 'I'm sure you have a reason for ringing. What's up?'

'I never needed a reason in the past... but you're right.' His hesitancy adds to my anxiety. 'I met Cassie earlier. She seemed out of sorts. Have the twins said anything to you about her?'

'According to Susanne, she's in good form. Where did you see her?'

'Out by Burly's Bend. I was cycling and she nearly stepped out in front of me. She didn't seem to recognise who I was at first. Maybe it was the helmet—'

'Did she say what she was doing there?' Anxiety is turning to fear.

'She said she needed to escape from the house. Apparently, Michael is teething and won't stop crying. I saw her on my way down as she was getting into her car. She'd parked it on the viewing platform overlooking the cove, so I'd say she's home by now. I just wanted to give you a heads-up about her.'

'Thanks, Killian. I appreciate that.'

'Talk soon.' He's gone before I can reply.

The silence he leaves behind zings with questions. I ring Cassie and listen to the message on her voice mail.

Michael is crying in the background when Susanne takes my call.

'What is it, Gaby? I'm in the middle of feeding Michael.'

'Is Cassie back?'

'No. She rang after mass to say she was calling into Jessica and having dinner with her. I *told* her to ring you. Has she not been in touch?' Her earlier buoyancy seems to have deserted her.

'Killian contacted me just now. He said he saw her up by Burly's Bend.'

'That's ridiculous. What in God's name would she be doing up there? Killian's obviously mixed her up with someone else.'

'He spoke to her...' I can't control my panic. 'He said she was out of sorts.'

'Out of sorts?' Susanne's tone changes. 'Don't tell me she's drinking again.'

'He didn't mention drink. More like she seemed kind of dazed.'

'I'll ring Jessica and see if she knows what's going on,' says Susanne. 'I'll be back in touch when I talk to her.'

'If she's not there, check Burly's Head. Remember where we used to picnic on the summit?'

'That makes no sense.' Susanne's exasperation is spilling over. 'Why on earth would she go there on a Sunday morning? Are you sure Killian—'

'*Susanne*, just do as I say and ring me after you've spoken to Jessica.' I end the call before she can ask any further questions.

The ten minutes I wait for her to call back seems interminable. As I guessed, Cassie is missing. She did not attend mass, nor did she visit Jessica.

Is it possible she has gone to the headland again? I grab my jacket and my car keys, unwilling to follow what's happening from afar and convinced my suspicion is right.

# TWENTY-FOUR

## CASSANDRA

I dislike the Sunday supplement magazines. All those recipes I'll never make, the quality wines I'd like to drink but don't because vodka has a quicker kick, and the celebrities in slinky dresses teetering on red carpets. This morning, flicking through the pages of a magazine I usually never read, your photograph leaped out at me. Large and in full colour, impossible to miss.

How could you? I recognised the man standing beside you. I had to press my fist to my mouth to stifle a cry in case Susanne demanded to know what was wrong. You looked radiant, in your element with the family you've chosen over us. They must have no idea who you really are. Otherwise, the media would be swarming all over Trabawn by now and I'd be in handcuffs. That's just a matter of time. Your ability to hide a secret can only be tested so far. Eventually, it'll explode in all its ugliness. Just as my secret was leached from me when Dominick arrived home on the night following Paddy Murdock's visit.

I'd asked Noreen if the children could sleep over so that me and Dominick could spend some time alone.

'Absence obviously makes the heart grow fonder.' Noreen winked as coyly as only she knows how to do.

You moaned about having to sleep in the same house as Noreen's boys. Aged thirteen, you were going through your hate-boys stage – apart from Killian, of course. Reluctantly, you went next door with the twins. The house was silent then. Silent as a tomb while I waited for my husband to return from the sea.

He looked tired when he arrived home. He smelled of salt air and fish. If possible, he looked even more unkempt than usual. I cried out when he tried to hug me. Paddy Murdock's kicks affected every breath I took. I needed a chest X-ray, and probably one for my head, but that was not going to happen.

Even now, driving too fast and with the windows open to cool my cheeks, I can remember every moment of that night.

Without speaking, I took my husband's hand and led him to our bedroom. He caught his breath as he entered the room. It was muggy with the scent of death and all that brought with it. He opened the window and turned to me.

'What's going on?' he said. 'That smell is—'

'The scent of a dead man.' I interrupted him brutally, uncaring about his shock. 'His name is Paddy Murdock. I killed him. He was going to take Gabrielle away from us. He claimed you stole her from her family. I believe him.'

Dominick remained rigid, as if my accusation had paralysed him. His mouth opened as he attempted to speak but he seemed unable to find the right words. He must have known that there were no right words and searching for them would inevitably lead to failure. He reminded me of the fish he caught and landed on the pier, cod-mouthed, opening on a last gasp.

He knelt and pulled aside the bedspread. I'd used the largest one with tassels that touched the floor and formed a fringe around the bed. One glance was all it took for him to arch his back and cry out. A sinner praying for repentance, I thought, seeking forgiveness from the god he'd rejected. His refusal to attend mass on Sundays when he was ashore was a constant niggle between us. Too late... too late...

'What happened?' Finally, he was able to speak.

I longed for the relief of tears, but I was hollowed to a husk. 'It was an accident. He was kicking me and would have killed me, if that was what it took to steal Gabrielle.' I pulled up my top to show him the bruises on my chest. 'I struck him with the phone. But I didn't kill him. He banged his head against the fire-place when he fell back from me.'

Dominick laid his palm against the mottled swelling between my breasts. Shock drained the colour from his sun-baked skin. His lines turned to furrows, aging him and affording me a glimpse of the old man he would become.

I could see the struggle he had to hold himself together as he began to tell me about his efforts to adjust to life outside the orphanage. George Blake had organised a flat for him and Paddy to share. They lived together for a year before drifting apart and losing touch. When Dominick – I had to call him Dominick even though Paddy Murdock had branded his real name on my brain – expressed an interest in joining the police, George helped him to be accepted into the Garda Síochána.

Maria married Aloysius Russell when he was minister for justice. Fate brought them together again after Dominick became responsible for her husband's security.

The excuse he made for taking Gabrielle – she would always be Gabrielle Grace and never, *never* Isabelle Russell – helped in time. Aloysius Russell was a brute and Gabrielle belonged to Dominick, as much as she did to Maria. It is possible to believe anything if the need is desperate enough. But the heaviness of the deceit Dominick laid on me never faded. It locked us into a mutually dependent partnership. One that was based on a dangerous secret that could destroy our world in seconds.

. . .

It comes again, that heaving guilt. I need to slow down. The hedgerows blur, the corners on Burly's Head sharp and dangerous. What does it matter? Slow or fast, the voices in my head are never silent. I've had enough.

'Poor, dear Cassie,' my friends will say at my funeral. 'She's found peace at last.'

I hope they'd be right, and it's not just another trite platitude.

The headland is busy with holidaymakers today. I'm anonymous when I leave my car. I don't see Killian until it's almost too late. The dear boy... so in love with Gabrielle... and she with him... mad teenage passions. I should have supported her that night... should have... should have... all the should haves and the what ifs... he's worried about me... the dear boy... but I send him on his way and return to the car for the bottle. My comfort and my consolation.

Dominick refused to allow me to help him to move the body to his jeep. He drove into the night and never told me where he laid Paddy Murdock and his camera to rest. I never asked, but it made sense that he'd brought him out on the *Sheila Rua* and given him a seaman's burial, his body weighted and never to be recovered. I haven't set foot on the trawler since then.

Dominick checked, but no car had been stalled at Burly's Bend, nor was one found abandoned near Trabawn. How Paddy Murdock reached Headwind remained a mystery. *On devil wings*, I often thought, as I struggled to forget him.

My ribs were so severely damaged it took two months before I could breathe evenly again... but did my breathing ever recover its normal rhythm? Was I any different from Paddy Murdock, who killed a young woman because she owed him money? I allowed him to die because he would have destroyed my family and separated you from us. Was that really an excuse for taking a life? Dominick assured me over and over that his death was an accident. I knew differently. I watched the light leave him and the prayers I said for his soul were as arid as dead ash.

The sun dances lightly over the waves, an ocean of spangles that won't waste time with me. One last stop. The enchanted circle. I open the bottle and taste the rush. What a beautiful day.

I can never decide what hurts the most. The fact that my husband lied to me about Mary Carter, who never existed, or that he only ever loved one woman. A love that he carried on his last breath. And, then, his final betrayal. *I stole you...* letting loose our secret, scattering seeds of doubt that turned into shoots, green and glistening with sap.

Shoots that have developed suckers strong enough to suffocate me.

# TWENTY-FIVE

## GABRIELLE

Four hours have passed without word from Cassie. Search parties have been organised. Killian's belief that she was entering her car when he cycled past her on his way down Burly's Head was wrong. Her car is still parked on the viewing promontory.

I'm almost halfway to Trabawn and the calls keep coming. Killian is worried about the fact that I'm driving in such a panicked state. He tried without success to persuade me to remain in Dublin. It sounds as if the entire community has joined in the search. He's positive Cassie will be found before long. Susanne repeats his reassurances, but I keep heading westwards.

Twilight is falling and Cassie is still missing when I reach Susanne's house. I find her in the living room, Michael at her breast, tears streaming down her face. Eddie has just phoned to say he's with a group of climbers, who are taking the downward trail to Burly's Cove. No trace of her was found on Burly's Head, including the picnic area.

'There's no way Cassie would tackle such a dangerous

climb.' I try to comfort her but she, like me, is picturing the slanting, twisting trail with its treacherous stony surface. There's a reason why such a magnificent beach with its crystal-clear water remains unused. Even those who venture down the trail discover that they are battling nature on both sides when they reach the cove: the cliffs are susceptible to rock fall and the ocean has perilous currents.

'What possessed her to do this?' Susanne sounds bewildered and anguished. I share her anguish, but mine is driven by the awareness that I'm responsible for what is unfolding. I've made Cassie 'out of sorts'. Time will tell what exactly that means.

The climbers who tackled Burly's Cove find no evidence that she made the descent. If her footprints marked the sand, the tide has washed them away.

The gardaí call off the search when darkness settles. It will begin again at first light.

I stay overnight in Jessica's house. Sleep is impossible. We sit up late and talk about Cassie. No other conversation is possible. We keep repeating ourselves as if, with each repetition, we'll be able to make more sense of her disappearance. Where is she sheltering from the night? What possessed her to go off the rails again? Neighbours come and go, and the chat continues until that by-now familiar pressure throbs in my head.

Killian is among the visitors. When he hugs me, all the tension between us since my return to Ireland disappears. I hold him tight and can't let go until he gradually prises me loose. I'm sobbing by then, harsh, hiccupping sobs that send me running from the room and out into the black night.

In the city that never sleeps, I've walked between towers of light. I've grown accustomed to neon and the ceaseless glitter of advertisements. Here, there is nothing to penetrate the night once I pass the shaft of light shining from Jessica's front door. I stop running when I reach the bottom of her driveway Here, in the silence, I can't ignore Cassie's threat. Her voice has a terrifying clarity.

*'If this scandal breaks loose, I won't hang around. I've no fear of dying. In fact, it would be a welcome relief from the voices.'*

'Gaby, where are you?' Killian's phone torch spears the dark.

'I'm here.' I step from the shelter of shrubs and wait until he reaches me. 'Do you think Cassie is still alive?' I ask.

'Hopefully, she is. It's not a cold night and, according to the forecast, no rain is expected. She could be sheltering in someone's house or may even be staying in a hotel.'

'I doubt that.'

'It's a possibility,' he replies. 'We have to be positive and believe in her safe return.'

'I know... I *know*.' Emphasis is essential. It adds weight to my conviction that Cassie is safe. If I think otherwise, I'll sink and be unable to rise again. The crush of guilt will see to that.

'Cassie's tough,' he says. 'She's familiar with this terrain. I'm sure she'll be found in the morning. I've taken the day off work tomorrow and will join you in the search at first light.'

'Thanks, Killian. I don't deserve you as a friend.' I lean into him, thankful that he can't see how flushed my cheeks have become.

He lifts his hand and cups my tears in his palm. His lips brush mine, a kiss that is almost imagined and yet I feel its tenderness even as he disappears into the night.

I must have slept, even though I watched the hours pass on the clock beside the bed.

Nicholas's advice that I eat breakfast before beginning the

search is ignored. The thought of food sickens me. I meet Killian as arranged at the foot of Burly's Head and begin the steep climb. Yesterday, our childhood picnic area was searched without success, yet I'm drawn back to it by an impulse I'm unable to explain. The sun is high and harsh. Cobwebs shimmy on the rocks as we walk through a mist that is already beginning to evaporate. Killian and his brother used to picnic with us when we were children. He is still surefooted as we make our way upwards. Once, when I stumble, he takes my hand and doesn't let go until we're inside the circle.

This childhood space is empty. We stand within the bleak limestone palisade. When flecks of mica flickered in the sunshine Cassie made it magical for us, and easy to believe that elves were mining gold.

We search the surrounding area, treading carefully on mulching leaves and evil-looking mushrooms that squelch underfoot. Whatever charms this place possessed when we were children have long vanished. Far below us, the ocean heaves its intolerance for those who dare take it for granted.

Killian calls me. My name has a hollow ring, laden with alarm. He's back in the circle and kneeling beside one of the tallest rocks. Its forward slant gives the impression that a sharp push could knock it over, but it's deeply embedded in its ice age roots. This, we used to believe, was the entrance to the elf mine.

He has removed a peaked cap, partially hidden by leaves, from the base of the rock. I recognise it instantly. I fall to my knees and press it against my cheek. We've often teased Cassie about this cap, which she wears throughout the summer. We've bought her floppy sun hats and chic visors, which she ignores. The canvas feels damp. I press harder as I breathe in her desperation. It must have blown off in the wind as she walked upwards to the headland summit.

An empty bottle also lies in this space. Vodka, the label still visible, and clearly dropped recently.

'She's dead.' My whispering words reach him before they are swept over the ocean to become at one with the shriek of seagulls. Where is her grave? In the silt of the Atlantic or at the foot of a headstone speckled with mica?

Killian hunkers down to gently take Cassie's cap from me. He rings Eddie and tells him to lead the search party back down to Burly's Cove. We know the tide patterns of these turbulent waves.

Back in Susanne's house, she cries when I show her the cap and clings to Jessica as we wait for Eddie to contact us.

He rings me directly. 'Gaby... *Gaby*...' His voice breaks. I know what's coming next. 'Cassie had an accident. We found her body... she's dead, Gaby... drowned... oh, my god... how am I going to tell Susanne?' He's trying to speak between sobs. The twins, seeing my expression, turn into each other and become one.

'I'll tell them both,' I whisper and hand the phone to Killian, who continues taking details.

The searchers believe it was an accidental fall from the summit and the currents washed her body to the cove.

'It was an accident.' Killian states this emphatically. He doesn't mention the empty bottle. 'You know how treacherous it is if you walk too close to the edge.'

How quickly Susanne's house fills. People in tears, people with food, people with open arms to embrace the twins and me. I allow them to wrap their sorrow around me. No amount of sympathy can silence Cassie's voice... *traitor... traitor... traitor*. How am I ever going to live with myself? Do I even want to try?

Cassie is severely bruised but still recognisable when we gather at the hospital morgue. The twins, united in grief, hold me upright every time I bend. Why won't they let me break? Why must they keep telling me how much Cassie loved me, missed me, longed for my phone calls? No one mentions the arguments that used to shake the air around us.

I've never cried like this. Such a fathomless well of tears when we bury her three days later. She will lie with my father. Is that what she wanted? An eternal resting place with the man who, along with his daughter, drove her to her death?

Killian has taken time off work to attend her funeral. I'm conscious of his watchfulness. Has he linked Cassie's death to the photograph in the magazine? If so, he never mentions it. Unlike my sisters, he is aware of ripples below the surface of my sorrow. Confiding in him will let loose the beast – that's how I envisage Cassie's secret: slavering, pawing the ground, ready to devour me should I betray her again. Now, more than ever, I'm bound to her.

Susanne and Jessica lift their sons' hands in waving gestures as I drive away. They are probably relieved, in a guilty way, that they'll no longer have to endure my tears and bleak silences.

Douglas has been trying to contact me. Two missed calls on my phone. I managed to ignore the first one. The second one came with a message.

'Gaby, this is Douglas Russell. My mother sends her apologies. She's unable to participate in the podcast. I did my best to persuade her, but she feels that this is not the right time for her. She specifically asked me to thank you for your interest in her foundation.'

I'm too tormented to be disappointed. Cassie is never out of my mind. The same thoughts churning over and adding to the remorse. It's crushing me. Each time I straighten my spine I wonder how that's possible, yet the longing to see Maria Russell grows in tandem with my guilt. Is it possible for such conflicting emotions to continue co-existing, or will my mind finally break under the strain?

# TWENTY-SIX

## GABRIELLE

My first podcast attracts attention when it goes online. A group of protestors who'd set up camp outside an empty building they believed was designated for asylum seekers were more than willing to speak to me. '*Ireland Says No!*' was painted on their placards and their venom soured the air they breathed. The second half of my podcast answered their fears and suspicions in the voices of those sleeping in tents as they wait to have their refugee status processed.

The Ireland I left ten years previously has a changing face that is as uplifting as it is dispiriting. These two elements are what I hope to capture with *Graceful Opinions*. Since then, I've released three more podcasts. On social media I'm accused of being either 'a rabid racist' or 'a wokey lefty liberal'. I'm touching the nerve of my listenership. It's almost like being back at NY Eyz.

The contradictory nature of my podcasts matches my moods. Maria is in my dreams, clashing with Cassie, as she does during the day when I'm plagued by these conflicting emotions. I build scenarios around her, but Cassie destroys them. Memories of those early years when she was the breadth of my small world keep surfacing and the troubled years pale into insignificance.

Unable to endure the guilt I feel over her death, and aware that Maria will always be a luring temptation, I've decided to return to New York. I can just as easily record my podcasts there. Same issues, same arguments. I will lay Cassie's ghost to rest by creating this distance between myself and my biological family.

As if aware of my resolve and how easily it can be undone, Douglas rings.

'Congratulations on your podcasts,' he says. 'I've been listening to them with interest.'

'Thank you, Douglas.' My reply is light and airy. 'That's high praise coming from the new minister for provincial growth. Congratulations to you, too. I'm amazed you've time to listen to me.'

No one, even the political journalists, were surprised by his victory. I observed it all from a distance – or so I convinced myself, until I heard his voice again.

'I make time for what's necessary.' He hesitates, his tone softening when he speaks again. 'I was interviewed by Killian Osmond yesterday. He told me about your mother's tragic accident. Please accept my deepest condolences.'

'Thank you.' My throat constricts when I think of his inadvertent role in Cassie's death. I owe it to her to end this conversation quickly.

'I admire your resilience in setting up your podcast at such a difficult time,' he adds.

'I cope by keeping busy.'

'*Graceful Opinions* has quite an edge to it. I like it. So does my father. He's the other reason why I'm in touch. He has an idea he'd like to discuss with you.'

'An idea? What exactly is it?' I hope Douglas doesn't detect the tremor in my question.

'He'd like to discuss it with you in person.'

Cassie is calling me to heel. *Let me rest in peace...* I must obey her wail from the grave.

'I'm afraid I can't take on any outside projects right now. Please give your father my apologies and thank him for considering me.'

'I understand.' Douglas sounds sincere, also regretful. 'I don't want to add to the stress you must be going through. I'll let him know your situation. He was hoping to invite you to Beech Park to discuss his ideas.'

'Your house?'

'It's where I grew up.'

He says it so naturally. Beech Park. My natural home. Don't I have a right to see inside the house where I should have lived... could still be living? The house my father desecrated with his lust for revenge. I've tried to understand his reasons. Revenge is the only word that comes to mind. He conceived a child with Maria. She must have turned her back on him, refused to leave her husband and her precious home. This father I adored, unable to tolerate her decision, came like a thief in the night to take me away. What other reason but revenge drove him to do something so despicable?

Hate scalds me. A flame I can't quench, just like my curiosity.

'Can I have time to consider meeting your father?' I ask. 'I'm incapable of making decisions right now.'

'Of course,' he replies. 'Hopefully, you'll change your mind. I look forward to hearing from you, Gaby.'

*One visit... that's all I need... Stop lying... one will never be enough... Yes, it will... it will... leave me in peace... Cassie... be quiet... quiet... let my house speak.*

I battle Cassie for days before giving in and contacting Douglas.

. . .

Gates open automatically. I enter a tree-lined avenue. Above me, branches intertwine and enfold me in a green, leafy tunnel. The sun, at its midday height, peeks intermittently through the leaves and flashes against the windows of my car. This is my last opportunity to see my birth mother before I leave for New York.

I slow down and fight off a dizzying spasm. *Drive away... drive away...* Cassie's voice fills my ears. I accelerate and drown her out.

The canopy of leaves lightens and there it is. Beech Park. This home where I first knew love. Could I have been any happier with Maria is this magnificent house? I played on sand and around the rocks, not on those spacious lawns that fan out on either side of me.

Beech Park is an Edwardian-style house with elegant bay windows. The grounds surrounding it have a natural wildness that must have seemed like heaven to my father, as a neglected boy. He would have climbed the trees and hidden in the maze of bushes. I blink back tears as I imagine him, a skinny urchin racing across the grass in pursuit of Maria. Did he kiss her behind the trunk of that wide-spanning oak? Paddy Murdock is nowhere in this vast, idyllic space. I can't allow him in. He belongs only to Cassie's story.

Aloysius Russell comes down the steps to meet me. 'Did you have any problem finding us?' he asks.

'Not at all. I used *Maps*.'

'Of course you did.' He chuckles. 'I guess people don't get lost anymore, which is good. But losing your way can also bring you in interesting new directions.'

'Has that ever happened to you?' I ask.

'Many times. But I always make sure I can find my way back to the old path.' Again, he gives that gravelly chuckle and ushers me inside with a slight bow.

A magnificent chandelier hangs from the centre of the hall. The doors leading into various rooms have a weathered appearance. Sturdy and built to last, they failed to protect me when my father closed the front door behind him, my three-week-old self in his arms.

I follow Aloysius into his study. 'Douglas is one of your admirers.' He sits behind a desk that is heavily carved and old-fashioned enough to qualify as an antique, and nods towards a chair in front of it. 'He thinks you have a unique talent. On his recommendation, I've listened to recordings of your morning shows and your recent podcasts. You're astute and feisty. Not afraid to speak your mind and develop an argument. I respect that.' My value is summed up with a benign nod. 'Thank you for agreeing to meet me.'

I wait for him to continue. I'm here for only one reason. When will the door open and reveal her?

'I'd like to work with you on a series of podcasts,' Aloysius says.

I force myself to pay attention to him.

'Since my retirement I've had time to think about problems that were outside my remit when I was a minister. As we speak, my research assistant is investigating concerns that have been ignored for too long or burdened with too much red tape. The media searches so hard for the big story that they overlook the little ones. Yet those are the ones that can bring prosperity to small, rural communities. Working together, we can highlight these issues through your podcasts.' He holds his palms outward to forestall my questions. 'You'll be the interviewer. I'll be the problem solver and will make sure there is a solution to whatever projects we undertake. It'll mean travelling to the counties I choose to visit, so we'll be on the road for much of the time.'

I need to leave now. He's a piper, piping as he lures me into his world. I've delved too deeply into Aloysius Russell's background to believe he's a good Samaritan. He's an ex-politician who has survived scandals and emerged relatively unscathed. His sudden desire to take the problems of small people onto his shoulders doesn't ring true. Why does he need me to shine his halo?

'It's a very interesting and worthwhile idea, Mr Russell but—'

'Call me Aloysius. No need to stand on ceremony, especially as I hear a *but*. I'd like to deflect it, if I may.'

'Unfortunately, my answer is no. I'm not comfortable with your idea. You've retired from politics and yet it sounds to me like you're embarking on a self-promotional journey.'

'Astute, as I said.' His teeth have been whitened. His smile emphasises their largeness. Cassie would have called them 'tombstones'.

She's inside my head, shrieking for attention.

'And you're absolutely correct about my intentions,' he continues. 'However, I'm not at liberty to say what they are right now. If you agree to work with me, I'll elaborate fully. You call what I've offered you a self-promotional journey but it's one that both of us can undertake together. I've already discussed this with *Bayview Communications*. I'm sure you're aware that it's one of the most powerful streaming platforms for podcasts. Its communications network will air our content in their print media and broadcasting channels. This will be a massive opportunity for you to extend your reach nationwide and beyond.'

'I'm afraid my answer is still the same. I plan on returning to New York. But I'm sure you'll have no problem finding a suitable podcaster.'

That should end our conversation. Instead, he continues outlining the podcasts we could make together.

'I only take on the best and Douglas assured me you'd be an ideal choice,' he says.' 'Why did you agree to this interview if you'd already made other plans?'

How would he react if I told him the truth?

*I'm here to catch a last glimpse of my birth mother whom my father loved behind your back. Her non-appearance will make it easier to leave this house of entrancing temptations.*

'Your son is very persuasive, and I was interested in hearing your ideas.' I speak too fast, and he leans back in his chair, as if my explanation has developed a strange propulsion. 'But I miss New York and, to be honest, I'm not that interested in politics.'

'Thank you for your frankness.' He stands to signal the end of our discussion, his hand outstretched. 'I'm sorry you're leaving us. I must say, you and Douglas made a striking couple at the auction.'

What is he insinuating? Does he really believe his son has an interest in me? I suspect it's wishful thinking on his part. I remember the unguarded spasm of pain that crossed Douglas's face when I asked about his personal life. His father takes a harsh line when it comes to 'traditional family values' and has been outspoken with his views many times. Does he deliberately ignore his son's right to love whomever he chooses or is he blinkered to the needs of those who don't fit into the narrow frame of his world?

It rained during the meeting. Fallen leaves glisten on the avenue, still green yet already edged with the russet tones of autumn. I see the hand of Maria in the freedom she allows the meadow grasses to create corridors of pollen and the order that Aloysius imposes on the sculptured shrubs. This is pure speculation, of course. I've no idea how my birth mother feels about nature and its demands. Like all my daydreams, I'm moulding her into an image that probably has nothing to do with reality.

I take a bend too fast and skid on a layer of fallen leaves. I veer to the wrong side of the avenue just as another car appears.

A white Porsche, it can only belong to Maria.

I catch a glimpse of her startled expression and hear her car tyres screech as she swerves towards the grass verge. She keeps control of her car before bringing it to a halt. I brake so hard that I'm thrust forward and bang my head against the steering wheel.

My forehead is bleeding and I'm slumped over the wheel when she opens my door.

'Oh, my goodness, you're bleeding,' she says. 'Can you straighten so that I can see how you are?'

'Forgive me.' I unclench my fingers from the wheel and lift my face to hers. 'I wasn't concentrating. This is my fault.'

'Gabrielle... I didn't realise it was you.' Her voice shakes and, yet, again, it comes to me like an echo, a dormant memory stirring. I know it isn't possible to reach back to my beginnings but that doesn't matter. In her womb I would have swayed and rocked and kicked to her words. I would have rested to her songs.

'Are you hurt, my dear? That curve on the avenue can be deceptive.'

'I should have been more careful.' Pain shoots across my chest. Is my heart breaking? Why would it not?

She moves closer to me. 'You're in shock,' she says. 'And you've quite a swelling on your forehead. You need to have it examined.'

'I'm okay... honestly... I'll be fine. I'm normally a careful driver—'

'I'm sure you are. But, right now, you're in no condition to go anywhere. I'm going to drive you to my doctor's surgery—'

'No... no.' She takes my breath away and leaves me gasping for air. 'That's not necessary.'

I protest all the way to her car. My feet reach into space. I'm surprised each time they touch the ground. Her arm supports me whenever I stumble.

On the drive to the surgery, she hardly speaks. Nor do I, yet the atmosphere between us is easy.

She's on first name terms with the doctor, who sees us after a short wait. I follow the directions of his finger and name the day and date. Other tests follow before he decides I'm not suffering from concussion or anything more damaging. X-rays or CT scans aren't necessary. I should be able to drive my car home.

I'm walking normally when we leave his surgery. I stumble again, though, doing so deliberately this time. The delight I feel when she steadies me is also radiant with pain.

'I presume you were at a meeting with Aloysius.' She starts the car and turns in the direction of Beech Park.

'Yes, I was.'

'Has he convinced you to work with him?'

'I'll be returning to New York, so it's not possible.'

'I understand the lure of New York. I've been there often.' She sighs, as if reliving pleasant memories. 'I'm sorry you're not available. I was looking forward to getting to know you on our travels.'

'Will you be travelling with your husband?'

'For the second half, yes. Aloysius has several engagements lined up and always likes me by his side when he's attending such events. I'm busy with foundation commitments but as soon as my desk is clear I'll be joining him.' She glances across at me. 'Douglas told me that your mother died recently. This must be a difficult time for you. Losing someone precious is a tremendous grief.'

Is she thinking about her daughter as she speaks? Impossible to tell. Twenty-nine years of wondering. What has that done to her?

We've reached the gates of Beech Park. 'Don't forget the doctor's advice. Lots of ice on your forehead and take time to rest.' She brakes beside my car. 'It's been nice meeting you again, Gabrielle.'

'Why don't you call me Gaby. Everyone does.'

'But Gabrielle is such a lovely name.'

'My mother was the only person to use it.'

'Then Gabrielle must always belong to her.'

My hands are beyond my control, fingers twining, pressing against the cuticles of my nails. 'I was very tempted by your husband's proposal.' I must stop fidgeting, or she'll wonder what's wrong with me. 'I can always postpone going to New York for a few months.'

'Oh, that would be wonderful, Gaby. Shall I tell him you're reconsidering your decision?'

'Yes.' The blast of regret that hits me when I think of Cassie almost causes me to moan aloud.

A web is being spun by circumstances I feel powerless to control. I shiver as I walk into its silky strands.

# TWENTY-SEVEN

## GABRIELLE

Throughout September, we've stayed in hotels in four counties where Aloysius has resolved local community issues. Apart from me, the *Red Tape Unreeled* podcast team consists of Aloysius; Colin Doyle, his comms officer; Liam Breen, the driver of our minivan; and Roy Doran, who looks after his security. Retiring from politics doesn't mean leaving one's enemies behind, it seems.

A shelter for homeless men has been opened after lying empty for a year due to local opposition. A bitter dispute over land allocated for affordable housing has been sorted to everyone's satisfaction and building is about to begin. Work has started on a new playground in a deprived area after years of lobbying without success by a local mothers' group.

Behind these success stories podcast on *Red Tape Unreeled* is Aloysius' slick and subtle touch. Months of advance preparation was carried out by a larger, as yet unnamed team of supporters. They have been working in the background to promote his image as an ex-politician who rolls up his sleeves and gets things done.

'What in the name of all that's *unholy* are you doing?'

Killian rang after the first podcast was released. 'Last I heard, you were thinking of returning to New York.'

'I changed my mind.' Stung by his tone, I was instantly on the defensive. 'A woman's prerogative and all that goes with it.'

'Come on, Gaby. I need a better excuse.'

'I received an offer I couldn't refuse.'

'Oh... so, it's about money, then? What a relief. I was worried it might be your obsessive interest in the Russell family.'

'*Obsessive?*'

'What else would you call it? You turn up on his son's arm at that auction and now you're acting as his father's propagandist.' His scorn was withering.

'Have you any idea how insulting that remark is? I'm a professional broadcaster and an—'

'Gaby, *please*, we used to confide in each other.' His interruption has bite. 'What's going on? If you want to highlight a politician, choose one with integrity and vision. Anyone but him. Rumour has it that he's thinking of running in the next presidential election and this is simply an opportunity for him to campaign before it begins officially.'

'That's nonsense. He's using his retirement to do something positive and all you can do is ridicule him. I'm going to hang up before we have an argument.'

'Goodbye, *stranger*.' With that gut-punch, he ended his call.

I wanted to ring him back. He's precious to me. My lifelong friend. When will I stop kidding myself? What I feel for Killian Osmond has changed. I won't recognise it, nor will I name it, except to say it's growing stronger as we draw further apart. He pricked my conscience with his criticism, but integrity is no match for a craving I can't control.

He apologises the next day, his words captured on my voice message. I don't ring him back. I can't handle what's going on in my heart when my mind scrambles to make sense of who I am.

Cassie never leaves me. First thing in the morning she lays claim on me before I can be distracted by other thoughts. That's when the pain of loss is most acute. Sharp nails, a lance, a stinging slap to my face: if death has a presence, that's how it would manifest itself.

Maria will join us tomorrow.

Maria has been part of the team for a week. It's impossible to be alone with her. Aloysius pins her to his arm at every opportunity. Was she just being polite when she told me she hoped to get to know me better? When we do manage time together, she is distant, her mind elsewhere. Even if she tried to talk to me, what would I say? What language is needed to end our years of separation? I rehearse the words in my mind, afraid to speak aloud for fear of being overheard. Killian is right – at times, I feel so lost I can't ever imagine being able to find my way back.

We'll spend a week in Clognua. It's typical of a town that once bustled but is now disfigured by boarded-up shop fronts and a general malaise. *Red Tape Unreeled* will record the efforts of a group of craftspeople who have been unsuccessfully seeking funds to set up a craft centre. By the end of our visit, Aloysius will have cut through the bureaucracy and the funding will be in place. No miracles – knowing Aloysius, I suspect that he'd had this funding deliberately withheld until he could ride to the rescue.

The web that traps me feels sticky, rather than silky, yet it's where I need to be.

I cling to the idea that Maria will recognise me as her daughter. A primal acknowledgement that bypasses all logic. As for Aloysius, the effect he has on me is disconcerting. He's courteous and considerate, appreciative of my podcasts, yet the feeling persists that I'm only touching his surface. And even that is rough and bristling enough for me to appreciate that I'm rubbing against the grain.

We're staying in a hotel with adjoining lodges. She and Aloysius occupy one of the lodges and the rest of us have rooms in the hotel.

Douglas and Jonathan have joined us for the weekend. I catch Maria watching me when I'm with Douglas. What does she make of us? Does she recognise something deeper in our friendship, and is puzzled because she's unable to name it?

Aloysius never loses an opportunity to link us together for photo opportunities and crack jokes about how I'm turning his son's head.

I'm convinced he was responsible for the photograph that finally destroyed Cassie. Foolish, selfish father, too engrossed in his own vision of the world to understand that love has many shades.

# TWENTY-EIGHT

## MARIA

I call her Gaby, as she asked. Her name does not sit easily with me. She unsettles me. I can't explain why. Maybe it's her gaze, her eyes so blue and intense. I'm aware of her sideways glances, full-on glances, shy glances that bounce off me and away again. Her podcasts are excellent. They tell a story of obstacles overcome and how my husband, astride his white horse, metaphorically speaking, rides to the rescue. The man with the power to smash bureaucracy… bam… slam…

We dine in the evening with councillors and local party members. He'll need their support when he makes his next move. I watch Gaby as she sits between Roy and Colin at a separate table and wonder what she's thinking when she looks over at me.

Last night she had a drink with Douglas in the hotel bar. Once again, I was struck by their closeness. Jonathan dislikes her. He arrived this afternoon in clacking boots, leather trousers, and Martian-like in his enormous helmet.

'She's nothing other than his cheerleader.' He made his feelings known in no uncertain terms. 'Why isn't she wearing a rah-rah skirt and waving pom-poms?'

'That's unfair.' I was surprised at how quickly I jumped to Gaby's defence. 'She's a professional. Her podcasts have created news items in the media and have a growing listenership.'

'I agree she's a professional. I've listened to some of her previous stuff. But these are puff pieces. Dad was pulling strings long before she began working with him.'

I didn't want to agree with him but, of course, it's true.

Tonight is important. Aloysius intends to reveal his intention to Jonathan. Douglas is already aware of his father's ambition. As usual, he has kept his opinion to himself. We'll eat in the lodge. I'll cook for a change.

Jonathan has been biking around Clognua for the afternoon. He returns to the lodge with a cheesy grin and the skunky odour of hash on his clothes. Aloysius will recognise it at once. A red rag to a bull, as Jonathan knows.

'You stink of hash.' Already, I can feel the evening slipping beyond my control. 'Have you done this deliberately to upset your father?'

He shrugs out of his leather jacket and flings it over an armchair. 'Why should I go to the trouble of annoying him? Since when has he needed an excuse to be angry with me?'

His truculent expression adds to my nervousness. Jittery – that's how I feel all the time now. I can't decide what's making me more nervous: Aloysius's plans, or the problems I'm experiencing with the foundation funds.

I've made lasagne, their favourite dish, and prepared a salad. I'd hoped the tomatoes and garlic would disguise the smell of hash but Aloysius's nostrils flare as soon as he enters the dining room. A warning glance from me keeps him silent as we gather around the table.

'I hope we can have a pleasant evening together,' he says to Jonathan, when they've filled their plates. 'I've some important news to share with you. I'll be announcing it publicly when the time is right but, until then, nothing that is discussed between us now is to go beyond this room.'

He pauses and waits for a reaction from his son, who continues eating. Douglas, trying to manage the atmosphere, as usual, puts down his knife and fork. 'You needn't worry. Jonathan won't—'

'Let me speak.' Aloysius curtly interrupts him and addresses Jonathan directly. 'I intend to run as a candidate in the upcoming presidential election.'

This blunt statement works. Jonathan raises his head.

'You're *what*?' He sounds stupefied.

'You heard what I said. I believe I've an excellent chance of winning. My record speaks for itself, and with my experience—'

'Stop... stop.' Jonathan half rises then collapses back in his chair. 'You're not standing on a platform, Dad. I don't need the spiel. I know it by rote. Why on earth would you run for the presidency when you've dipped your fingers into so many scandals? The media will crucify you.'

'Well, it's a relief to know I have your backing, Jonathan.' Aloysius seems relaxed, smiling. 'What scandals do you mean?'

'Glenpora—'

'Put to bed, as you well know.'

'The bullying accusations—'

'Allegations, you mean. Nothing was ever proved.'

'What if someone asks you about Katie Corcoran?'

Aloysius's stillness is the giveaway: like a cat watches a bird, that utter focus before the fatal spring forward.

The crash of his fist on the table finally breaks the strained silence that followed Jonathan's question.

'I'm not going to have this argument with you again,' he says. 'Instead, I'm going to state some simple facts. I intend to run for president and win that election. To do so I need the support of my family. For starters, you must clean up your act.

I've supported your idleness, your inability to hold down a job, and your ridiculous Hell's Angels posturing for long enough.'

'I have a company—' Jonathan attempts to speak.

'You have a *hobby*.' Aloysius's interruption and his scornful tone diminish the efforts Jonathan has made to establish his own business. 'Don't tell me that organising rallies for a bunch of thugs can ever equate with real work. Finally, if you dare to mention that woman to me again, you'll be disinherited. The fancy apartment you occupy is in my name. You'll have to look elsewhere if you want a roof over your head.'

'My *hobby* earns me enough to move out of *your* apartment,' Jonathan retorts. 'As for being disinherited, do you think I give a damn? I'll mention Katie's name as often as I like. I'll never stop blaming you for her death.'

Teenage love is such a powerful keg. All it needs is a flint and the explosion will shadow every relationship that follows. I'd hoped Jonathan's heartache could be eased with time, but the women who've followed Katie Corcoran are simply shallow replicas.

'Stop... both of you... please, stop.' I lean towards Aloysius and press my hand to his chest to prevent him reaching across the table to strike Jonathan. To my surprise, he falls back into his chair. Looking at Jonathan, I understand why. My younger son is no longer a sapling, easily felled, and Aloysius, with his ability to stay one step ahead, realises that fact.

'We will mention Katie's name as often as Jonathan wishes to speak about her.' I don't shy from my husband's enraged expression. 'We will *always* give her memory the respect she is due.'

'This is the worst possible time for us to argue.' Douglas finally speaks. 'Once the news breaks about the election, we'll be in the eye of a media storm. They'll be watching us and hoping for a chink that will give them fodder. That's what we are to them... *fodder*.'

He's young to be so bitter. Does he long to go public and tell them he wants to marry the man he loves? Three years of waiting for that right moment yet held tight by Aloysius's determined grip. I met him once; at least, I think it was him. A writer who seems to be in every newspaper and chat show these days. He held my hand for a fraction longer than was necessary when we were introduced at a husting during the by-election Douglas won.

'Douglas is right.' Aloysius nods. 'We must present a united front as a family. Running for the presidency of Ireland is the most important decision I'll ever make.'

'Whatever.' Jonathan shrugs with the usual indifference he displays after causing an argument. 'But I don't understand why you're making it. Power is your opium. As president, you'd be under the thumb of the government—'

'How dare you denigrate the importance of the presidency?' Anger radiates from Aloysius even as he struggles to control it. 'You've no idea what you're talking about. My role—'

'—is mainly ceremonial.' Jonathan begins to read from his phone. '*Many of the powers of the President can only be exercised on the advice of the Government.*'

'If you read on, you're discover that a president has *absolute* discretion in other areas,' Aloysius states. 'But I shouldn't expect you to understand anything as important as the Irish constitution when your reading abilities never stretch beyond the dummy's guide to motorbike repairs. Now, if you'll excuse me, I've an election to plan.'

Aloysius's departure from the table is followed shortly by the slam of the bedroom door. Dinner is ruined. Lasagne needs to be eaten when it's piping hot, not congealing in the conflicting emotions around the table.

'I'm sorry, Mum.' Jonathan sounds repentant but only on my behalf. 'I didn't mean to spoil the evening.'

'Don't come near me.' I hold my hand, palm out, to keep

him away. 'Once again, you've managed to destroy another family meal.'

'A self-destructed meal is nothing in his grand scheme of things.' He jerks his thumb towards the bedroom. 'What he's planning is pure madness. The media will bring up those property deals with Glenpora, not to mention the staff who claimed he was Mr Bully. And you can bet there are other scandals waiting to be savaged. The skeletons in his cupboard must be rattling their bones with delight.'

'He'll survive them all and come out smiling,' Douglas reminds him. 'You must know by now that he's a fighter when the decks are stacked against him.'

'Why haven't you talked him out of it?' demands Jonathan.

'Don't you think I've tried?' Douglas shrugs. 'You know how stubborn he is when he decides on a course of action. He's been planning this for months. The podcasts he does with Gaby Grace are part of his campaign, unofficially, of course, and they've certainly raised his profile. When the election is called, he'll have had an important head start.'

'It's madness.' Jonathan repeats himself. 'I'm out of here. Unlike you two, I'm happy to depart a sinking ship.'

*Be a rat, if that's your decision.* I bite back the words and allow my anger to smoulder. A kindling anger, waiting for a spark to ignite it. My emotions are so suppressed, I've almost forgotten their function.

After Douglas has returned to the hotel to meet with the podcast team, I pour the last of the wine for myself and Jonathan.

'I must admit, I couldn't figure out what this "Russell Rides to the Rescue" trip was about,' he says. 'I knew there had to be a motive behind it. Now, I understand. He's been canvassing the necessary nominations from the councils for him to run for election.' His laughter is hollow enough to make me wince. 'How long have you known?' he asks. 'Did he tell you about this before he retired?'

'Yes.'

'Why didn't you talk him down?'

'Like Douglas said, he'd made up his mind.' My son doesn't need to know that any effort I made to dissuade Aloysius would only have sealed his determination. Now, I must depend once again on my self-control to see me through this ordeal. Fury is a useless emotion and one that has never served me well.

Presidential elections are filled with spite and bite. Reputations can be thrashed, careers ruined, family secrets exposed. How will we survive this forensic scrutiny? How will Douglas? We are a rainbow nation, yet Aloysius has a base of followers that refuses to bend to the will of the people. And journalists are always looking for the loose thread they can pull and weave into a news story.

The wine bottle is empty. Jonathan shakes his head when I suggest opening another.

'Is everything okay with you and Amy?' I ask.

'As okay as they'll ever be,' he replies.

'I presume that means it's over.'

'Almost.' He nods. 'She believes I'm incapable of commitment.'

'She's right... and wrong,' I reply. 'You made a commitment once. Ever since then you've been carrying it like a cross on your back. It's time to lay it down, Jonathan, and learn to love again.'

Should I laugh at my hypocrisy? At my own failure to banish a memory that never grows cold?

I only loved once. He's dead, now. Not that I received notice of his passing.

All I have is a dream that came to me with such clarity I accepted it as a sign that the chain holding us together had finally broken.

In my dream, Cormac was standing on the lawn at Beech Park. A young man still, untouched by the years that must have changed him. Mist was rising from the grass and eddying around his feet. He joined his hands, as if in prayer, then lifted them above his head before bringing them back to rest against his heart. I watched him from the bedroom window. No matter how hard I banged on the glass, it refused to break.

I awoke on that instant. Aloysius was leaning on his elbow, staring down at me. For one mad moment I wondered if he'd witnessed my dream. It was a crazy thought, yet I gave it merit. He's only occasionally hit me or handled me roughly since Isabelle was taken, yet my body feels constantly battered.

Insults leave bruises that discolour my mind. Coercive behaviour is a recognised crime, but how do you pin it down? He serves as my repentance. I'm shriven for as long as I stay with him.

Those two boys, Cormac and Paddy. I remember them clearly, shabby tracksuits and runners thick with grime. My father dressed them each time they visited Beech Park, yet they always returned in threadbare, hand-me-down clothes. They seemed to be friends at first. Later, I would come to understand they were bound by nothing more than a shared, cruel experience.

My father wanted me to understand that life was not a cossetted pathway. This was his way of introducing me to the more brutal side of it. In the beginning, they scared me, those sullen urchins with their flat voices and cropped haircuts. I soon realised they were equally scared of me, and, somehow, over that first summer of weekends, we became friends. I was always more at ease with Cormac. Paddy was tougher and louder, more demanding that I side with him in the arguments that always erupted when he was annoyed.

He stole money from my father and accused Cormac of

being the instigator when the theft was discovered. George believed Cormac's denials. He decided that Paddy would no longer be invited to Beech Park, but the authorities at St Alexis decided that both boys were responsible and stopped their visits.

The boys who replaced them had no time for a girl and I'd even less for them. My father decided to send me to a boarding school, which proved to be an even better exercise in self-survival.

I was twenty-one when he died suddenly. After I recovered from the shock and was able to think clearly again, I discovered the debts he left behind, the bad investments that could never be recovered. I decided to sell Beech Park. Before I could put it on the market, Aloysius had made me an offer on the house. One that was high enough for me to decide on a quick sale.

My father had believed Aloysius had the wiles and the wisdom to be a leader-in-waiting and I, working so closely with him, was swayed by his rapid rise within the party. I was used to living with a powerful man. I've looked for other excuses to explain my decision to marry Aloysius and found none. Had my father added 'ruthlessness' to his list of attributes would I have believed him?

Would it have changed my decision?

Douglas was two years old when Cormac became part of Aloysius's security squad. Who could have anticipated such an encounter? His black hair was still cropped but it had style, his voice was tuneful, and his eyes, dark blue and steadfast, were instantly familiar to me. Not that I pretended to recognise him. Marriage had acquainted me with my husband's jealous moods and sudden acts of violence.

I found time to be alone with Cormac, snatched interludes when Aloysius was looking the other way. He accompanied us on trips abroad to Geneva, Brussels, New York, Sydney, his eyes always on Aloysius, except when he was off duty.

At first, we simply reminisced about our childhoods. But we could feel it coming, a dangerous torrent that must be stopped before it overwhelmed us.

Aloysius was passed over for a ministerial position he craved. He turned his attention back to me. His beatings left no visible marks. No midnight dashes to hospital with crushed ribs or a throbbing head. Threats to leave him were handled easily by reminding me that I'd lose custody of Douglas. He had the power to do so. We both understood he would use it.

He was abroad on governmental business on the night I confided in Cormac. His anger was explosive, but Aloysius was not there, and something was needed to release it. I led him up the stairs and into the guest bedroom. No pretence. We had both yearned for what was to come and had no time to think of the madness that would follow. He came into me with a force that lifted me to a place of splintering stars. I held him with that same ferocity, finding relief in a surge that stole all reason from us. We lay together until our breathing quietened and, when we'd rested, we made love again, slowly this time, his fingers stirring my skin, his mouth seeking my tongue, causing me to moan so loudly he had to press his palm to my lips for fear of awakening Douglas.

He was gone by dawn. Our short, consuming love never stood a chance. Would I have turned my gaze away from him had I known what would follow? One night of passion could never be balanced against the heartache that was waiting. So, yes... yes... I would have blinded myself to his passion had I possessed a crystal ball.

I never saw him again. Some days later, a new garda detective was allocated to Aloysius. He told me that he'd been informed through official channels that Cormac was in league with drug dealers and had been dismissed from the Garda Síochána. Had Aloysius suspected us? He had the ability to create such an impression, but I held my silence and shrugged at the news. Deadpan – it went with the territory of being married to a monster.

When I held my new-born baby in my arms, I was embalmed in her scent. I've never lost it, that sweet, milky scent of pure innocence. I was never in any doubt that she was Cormac's child.

# TWENTY-NINE

## GABRIELLE

A loud knocking on my bedroom door startles me awake. It's six thirty in the morning, too early to be summoned by Aloysius. Roy Doran stands outside. We've barely spoken since we met. The efforts I made in the early stages to be friendly were rebuffed by his stony silence.

He pushes past me into the room without asking permission. His eyes scan over the clothes I tossed across a chair last night, and the table where I left my laptop. In a few strides, he picks it up and asks for my phone.

'Orders from above,' he replies when I demand to know what's going on. 'If you've any issues, contact Mr Russell. My advice is to cooperate, and this can be done without any fuss.'

His movements are quick and efficient as he opens drawers and checks the wardrobe. It's a small room, sparsely furnished, and his search is brief.

His voice is flat, expressionless, his eyes never still. 'Mr Russell wants to meet you in room 33 in thirty minutes,' he says when I hand him my phone. 'You'll get your phone and laptop back then.'

'What's this about, Roy? I've a right—'

'Thirty minutes. Room 33.'

He must be skilled at carrying out such searches. My bedroom doesn't look as if it's been disturbed yet his invisible fingerprints are everywhere.

I stand under the shower and wash off the clingy feel of his presence.

Roy Doran is sitting with Aloysius when I enter the room that's used as an office. My phone and laptop have been left on the desk.

'I apologise for this sudden intrusion into your privacy.' Aloysius signals to me to come forward. 'You can take your phone and laptop back. None of your private content has been touched. We were looking for specific information and Roy is happy to clear your name.'

'Why should my name need clearing?'

'My intention to run in the upcoming presidential election has been released on social media.' He states this coldly, but his reddened cheeks reveal his fury. Killian was right when he stated that the presidency would be Aloysius's ultimate target. I think about him far too often. Bad idea, bad, bad!

'It's essential that we find out who's responsible,' Aloysius continues. 'We're satisfied that you're in the clear, Gaby, as I knew you would be. But procedure needed to be followed. A press conference has been called for later this morning. Colin will fill you in on the details.'

Colin is just finishing his breakfast when I enter the restaurant. He must have undergone a similar experience if his grim expression is any indication.

'I've already been fired and rehired,' he admits. 'I've never seen Aloysius so angry. He'd planned to launch his campaign with a public rally and a massive outdoor concert in the Phoenix Park. Instead, the media are now on their way to this town that time forgot and I've to organise a press conference for this afternoon.'

'Has word spread that quickly?'

'A bushfire is an apt description.' Colin flings his arms in the air for emphasis and sighs. 'He's going to have to declare his intentions without any fanfare. Douglas had to leave for Dublin this morning. Ministerial business takes precedence over his father's problems. Aloysius has ordered Jonathan to stay put until after the press conference to provide the usual family back-up. You can imagine how that went down with Jonathan.' He takes a last gulp of coffee and hurries back to his room to work on a press package.

It's after ten in the morning when Aloysius calls me back to his office. His complexion is back to normal and his mood as buoyant as it usually is.

'That information about the election was not meant to be made public until a specific date,' he says when I'm seated. 'I intended discussing it with you after this trip. However, events have overtaken us. My hope is that you'll work closely with me on the presidential campaign I intend to run.'

'It seems to me that you're running it already. Those podcasts—'

'Have nothing to do with it.' He brushes the air with the back of his hand as he interrupts me. 'We're talking about two totally separate endeavours.'

'I disagree.' I refuse to tolerate this pretence. 'I couldn't understand your motivation for choosing the projects you've undertaken but *Red Tape Unreeled* finally makes sense to me. It's your lobbying platform for garnering the support you'll need from the councils to stand for election. The podcasts we've made are nothing more than an exercise in propaganda. Please don't insult my intelligence by pretending otherwise.'

'The last thing I'd do is insult your intelligence, Gaby.' If my comments have angered him, he's not showing it. Instead, he seems even more relaxed as he leans back in his chair and folds his arms. I'm not fooled by his composure. His fury this morning is still too fresh in my mind.

'If, as you appear to believe, you're my propagandist, why did you agree to work with me and, if I may add, work so successful that we've created an ever-increasing listenership?'

How am I supposed to answer that question? I'm aware of his scrutiny, and there is something deep within his eyes that warns me to be careful. I'm sinking into a marsh. Down... down... so much slush and fetid undergrowth.

'I like a challenge and you provided me with one,' I reply. 'The financial offer was an even better inducement.' Am I as shallow as I sound? It's becoming so hard to understand myself these days.

'I admire your honesty,' Aloysius says. 'That inducement will be substantially increased should you decide to work as my official podcaster for my presidential campaign?'

His team has been assembled: strategy, communications, donations, budget, research, management, security – all areas covered by people he trusts.

'I want you to record the rough and tumble of this election campaign when it begins. We'll have face to face interviews at the end of each day and you'll challenge me on the questions the voters will bring up.' His smile broadens as he invites me to become a cog in his machine.

'It can only work if I've full editorial control.' Remembering Killian's taunt, my tone sharpens.

'That's a given.'

'What if you're not happy with my questions?'

'I'll answer them as honestly as possible. Don't worry, Gaby. There'll be no lack of material to dissect as the campaign progresses. In the political arena, enemies sprout like mushrooms. Not the happy-clappy variety, unfortunately, just the poisonous fungi.'

Apart from the leak, something else has rattled him. The family get-together in the lodge yesterday was a disaster, according to Douglas, when we spoke last night. He was short on detail, but I gathered that Jonathan was responsible for spoiling the mood. Such confrontations, according to Douglas, occur regularly. The only reason Jonathan attends these family meals is for Maria's sake.

So much for my idealised concept of a perfect family.

We gather in the hotel conference room. The press conference will begin at one o'clock. Television and press, alerted by social media, have assembled in Clognua to interview Aloysius. Killian is already seated and speaking on his phone. He waves casually but makes no effort to join me. So be it.

Aloysius, Maria and Colin sit down at a table and face the press. The clicking rhythm of cameras reminds me of a drum solo, the soft tap before the beat goes wild. Anything can happen here.

'Are you aware that Edward Kinsella is seeking a second term as president?' A female journalist asks the first question. 'Why would you go up against a candidate who has full party support behind him?'

'We are a democracy with a free press.' Aloysius's rage this morning could have been imagined. 'The role of the president is open to anyone over the age of thirty-five and, as I qualify in that respect... much as I would love to state otherwise' – he waits for the obligatory laughter which is slow to come and faint when it does – 'I also qualify in terms of experience, commitment and knowledge gained through the decades that I served my country.'

Killian is on his feet. 'What about the findings of the Glenpora report? Do they not preclude you from running for presidential office?'

'Absolutely not. Nor should they.' Aloysius sounds relaxed and assured. 'A journalist with your reputation must be aware that I was fully exonerated by that enquiry.'

'I'm aware that no criminal charges were pursued against you,' Killian continues. 'However, the report made references to improper contacts between you and Glenpora Properties.'

'That's a ludicrous insinuation. That claim was later amended and was deemed to have been caused by human error.'

Aloysius always looks confident in photographs but, up close, I see his bullishness. He is borderline between being a thug and a suave politician who will cut the legs from under anyone who tries to take him down. 'I was awarded full recompense for the anguish caused to my family, and the reputational damage I could have suffered.'

Before Killian can respond, Colin signals to another journalist whose hand is raised.

I sit beside Jonathan, who taps his feet with increasing impatience as the press conference drags on. This is my first opportunity to be close to him. Unlike Douglas, he's hardly acknowledged me since we were introduced.

'Why put yourself through such an arduous campaign when you've just retired?' Another journalist is on her feet.

'Because there's always another greasy power pole for him to climb,' Jonathan mutters into my ear while Aloysius jokes about how he'll consider golf and gardening after he's served his seven-year term. He goes on to stress that he's limbering up for the campaign of his life. He's never felt fitter, more energetic and determined.

Maria's smooth skin is highlighted in the sheen of publicity. Her eyes have narrowed slightly. Their cat-like slant is more accentuated as she stares from me to Jonathan. She moves her shoulders slightly, as if she is shrugging off her husband's robust promises.

*She is going to faint.* Even as I register this thought, she stands and moves back from the table. Aloysius tries to hold her, but she slips eel-like from his grasp and sinks to the ground.

I run with Jonathan towards the stage. She lies, motionless, her eyes closed now, her skin ashen. When I kneel beside her, I'm pushed away by Aloysius, who has a glass of water in his hand.

'It's her blood pressure,' he tells Jonathan. 'Her doctor told her it's too low.'

'An ambulance is on the way.' Colin speaks softly to Aloysius, who nods, his eyes fixed on his wife.

The ambulance arrives quickly. The paramedics disperse the crowd around Maria and speak briefly to Aloysius. I move to one side as they carry her past me on a stretcher.

What if she dies before I have the chance to tell her who I am?

Aloysius climbs into the ambulance and the doors are slammed closed. He has left instructions. Colin will answer any further questions and Jonathan will follow on his Harley to the hospital.

'Can I come with you?' I ask Jonathan. 'I might be able to help in some way. She'll need toiletries if she's kept in overnight.'

He considers my request for a second before nodding and unhooking a second helmet from the side of his motorbike.

A nurse leads us to a waiting area. Maria's condition is stable, and Aloysius is speaking to the doctor who's attending her.

'If anything happens to her...' Jonathan stops, afraid, perhaps, of uttering his fears aloud. His hands, clenched in fists, rest on his knees.

'Low blood pressure is something that can be addressed very quickly,' I assure him. 'She's in the best possible place.'

We should be sitting close to each other in a comforting embrace. My father's actions so long ago have made this impossible. Hate has teeth that never stop gnawing at the love I once felt for him. Instead, all I can do is offer my half-brother platitudes that are stilted and meaningless.

'How's the podcasting going?' he asks.

'It's getting a good response from listeners.'

'That's what I hear. Where's Superman's next destination?'

'Have you listened to the podcasts I've made with your father?' His rudeness doesn't bother me. Isn't that in the nature of a younger brother?

'What do you think?'

'I think you can't be bothered.'

'Got it in one.' His shrug is exaggerated and meant to be annoying. 'Red Tape Unsealed... or whatever it's called, is just one of many tactics he's using to build up his image before the campaign starts.'

'Did you leak that information?'

He laughs. 'If I did, I'm hardly likely to admit it to my father's spin doctor. But, *actually*, no. I didn't. Whoever did it had to be tech-savvy enough to protect their identity. This is way out of my league.'

I've no intention of arguing with him. His posturing irritates me: his tattoos and over-studded leather jacket with his skull head badges, the aggressive buckles on his boots. His image is a stark contrast to Douglas's, whose Italian-designed suits project an image that is stylish yet safe. Suits that remind me of armour, crafted for protection.

'Sorry if I offended you.' Jonathan breaks the chilliness that has settled between us. 'You were a cool presenter on that wild phone-in show you used to host. What was it called?'

'*Gaby's Good Morning Wake-up*.'

'Yeah... I've listened to it online. You didn't take prisoners then.'

'And I do now? Is that what you're implying?'

'My father never does anything without a motive. These podcasts are nothing more than a publicity stunt. Oh, they sound genuine, I'll grant you that, but you and I know differently. You're sharp and opinionated. Working for my father simply doesn't make sense.'

'Why do you dislike him?'

'Dislike...' He pauses, as if the meaning needs to be digested. 'Families are weird, don't you agree?'

'That depends.'

'On what?' he asks.

'Circumstances... like losing a child.'

'Ah, yes.' He draws in his breath, his cheeks puffing as he releases it. 'Isabelle, our family ghost.'

'You believe she's dead?'

'My father believes that's what happened soon after she was taken.'

'Do you agree with him?'

'He's never wrong. You must have discovered that by now?' His laughter grates with bitterness. 'And the dead stay dead, no matter how much we demand that they come back to comfort us.'

He's no longer talking about his lost sister. Not if the sudden stiffening of his features is anything to go by.

'Did you lose someone who was very close to you?' I ask.

When he nods and faces me, I feel as if he's seeing me for the first time.

Before he can reply, Aloysius appears. His purposeful stride adds to the impression that he has responsibilities beyond the hospital that demand his attention. I stand to greet him, but Jonathan remains in a sprawled position, his legs crossed at the ankles.

'According to the cardiac specialist, her heart is sound.' He stares pointedly at his son's boots and steps around them. 'Low blood pressure caused her to faint. She'll be kept under observation overnight. Colin has already sent out a press release that explains the reason for her collapse.'

'What reason?' Jonathan asks.

'Food poisoning. A mild attack that brought about a sudden lowering of her blood pressure. All due to circumstances not of her own making.'

'That's rubbish.' Jonathan argues. 'She was perfectly fine at breakfast.'

'Apparently not. She'd like to see you. Just don't tire her out.' Aloysius turns and speaks directly to me. 'Come back with me, Gaby. You'd no reason to be here in the first place.'

'I thought Maria might need some toiletries—'

'No matter... no matter. I've arranged with one of the nurses to bring her anything she needs.' He's already walking away, without checking to see if I'm following him.

'We're going to make an extra podcast when we're back at the hotel, but we'll change its format,' he says. 'I want you to focus on the foundation. It's what you wanted to do originally. This is your opportunity. Make it your best. I'll speak for Maria and give her the credit she deserves. You can release it under *Graceful Opinions*.'

I want to protest. I decide what is podcast on *Graceful Opinions*. But he's offering me an opportunity to understand the circumstances that persuaded my mother to establish Isabelle's Quest and I'm unable to resist it.

The press group has gathered outside the hospital. They move as one towards us when we emerge. Killian is in their midst. They shout questions about Maria's collapse. Is it a heart attack? A stroke? Stress? Is Maria Russell too fragile for the demands of a potential president's wife?

. . .

The podcast reveals how much of Maria's life has been dedicated to the foundation. She's been involved in dangerous situations, entered dangerous locations, confronted dangerous people. I'd no idea her reach was so widespread.

Aloysius is a smooth performer. For once, the attention is not on himself, but he's doing this for only one reason: if rumours still exist about Maria's frailty, he hopes they'll be dispelled as soon as the podcast goes live. I try and steer the conversation to the early days of my kidnapping and discover that Marie never left her room for months afterwards. Isabelle's Quest saved her sanity.

When I finally reach my hotel bedroom later that evening, I write a text to Maria. Reading it over, I delete it. Within five minutes I'm rewriting it. I was never a ditherer but I'm incapable of deciding what I want to do.

Finally, it's sent.

*Maria, I hope you're feeling better. Today's podcast gave me an opportunity to get to know you better through the work you do with your foundation. I have something to discuss with you. Can we meet privately when you return to the campaign? Gaby*

She replies shortly afterwards.

*What a mysterious request. Of course, I'm happy for us to speak privately. Is everything okay with Aloysius? I'm aware that he can be demanding. Producing a regular podcast and always making it interesting isn't easy but you're doing a splendid job. Why not visit me tonight? I've insisted that the men in my life stay away. They will only argue about politics and my head needs rest. Some female company will be welcome. I hope to see you later. Maria*

Killian rings. I ignore his call and let it go to voice mail – again. I'm still angry over his accusation that I'm obsessive, even though it's true. I don't know where I'm going but if I slow down long enough to think straight, I'll lose my nerve and begin to think objectively, logically. I'll sum up the possibility of being rejected by her; the possibility that she would prefer to suffer the gaping wound my disappearance created in her psyche rather than acknowledge me and admit to her affair with my father.

I stamp on such thoughts and read her reply again as the taxi driver brakes outside Clognua hospital.

# THIRTY

## MARIA

Gaby wants to see me. Why? A private matter, that's what her text said. Her intensity when we're together worries me. I feel as if I'm under a microscope and she's peering into my soul. Is Aloysius working her too hard? Same bullying tactics that landed him in trouble when he was in government? I'm surprised she's so docile. He doesn't scare her, from what I can see, yet she's surprisingly biddable for someone with her shock-jock reputation.

I compliment her on her podcast when she arrives. It could have been a syrupy interview about the foundation and my role in it. Instead, it made compelling listening. At times, I hardly recognised myself or the cases that have been undertaken by the foundation team, yet they are true and have been my salvation.

She's casually dressed in a jacket and jeans, her hair drawn back in a high ponytail, as it was this morning. It's clear that she's upset. She's wearing make-up, which is unusual, but it does not hide the mottled redness around her eyes. Was she crying before coming here?

She was leaning over me when I recovered consciousness. It happened so suddenly. I tried to fight it off... slow breathing...

focus... focus... a cold sweat tracking across my forehead... but there was no way to stop that drift into the dark.

Low blood pressure equates to stress, said the doctor who attended me at the hospital. The right medication would put pep in my step. Aloysius thanked her and shook hands with all the medical staff within reach.

Gaby sits on the edge of the chair beside my bed. Stretching towards her, I take her hand. It's icy cold yet her fingers move with an unexpected firmness and twine around mine.

'I don't know how to begin.' Her lips quiver, their fullness more pronounced.

I shudder suddenly, unable to control a sharp feeling of déjà vu. It goes nowhere. Gaby is a stranger who, for reasons best known to herself, has decided to lionise Aloysius.

'I've been planning what I would say to you if we had a chance to be alone,' she says. 'Now that I'm here, it sounds too ludicrous...'

'It always helps to start at the beginning, Gaby.' I sense the effort she's making to stay calm.

'I don't know how to begin.'

'I know that Aloysius can be demanding at times. Has he upset you?'

'No, things are fine with Aloysius,' she says. 'It's to do with my father. He died some months earlier than my mother. He'd been ill with cancer for months. I arrived home from New York to be with him at the end, but he was drifting in and out of consciousness.'

The loss of her father, followed closely by her mother's death, has obviously affected her. She eases her hand from mine and pulls at a tendril of hair that has escaped the ponytail.

'I don't know if he was aware I was beside him,' she continues. 'Yet I haven't been able to forget the last words he spoke to me. He was delirious... but still... he's tormenting me...' Her voice trails away.

'How upsetting for you.' Why has she come to me for solace? Her emotional turmoil is beginning to impact on me. 'Last words are precious, Gaby, even if they are spoken when someone we love is delirious.'

'I can't make sense of what he said...' Her abrupt pauses are unnerving. 'I can't talk about it... I want to... but I can't.' Tears are running down her face, as they must have done before she arrived. 'You're ill and I'm not helping your recovery by being here.'

'I'm perfectly fine. My blood pressure has improved and if talking about your father can help you, I'm happy to listen.'

'Thank you but I've stayed long enough. Please don't tell the others I came here. It was a stupid thing to do. I'm sorry...'

The speed with which she leaves the room makes it impossible to reply. I can't understand her behaviour. She is normally so self-possessed, yet I remember the first time we met, and how her hand trembled in mine. Tonight, her hand was steady and her clasp fierce.

At the press conference, as Aloysius spoke about humility – it's a word he frequently uses, even as he boasts about all he has achieved and will achieve when he's elected president – the back of my neck tingled. Goosepimples. Gaby and my younger son were sitting together. Jonathan's thoughts were elsewhere, as usual, but she had the same fixed stare that always disturbs me. She was unable to avert her gaze and once again I had that sense of being sized and judged.

Why do I remember that so vividly? And how, when I came too and saw her bending over me, her face seemed to dissolve into... what...? Molecules? I remember thinking about atoms conjoining, bonding, but that impression vanished quickly, and I could see her clearly again. She was scared and concerned, as was Jonathan, who was kneeling beside her.

She was dressed in black: trousers and a tailored jacket, an efficient uniform she's worn throughout the tour. Jonathan was in his usual black leathers. After the row with Aloysius, he'd shaved off his beard but refused to have his hair cut. Instead of the usual untidy mop, he'd compromised by tying it back in a ponytail. She'd styled her hair the same way and I was struck by the similarities between their high foreheads and narrow chins, the fullness of their lips, the wide-set slant of eyes that differed only in hue.

In the instant before I fainted, as I stared from one to the other, their features blended with cameo sharpness into a silhouette that seemed as chiselled as a face on a newly minted coin.

How could I have forgotten until now the sudden, stunning notion that Gaby Grace, with her forceful dark-blue stare and eerie resemblance to Jonathan, could be my daughter? Even as this fantastical thought came to me, my senses fell away, and I collapsed.

That same sensation returns now, a cloud-like floundering through thin air, all sound muffled except the hard, rapid strokes of my heart.

Is it possible the search that has defined the last twenty-nine years of my life could be over? Or have I finally lost my wits?

It's a question only one person can answer.

# THIRTY-ONE

## GABRIELLE

I blew it. Eye to eye, I faced Maria and was unable to utter those few simple words.

*Your search is over*.

Why did I falter? The answer is easy. Pull one brick from a finely balanced edifice and it signals the beginning of a collapse. My father removed the first brick with his last words to me and I've been dislodging them pell-mell ever since.

I can't bear to think about Cassie. I've pushed away her warning voice. *You sent me to my death. You owe me*. Tonight, I could no longer ignore her. She was there between us; an inflexible presence, demanding to be heeded.

I take a taxi from the hospital back to Clognua. The streets are quiet. Aloysius claims to have visited every small town in the country when he was a government minister and, according to him, Clognua once had six pubs. Only two remain.

Heads turn when I enter the first one. This must be the pub favoured by locals. All men, caps pulled low over foreheads, they stare at me briefly before turning back to their conversations and silences.

The second pub is livelier. Music streams from the interior

onto the street. The thud of a bodhrán matches the tempo of my heart; such a crazed, ferocious beat pulling me towards the entrance.

This time, heads don't turn. People are too busy talking or listening to the small band of musicians huddled in a circle. Oblivious to the chatter around them, they're playing for their own enjoyment.

In the hospital, face to face with Maria, I realised the impossibility of doing this alone. I need a shoulder to lean on. An ear to listen. A voice that will make sense of what I've uncovered.

*Killian* was the only name I breathed as I ran from the hospital.

Earlier, he'd messaged me and suggested we meet for a drink in one of the pubs. I spot him among a group of journalists standing around the bar. He's holding forth; others are laughing in response. How passive they look, rival bloodhounds winding down for the night. Tomorrow, they'll pick up the scent again, sniffing and snarling around the Russell family.

They respect Killian. Captain of the bloodhounds. I can't think straight. My mind veers from one scenario to another, all equally catastrophic. Confiding in Killian would put the pressure of secrecy on his shoulders. Such a momentous burden. Once again, I remind myself that it would go against all his instincts as a reporter to keep such a secret.

He turns in my direction and leans around one of the journalists to see me more clearly. He pushes through the crowd separating us and grabs my hand.

'Glad you made it!' he shouts above the noise. His too-wide smile and flushed cheeks proves he's been drinking for a while. 'Come and meet the guys.'

'That's not a good idea.'

'Why not? Surely, you're allowed to fraternise with the enemy.'

'Are you serious?' I demand. 'You, of all people, can appreciate how anything I say here could be twisted into a news feature that could affect Aloysius.'

'Smash his glass house, you mean.' He's no longer smiling. 'When you told me you were going to become a podcaster, I'd no idea you were setting up the Aloysius Russell fan club.'

'I didn't come here to be insulted, Killian.' I need to leave right now.

Otherwise, his scorn will break the last of my resolve and I'll become a helpless sack of tears.

'Why are you here?' His eyes, slightly glazed, have the fixed stare of someone struggling to concentrate. How long has he been soaking up the drink and the atmosphere with his 'guys'?

'I thought we could talk...'

'What about? '

'Nothing important. And not worth interrupting your drinking session.'

'I'm celebrating good news and, yes, I've had a few but we can leave—' His phone rings before he can continue. 'I'm sorry... give me a moment.' His face lights up when he takes out his phone and checks the screen. 'Shauna...' He forces his finger against one ear to drown the sound and waves at me to wait. 'Yes, the news is out here as well. Congratulations are the order of the day.' He listens intently to her and laughs. 'Oh, the usual slagging. They're convinced I'm inheriting a ball and chain. Time will tell. Listen, it's impossible to talk right now. I'll ring you as soon as I return to the hotel.' He nods at the phone and laughs again before ending their conversation.

'I'm not drunk, Gaby,' he says. Shauna's call appears to have steadied him. 'It's obvious you're upset. We can go somewhere quiet and discuss whatever is bothering you.'

'No, we can't.' Coming here was as foolhardy as my decision to visit Maria. 'Go on back to your friends. I'm tired and it's been an upsetting day.'

'How's Maria?' Does he know about my disastrous visit to

her? A glance at his expression reassures me he's making a genuine enquiry.

'Are you asking as a friend or a journalist, Killian?'

'I'm asking as a human being,' he replies. 'She took quite a knock when she fell.'

'She'll be discharged tomorrow so she's fine.'

'Is everything fine between us?' he asks.

'Of course.' It's a stock answer that is as hollow as his question.

My phone rings. By the time I find it in my jacket pocket, it stops. Maria's name comes up under Missed Calls.

A text arrives while I'm staring at her name.

*Gaby... I need to see you. Please come back now.*

'I must go. Something has come up, workwise.' The lie slips easily from me. I hurry from the pub before he can ask questions and head to the taxi rank.

The same taxi driver opens the back door for me. 'You're having a busy night,' he says. 'Has that poor woman taken another turn?'

'No, she's *absolutely* fine,' I reply. 'I left something behind when I was with her earlier and I need it now.'

He shrugs and stays silent for the rest of the journey.

Visiting hours are just ending but I arrive at Maria's room without being stopped and asked to leave.

In the hour that passed since I saw her, she has developed a fever. At least, that's what I attribute to her pallor, the sheen of perspiration on her face, and the tremble in her hands as they rest on the bed cover. Pillows are propped behind her, yet she struggles to sit upright. Has she received bad news about her health? News that has bent her spine like a bow?

'I came as soon as I saw your text.' I pull a chair closer to her bed. 'Is something wrong?'

'I can't tell.' Her voice is husky, shaky. She coughs to clear her throat but still sounds raspy when she speaks again. 'You came here to confide in me then left without revealing what's causing you such distress.'

'I shouldn't have bothered you—' I begin but she quickly interrupts me.

'You came to me for a reason. You left without discussing it. Please, be honest with me. What did you want to tell me about your father?'

'I'm afraid...' Every step I've taken since his deathbed confession has led me to this moment. Every lie I told to reach it clogs my throat.

'What did he say to you before he died?' Her fingers join as she waits for my answer. Is she praying, or tensing her body to reject what I have to say?

'"I stole you."' Three words take flight, soaring and falling like a bird that has been speared yet is still alive.

The swallowing noise she makes ends in an audible gasp. 'You told me he was delirious...' She finally manages to speak. 'How could you give credence to something so... so... shocking?'

'I didn't.' I'm unsure if my voice will reach her. 'Not at first, that is. I convinced myself he only meant to tell me he loved me. That was believable for a while but then... well... I started asking questions, and found out something...' I stop, too frightened to continue.

'What did you find out?' She is sitting straighter now, her head erect.

'I don't know... I don't know... I'm sorry... sorry... I don't know how to say it.' I'm parroting nonsense when I should be concise. A clear statement. *I am your daughter. My father stole me from your arms.*

'Do you believe you're Isabelle?' she asks.

I can only nod.

She leans back on her pillows. 'Have you any idea how

many young women have contacted me over the years with a similar story to yours?' She speaks so low I must lean closer to her bed. 'Some are liars, cruel and manipulative. Others are delusional, lost souls with no sense of their own identity. I suffer from post-traumatic stress and such encounters always affect me.'

'I'm sorry...'

'Please, Gaby, just let me talk.' She waves aside whatever attempted apology I was about to make. 'You don't belong to either category, so I can't understand how you came to this conclusion. Those words your father spoke could be interpreted in many ways. How did they bring you here?'

'His surname was not Grace.'

'What was it?'

'Does the name "Cormac Gallagher" mean anything to you?'

Maria closes her eyes. Is the sight of me too painful to bear? Cassie's presence is so close I could reach out and touch her. I banish her spectre, but she hovers near, as she has done since she left me bereft.

The silence lengthens between us. I've pulled the last brick and upended the two separate worlds that held us secure until now.

'I believe he loved you very much,' I say.

'I knew he was dead.' She sounds as if she's emerging from a trance when she opens her eyes. Unshed tears tremble on her lower eyelids, the irises so enlarged they engulf me in their dewy green depths. I want to see love shining, hope realised, a longing fulfilled, but there is nothing to guide me forward.

'He came to say goodbye to me in a dream,' she says. 'And you are right, Gaby. He was only a boy when he fell in love with me. He was briefly in my life and was the best part of it. You are his daughter. I see the resemblance. But I don't understand how you came to believe you are mine. Cormac would never have hurt me so cruelly. Never... *never*... not in a million years.' She says this gently but decisively. 'You've lost both of your parents in such a short space of time, and you've allowed your imagination—'

'No... stop. Please stop. The woman who mothered me – Cassie – she wasn't my birth mother. I had her DNA tested, also my father's. We could test—'

'No... *no*...' She recoils slightly, as if appalled by what I was going to suggest.

It was not supposed to be like this... but what had I expected? To be enveloped in her joy? Instead, she is rejecting me. Brick by brick, another wall is being built. I see it rising in her determined stare, the rigid set of her lips, the composure she has gathered around her.

'Cassie is dead because of him.' This admission is torn from me. 'He stole me from you and forced her to live with that secret. I kept pushing... pushing her to tell me what she knew... and that's what killed her... how *I* killed her...'

I've said it aloud, at last.

'It's my fault she's dead. She begged me to stop all contact with you and your family because of the harm it would do to mine. I was too selfish to listen. She died alone, drowned in the ocean she loved, and, even then, I went ahead and agreed to work with Aloysius because it gave me a chance to be with you.'

My voice is a torrent finally released.

'I found this photo among my father's possessions and that's how my search began.' I show her the newspaper clipping.

Maria holds it tentatively in front of her, afraid, perhaps, that it will disintegrate under the force of her gaze. She trembles so violently as she looks at it that I'm afraid she'll convulse or pass out again.

Instead, she puts the photograph to one side and holds out her arms to me. She drowns me in her tears.

Time is immaterial. How can it be measured in the passing

of minutes when we must compress twenty-nine lost years into our embrace? Maria is racked with sobs and her distress helps to calm me down. The wrench when I ease myself from her arms must be akin to the slash of a blade through the umbilical cord.

I fill a glass with water. She shudders at its coldness when I bring the glass to her lips.

'Will I call a nurse? Your blood pressure—'

'Don't.' Her hold is surprisingly strong when she grabs my wrist. 'I don't want them to contact Aloysius. He asked to be told if there is any change in the readings.'

'Does he believe he fathered me?'

'I could never admit the truth to him.' She nods and arches her shoulders. 'His grief was as deep as mine. He blamed himself for your disappearance. You would have been safe if he'd been home on time and working in his office. He never went to bed before two in the morning back then. A vote was being passed in the Dáil that night and he had to stay late. You'd been taken by the time he came home. I've been tormented by those same feelings. How could I have slept through such a terrible crime?'

Our reflections are visible as the night presses against the window. Her mask is off, and I see the toll those lost years have taken.

'"I stole you."' She repeats my father's words. 'How could Cormac do that to me? I loved him. I believed he loved me. One night together, that was all we had. I never saw him again. How did he know I gave birth to his child?'

She doesn't sound angry, just bewildered.

'I don't know.' I've asked myself this question so many times. Now, she too will be plagued by this mystery. 'Did you ever suspect he could be responsible for my disappearance?'

'No. How could I? He was out of the country. Disgraced, according to Aloysius, though I never believed the accusations that were made against him. Aloysius said he'd been involved in passing information to a drugs gang. I kept my head down and said nothing. I'm not a brave person, Gaby...' Her voice slips on my name. It must sound so strange to her now.

Will she ever be able to call me *Isabelle*?

'You've troubled me since we first met,' she continues. 'I couldn't understand why until this morning when I saw you and Jonathan together. Douglas takes after his father, but Jonathan resembles me. It's hard to notice the likeness with the beard he usually grows and all that hair around his face. At the press conference, when I saw you sitting with him, I was struck by the likeness between the two of you.' She leans forward and cups my face. 'Can a thought have so much power that it steals away your senses? That's what happened when I found myself thinking that you and Jonathan could be brother and sister. The thought had been wiped from my mind when I recovered. Self-preservation, probably. I was afraid my heart would be unable to take the strain. I was wrong. It's overflowing now and has never felt stronger.'

'I hate my father for what he did to you and to me.'

'I can't hate him,' she says. 'It's too big a burden to take on. Maybe later... when I can think clearly again.' Her voice sinks to a whisper. 'No one must know about you. Do you understand, Gaby? This must be our secret. Can you imagine the reaction if the truth came out? We'd be tested for DNA, Aloysius included. I can't even begin to think of the consequences that would flow from such a revelation.'

I understand her fear, her dread at his reaction should he find out she once loved so recklessly. I've handed her a chalice as poisoned as the mind of the man who took me from her.

'I owe Aloysius,' she says. 'It's a debt I've been paying back since you were taken. It doesn't end now.' Her hands flutter to her cheeks and away again. Her terror is stark behind the gentle words she uses to disown me.

She has barely scratched the veneer that lies over our secret.

The nightmare that would follow the revelation that Isabelle Russell had been found and reunited with her parents – what a field day for the journalists. But this would only be the start of the investigations. The twins would be interviewed. I imagine journalists swarming over Trabawn, my father's life story, and Cassie's death, sensationalised. Aloysius's presidential ambitions turned to ash. And what of Maria, her lie publicly exposed on front page headlines? A cheating, adulterous liar, who had the audacity to believe she could be a presidential wife.

I fold the newspaper clipping into my wallet as the door opens. Maria's shock, the rigid jerk of her body as she stares over my shoulder, tells me it's Aloysius. My bag slides from my hand to the floor as his wide girth fills the entrance.

Maria is the first to move. Her lips slide into a welcoming smile. From where does she draw such composure? Is it only achieved through the honing of deceit?

'You're full of surprises, Aloysius,' she says. 'I thought you were spending the night strategising.'

'I'm all strategised out and everything is under control for tomorrow. I was anxious to see how you're doing.'

'Good enough to be discharged in the morning.'

'I was under the impression you needed to rest.' His disapproval is clear when he stares at me. 'The last thing you needed was a visitor.'

'Gaby's here at my request. After listening to the podcast, I rang to thank her in person. She was kind enough to agree to visit me.'

'Would a similar call to me not have been in order?' He smiles, as if his question is of no importance.

'I intended to do so as soon as Gaby left.' Is her stomach clenching, as mine is, when he bends to kiss her cheek? He must notice our tear-flushed faces and how closely we are sitting together. Can he sense the fervour that has consumed us? It must hang in the air, a miasma of emotions that threatens to choke me if I don't leave this room, where my mother has no option but to reject me.

'I'm leaving now.' My lips feel stiff, incapable of smiling back. 'I hope you have a good night's sleep, Maria, and are discharged in the morning.'

'Thank you for visiting me, Gaby. I enjoyed our conversation. I'm sure we'll have an opportunity to return to it again soon.'

Speaking in code, is that how we are to continue?

I've finally stepped over the edge of the precipice. I still have no idea what will happen when I stop falling.

# THIRTY-TWO

## MARIA

I'd imagined it so often. That heart-stopping moment when I'd hold Belle in my arms. At first, when she was taken, all I could envisage was being reunited with a baby. As time made this impossible, she became a willowy child, still unformed, and without too much history to unwind. That was how she stayed, even when technology made it possible for me to view face-aging apps that defined her passing years.

Belle is no willowy child. No lost soul – though she is deep in grief and confusion, not to mention remorse over the death of the mother who reared her. Cassandra, prophetess, who warned her to leave stones unturned and died because my daughter was unable to do so.

I didn't doubt her claim, even as I tried to deny it in the beginning. I needed time to control the fervour within me, yet the normality of our coming together was astonishing. Yes, we cried. We clung together. We held each other's faces between our hands and felt the strangeness of contours that should have been familiar to us.

Then, I rejected her.

What else can I call it, this betrayal of blood and kinship?

She understands, but does that make it right? A thousand times, no; and yet we both agreed that the truth, for now, is too dangerous to reveal.

Aloysius is suspicious. He's always had the ability to sense the atmosphere in a room, and the walls of this small room – where an appalling crime was exposed – must have been expanding from the pressure of our emotions.

'Why the tears?' he asks, after she leaves. 'What's going on between the two of you?'

'She's recently lost both parents and became quite upset when I began to talk about Belle,' I reply.

'That's the last thing you need to do.' He sits on the edge of my bed, close enough for me to notice the deepening lines on his face: furrows of displeasure that I can read like a book. 'I worked hard on that podcast to present you as the strong woman you are,' he says. 'Hopefully, that will mitigate the media speculation that you don't have the stamina for this campaign.'

I'm disconnected from his warnings. In my mind I keep replaying the extraordinary miracle that just took place... and how it has the capacity to destroy me.

'It's obvious that you're more concerned over your campaign than about my health,' I say.

'On the contrary, I've very concerned about you. You look shattered.' He winds strands of my hair around his index finger and gives them a gentle pull. Teasing me in a loving way, that's what he'll call it, if I protest. 'I've organised a hair stylist and a beautician to tend to you in the morning before you leave here.'

'I don't need—'

'No arguing, Maria.' He tugs my hair again, not so gently this time, before untangling his finger. 'Perception is everything, especially as the press is now aware that I'm in campaign mode. It's essential that doners are not discouraged from funding us.'

He glances down at his feet and bends to pick something up

from the floor. It's the wallet Gaby opened to show me the newspaper photograph. It must have fallen from her shoulder bag.

'She forgot this,' he says. 'I'll take it back to her.'

I resist the temptation to grab the wallet from him. What if he opens it… sees the clipping… begins to question her as to its relevance? But he has no reason to check it. The podcasts she's made have added a different slant to his reputation and he trusts her.

How did she manage to stay under cover, after what she discovered? Does she possess the same self-containment I acquired so painfully? Hers seems effortless but what do I know about my daughter? Practically nothing… except that a man we once loved in our different ways betrayed us both in the cruellest way possible.

# THIRTY-THREE

## GABRIELLE

I don't do pretty-crying. My skin is blotchy, and my lips parched from tears. I look untethered, rootless. In the hospital bathroom I wash my hands and stare at my reflection. How did I get from there to here? The steps along the way have receded, as if unseen hands have pulled away the ladder I climbed. *Nowhere woman.* Keeping secrets from half-sisters, half-brothers. Belonging to neither Beech Park nor Trabawn.

I need to repair the damage with make-up. I reach for my shoulder bag and discover that my wallet is missing. It must have slipped out when I dropped my bag to the floor.

The hospital is quiet now. I'm the only person in the elevator as it rises towards St Brendan's ward.

Aloysius is waiting to descend when I step from it.

'I came after you to return this.' He hands my wallet to me. 'I didn't want you worrying when you discovered it was missing.'

'Thank you.' I take it from him and slide it into my bag.

'I want to say goodnight to Maria,' he says. 'I'll see you back at the hotel. Meet me in the bar in an hour.'

His request unnerves me. Not that there is anything

unusual about it: we often brainstorm at night about the podcast for the following day. But everything is different now.

I still feel Maria's arms around me, those few precious moments when we clung together and acknowledged the past. Has her embrace left a patina on me, an aura that will betray our secret when I sit down with him?

Outside the hospital, Roy Doran is waiting for him. He shadows Aloysius, as my father once did. Apart from this morning, he hardly ever speaks and when he does, his gravelly voice has an unpleasant timbre. I wasn't surprised to hear he served in the army. He ignores me, as he usually does, but I'm aware that he's watching me as I phone for a taxi.

An ambulance, headlights blazing, is parked beside the accident and emergency department. An elderly man in a dressing gown huddles behind a pillar with a *No Smoking* sign attached and lights a cigarette, a glowworm that betrays his sanctuary.

Later, when I enter the residents' bar, Aloysius is waiting for me. Roy is seated beside him, their expressions intent as they lean towards each other. It's impossible to hear what they are saying and Aloysius, noticing me, raises his voice.

'Ah, Gaby, Roy and I were just putting the final touches to tomorrow's schedule.'

That's when we reach Trabawn where we plan to visit EOM Analgesics. Ted O'Mahoney has flown from New York for the occasion. A welcome reception has been organised for Aloysius, and for Douglas, who will fly into Kerry Airport in the morning.

When the reception is over, we'll travel further westward to a small village that floods regularly and needs a long-promised ecological drainage system. Aloysius has made sure that all will be in order before we leave. Job done.

He raises a finger towards the barman. 'You'll have a nightcap with us?' he says to me.

This is not a request, nor is it meant to sound like one.

'Thank you,' I reply. 'A glass of sparkling water, please.'

'Nonsense. Something stronger, I insist.' He settles back into the armchair and nods towards the one opposite him.

'I'll leave you to it, boss,' says Roy. 'Tomorrow's a busy day and I need my beauty sleep.'

'See you bright and early in the morning.' Aloysius nods goodnight to him and turns his attention back to me.

'What's it to be then, Gaby?'

I settle for a glass of Pinot. Aloysius orders whiskey for himself and waits until the drinks are served before speaking again.

'Cheers.' He clinks his glass against mine and takes a long sip. 'I only have one question to ask you,' he says. 'I expect you to answer it truthfully.' His gaze is compelling, not even a hint of a smile now. 'What were you and Maria discussing when I came into her room?'

He must have asked her the same question. I will answer it honestly and hope she did the same.

'We were talking about Belle.'

'In what respect?' he asks.

'Her disappearance was the catalyst for setting up Isabelle's Quest.' My voice doesn't falter. 'She was on both our minds after the podcast.'

He drains his glass and signals to the barman for another whiskey. 'Twenty-nine years is a long time to mourn the loss of a child,' he says. 'To learn to live again, it's necessary to find closure. I found it through my work in government and encouraged Maria to establish the foundation.'

'In the podcast you claimed it was her idea.'

He frowns, his disapproval so palpable I instinctively push back further into the chair. 'A narrative must always be attuned to the occasion,' he says. 'Through no fault of her own, Maria displayed weakness today. It was necessary to dispel that impression.'

'So, you were lying on the podcast?'

'I was supporting my wife. This campaign, when it begins officially, will be as important to her as it is to me. To return to my question, you were both in quite an emotional state. Why should a tragedy that occurred so long ago affect you so much?'

'I wasn't aware that tragedies have a time limit,' I reply. 'Our podcast triggered so many memories in Maria that I was moved to tears when she spoke about your daughter. I cry all too easily since the death of my parents.'

The web of lies becomes stickier each time I add another one.

'Leave Maria be,' he says. 'She can't afford any more mishaps. You may believe you're doing her a favour by being so empathetic but it's quite the opposite. She's at her strongest when she's looking forward, not back.'

'Don't you ever look back?'

'One doesn't need a handkerchief to express grief,' he says. 'Belle will be with me until the day I go to my grave. She gives me strength to face any odds that come my way and encourages me to be the best at what I do. I turn to her when I'm down. Without fail, she brings me comfort.'

What am I supposed to say in response? After a month of probing and prodding to find out what makes him tick, I'm moved by his belief in a lost child whose soul lived on as his lodestar. It's surreal yet real, this power I have to end the mystery, but Maria has bound me with chains of silence.

I've finished my wine and he, it seems, has finished confiding in me.

'You're tired,' he says. 'And to be honest, you look as though you're about to collapse. We've an early start in the morning so, like Roy, you need your beauty sleep. Thankfully, you'll benefit from it but Roy' – his twinkling smile is the one he usually reserves for voters – 'I guess in your line of work you could say he has a face made for radio.'

The hotel is hushed as I walk along the corridor to my room. My head is pounding again. I need to confide in someone... not someone... just Killian... But, after tonight, how is that even possible. The heft of such a secret. How could he keep it from Shauna? And what about her reaction? Would she find it impossible to work so closely with Douglas and keep something so overpowering from him?

My phone bleeps as I'm struggling to sleep. A late-night text message from my former producer.

> *Hi Gaby... long time no hear. Love* Graceful Opinions. *Not too sure about* Red Tape Unreeled *but I guess you know what you're doing. I've arrived at Trabawn with Ted. Tell all when I see you tomorrow. Miss you... as do your listeners. We should talk. X Emily*

# THIRTY-FOUR

## GABRIELLE

The ocean is a silver glint in the distance as we approach Trabawn. The glint widens into the reach of the Atlantic and the tossing spume hazes the windows of the minivan. Once through the town, where tourists crowd the narrow streets and traffic slows our progress, we reach EOM Analgesics.

A red carpet has been laid in welcome. Ted O'Mahoney and his management team are waiting to greet us. No signs of stress from Maria as she steps down from the minivan to be greeted by him.

Last night she cried in my arms. Now, she is serene in an elegant two-piece suit, a box jacket with trim and a tailored knee-length skirt.

We talk with our eyes. *I love you.* We say it over and over. I'll never grow tired of repeating those words, yet, already, I feel the distance widening between us. A physical distance that will make it impossible for us to continue living our shared lie.

Douglas has already arrived in Trabawn. Yesterday, he had to be present in the Dáil for a government vote and this morning he flew directly into Kerry Airport where he picked up a rental car. Jonathan arrived on his motorbike. The shock of Maria's collapse has subdued him. He's agreed to remain with us until the last podcast has been recorded.

I'll meet my family again, my sisters and nephews, their husbands. They'll mingle with the Russell's, and all of them, apart from Maria, will be unaware that there is a cuckoo in their midst.

Inside a glass-domed reception area we gather alongside EOM Analgesics staff. They are mainly young, both multinational and local, dressed either in white coats or business casual coordinates. The atmosphere is relaxed yet has a sense of purpose that I remember from my years with NY Eyz.

I recognise neighbours from Trabawn who have been invited to the reception. Wine is poured and waiters glide past with trays of hors d'oeuvres. I notice Emily in the crowd, but my attention is on Jonathan, who has just arrived. He must have changed his leathers after his journey, probably at Maria's insistence, and he's wearing a suit and shirt for the occasion. Out of his leathers, he looks surprisingly urbane. It's a coating they all have, this casual elegance Aloysius acquired over the years, but which came naturally to the others.

I can't see the resemblance that triggered Maria's collapse yesterday. I look like my father, that young man in the photograph I found in his desk. Admittedly, Maria and her son, my sullen half-brother, have oval-shaped faces and prominent cheekbones but mine are edgier, a rougher cast that I tame with skilful contouring. Such similarities are superficial, but Maria knew the difference and it brought the knees from under her.

Killian's parents arrive, along with his brother, Jamie, and his partner, Alicja. Noreen Ferguson, majestically large in a geometrically patterned dress, is here with her sons.

'It's classier than ever you're looking, Gaby.' Her glance, rapier-sharp, narrows as she nods towards Douglas. 'The pair of you cut a fine dash, I must say. Is it true he's going to put a ring on your finger?'

'I can assure you, a ring on my finger is the last thing on both our minds.'

'From what I hear, it's not the last thing on Killian's mind,' she says. 'Looks like I'll finally have a chance to wear my fascinator.'

Jessica appears in a skirt and slim-fitting jacket that reveal the weight she's lost since Josh was born. Susanne is minding the boys until they can organise a full-time childminder. She arrives soon afterwards with a twin buggy and two sleeping babies. I hug her and marvel at how my nephews have grown.

Aloysius beckons me forward for a group shot and positions me beside Douglas. My lips form a smile. I *am* my mother's daughter and will join in the masquerade. I notice Killian among the reporters. Pale and bleary-eyed, he must be in the throes of a hangover. His eyes settle on Douglas, who has placed his arm casually around my shoulder. A television cameraman moves a camera closer to us.

The leaking of information on Aloysius's presidential aspirations means that everything he does from now on until the election is called will be scrutinised. Who could have leaked such carefully guarded information? It remains a mystery, according to Colin, whose grim expression hasn't relaxed since yesterday.

Emily appears and holds out her arms. 'I was going to surprise you but decided to text in advance in case you cracked your jaw off the floor when you saw me,' she says.

I nod in agreement. 'That was highly probable. What are you doing here?'

'I travelled with Ted.'

'That much is obvious.' I digest this information and the fact that a diamond is glittering on her ring finger. 'Are you and he... like... an *item*?'

'I can think of a more flattering term. How about *fiancée*?' She holds up her hand to show me her engagement ring.

'I don't believe it.' The solitaire dazzles. 'When did that happen?'

'About a fortnight ago. I warned Zac not to let you know. I wanted it to be my surprise.'

'Well, you've certainly succeeded. Congratulations.'

I've never seen her so happy. How have his three teenage daughters reacted to a new woman in their father's life? This is not the time for such a discussion and Emily is already updating me on NY Eyz.

'The ratings for the early morning slot are falling,' she says. 'Libby doesn't suit the grouchers who listened to you. Too tame is the feedback we're getting. Unlike you, she's not a good listener and misses the vital signs that can trigger an important discussion.'

'I thought they hated me.'

She laughs and shrugs. 'They recognised themselves in what you said to Lucas. *Your show* is akin to a complaints department. That's what made it zing, whether you were batting their complaints back at them or encouraging them to take action. We're moving Libby to a late-night slot that's become vacant and *Gaby's Good Morning Wake-up* will be restored, if you're willing to take it on—?'

'I don't know...' I stop as Ted calls for attention and silences the crowd. He introduces Douglas, who joins him on a make-shift stage that has been erected in the centre of the glass-domed reception area.

Douglas's speech is short and focused on the prosperity that EOM Analgesics is bringing to Trabawn thanks to Ted but, also, he says, thanks to his father's efforts before his retirement from the Department for Provincial Growth. He offers the stage to Aloysius, who embraces the crowd with his arms and makes them laugh when he refers to the maw of social media and how it leaks like a sieve. He's joking ruefully with the crowd, asking them to share his shock when he discovered that the 'still-not decided' question as to whether he would consider running for the presidency had been released without his knowledge.

He's turning his fury into an anecdote and inviting them to journey with him on the campaign. It's working. Hoots and hollers rise from the listeners as he outlines the reason why he's the perfect candidate.

Maria's smile is as fixed as plaster. Does anyone else notice? Probably not. Did they notice Douglas's discomfort when he laid his arm on my shoulder? I felt the weight of it, his clenched determination to submit to his father. Did they notice Jonathan's loathing glance at Aloysius when he insisted on the two of them being photographed together, or just see a father and son enjoying a moment? Do they notice Maria's eyes moving over the crowd to rest on me? Can they see love flowing across the void that separates us?

Eddie is looking after the boys when Jessica and Susanne weave through the crowd to my side. 'How much time have you got before you leave?' Jessica asks.

'We've to make Port Millington by two o'clock and we're already behind schedule. We'll have to leave as soon as the reception is over?''

'Then why doesn't his lordship shut up?' Susanne frowns as Aloysius raises his voice to make a point about the importance of locating businesses in small, regional communities like Trabawn. 'Doesn't he understand the concept that less is more?'

'We were hoping you could slip away and have a chat in my office,' says Jessica.

I check my watch. He'll be speaking for another ten minutes, and our departure will take about half an hour.

We ride the elevator to Jessica's office. Once inside, Susanne hugs me so tightly I can hardly breathe. 'We've missed you,' she says. 'And we're *really* proud of you. Those podcasts are so interesting, though I must admit I can't stand him.'

'Why not?'

She shrugs. 'I guess it's Cassie's influence. She always said he was a waste of space. What's going on with you and his son?'

'Nothing at all. He's just a friend.'

'That's not what his father thinks.' Jessica perches on the edge of her desk. 'I saw the guest list he sent to Ted when we were planning this reception. He has you down as his son's partner.'

'Well, he's wrong. Very wrong.'

'I believe you, even if thousands wouldn't.' Susanne grins. 'Seriously, I'd always tagged you to Killian but that ship never sailed. Now that he's engaged, I guess it's marooned in dry dock.'

'Stop with the metaphors.' Jessica groans and speaks directly to me: 'She's joined this writers' group and it's impossible to have a conversation with her that's metaphor-free.'

But I'm not really listening. 'Did you say Killian is engaged?'

'According to Noreen Ferguson,' Jessica replies.

That was what Noreen meant, when she mentioned her hat. I was so preoccupied by Maria's nearness that her words hadn't penetrated. No wonder he was celebrating in Clognua. A ball and chain, and a ring for commitment.

I'll return to New York. My time here is done. I love too much. Killian and Shauna will marry. Maria will continue to carry her secret but will no longer grieve for her lost baby.

'I must congratulate Killian.' Somehow, I manage to speak clearly.

My phone rings. It's Colin. Aloysius has finished his speech and is demanding more photographs before we leave for Port Millington.

The twins are already on their feet. 'No rest for the wicked, it seems,' says Susanne. 'How do you cope with all this rushing around? You look a bit tired. Are you getting enough sleep?'

'Don't worry about me. I'm on top of everything. Emily has just offered me my old job back. I'm taking her up on it.'

'Oh, no!' They speak in unison, their dismay evident.

'I thought you'd settled here for good,' says Jessica.

'I'll be back and forth. And I promise not to neglect my auntie duties.' I link arms with them as we walk towards the elevator. I love them unconditionally.

When it comes to choices, there is only one for me to make.

The noise is overwhelming as I make my way over to Killian.

'I'm sorry about last night.' He holds up his hands apologetically. 'I was celebrating.'

'I heard. Congratulations.'

'Is the word out on the street already?' He sounds surprised. 'Typical Trabawn. I wanted to share the news with you in the pub, but that didn't work out too well, did it?' He jerks his thumb towards the press group. 'You should have stayed and had a drink with us.'

'I'd other things on my mind.'

'That much was obvious.'

'I hope you'll be very happy, Killian.' My phone is ringing. Colin again and sounding even more harried. The photographer is waiting and Aloysius wants me in the group.

Killian frowns and stares hard at me. 'Happiness can never be guaranteed,' he says. 'I've wanted this for a long time, and I intend to give it my best shot.'

'I know you will. Have you been talking to Emily?'

'Apart from admiring her rock, no.' He shakes his head. 'Why?'

'I'm returning to NY Eyz.'

He takes a step back. 'I thought you planned on building your career here.'

'Circumstances change. So do minds, as I've discovered.'

'And is yours definitely made up?' He doesn't even try to smile.

'Yes. There's absolutely nothing to keep me here.'

'I see.' He nods slowly. 'I thought maybe there was... but that was obviously my mistake. When are you leaving?

'In a few days.'

'Will I see you before you go.'

'I doubt I'll have the time—'

'And there's *absolutely* no reason why you should. Good luck, Gaby.'

'You, too, Killian.'

And that's it. Another cutting. Heartbreak is not a single fracture. Its fissures are many and I'm amazed that my heart is still beating at a regular tempo.

'About time.' Aloysius speaks softly when I join them. His gaze is intimidating, as is the sudden hardening of his mouth. 'Stand in there beside Douglas and let's get this show back on the road.'

I walk past him without replying and stand between Maria and my half-brother. This is where I always belonged, but what should have been my natural stance is now a stilted imitation.

'Are you ready, folks?' a photographer shouts. They pose and smile, the perfectly manicured Russell family. How easily they project the confidence and harmony that armour-plates them against the gaze of the public. I want to own that same self-assurance, but I feel gauche in their presence, rough-edged and a stranger to their world.

Once again, that swell of rage rises within me when I think of my father's actions and their far-reaching consequences.

'I'll be returning to New York next week.' I tell them when the photographer has walked away. I speak to all of them, but my words are for her ears only. 'This podcast in Port Millington is the final one I'll make.'

# PART 4

# THIRTY-FIVE

## MARIA

My daughter's voice guides me through the morning. NY Eyz is so clear that Gaby could be broadcasting from the next room. It's 5 a.m. her time, 10 a.m. mine. I focus on my work as I listen, but not to the words or the arguments that sometimes flare online. It's her tone I hear, the rolling vowels that still bind her to Kerry but are now overlaid with the sharper inflections of New York. I use my phone radio, earbuds in place, in case Aloysius enters.

A report has come through from one of my agents in Pakistan. A young girl with Irish citizenship was taken there by her father after a contentious divorce. Prime custody for the child had been awarded to his ex-wife and Isabelle's Quest is funding her legal costs as she fights for the return of her daughter. Such cases once invigorated me but, lately, I long to hand the responsibility over to someone else. I intend to discuss this at the next board meeting.

I take a coffee break at 11.30 a.m. and engage fully with Gaby's early morning conversations. She reminds me of a conductor, her voice rather than a baton controlling the flow of the phone-in conversations. I hear music in the sounds her callers create and long to be one of those voices, free to air my views, proclaim my truth, and savage what I hate. Sometimes she's gentle, but she can be rough, a street fighter at heart, as her father was, dragging himself upwards from beginnings that offered him nothing but disdain and hardship. I hear echoes of him in her way of saying things, and in the husky reverberations of her laughter.

Unable to see a future with her birth family, she fled from me. I've heard nothing from her since she returned to New York. Does she know I tune into her at every opportunity? That I can't stop thinking about her and reliving that hour we spent together? Sixty minutes to make up for twenty-nine years. I ache all over. It's as though I'm infused once again with the pain I experienced when Cormac stole her from me. Explaining my symptoms to a doctor would be impossible, nor would I want to do so. It binds me to her, a physical bonding that continents can't break.

Her early morning show is ending. I can't call her Belle, nor Isabelle. She is a creation of her own making. My tongue twists when I try to place her back in the cradle that held her for three weeks. She always ends with a song. I smile when I hear what she has chosen this morning. 'Maria' from *West Side Story*. She's hoping I can hear her and is sending love on powerful wings.

I remove my earbuds and stare at my laptop screen when Aloysius enters. He's been rehearsing with his team in his office for an important interview on television tonight.

The presidential campaign began officially at the start of November. Edward Kinsella, who's seeking a second term in office, is his main rival. They'll also compete against Caroline Slone and Jack Ellis. Caroline runs a charity for the homeless and Jack has made his fortune from wind energy. The election will be held at the end of January, with a ten-day break for Christmas.

So much time on the road, standing by his side and smiling until my lips are aching. Happy days.

He coughs to attract my attention. 'Can you leave what you're doing and join us?' This is a command, not a question. 'I want your opinion on my performance.'

Politics, again. I'm a politician's daughter, a politician's wife, and a politician's mother. Where am I in this web of intrigue? I was held together by grief, guilt and hope. Now that I'm no longer carrying that weight, I'm free-falling. I long to run away to New York and get to know my daughter. It seems so simple. *Just go... do it... stop living an uncontrollable lie... Can't... can't...*

The campaign team is assembled in the living room. Video cameras follow Aloysius's every movement. A sound engineer controls the audio feed. Tonight, he's appearing on *Hunter's Hour,* a television programme that consists of questions from the audience. Declan White, his chief strategist, has assumed the role of the television presenter, Gemma Hunter.

The fake question and answer session gets underway. Aloysius is in complete control, no matter what questions are batted at him. He looks distinguished, trustworthy, powerful. I've felt his power. It swept me off my feet and then, laid me low. He will fare well on *Hunter's Hour*, high on the tension such exposure creates.

The anticipation of the television studio's audience sends a tremor through me. A guillotining comes to mind, knitters on the sideline, plain and purl, a dropped stitch, decapitation. I've seen it happen often. The wrong question and the wrong answer that can instantly destroy even the most experienced politician.

Their audience's questions are as predictable as I'd expected. Aloysius stays composed when he's asked about

Glenpora Properties and gives his usual reply about his exoneration. He is slick, fast, and convincing.

The question-and-answer session is nearing an end when a man in the audience interrupts the presenter.

'What about Katie Corcoran?' He speaks fast, loudly. He knows his time on air is limited and it's clear from Gemma's startled expression that his question was not pre-arranged. 'Aloysius Russell has my daughter's blood on his hands. All because she had the nerve to fall in love with his son. He ran her from his house, and she was forced to use her motorbike on a night when a blizzard was blowing, and the roads were thick with ice.'

This is exactly what Jonathan warned could happen.

A television camera zooms in on the questioner. Robert Corcoran has aged considerably since he stood by the edge of his daughter's grave. Tears were visible on his cheeks, then, as they are now. His mouth works but his hunched shoulders suggest that the courage it took to interrupt the interview has left him and he's unable to continue shouting.

A camera turns on Aloysius for a close-up. Outwardly, he seems unruffled, just slightly bemused by this unexpected attack. Security guards are already heading towards the man, who is quickly escorted from the studio. He doesn't resist, nor shout any further accusations.

Gemma has recovered her composure when she speaks directly to Aloysius. 'I'm sure you'll want to avail yourself of the opportunity to address the allegation that has just been made about Katie Corcoran's accident.'

'I will, of course.' He has perfected the ability to hide his turmoil, yet he must be seething. 'My apologies to everyone for this unforeseen interruption.' He inclines his head towards the seated audience. 'But I'll need time to address the charge that has been made against me. Before I deal with it, however, I'd like to extend my deepest sympathy to the Corcoran family for the tragic loss of their beautiful and beloved daughter.'

'Katie Corcoran died in a motorbike accident seven years ago.' Gemma must be receiving information on her earpiece. 'Was she in a relationship with your son, as her father stated?'

'A brief relationship, as I recall, when my son, Jonathan, was in his teens,' Aloysius replies.

A camera is zooming in on me. I'm in the middle of this unfolding drama and must control my expression. Like Aloysius, I've learned the value of a façade. It's essential to look sympathetic rather than horrified by Robert's accusation. This is a fast-moving story, and his brusque removal has added to the authority of his claim.

*A blonde elf*, that was my first thought when Jonathan introduced Katie to us. A tough, punkish elf in leather and wearing a helmet that looked too heavy for her petite head. They'd met at a motorcycle rally. Jonathan was a beginner and Katie, four years older, eased his way into that tight circle of motorbike enthusiasts. The two of them remained inseparable until her fatal crash eighteen months later.

She was riding a Harley Davidson Street Glide on the night she died. I've never been able to forget the name – a piece of trivia that triggers me every time I see one. I remember how tiny her face looked under her helmet and how her hands trembled as she removed it in the hall before going upstairs with Jonathan. They stayed for hours in his room. When I called them down to dinner, they were quiet at the table. Jonathan's apprehension became more obvious throughout the meal. Not that Aloysius noticed. He was angry and preoccupied about a bullying allegation that had been made against him by two staff members in his department. He was determined to fight back, as only he knew how to do.

Jonathan chose the wrong moment to break the news that he would be a father by his twentieth birthday. He would also be a husband. He held tightly to Katie's hand as he made this announcement. I saw the fear on both their faces as they waited for Aloysius to react – which he did before I'd time to speak.

His rage was chilling. How was he supposed to hold his head up in government where his reputation was based on family values? How could his son have been trapped by the sly antics of a *slut* who was old enough to know what she was doing?

The ugliness of the word left spittle on either side of his mouth.

I thought he would die from a stroke or heart attack and was unmoved by this possibility. But it was Katie who died, his scathing anger and insults driving her from Beech Park in tears. When Jonathan tried to follow her, he was brought to the ground by his father's fist. He saw through to the core of Aloysius that night, his brutishness no longer hidden behind an urbane front.

Before Jonathan could recover, Aloysius dragged him to his bedroom and locked the door. I ran after Katie, but she'd vanished into the icy air.

Ten minutes later, she skidded and crashed her motorbike into a wall.

The next morning, when news of her death reached us, Jonathan called his father a murderer and has not changed his mind since then.

'Katie, as I recall, was quite a few years older than my son.' Aloysius is back on screen. 'Her death shocked us all. I fully understand her father's grief. To lose a daughter is heart-breaking, as I and my wife know only too well.' He pauses, as if waiting for the wave of compassion that usually follows this reminder.

The audience is showing no inclination to oblige him.

'Was she in your house on the night of her accident?' Gemma asks.

'She came to dinner, and we had a pleasant evening together.' Aloysius nods. 'To say that there was any animosity between us is *absolutely* untrue. Her father's assertion that her accident was caused by me *running* her from our house is absurd and a lie. Maria and I always made her welcome whenever she called.'

'Were you aware that she was pregnant?' Gemma's tone is as sharp as her gaze.

'Pregnant?' Aloysius sounds astonished but a camera has turned to Jonathan, who is seated beside me in the front row. His hair is as unruly as ever and he's growing his beard again. Instead of a suit, he chose to wear his leather jacket tonight. He looks tough and rough, but this image is quickly dispelled by his stricken expression. The tear that rolls down his cheek is quickly followed by another.

'She was two months pregnant.' Gemma addresses Aloysius and he is back in the frame of the camera. 'Had she discussed her pregnancy with you?'

'This is a tremendous shock.' Aloysius's Adam's apple bobs once but, otherwise, he answers calmly. 'I'd absolutely no idea that that was the situation. It's heart-breaking to hear it now under these conditions. We would have welcomed a grandchild. Somehow, I've always believed that he or she would heal the wound that the loss of Isabelle inflicted on us.'

The candidates who are running alongside him will be sharpening knives. He should be careful about turning his back on them from now on. He continues to deny any knowledge of Katie's pregnancy.

'A passion and a cause are necessary to find closure when a child is taken from us,' he says. 'One of the most worthwhile decisions we ever made was to set up Isabelle's Quest. The work we do to reunite children with their lawful parents gave us the strength to heal our grief.'

Gemma brings her attention back to the audience and winds up *Hunter's Hour*.

'The media is watching our every movement.' I speak quietly to Jonathan. 'We mustn't give them any more ammunition. Shake your father's hand and congratulate him on his performance.'

He does as I ask. We're a political family who understand the rules of engagement. Appearance versus perception. We appreciate the fine line that creates the difference. Aloysius responds with a broad smile and a hearty handshake when Jonathan approaches him.

An invitation to the green room is politely declined. Aloysius insists we return to Beech Park to discuss how this situation is to be handled. Staying ahead of the story the media will report is the only thing on his mind. Fire-fighting tomorrow's headlines. Killian Osmond is probably already at work, scouring the internet for information on Jonathan and Katie. His appointment as the political editor at *Bayview Dispatch* has been like an itch on Aloysius's skin.

Roy Doran drives us back to Beech Park. His presence soothes Aloysius. I've never understood their closeness. Aloysius is so gregarious in public, and Roy, his taciturn shadow, is akin to his dark side. At least, that's how I view them.

Douglas arrives shortly after them and is followed by Jonathan. For once, he enters quietly, his helmet already removed.

'You're a lily-livered, slobbering idiot.' Now that the camera is no longer on Aloysius, his mouth is contorted with a barely controlled fury when he speaks to Jonathan. 'Are you happy now that you've destroyed my reputation?' he demands. 'You turn up looking like a thug, then cry like a baby when I'm attacked. You made a spectacle of yourself tonight.'

'Unlike you, I suppose.' Jonathan's anger flushes raw on his cheeks. 'Lying is second nature to you, so you were more than able to handle Robert's accusation.'

'You told him about that night?'

'No, I did *not*. I've been a good boy and did what Daddy ordered me to do.' Jonathan taps his lips with his index finger. 'Robert Corcoran didn't have to hear it from me to figure out how you treated his daughter that night. He just had to look at your political record to know what a bully you are.'

'Stop, both of you.' Douglas steps between them. 'I've arranged a meeting here with the campaign team but before they arrive, we must agree among ourselves how to kill that story. Insulting each other isn't going to help.'

'Perhaps this will.' Aloysius moves with such suddenness that Jonathan is knocked against the wall before he has time to avoid his father's fist.

I'm back again to the night Katie left us and how, in that aftermath, I decided to end my marriage. I didn't, of course. I gave in to Aloysius's entreaties, bound to him by our shared loss, and a lie I could never admit.

'Oh, for God's sake, stop this madness!' Douglas shouts as he grips his father's arms and manages to restrain him while I help Jonathan to his feet.

'Leave now,' I tell him. 'We'll talk about what happened when we're calmer.'

'Don't you dare set foot in this house ever again or you'll get more of the same,' Aloysius shouts as Jonathan is leaving.

I open the front door for my son and slam it on his father's threats.

'Jonathan will come here as often as he wishes.' I speak directly to Aloysius when I return to the room. 'If you ever dare to lay a hand on him again, I'll report you to the police for assault and stand witness to it.'

Before he can reply, I turn to Douglas. 'Use your constituency clinic to discuss all this. Enough mud has been slung here tonight. I want the air cleansed. Now, all of you, get out and leave me alone.'

'We'll continue this discussion later.' The steeliness in Aloysius's gaze as he looks at me is a warning that our already shattered relationship is capable of further breakage.

I check social media after he leaves. Robert Corcoran's interruption on *Hunter's Hour* is trending. Unable to deal with the online venom, I close my laptop.

Aloysius must also have been on social media, if his grim expression when he returns from the meeting is any indication.

'This debacle is on you,' he says. 'Attending that girl's funeral was a mistake. God only knows what conclusions her father reached when you kept nattering on at him about the accident.'

'I didn't *natter*. I merely expressed our sympathy to him.'

'You mean our *guilt*. We'd nothing to be guilty about, yet you carried on as if it was all our fault.'

'*Your* fault, Aloysius. The way you spoke to Katie that night—'

'I told her our son was too young to marry. We both know she trapped him—'

'All I know is that I lost a grandchild who never had a chance to grow because you were more interested in your reputation than in the happiness of your son and the woman he loved.'

'He was a pup. Nineteen, for Christ's sake. What did he know about fatherhood?'

'What do *you* know about it?' I lean against the breakfast

bar and allow the words to escape. 'You refuse to acknowledge that Douglas is gay and is trapped by your determination to keep it secret. As for Jonathan—'

I'm cut off in mid-sentence as he moves closer.

'Don't you ever say that again.' His quiet voice belies his fury. 'I've seen how women fawn over him. Gaby Grace couldn't keep her hands off him.'

'It wasn't what you think—'

'What was it then?'

'Friendship, nothing else. We both know that. You must allow Douglas to own his truth.'

'Own his truth...?' His scoffing tone quickens. 'That's woke garbage you're spouting. I assure you there *will* be consequences if you dare to repeat that again. Do you understand what I'm saying?'

'Yes, I understand perfectly.' My stomach will become his punchball if a wrong word sets him off again. I've seen the signs, his outbursts of temper as the pace of the campaign increases, his balled fists if I question him about the foundation funds. He could just as easily have brought me to the floor tonight.

Douglas is no longer here to protect me. My earlier courage has turned to self-preservation and an appeasement born of practice. 'This election campaign is stressing all of us,' I say. 'It'll soon be over and, hopefully, we'll be able to get our lives back on track again.'

'But before then, you need to shape up and support me. You looked like a wooden puppet when the camera picked you out tonight. Have you forgotten how to smile?' He presses an index finger from both hands to my mouth and stretches my lips. 'There... see? It's easy peasy.'

Jonathan calls me early in the morning. 'Are you okay?' he asks. 'What happened after I left?' He has heard the rough side of his father's tongue on too many occasions to believe that Aloysius went meekly to bed after I defied him.

'We went to bed. We'd nothing more to discuss.'

'I don't believe you. He was angry enough to...' He stops, as if what he imagines is too stark to consider.

'We were both exhausted. Nothing more was said. Have journalists been in contact with you?'

'They were waiting outside the apartment when I returned last night.'

'Did you answer their questions?'

'No. But he's lucky I didn't tell them *exactly* how he treated Katie.'

'*Please*, Jonathan... you know how the media will react if you—'

'Why do you always defend him?'

Jonathan is not prepared to listen to me. I don't blame him. I'm sick of listening to my own efforts to control the undercurrents that drag at the remnants of my marriage.

'I don't understand why you stay with him,' Jonathan continues to echo my own thoughts. 'You're still young enough to start over if only you had the courage to walk away from a marriage that gives you nothing back.'

'What about you?' I don't bother contradicting him. 'You've never moved on from Katie's death. All you do is replicate her and then end your relationships when you discover that's not possible.'

The silence that falls is laden with the memories Katie left us. 'You're right.' Jonathan finally breaks it. 'Amy pointed that out to me on the night we broke up. Time to move on... literally. I'm going to New York for a while. My ESTA's still valid so I've booked a flight for tomorrow.'

The suddenness of his announcement startles me, yet I'm not surprised. He's always on the move, restless when standing still.

'You can't leave until after the election.' I imagine Aloysius's fury if he doesn't have the full family complement behind him. 'Your father will expect us to support him until it's over.'

'It's over already,' Jonathan replies. 'Have you seen social media?'

'Not since last night. I don't intend checking it again.'

'That's probably a wise decision. I'm leaving, regardless.'

He complains about Aloysius's stubbornness, yet he's shaped from the same mould.

'Darling, listen to me, please,' I plead with him. 'Last night was a disaster for your father. If you leave now, it's only going to add fuel to the fire. Please, for my sake, just hang on until this nightmare is over. As a family we need—'

'We were never a family,' he replies. 'I'm sorry, Mum, but I'm tired of pretending otherwise. I'll phone you when I reach New York.'

Over the following days, Aloysius fobs off questions from journalists about Jonathan's absence by claiming his son has business commitments in New York. Nothing in his tone reveals the anger that consumed him when he heard Jonathan had left.

Our son is sofa surfing in a friend's apartment and checking out the possibility of organising a motorcycle rally from New York for the members of his motorcycle club. The rally will include workshops on motorbike safety and will end with a massive, outdoor concert. The numbers who want to participate continue to grow.

If only I could switch places with him and hold my daughter in my arms again.

# THIRTY-SIX

## GABRIELLE

Esther O'Neill from Flatbush is one of my regular callers. She's thin to the point of boniness, is a hoarder, has seven cats she adores and a world of humans she despises. None of this is true, of course, but it's what I picture every time she rings *Gaby's Good Morning Wake-up* with another rant. The only thing I know for sure is that she has Irish roots and never misses an opportunity to refer to me as an "*amadán*."' This morning, she's too annoyed to call me an idiot. Instead, her target is the "rough sleepers" who are 'cluttering up' the subways. A homeless woman rings in to explain her situation. Esther won't listen and is so abrasive that I'm forced to mute her.

The morning passes swiftly, and I'm surprised to see the next presenter frowning at me through the glass as he taps his watch.

'That was a spirited performance,' Emily says, when I emerge from the studio.

'I went the full ten rounds, all right.'

'You're well able to take it.'

'Esther called me "an ignorant spud-eating leprechaun." Does that qualify as a racist comment?'

'We'd need to check that out, though I doubt it'll be an entry in the directory of racism.' Emily laughs. 'Stop brooding on the negatives. Your ratings are rising all the time.'

After leaving the studio, I make my way to the Lucky Black Cat for breakfast.

'Morning, Gaby from Trabawn.' Sophy Robinson, the owner, shouts a welcome when I enter.

'Morning, Sophy from Bed-Stuy.' It's our standard greeting, a joke that never grows stale. She's a regular caller who listens to the show while doing preps before opening.

I sit beside the window and order a double expresso.

'This will put pep in your step.' She brings me coffee and pancakes with bacon. 'On the house,' she says. 'You were really bussin' this morning. That Esther sure has it in for you. What was it she called you?'

'An ignorant, spud-eating leprechaun.'

'I know what a leprechaun is, but "spud" is a new one on me.'

'It's the Irish term of endearment for a potato,' I reply.

She shrieks with laughter as I drizzle maple syrup over the bacon. 'Esther from Flatbush shovels more B.S. than the rest of your callers put together.'

I allow her to soothe me while I eat my breakfast. I reach the apartment as Zac is on the way out to his afternoon show.

'How'd it go?' he asks.

'I'm an ignorant, spud-eating leprechaun.'

Zac also finds this hilarious. 'Sounds like you were on top form. I'll listen to the catch-up later.'

I'm beginning to enjoy the sound of it. Maybe I should have it printed on a T-shirt. Own my identity... but which one?

Yesterday, eager for a glimpse of Maria, I watched Aloysius's episode of *Hunter's Hour* online and was immediately swept back into the cauldron of politics.

It wasn't until the interview was suddenly interrupted by a protester that I saw her at last. The usual conflicted feelings rushed over me. She was sitting beside Jonathan, who had turned to face the protester. Tears were visible on his face. Maria's shock was fleeting, yet I noticed how she bent her head, as if the force of the man's words had battered her. She recovered quickly and assumed a fixed, sympathetic expression. Even after the man was led from the studio, the reverberations remained.

If Robert Corcoran's accusation is true, I can understand Jonathan's antipathy towards his father.

I shouldn't ring Killian but my willpower has taken a hit this morning.

'Hello, stranger.' He answers immediately. 'How're you doing?'

'All good. Sorry for not ringing sooner. You know how it is.'

'I don't, actually, but it's nice to hear from you.'

'I watched *Hunter's Hour*. That was some roasting Aloysius took.'

'It certainly made for good television viewing. Gemma was thrilled, that's if the grapevine is to be believed.'

'How do you think it will affect his chances?'

'Hard to tell as yet.'

'Are you going to investigate that man's claim about his daughter?'

'I've an interview with him lined up for later today.'

'Of course you have.'

He laughs, then sighs. 'How are you *really* doing, Gaby?'

'Settling down again.'

'Not homesick?'

'No time to notice. What about you?'

'Busier than usual, obviously. However, I managed a weekend in Trabawn. Your nephews are thriving.'

'I know. I receive a daily video. How are the wedding plans going?'

He pauses, as if my question has taken him by surprise. 'Good, so far. All I need to do is turn up at the altar and give a witty yet profound speech at the reception. No pressure...'

'I'm sure that's exactly what you'll do.' Phoning him was a gigantic mistake.

'It's not until June, and your name is on the guest list,' he adds. 'You'd better come.'

The only way to deal with such a call is to go for a run.

I change into my running gear and head for the park. It's usually busy in the afternoon but not today. The wind is sharp enough to chase the last leaves from the trees. They rustle beneath my feet, a carpet of russet and gold. My pace is steady rather than fast. I'm used to being overtaken by other joggers. I pass an elderly man, muffled in a woolly hat and scarf, his long overcoat buttoned against the wind. He's walking an XL Bully, who, thankfully, is muzzled. The dog snuffles as I pass by and the man nods a greeting.

The cold is a blast that bends the grass and tosses petals from the bloodroots. I won't run my usual route. I veer towards the path that serves as a short cut to the park entrance. It's narrower and more bendy. It will save ten minutes, then a takeaway coffee to dispel the chill.

I wait to be overtaken by a runner behind me. The footsteps move at the same pace as mine. A quick glance over my shoulder confirms that he's male and wearing a black tracksuit and ski mask. I swing to one side to allow him to pass.

Despite the cold, the sky is now clear of clouds and the sun has a blinding glaze. His shadow falls over mine as he increases his speed. But instead of running by me, he catches me from behind. I stumble backwards, off balance, and am held steady as he tightens his arm around my neck and pulls me into a thicket.

Disbelief, that's all I feel initially as my heels drag on the earth. By the time I scream, he's hauled me through the shrubbery onto a mulch of dead leaves. He flips me over and presses his hand to my mouth to stifle me. Above us, the trees cast a filagree of branches against the blue sky and expose the nests that were abandoned when fledglings flew. The sun dances in a dazzling haze until it's blocked by his shoulders. Rape, that's what I believe is his intention, until his hands close around my throat. His gloves have the soft feel of leather, his grip merciless. When the sleeve of his top rises, his pale, freckled wrist is etched with veins. His concentration tells me that this is not the first time he's killed.

Such determination in his eyes as he stares down at me and squeezes harder.

Maria. She will be my last vision before I die. But she is already blurring and the face that stares down on me with such compassion belongs to Cassie... so sweetly familiar as she waits for me to join her.

She took a stick to me once, lashed it at me then ran crying from the kitchen when I wrestled it from her. I broke it over my knee and threw it into the fire. Such fights... she's remembering them, too. My right hand, free from his grasp, scrabbles in the mulch. My fingers close around the broken branch of a tree. I don't have the strength to lift it but Cassie urges me on... *Remember your fury... remember the strength you gained from it... use it now... use it now.*

I try to aim my cudgel at him and pray it has a knot as hard as a hammer. Did I hear the whack of wood against his head or imagine it? I've entered a dream-like state, a gossamer-thin reality that is powered by instinct. His curses are muffled behind the ski mask, but I recognise an Irish accent. He grabs the branch from me and flings it aside. Has his grasp loosened enough for me to scream? The sound I make is riven with pain and as harsh as the cawing crows swirling overhead. So many of them, beady-eyed witnesses to my death.

'Stop what you're doing right now. Disobey me and you'll be dealing with my dog.' The voice that penetrates my terror is followed by a low, phlegmy growl. 'Make no mistake, dude,' the voice continues. 'Liberty doesn't hang about, and he'll have your arm off in a split second.'

As if adding credence to this threat, the growl becomes a bark that sounds ever more threatening. My attacker doesn't hesitate as he loosens his grip and springs to his feet.

Liberty is close enough to see that his muzzle and lead have been removed. He opens his mouth to reveal his fangs and a glistening tongue. As the dog takes a few steps forward, this stranger who wants to strangle me crashes through the shrubbery and out of sight.

'You're safe now, miss.' The elderly dog owner bends over me and helps me up. My eyes sting with sweat and tears. His expression is an indistinct mass of concern as he supports me when my knees threaten to give way. Despite his age, he's strong and in complete control as he orders his dog to heel. I remember passing him earlier and being relieved that his XL Bully was muzzled.

When we reach the path, I collapse onto the bench and lean into the stranger who saved my life. His name is Wayne. He takes a flask from a pocket inside his coat and hands it to me.

'Brandy,' he says. 'Take a good slug, then I'll go with you to the police station.'

He was mugged three years ago. When he recovered and was released from hospital, he figured he had two options. To hide inside his house or claim his freedom to walk the park by buying an XL Bully.

'Don't run alone,' he advises me. 'Go with a friend or, better still...' He pats Liberty's head. 'A dog.'

The police want a clear description. Black, that's all I can say. Black everything, except his skin. I'm photographed, swabbed and finger-printed so that mine can be eliminated.

I accompany the cops to the crime scene. I show them my cudgel. Evidence. Who knows what it will reveal. A single hair, maybe. DNA... it has the potential to change a life forever.

*Don't run alone* is the advice that follows me from the police station and is repeated at the hospital. Maybe I should consider an XL Bully. My neck looks as though it barely survived a hangman's knot. I'm thoroughly checked before being deemed well enough to be discharged.

I'm on a strange high, almost giddy from relief and adrenaline as I hail a taxi to take me back to my apartment.

The only person I want to contact is Killian. I need to hear his voice, see his face. No... no... what can he do but upset me even more? I can't worry the twins, who'll insist that I return to Trabawn immediately.

Emily arrives with a Thai takeaway as soon as she hears about the attack. Zac joins us with beer, cold from his fridge. They have stories to tell of muggings they endured and, as with Wayne, I don't contradict them.

I was not mugged. A psychopath attempted to murder me. I was never in doubt about his intentions. Was I chosen or attacked randomly?

Emily and Zac rush to reassure me. I was just in the wrong place at the wrong time.

Today, only one subject is explored on *Gaby's Good Morning Wake-up*. I've no shortage of callers who want to answer the question I put to them: As women, do we have the right to run alone?

It's contentious enough to last the entire three hours, but my attention is elsewhere. My attacker's voice has become an earworm in my head – an accent that is harsh and has a faint echo of familiarity.

# THIRTY-SEVEN

## GABRIELLE

New York has become a place of shadows. They lurk in doorways and in the chinks of light that spill between the towers. My apartment is no longer a refuge. Old brownstones carry sounds: gurgling pipes, rattling radiators, the whine of hinges, footsteps on the stairs. Three days have passed since my attack, and I've become convinced I'm under surveillance. I can't decide if this suspicion is paranoia or fact. I want to believe my mind is playing tricks. Who can blame me for overreacting after such a traumatic attack? The conviction grows stronger whenever I leave my apartment or the studio. I keep imagining his breath on my neck, his arms closing around me and forcing me to the ground. I still haven't returned to the park.

Tonight, I need to concentrate on tomorrow's phone-in. The stairs creak again. I'm three stories high in a brownstone with no elevator. Each flight has one or two steps that give off an individual creak. This one belongs to the fifth step on my stairs. Davin, my taxi-driving neighbour, must be returning earlier than usual from his night shift.

I shower and wash my hair. The flow of water is weak and

not hot enough. I must talk to Zac about the plumbing. I dry off and slip into my dressing gown.

Opening my bedroom door, I have only an instant to wonder if I'm experiencing a flashback. Same stance, same tracksuit, same sturdy frame: is this post-traumatic stress at its most horrific?

When he reaches for me, I expect his hands to pass through me and prove he is nothing more than an apparition. Instead, his grip has a terrifying familiarity, iron-strong and determined as he lifts me off my feet and flings me down on the bed. Before I can react, he straddles me. He reeks of drink. His knees trap my arms so securely that I'm unable to flail at him.

I know what he is capable of doing. Once again, death seems so close, a black cloud forming and blotting out my future. The pressure pounding in my chest should be loud enough to deafen us both but I'm the only one who hears it.

I think of Cassie, beg her for the assistance she gave me the last time. She knows what it's like to feel a man's hands on her throat, his fetid breath scalding her face, but her energy is a frail thing that I'm unable to grasp.

A blow to my cheek stuns me and silences my screams. His hands fasten on my neck where the bruises he inflicted before have formed a mottled necklace. All I can see are his eyes through his ski mask, the glitter of their deadly intent.

He removes one hand from my neck and lifts a pillow. The pressure is unrelenting as he presses it over my face. The mattress muffles my kicks. I can't breathe. Slowly and deliberately, he is suffocating me. The attack in the park was not random. This man wants me dead. But why me? Did I annoy one of my listeners? Rouse him to such an extent that he's willing to wait until I go limp before releasing his hold on me? It will happen soon. His weight on my chest makes it impossible to breathe. I try and twist my face to seek air in the folds of the pillow. He presses down even harder, flattening my nose, forcing my mouth closed. His accent is still distinguishable behind the ski mask, his rasping voice cursing me for struggling against him.

I'm going to die. This time there is no Wayne, or Liberty with his drooling jaws. No Cassie to lend me her fury. No Maria to give me the love we were both denied. All I have is white noise and terror.

When he loosens his grip and falls away from me, I'm too dazed to understand what's happened. The breath I take into the loosening pillow is as pitched as the mew of a new-born kitten. When I push it away and attempt to rise, I see my attacker on the floor. He is on his knees, his movements slow and uncoordinated. I understand why when I see Zac standing above him. My landlord is the reason I'm still alive. He told me once that he was a leadoff hitter on his high school baseball team, and now he's about to swing his baseball bat for the second time.

His aim is deflected when he hears my mew-like breathing and turns. My attacker ducks just in time and scrabbles out of range. The room swirls. I close my eyes and fall back into an impenetrable darkness. No shadows. I want to hide in it forever, but other sounds begin to filter through: Zac's voice filled with concern, and footsteps, running fast then fading.

'It's okay... he's gone... Gaby... Gaby... open your eyes... he's gone.' Zac's concern eventually persuades me that I'm safe and free to see again. My breathing slows as the wheezes I've dredged from my lungs begin to ease. He brings me water and helps me into a sitting position. The police are on their way.

'He's gone,' he repeats. 'Is he the same guy who attacked you in the park?'

I nod.

'I should have followed him.' Zac sounds regretful. 'He was right to run when he did. I wouldn't have missed the next time.'

'Thank you...' My throat feels as if it's been scoured with

sandpaper. 'How did you know... I thought you were spending the night at Rosa's?'

'We'd a row.' He shrugs, too shocked to sound rueful. 'I came home and discovered the lock had been damaged. The front door was closed but unlocked. I immediately thought of the death threats you get on social media, and the attack in the park. I picked up the bat and opened your door with the master key.'

Random acts, random decisions – how can anyone believe that the world is not in a permanent state of madness?

Why is this man determined to kill me? He must be a crazed listener to *Gaby's Good Morning Wake-up.* No other explanation is possible.

The police who interview me are from a different precinct. They ask the same questions and look dubious when I tell them I've no enemies that I can name. Just a faceless listenership with their angst and anger. But they are not voiceless. I agree to replay my on-air conversations and see if I can recognise that rasping voice. In the meantime, they take Zac's baseball bat for a forensic examination and will check if anyone with a suspicious headwound contacts a hospital.

Unlike the last time, I have no bruises, just sudden spasms that convince me I'll be unable to draw breath. By the following day, Zac has changed the lock on the front door. Security cameras will be installed outside the entrance and in the hallway.

I ask my listeners a question: Do you feel safe from attack in your own home? The lines light up. Tensions are high as women relate to my question. Their stories are grim but also inspiringly brave. The flow of callers continues through the following morning's show. *Gaby's Good Morning Wake-up* is becoming oppressive and alarming, Emily believes. The powers-that-be are anxious in case ratings drop.

'Talk your experiences through with a counsellor,' she says. 'NY Eyz will cover all costs.'

'No, I don't need counselling. It won't make my life any safer. I'd be better off joining a kick boxing gym or karate club.'

I plan to do so yet don't take any action. I present my show, then take a taxi to my apartment where either Zac or Davin accompany me up the stairs. Once my small apartment is checked and declared empty, I lock the door.

Has it become my haven or my cage?

My buzzer sounds one night as I'm getting ready for bed. Rising in the small hours to go to work leaves little room for partying, and friends never call after nine. I check the intercom.

A man stands under the exterior security light that Zac installed after the second attack. My attacker has hardly come calling to complete his murderous task yet I'm trembling as I check the blurry image on the screen. I make out a bulky biker jacket with the distinctive buckle and zip adornments. Surely it can't be...

No mistake.

Jonathan Russell is outside, waiting to be admitted.

# THIRTY-EIGHT

## GABRIELLE

'Oh, my god, you were getting ready for bed,' he says, when he sees me in pyjamas. 'I'm sorry for barging in on you without warning. I should have realised you've an early start in the morning,'

'Up with the larks, that's me.' I'm uncomfortable in his presence yet also affected by a giddy excitement that lends an unnatural pitch to my voice.

'Same here,' he says. 'I won't stay long. Douglas asked me to look you up and find out how you're doing.'

'That was kind of him. As you can see, I'm good.'

'You left so abruptly that he was worried in case our father upset you in some way.'

'Tell Douglas that my decision to come back here had nothing to do with your father.'

We're still standing in front of each other and he, as if conscious that I should be in bed, checks his watch. 'He'll be relieved to hear that. I'd better not keep you up any longer.'

'I'm not ready to sleep yet.' Why am I doing this? His sudden presence is triggering everything I'm trying to keep under control. 'Have a beer before you go and fill me in on the campaign. I've been following it online, but I *do* miss the smell of the greasepaint.'

He smiles and nods. 'A beer sounds good. Thanks, Gaby.'

He follows me into the living room and stands for an instant to observe my surroundings. I'm relieved that the blown-up photo of Maria hangs in my bedroom. The only ones on display are of the family I love and will never harm... so why have I invited him into my space? As always, in the company of a Russell, my mind twists with contradictions.

I hang up his jacket and gesticulate towards an armchair. 'How long have you been in New York?'

'Over a month now.'

'How does your father feel about that?'

'I haven't asked him, nor do I intend to find out.' He's defiant and yet I sense that he's equally as adept as his mother at hiding his feelings.

'I'll get the beers, or would you prefer a Guinness?'

'Beer is fine.'

He's studying a photograph of the twins with their babies when I return from the kitchen with two bottles.

'I saw you with your sisters at the EOM reception.' He points at the photograph. 'You're obviously a very close-knit family.'

'As you are, Jonathan.'

'Hah!' He takes the drink from me and flings himself into the armchair. 'You were close enough to us to know better.'

'I don't make judgements,' I reply, which is a lie, of course, but I want him to keep talking. 'Every family has issues. I watched *Hunter's Hour*. I presume the reason you came to New York was to escape the media backlash?'

He studies the bottle before raising it to his lips and taking a long gulp. 'No one escapes that kind of backlash. My father could have done with another episode of *Red Tape Unreeled* after that incident.'

'More propaganda, you mean?' I can't forget the verdict he and Killian attributed to those podcasts.

'You can't pretend otherwise,' he says. 'My belief is that you left because you could no longer handle the faked scenarios you were inventing with him. You're a professional broadcaster. I listen to your morning show on my phone when I'm running.'

'Be careful where you run.' For an instant, I'm tempted to tell him about the attacks. But that will consume the time we have together.

I offer him another beer. 'Tell me about Katie. From your reaction when her father spoke about her, it was obvious you were very upset.'

'It was shattering,' he admits. 'I've never been able to forget her. I'll carry the regret I feel over her death to my own grave.'

I listen without interrupting him as he tells his story. I'm no longer counting the beers we consume as he relates the events of that fateful night. I should have been part of this family tragedy. Could my presence have made a difference to the outcome? Thinking like this will drive me crazy.

'Robert Corcoran wasn't the reason I left,' he says. 'My father...' He sighs and slaps his hand against the side of his head, as if the thought of Aloysius, and the ill-feeling between them, can be dispersed by such a gesture. 'He was never easy to be around, but this campaign has brought his obnoxiousness to the fore. I can't handle my anger with him anymore.'

'Is Maria all right?' Finally, I allow myself to ask the question that has been on the tip of my tongue since he arrived. 'How is she managing the campaign? That incident on television must have also affected her deeply.'

He raises and drops his shoulders as he reaches for another beer. 'She pleaded with me to remain at home for the campaign, but I just had to get out. I talk to her every day. She seems to be coping okay. She's steeped in politics and knows what's expected of her.'

'You make her sound like a robot.'

'Do I?' He sounds surprised. 'That's not what I intended. She's amazing but sometimes...'

I'm almost afraid to breathe in case I intrude on his thoughts.

'Don't get me wrong,' he continues. 'I've never doubted her love or been neglected by her in any way, yet there's always been a space between us that I've been unable to fill.'

'In what way?' The beer has relaxed him and he's beginning to open up to me.

'This may sound weird,' he says. 'But I've often thought the reason is linked in some way to my sister's disappearance. It's overshadowed my whole existence. To be brutally honest, Gaby, there are times I've *actually* hated her. I mean, she's a ghost so I know that's kind of sick. But I've never had a chance to know the woman my mother was before Belle was taken.'

'I'm sorry you've had to endure—'

'No, I *didn't* endure anything.' His interruption is abrupt. I must hide the wildness that has overtaken me since I saw him standing outside and allow him to continue at his own pace.

He finishes his beer and accepts another. He snaps the top off and does the same to mine. Tomorrow morning, my head will ache. Theo, whose show goes on after mine, will complain about the rank smell of stale alcohol I'll leave behind in the studio. I don't care. Nothing matters except the slightly slurred sound of Jonathan's voice as he fills the void in the life I should have lived.

'My parents were the ones who endured,' he says. 'Their marriage, for instance. I've often wondered if Belle was the only reason that held them together. My mother told me once she's bound to him by guilt. She slept through their child's kidnapping and deprived him of his daughter.'

He stops and stares at the bottle, as if surprised by how far the level has dropped. 'I'm drinking too much. Sorry for bending your ear.'

'You're not doing that, Jonathan.'

'But I *am* talking too much. I don't usually go there... I mean where Belle is concerned.'

'Do you talk to Maria about your sister?

'No. I listen when she needs to unload. That usually happens around the anniversary but, to be honest, I've nothing to give back. I often wonder if I exist purely because she needed a replacement child.'

'I'm sure that isn't true,' I say. 'I've seen the two of you together. Maria obviously adores you. Is she really coping with the campaign? I know how difficult she found the podcasts.'

'According to Douglas, she's holding it together very well. He thinks she's changed in some way. I noticed it before I left but I wasn't sure if it was my imagination. Now, when we speak on the phone she sounds... how shall I put it... more upbeat... and resolute.'

'What do you think has caused this change?'

'I'm not sure,' he says. 'I think it's related to that time she collapsed in Clognua. It probably made her realise that she needs to take care of her health.'

I want him to leave. Otherwise, I'll crash. A pretence can only last so long and I'm abusing his trust. Perversely, I want him to stay. A pretence can help me to probe his psyche and get to know my mother through the life they shared.

'Does she think Aloysius will win?'

'Hard to tell,' he replies. 'He's weathered the publicity that followed *Hunter's Hour*. He has a base that will support him, no matter what dirt is flung in his direction.'

He stands to leave. 'I've an important meeting tomorrow and you have a show to present. Thanks for the beers.'

'Will you go home for Christmas?' I ask.

"My mother's pleading with me to show my face. I haven't made up my mind. What about you?'

'My sisters are doing their best to persuade me to make the trip. I'd like to see them. This is our first Christmas without our parents. My problem is time. Unlike Ireland, New York doesn't party for a week over the Christmas season. I'd be expected back on air by the twenty-seventh and wouldn't be able to catch a flight to Ireland until Christmas Eve. It's not worth the stress.'

'Maybe it is,' he says. 'A first Christmas without your parents will be difficult. It should be shared with your sisters.'

'Maria would also want you there, Jonathan.'

'That's the problem.' He sighs heavily. 'But I can't always be there when she needs me. I don't want my father to win this campaign. I don't even want to hear him talking about it or to see those fucking election posters everywhere I look.'

I should let him go. Curtail this visit to a one-off.

'Don't be short of a sofa while you're here, Jonathan.'

I write down my phone number and hand it to him. 'Mine pulls out into a bed and you're welcome to use it if you're ever stuck.'

So much for resolve.

'That's kind of you.' He smiles and unexpectedly holds out his arms. 'I'm glad I called. New York can sometimes feel like the loneliest place in the world... so thanks for listening.'

I walk into his embrace. One step back, two steps forward would appear to be the only way I'm travelling.

The more I attempt to move away from my family, the more I allow myself to be drawn closer into its centre. Will my neediness ever be satisfied?

# THIRTY-NINE

## MARIA

Tonight, Aloysius is addressing the Hearth and Home Women's Alliance at their annual Christmas party. He speaks about the family, the core of society, and how that core can disintegrate if it's attacked by those who wish to bring it down. I've heard variations of this speech many times, yet he delivers it with an enthusiasm that suggests it has just been freshly written.

Afterwards, he mingles with the audience, drinking tea and tasting the array of pasties that the members baked for the occasion, and are now being sold to raise funds for his campaign. Will this night, and others like it, ever end? I want to be in bed where I can dream about my daughter. I let her go too easily. Twenty-nine years of holding my silence was too hard to break.

'I came here tonight to hear your husband speak.' The woman standing beside me is elderly. Her hand trembles slightly on her walking stick. 'He's as eloquent as ever and has wooed his audience by repeating their aims and aspirations back to them. A clever orator, wouldn't you agree?'

It's hard to tell if she's insulting Aloysius or praising him.

'Clever and sincere.' I smile benignly at her.

'How do you feel about becoming a presidential wife?' she asks.

The expression 'lived-in face' comes to mind, all those embedded lines with their own histories. 'You look the part, I'll grant you that,' she continues. 'But what do you think about the role you'll have to fulfil?'

'Firstly, I'm not sure it's a role I'll have to assume but, if I do, I'll serve it with both humility and commitment.' I'm paraphrasing Aloysius but, unlike him, my answer sounds insincere.

Her gaze is unnervingly direct. 'Do you really want him to win?'

'Of course I do. Running for this election is the most important decision Aloysius ever made.'

'I would have imagined his most important decision was to marry you.'

'Of course it was, but this...' I gesture towards the audience. 'He believes he's the right person to win this election. His expertise—'

'I'm aware of his expertise so let's not waste time discussing it.' She grips my elbow with her free hand as the noise level increases. 'I knew your father. Let's find a quieter spot to talk.' She steers me away from the group to an area in the auditorium where the voices can't reach us.

'Georgie – that's what I called your father – was my first boyfriend,' she says. 'We were both in our teens but, even then, I recognised the honesty that would bring him through his political career. As his daughter, I suspect you've inherited that same trait.'

'When did you stop being his girlfriend?' I'm surprised by the woman's bluntness.

'When he met your mother. No battle there. I was heartbroken but teenage love can be an ache that heals remarkably well, even if that doesn't seem possible at the time. I followed Georgie's career until he died. I must admit, my attention then switched to you and your husband. I can't pretend to have the same regard for Aloysius as I did for your father. But I was heartsick for both of you when your baby was taken.'

'Thank you... I'm sorry... I don't know your name.'

'Kathryn Bryant.'

'Your name is familiar, though I don't remember my father ever mentioning you.'

'I guess that's not surprising.' She shrugs, unperturbed. 'Like you, I set up a foundation. It's called Bryant's Haven.'

'Yes, of course. I recognise your name now. You run a refuge for victims of domestic abuse.'

'Actually, I prefer to call them survivors. I retired some years ago. However, the refuge is still going strong... more's the pity. I'd die happy if Bryant's Haven had helped to end such brutality but, sadly, the light at the end of a long tunnel has yet to glimmer.' She taps her walking stick against the floor and frowns, her expression thoughtful. 'Age brings some privileges and one of them is insight. The other is plain speaking. Do you mind if I engage in both?'

'Please do.' I tense, certain that what comes next will be disturbing, yet anxious to hear what this forthright woman from my father's past has to say.

'I gave shelter once to Aloysius's first wife. I know I shouldn't tell you this but you're Georgie's daughter and it's important that I protect you. Your husband had expected to become a government minister after his party won an election and was bitterly disappointed when he was passed over. He took his frustration out on Julia. She managed to escape and made her way to my shelter. Like many abused women, she believed his weasel words and returned to him. I never saw her again. Two years later she was dead, and I often—'

'Julia suffered an asthma attack.' I quickly interrupt her, upset by what she appears to be implying. 'I was working for Aloysius at the time. I saw how her death affected him.'

'Enough to marry you a year later?' She says this quietly, without emphasis, but I hear the condemnation in her question.

'There was never any suspicion over her death.'

'I'm not suggesting there was,' she replies. 'She told me about her asthma and how it flared up when she was stressed. I'll always remember her eyes... the pain she allowed me to see there. Your lovely eyes are remarkably similar. Your husband will not win this election. Please, be careful that you come to no harm. Now, then, I've said enough and it's way past my bedtime. It was a delight to meet you, Maria.'

Aloysius is constantly on his phone as we journey home. Meeting Kathryn Bryant has disturbed me. Insightful and outspoken, she certainly proved her reputation in our short time together. My mind churns over the information she revealed.

Julia Russell has always seemed like a ghost. Aloysius never speaks about her, and moved into Beech Park without trailing any of her possessions behind him. He erased her from his life, just as he erased Belle – until it became apparent that her disappearance could be used for his political gain.

His elbow jogs against mine as the driver turns a corner. I shift further from him, a movement he'll have noticed. Let him stew. Something is stirring in the air and I'm beyond caring where it carries us.

I listen to *Gaby's Good Morning Wake-up.* Esther from Flatbush is giving out again. She rants regularly on the show. I get the feeling that her phone calls to the station are the highlight of her day. She's irritating yet a relief from the topics Gaby recently introduced. At times I wanted to turn her off. All those calls she took from listeners about violence endured by women. Such an unrelenting stream of oppressive calls. I didn't want to recognise myself in the centre of them, but how could I not?

This morning, opinions are divided on street gentrification, yet violence still hangs like an uneasy spectre over the show.

# FORTY

## GABRIELLE

The arrival hall at Kerry airport is crowded with reuniting families, who wait at the barrier with their *Welcome Home* balloons and banners. A choir singing Christmas carols is almost drowned in tumultuous cheers as another cluster of passengers emerges. Returning sons and daughters rush towards their families with outstretched arms. The winking fairy lights are a pale reflection of the joy that sparkles from everyone's eyes as hugs are exchanged and tears wiped away.

I search for Jessica among the waiting crowd. She promised to pick me up when we last spoke on the phone. People are beginning to disperse yet there is still no sign of her.

I notice Killian as the crowd separates. No balloon or banner in his hand, just one red rose which he holds with a certain awkwardness. A single red rose to signify his love. Shauna must be spending Christmas in Trabawn. I hadn't noticed her on the flight. She could be coming in on a later one.

This is unendurable. I'm likely to burst into tears if he sees me. I soak him in, his face so dear to me, his body once so lanky now filled into its solid frame. I want to rush into his arms and never let him go. I've been staring at him like a love-struck teenager and left it too late to hide. He catches sight of me before I can move or avert my eyes. Greedy eyes, sizing him up, stark with longing.

He doesn't seem surprised to see me. Trabawn and its drumbeat again. The close-knit gossip network always takes me by surprise whenever I return home.

I wave at him, keep it casual at all costs, and look beyond him for Jessica. I'm furious with her for being late and furious with him for turning me into a victim of unrequited love. Is there anything more pathetic? Most of the waiting crowd have left and new families are arriving to await the next flight.

He walks towards me. 'Happy Christmas, Gaby,' he says. 'I told Jessica I'd pick you up.'

The rose he offers me is an opening bloom with a sprig of white gypsophila and glossy green leaves that tremble in anticipation... of what?

'I thought you were waiting for Shauna—?' The stem of the rose is wrapped in cellophane but I still fear its thorns.

'Shauna?' He frowns. 'Why on earth would Shauna come to Trabawn for Christmas?'

'To be with you and your family.'

'Ah, so Shauna is the name of my phantom bride.'

'Phantom?'

'I'd a chat yesterday with Susanne. Apparently, she was under the impression that it was me, not Jamie, who got engaged and told you so. She blamed Noreen Ferguson for initially starting the rumour.'

'I don't understand.'

'Word spread about Jamie's engagement to Alicja at the EOM reception. Shauna and I haven't been together for months. We should have parted sooner but we like each other too much. It seemed easier to drift, especially when we were both so career driven.'

'I'd no idea—' I touch my throat. The bruising has gone but it's still difficult to swallow.

'Susanne said you looked devastated when you heard I was getting married,' he says. 'Is that why you told me you'd nothing to keep you here?'

'Yes.'

'For crying out loud... what were you thinking, Gaby?'

*They're convinced I'm inheriting a ball and chain.* That was what I heard him say when Shauna rang. The music was loud, the voices raucous, yet his words were distinct. 'That night in the pub in Clognua, you told me you were celebrating,' I say. 'Next day I hear you're engaged. I assumed—'

'I was celebrating my promotion.' His interruption has force, yet he speaks quietly, his expression a mixture of affection and exasperation. 'I got the political editor's job. I thought that was why you showed up. Then you hurried off before I'd a chance to talk to you about it.'

The same night that I was held close in Maria's arms.

'Do you know how I felt when you told me you were returning to New York?' His eyes are on me, moist like mine, but steady.

'Tell me.'

'As if the bottom had fallen out of my world.' He waits for my response. He doesn't need words. My answer must be visible in the glow that warms my face.

'My world also collapsed when I thought I'd lost you.' I whisper my reply but he hears me clearly.

'I love you, Gaby.'

He says it simply and it seems so natural, so right. When Maria acknowledged me, I felt as if a violent thirst had finally been quenched. Now, when I tell him I love him, it's as if I'm emerging into light, a maze of wrong turnings behind me.

'This rose was always for you.' He extends it once more. 'Please take it or I'm going to look like a right idiot.'

'Some would call you an "*amadán*."' I laugh and push Esther from Flatbush clear away as I reach forward and accept his rose, thorns and all.

What lies before us? Can I truthfully claim to love him yet continue to carry my secret? How do I even begin to explain the journey I've been on? A journey that excluded him. A journey I was afraid to share in case he abused my trust and used my story as his greatest exposé.

I was wrong not to trust him. His arms are strong, as is his word. No more secrets. We walk hand in hand from the airport.

The bedroom of his youth, an annex at the side of his family house, was once as familiar to me as my own. This is where we move seamlessly from friendship back to passion. As we slowly undress, it's as if I'm seeing his body for the first time. His gaze holds that same wonder as we lie on the bed where we used to listen to Coldplay and Arctic Monkeys, the volume turned up because his once-grunge bedroom was separated from the main building by a passageway. Those echoes are silent, and the sound of our breathing quickens as we remove everything that could come between us. Desire has a depth that demands as much as it gives and we, greedy with need, lose ourselves in the breakers. Again and again, we explore the curves and crevices of our bodies, seeking an ever-deepening fulfilment until we are spent with bliss. How wonderful it is to discover that friendship and passion can blend without effort and create a new connection that feels unbreakable.

I will time to stop its thieving and for others to leave us alone but, of course, that's not possible. The twins are tolerant of my absence up to a point but my presence at the Christmas dinner is an order, not a request from Jessica, who is hosting it for the first time. Nor is Killian able to ignore his parents' wishes that he leave the annex and take his familiar place around their table. So much to catch up on. I try not to resent the hours I must spend away from him.

Nudges and winks follow us wherever we go. The twins demand to know why we'd taken 'forever' to realise we're crazy about each other. Noreen Ferguson, looking sheepish, apologises for her mistaken belief that Killian had become engaged to Shauna.

'Am I losing my marbles or what?' She taps the side of her head when we meet outside St Finbarr's Church on Christmas morning. 'It's no good being the town crier if you don't get your facts right.'

I attend mass with Susanne and Jessica. Cassie and Dad are among the list of departed parishioners whose names are read from the altar. On either side of me the twins squeeze my hands until the telltale tears sting my eyes. Happiness and sadness, they move in tandem through those two days and nights.

I play peek-a-boo with my nephews. They will soon be crawling. Who will make the first move? Michael or Josh? This is a friendly rivalry, based on tooth averages and mobility. I sit on the floor between them and watch them playing with toys that emit ear-numbing tunes that are only slightly shriller than their own cries when they're hungry.

I wait for an opportunity to tell Killian about my 'other' family. That's how I think of them: an attachment I've acquired without having any idea how to manage it. So far, lies and deceit have brought me to this stage but once a secret is shared, it can take a different shape. It will dominate our short time together. A starter gun that will drive Killian forward into my search. Can I take that risk... and is it possible to condense my story into the five questions that are fundamental to good journalism?

Who am I? Isabelle Russell.

What happened? I was stolen.

When? Three weeks after I was born.

Where? Beech Park.

Why? My father wanted revenge.

Killian's arm tightens around my shoulders as I chart each step I took along the crooked path that led me to my mother. He's a good listener, always was, but this is different. How will he react? Amazement that I was hiding in plain sight for twenty-nine years? Disbelief at what he finds too far-fetched to be real? Anger that I didn't trust him sooner?

Occasionally, he sighs and shakes his head, as if recalling specific incidents when his suspicions were aroused.

'Maria was terrified of what would happen to her if the truth came out.' I must impress on him the ramifications should this become public. 'I promised it would stay between the two of us. Also, I believed you were engaged to Shauna and that I'd no right to involve you.'

On and on I go until my breath catches and I fall silent.

'I'm still trying to take it all in,' Killian admits. 'What you've told me is extraordinary, and yet I'm not surprised. I always felt I was just a step away from understanding your relationship with the Russells. Now it makes perfect sense, except for one critical fact. Your father wasn't a vengeful man. Why would he put the woman he loved through so much torment?'

'It's a question that's haunted me, too. I don't know how to answer it. He stole me, Killian. If he hadn't uttered those last words to me, I'd never have known any better and Cassie would still be alive.'

She appears before me, my ghost, constant and watchful, but it's my father who causes my voice to shake with rage. 'I'll *never* be able to forgive him.'

'What will you do now?' he asks. 'The truth has to come out sooner or later.'

He's right. A truth that will have the velocity of a bullet. Where will it penetrate?

'I must think of the twins and how it will impact on them.' He needs to appreciate all that is at stake. 'You know what Trabawn is like for gossip. This would hit the community like a hurricane, especially when the media descend on the town.'

'I know what you're saying but this is an enormous revelation,' he says. 'If you decide to go public, I can help you to handle it—'

'This can't come out, Killian.' I'm seized by panic. 'Promise me you won't tell anyone else.'

'Gaby, you have my word. All journalists dream about breaking such a story but you're not a dream. You're the most important person in my life. That's all that matters to me.'

'I need to tell you something else, Killian. It's something I should have shared with you years ago. I tried to pretend it never happened and almost succeeded... but all this – everything that's happened since my father died kept pushing it forward and forcing me to acknowledge its importance.'

As I tell Killian about the baby we conceived so heedlessly in the boathouse, and how easily she slipped from our lives, the tears on his cheeks speak of his sadness more clearly than words could ever express.

The last barrier between us has been removed. I'm lightheaded with relief, weightless as I sink into the strength and hardness of him, eager for his lips, opening myself to all that is within him to give me.

# FORTY-ONE

## MARIA

I awaken early on Christmas morning. Pixels of light glimmer in the dawn. Somewhere in this Christmas Day glitz, my daughter waits for me. I long to tear down the lights on the Christmas tree, and those that loop around Beech Park and outside, too. Such a mocking reminder that the season is about merriment, joy, revelry.

Douglas arrives late for Christmas dinner, which is unusual for him. He's wearing a festive jumper with reindeers whose eyes wink in coloured lights. A Rudolf nose in the centre gives a 'Happy Christmas' grunt when pressed. Jonathan would have worn such a jumper rakishly but on Douglas it looks like a disguise.

Jonathan refused to come home for Christmas. The rift between him and Aloysius has grown too wide. For once, my powers of persuasion failed. I heard his regret that he must disappoint me, but he was steadfast in his determination to remain in New York.

My suggestion that Aloysius ring Jonathan and apologise for attacking him was met with a firm shake of his head. 'What exactly am I meant to apologise for?' he demanded. 'His behaviour during that programme was bad enough, but his decision to run away from the media could cost me the election. How can you expect me to kowtow to him when he should be doing his upmost to limit the damage that he's inflicted on me.'

He blames Jonathan for the dip in the polls since *Hunter's Hour*. Trying to reason with him is impossible. Apologies in any form, according to Aloysius, mean acquiring an Achilles' heel – something that will be exploited by the media. What happened, happened. Move on.

If Aloysius loses the election, I'll leave him on the day after the results are announced. But if he wins... that possibility is my waking nightmare.

Leaking the information on social media about his election plans focused too much attention on him before he was ready for it. I don't regret my underhand stroke. Nor do I regret the meeting I had with Robert Corcoran and the apology I made for the treatment that was meted out to Katie in Beech Park on the night she died. He is an activist on road safety. I knew he'd act to highlight my claim. Am I as monstrous as my husband, or simply a woman who is desperate to outwit the man who has caged her?

Presents are exchanged before we sit down to eat. Candlelight casts a kindly glow over us as we give the traditional clap when Aloysius carries the turkey to the table. We pass dishes to each other with exaggerated politeness. I've asked them not to talk about politics during the meal. They agree yet there is a suspended atmosphere in the air as we seek safe subjects to discuss. Our voices are pitched higher than usual, our laughter more inflated. When silence falls it's strained from the effort of finding the next topic of conversation. Jonathan's absence is like a hole in the room that no one dares approach.

It's a relief to leave the table and return to the living room where the television distracts us. As bad luck would have it,

Aloysius turns it on just in time to see Edward Kinsella standing in front of a glittering Christmas tree.

The campaign is on hold until the new year. No more polls, explosive interviews, postering and posturing. Edward has the advantage of being the incumbent and he delivers his presidential Christmas message to the nation with gravatas.

'He doesn't deserve another seven years at the helm.' Aloysius is unable to restrain himself. 'Jonathan will be wholly responsible if I lose this election. I'd a hefty lead in the polls before *Hunter's Hour*. That would have continued to grow if he'd stood his ground and supported me against the vile allegation made by that woman's father.' His voice goes like a needle through my brain.

'Her name was *Katie*,' Douglas says. 'And it was an *accusation* he made. One that was well founded, as we all know.'

'Please don't fight on today of all days.' I try to head them off but Aloysius's anger matches his reddening complexion.

'I've always done what's best for my family and that marriage, had it taken place, would have been a total disaster within twelve months,' he states.

'You've no way of knowing that.' Douglas stares at the television screen as Edward Kinsella welcomes the Irish diaspora home for Christmas and sends a message of goodwill to those who sleep in cardboard boxes. 'It's Kinsella you should be studying, not heaping blame on your son. According to the polls, it'll be your intransigence that'll cost you the election. That's probably the reason Gaby decided she was no longer interested in working with you. That reminds me. Jonathan called to see her in New York.'

'How is she?' I reach for the remote and lower the volume. This should be a normal question, yet it feels loaded. It opens the door to another. How did she and Jonathan get on? Did they talk about me? Did Gaby by word or deed reveal what took place between us at the hospital? The room melts and all I can see is my daughter's face.

'She's doing okay, from what he said,' Douglas replies.

'And what reason, may I ask, had he for calling on her?' Aloysius prizes loyalty above all else. Gaby's sudden departure is an insult that still festers with him.

'I asked him to look her up,' Douglas replies. 'She seemed upset before she left. I was worried that you were the reason.'

'The *reason*?' Aloysius stiffens. 'Elaborate, please.'

'I'm talking about me and Gaby, and how you pushed us together at every photo opportunity.'

'I *pushed* you together.' The mood, already strained, is becoming charged. 'What about you? You lead a girl along then don't make the slightest effort to follow up on her interest in you.'

A momentary silence greets this accusation. I think of a balloon. The sudden jab that brings instant deflation, and am aware, with ever more certainty, that my family is broken in a way that can't be healed.

'Firstly, Gaby is a woman, not a girl,' says Douglas. 'Secondly, she understood from the beginning that my interest in her was nothing more than friendship, just as you did. But, as usual, you forced us to dance to your tune.'

'From where I was standing, it certainly didn't look like friendship.' A nerve twitches at my husband's temple. 'Obviously, I was wrong. She wasn't your type. Too stroppy, I guess, but that's no reason—'

'Stop!' Douglas has never raised his voice to his father and the harshness of his tone creates a charged hush. 'I want to share something with you now,' he says. 'I won't be here next Christmas. I'll be spending it with Oisín, my partner.' He states this with an unflinching determination as he stands and faces his father.

'What exactly are you implying?' Aloysius breathes heavily. A harsh intake, an explosive exhalation.

'I'm not implying anything. I'm stating a fact. My partner's name is Oisín O'Sullivan. We've been in love since we met—'

'What can you possibly know about love?' Scorn or mockery, or both, are implicit in Aloysius's interruption.

The room seems primed, as if any gesture will shatter the glassy atmosphere.

'More than you, Dad. Much more than you ever will.' Douglas is determined to finish this conversation, no matter where it leads.

'I'd like to meet Oisín.' I try to rise from the sofa to go to him. Aloysius grabs my arm and forces me down. His complexion, deepening to an unhealthy mauve, is alarming.

'Take your hands off me.' I'm beyond caring about his anger. I try to wrench my arm away from him. His grip has a ferocity that will leave marks on my skin. For an instant, it seems as if he'll prevent me rising. I hold his gaze and repeat myself. Slowly, his fingers uncurl. His hand falls to his knee. I leave his side and cross the floor to my son.

'Oisín will always be welcome in my house.' I take Douglas in my arms and hold him as closely as I did when he was fifteen and confided in me. I wasn't surprised then, just saddened that he was afraid to speak to Aloysius. And then it was more than fear, I realised, as time passed, and his father's views became more rigid on his interpretation of traditional family values.

It's over an hour since Douglas left. I'm relieved that this subterfuge has ended but the uneasy reverberations of his announcement still hang in the air. I clear the dishes from the table and carry them to the kitchen. The turkey has hardly been touched but, already, it looks unedifying.

'Why do you always undermine me in front of my sons?' Aloysius enters the kitchen as I'm stacking the dishwasher. 'You do it all the time and today, when your support was needed, you let me down once again.'

'Are you serious?' Straightening, I resist the urge to slap his face. He's baiting me, hoping I'll provide the trigger that will give him a reason to strike me back. 'If standing up for our son's right to be treated with respect is undermining you, then so be it. Guilty, as charged. Douglas has the right to love whomever he chooses. You have no say in the matter.'

'Oh, really.' He's no longer angry, just bloated with self-righteousness. 'Have you any idea what being *gay* will do to his prospects? Not to mention how it will impact on me! I worked tirelessly to create a ready-made career for him in the Dáil based on those values you so evidently despise. Why do you think my supporters elected him? They certainly didn't do so on the basis that you could entertain his so-called partner to *afternoon tea*.' He adds emphasis to the last two words with a languid flap of his wrist. 'You'll entertain him in this house over my dead body.'

'I'll entertain whoever I wish. You're my husband, not my custodian – not that I've ever experienced much difference between the two.'

He moves closer. He's losing control yet still aware that he needs me upright by his side until the campaign ends.

'What kind of wife are you?' he asks. 'A husk...' He pauses to allow his words to sink in. 'That's the best description I can come up with. I can't figure you out anymore. Where are you?' He clenches his fist and knocks his knuckles lightly against my forehead, a playful gesture with deadly intent. 'What's going on in that noggin of yours? I need your support, yet your mind is elsewhere the whole time.'

He's right, of course. I exist from one day to the next. If he mind-travelled with me he would see that I head in only one direction. She has captured my thoughts and the longing I feel when I think of my darling girl is my comfort as well as my ache.

# FORTY-TWO

## MARIA

Colin comes to me every day with my itinerary: interviews with the leading newspapers, walkabouts, visits to office blocks and factories, schools and hospitals. The interviews are as tedious as are the subjects I'm expected to consider. Who is my favourite fashion designer? Name my favourite food, book, play, television series? How will I transform the décor in Áras an Uachtaráin if Aloysius is elected?

When a WhatsApp message arrives from Shauna one night, I experience a shift in the atmosphere. It is the calm before the storm or, perhaps, the pause between a bolt of lightning and the clap of thunder.

> *Douglas asked me to give you a heads up. He and* Oisín *will be on* Hunter's Hour *shortly to speak about their relationship. He wants to be upfront with his constituents and create space between his aspirations and Aloysius's dogmatic views.*

The theme music is playing when I turn on the television. No need to tell Aloysius. The wide-screen television will be on in his office, where he's analysing the latest polls with this team.

I recognise Oisín O'Sullivan instantly from the husting I attended. A slightly built man with glasses and a receding hairline, he's smaller than Douglas, his head only reaching my son's shoulders, yet they look perfect together. He speaks quietly about the beginnings of their love story, which began when Douglas attended the launch of Oisín's debut novel. Two novels later, and a television series in the pipeline, he, like Douglas, has become used to publicity and looks at ease as they discuss their plans to marry.

I turn off the television and wait for Aloysius to emerge from his home office. His team leaves silently, no shouted goodbyes or bursts of laughter. The front door is closed quietly.

Earlier, they ordered pizzas and the kitchen is filled with empty plates. I load the dishwasher and clear away the scraps. I've finished tidying up when Aloysius enters, a glass of whiskey in his hand.

'I suppose Douglas told you in advance what he intended to do?' He raises his glass in a mock salute to me as he makes this accusation.

'No, he did not. I received a text from Shauna just as the interview was about to start.'

'How *very* kind of her.' His sarcasm has an alarming timbre. He's barely holding his temper in check. 'I hope you're proud of your sons. Between the two of them, they've destroyed my chances of winning the election. But I suppose you'll defend them to the hilt, like always.'

'That's exactly what I'll do. Someone needs to defend them against your violence and prejudice. Douglas never wanted to be a politician. But that wasn't your concern. You were determined to mould him to your image. You refused to acknowledge his right to be him—'

'I wanted to protect him.' His interruption demands my silence.

'That's a lie.' I refuse to allow his views to overwhelm me.

'You've never protected anyone other than yourself. But we're not going to have this conversation tonight. I'm tired and the post-mortem on our son's interview can wait until morning.' I slam the dishwasher door closed.

'You don't want me to win.' He's edgy, determined to spar.

'How can you say that? I'm working as hard as anyone else on the team to support you.'

'While conniving with my sons to ruin my reputation and the traditional family values I represent. Douglas is trending on social media. I hope you're happy now.'

'It's a long time since I've been happy, Aloysius. Why should now be any different?'

He ignores the inference, yet I see its effect: his rising flush and the lift of his shoulders. 'All I've ever asked from my family is loyalty and support. Not once, not even *once*, have you even *pretended* to believe I'll succeed.'

I should appease him. After all, it's my area of expertise. Kathryn Bryant's warning sounds in my ears but it's diminished by a raw, primal anger. 'You're wrong, Aloysius. I pretend as hard as anyone else that you'll win. But I'm not prepared to do so any longer. I hope you're defeated. It would be unbearable to live in a country that elected you as its president.' I'm filled with an unfamiliar recklessness and am unable to stop. 'Is that what you want to hear, or should I continue with the manufactured lies that hold our marriage together?'

He moves closer. No holds barred now. I reach towards the knife block but he's faster. My stomach takes the brunt, three blows that bring me to the floor. Instinctively, my body coils into a foetal position, as it did many times when I was carrying Belle in my womb. He walks from the kitchen without speaking.

I lock the door of the guest bedroom and lie down on the bed, turning my face into the pillow. This is the first time I've slept here since the night Cormac stayed with me. I think about the knot we formed as we lay together, limbs entwined, sated, a new life seeding.

Later, Aloysius pleads with me to allow him in. 'Please... please... I'm sorry... my dearest... please forgive me... we hurt each other tonight but we can get over this... don't you understand how much I love you...?'

I pull the duvet over my head to drown him out. Will he kick the door down? Is he aware that the sharpest knife from the block in the kitchen is under my pillow?

# FORTY-THREE

## MARIA

The pain in my stomach awakens me. It's sensitive and taut when I press my hand to it. Unable to remain in bed, I unlock the bedroom door. Aloysius is snoring in the next room. The scene from last night fills my mind. How dare he sleep so soundly after what he did to me?

I can't face breakfast. Even the thought of my normal morning coffee sickens me. I lock my office door behind me. This will be my sanctuary for the day. I listen to Gaby handling calls about adults behaving badly in public, a growing problem on New York streets, apparently. Such anger... I'm not able for it this morning. I turn her off and prepare the foundation's finances for a forthcoming audit. On the surface, the accounts seem balanced. Aloysius's terse assurances throughout the campaign that there was no need to worry appears to be true, yet I suspect something is hidden behind those figures. Not knowing the shape of it adds to my determination to find out what's going on.

I sit still when he knocks on the office door. He turns the handle a few times, his movements becoming more forceful. The lock holds.

'Maria, listen to me. I was overwrought last night and behaved appallingly. I'm deeply ashamed of myself. Come out, please. I'm worried about you. I want to know if you're okay.'

I ignore his cajoling. His words have always proved to be as empty as his promises and I endure them in silence until he runs out of apologies.

'I'm leaving now,' he says. 'Douglas has agreed to meet me. You're right about my attitude towards him and... and... Oisín.' He stumbles over the name, unable to control the bite in his tone. It warns me not to heed him. 'I intend to make peace with my sons,' he continues. 'Family is everything to me. I've allowed my ambition to overshadow that love. We must move on from last night. What you said was difficult to hear but I can't blame you for speaking your mind.'

What an effort it must take him not to lay the responsibility for his violence on me.

'My behaviour was unforgiveable yet forgiveness is what I beg

from you.' His pleas sound sincere, almost believable. 'I love you more than you can ever appreciate. This cannot be the end of us. I'll be back in the afternoon. *Please* welcome me home and tell me I'm forgiven.'

Eventually, when I refuse to respond, he walks away. Shortly afterwards, the front door is slammed. Unable to believe he's finally left, I check the window and watch his car until it disappears.

I need coffee, strong and black. Aloysius insists that I drink too much caffeine, saying it's the reason I'm so nervy all the time. In the kitchen I grind coffee beans. Halfway through, I switch off the machine, unable to breathe in an aroma I always enjoy. I feel nauseous. I brew a cup of herbal tea in the hope that it will ease the pressure in my abdomen.

Belle's disappearance modified his violence and reduced it to occasional outbursts when he was under extreme duress, or so he'd claim afterwards. But the threat has always been there, along with the awareness that there are other forms of cruelty. Not all are administered with a fist.

After drinking a cup of ginger tea, I decide to lie down and put a hot water bottle on my stomach. As I walk down the passageway towards the stairs, I notice a chink of light behind his office door. He always locks it whenever he goes out, convinced that the number of people who come in and out of the house are a threat to his privacy. There must have been too much guilt on his mind to remember to do so this morning.

I push open the door. His computer is still on. The screen lights up when I hit the keyboard. We share the *Foundation Donations* file. After a quick check, it's clear that his figures tally with mine. I open a second file titled *Campaign Donations.* A close examination of these accounts prove that I was right to be suspicious: Aloysius has corrected the discrepancies I'd noticed in my earlier inspections and has replaced the missing foundation funds with money from his donations account. Once the audit is complete, he'll plunder that account again and will transfer the funds he needs back to his campaign account.

The pain under my ribs has become sharp and persistent. I breathe shallowly as I copy the second file onto a USB flash drive that I find in my office. While it's downloading, I notice an onscreen album of photographs from the *Red Tape Unreeled* project. I study one of Douglas with his arm around Gaby. How vibrant they look, how happy. A picture paints a thousand lies. My eldest son is still unaware of what Gaby unconsciously stirred in him. Familial love, as equally passionate as it is destructive.

I recognise a copy of the newspaper clipping Gaby showed me on that fateful night in Clognua hospital. I stare blankly at the screen, unable for an instant to believe what's in front of my eyes. Restoration work has been done on the original photo of Cormac with Aloysius and the other politicians, if the improved clarity is any indication. I enlarge the image. Could Aloysius have his own copy, a piece of archive material he unearthed for research purposes? Much as I wish to believe that was the case, I know this photograph came from only one source. This realisation is terrifying, as is the knowledge that it has been photoshopped.

Technology has brought Cormac from the shadows into the light. This newer image shows him on his own, his face so distinct that I can make out the faint lines around his eyes. His close-cropped hair is startlingly recognisable, as is the direct gaze our daughter inherited. My horror increases as I come upon other photographs that have also been altered. Cormac's face has been positioned next to an image of Gaby. The sheen of perspiration on my forehead oozes into my eyes. It's possible for a blurred instant to believe I've mistaken the next configuration. I blink hard and see it clearly again. One single photograph. Three faces side by side, mine in the centre, Gaby to my left, Cormac to my right.

My heart is beating too fast. I touch my chest, convinced I'll feel its painful throb. What thoughts went through Aloysius's mind as he studied us? Three faces with distinctive features yet with identifiable similarities.

Clognua, that must be where he discovered Gaby's secret. He followed her to return her wallet. I remember how he questioned me about what we'd been discussing when he'd arrived so unexpectedly to the hospital.

'We were talking about Belle,' I'd told him. 'That's hardly surprising when you devoted tonight's podcast to her. Gaby became emotional. Considering she lost both parents within the last year, that's understandable.'

I thought he believed me. Such a foolish assumption to make. He'd searched Gaby's wallet and found the spark that began her search. But, surely, that would not be enough for him to leap to the conclusion he's laid bare on the screen?

I notice an app titled *Permeation Safety Core*. Opening it, I realise the contents of the phones belonging to the *Red Tape Unreeled* team were downloaded onto this app. This was done on the same day as details of Aloysius's plan to run in the presidential election was leaked on social media. The same day I collapsed and, later that night, was reunited with my daughter.

Perhaps, if I wasn't in such pain, I could figure out how to access the material on the app. Somewhere within that maze of information, Aloysius has found enough evidence to piece together my relationship with Gaby and the only man I ever loved.

How has he contained all that rage until it finally ran out last night?

I remove the USB flash drive and shove it into a pocket in my trousers. The room is moving, a dizzying swirl that rushes bile to my mouth. It tastes of iron. Something is wrong. This is not fear or panic, though I'm experiencing both. I remember the sensation that came over me in Clognua during Aloysius's press conference. The belief that everything around me was falling away. This is similar but worse. I close down the computer and hold on to his desk to steady myself when I stand.

Pain jolts though me with every step I take. I manage to leave his office door slightly ajar, just as I'd found it.

I must warn Gaby. I need a phone number for her. If I ring NY Eyz will they give it to me? Jonathan said he'd called to see her. Would he have it? The floor is moving, waltzing me towards the hall chair and landing me between its winged arms.

The blows I received last night must have injured my stomach internally. I need an ambulance. Help must arrive before Aloysius returns.

I call the emergency number. My knees threaten to give way. I hold tightly to the wall as I make my way to the front door. A glimpse at my reflection in the hall mirror confirms my fears. My skin is waxen and sweaty, my face scrunched with pain.

Aloysius stands outside. A monster with a bouquet of flowers in his hand and an apologetic grimace. He drops them when he sees me and catches me in his arms. I reach for his eyes when he tries to carry me back into the house but I'm too weak to struggle.

And then, thank God, an ambulance comes into view, the siren keening. He's too late to hide the evidence of his brutality. I'm safe in other hands, gentle hands that lay me down and help me to breathe. Doors slam.

Aloysius sits beside my stretcher as I'm driven away from the house where my past is exposed on a computer screen. I should scream and demand that he be removed from my sight. My mouth opens but I'm soundless, muted through pain and the belief that I'm about to die. His face fades into a blurred grey sphere yet I know he's still there, his unblinking stare warning me... warning... warning...

# FORTY-FOUR

## GABRIELLE

In the Lucky Black Cat, diners are discussing the snow forecast. Sophy brings me my usual breakfast and gives me a thumbs up. 'You handled this morning's fireworks well. I didn't know you were such a lefty leprechaun.' She grins and hurries on to the next table.

It seemed like such a simple question to ask my listeners. How had the word "woke" turned from its affirming origins to become a mocking, pejorative term? Opinions were divided and heated enough to scald my ears.

I sip my coffee and think about Douglas Russell and his partner Oisín O'Sullivan. The courage it must have taken them to speak about their relationship on *Hunter's Hour*.

'Did you know about Oisín O'Sullivan?' I'd asked Killian when I caught up with the interview on playback.

'Of course,' he'd replied. 'But it was never a story in the print media until Douglas made it one.'

The interview has been trending on social media. As Killian said, Douglas has made his sexuality into a news story and the press is concentrating on his father's reaction. How does his son's public disclosure tie in with the slogan Aloysius has been using on the election campaign: *Reclaim our Right to Traditional Family Values*?

I sit by the window in the Black Cat and watch a flotilla of clouds stream by. I'm still nervous, watchful, my eyes constantly sweeping over the customers. It took weeks before I had the courage to come back here and sit alone. Sophy is my guardian, aware of the identities of those who come and go from her diner. When I finish, a cab driver will take me to my apartment where Zac or one of the tenants will walk with me to my door.

Killian rings to begin our first conversation of the day. Sometimes these are short, snatched moments when we have a time break that suits us both. Our longer conversations are reminiscent of our teenage years when everything we did was significant enough to be discussed.

As soon as I hear his voice, I know the news is bad.

'It's Maria,' he says. 'She's had an accident in her car and been taken into hospital.'

'Oh my god... my *god*. Please don't tell me she's seriously injured—?'

'She braked too hard in a traffic jam and took a blow in her stomach from the steering wheel,' he says. 'According to Shauna, she damaged her spleen.'

'When did this happen?'

'Yesterday.'

'Are you sure she's going to be okay?'

'Calm down, Gaby. Shauna says they're hopeful she'll make a full recovery. She should be back on the campaign trail by next week.'

A steering wheel to the stomach. Could it do that much damage? I remember swerving to avoid crashing into Maria on the afternoon I visited Beech Park and the blow I took to my head. I've no reason to be suspicious yet I sense there's more to what Killian has revealed. I question him further and he reluctantly tells me that she suffered internal bleeding.

'I'll ring as soon as I've any further word on Maria,' he promises. 'Believe me, she's going to be fine.'

Maria's accident releases the mad dogs of social media. How could a woman who was such a careless driver expect to become a presidential wife? She'd been involved in a hit and run, caused a motorway pile-up, ran over a beloved cat, and been arrested for drunk driving. On and on they go, each claim more ludicrous and vicious than the previous one.

Why didn't I guess something was wrong? A delayed reaction is turning me to jelly. My mother, who is never out of my mind, was in danger, yet I remained oblivious. What does that say about kinship? Frail links, unacknowledged, that's what's wrong.

# FORTY-FIVE

## MARIA

I still have my spleen. It was touch and go regarding its removal, according to Professor Dillon. A decision was made to repair the rupture and the internal bleeding is now under control. All I need to do is ensure I don't brake so suddenly in traffic that my stomach suffers the brunt of the steering wheel.

It's a regular cause of stomach injuries, apparently.

Professor Dillon doesn't add that such injuries can also happen in the privacy of one's home. Has that suspicion crossed his mind, or has he taken Aloysius's word about my brake-slamming episode at face value?

I remained in intensive care for two days. When I finally recovered my senses, Gaby's safety was my only concern.

'Absolutely not,' Aloysius said, when I asked for my phone. 'Too much stress. You need to rest and regain your energy.'

'All I want to do is check my emails—'

'Your emails can wait until you're well again.' His interruption was firm and deliberate.

'Are you refusing to give me my phone?' I gathered enough energy to shout at him.

'Of course not.' His tone was understanding, the one he

uses when he claims I'm being difficult. 'I'm simply obeying Professor Dillon's orders. It's important that you concentrate on your health, which is what you should be doing right now, instead of getting hot and bothered about a few emails.'

It's useless arguing with him. He's right about one thing. Being strong will be essential when I walk away from my marriage. That can't happen if I'm exhausted and shaky.

The tiredness is extreme, as is the pain from my surgery. All I can see when I close my eyes is the triptych of those three faces linked together by one undeniable fact.

Douglas left for Brussels as soon as I was deemed stable after surgery and Aloysius snatches moments from the campaign to visit me. He warns the nurses not to listen when I ask to borrow their phones; that social media is filled with speculation about my absence from the campaign and I mustn't be exposed to such drivel.

His visits are a warning and a taunt. No words are necessary to understand his intentions.

Four days after the operation, when I awaken from a doze, Jonathan is sitting by my bed. I've longed so much for his arrival that I'm convinced for an instant he's an illusion. Distinguishing between reality and fantasy is difficult when my mind is fevered with fear.

'I'd have come sooner,' he says. 'But Dad told me your accident wasn't serious. I only realised how ill you've been when I managed to contact Douglas between meetings.' He sighs, an exaggerated huff. 'What else do politician do besides sitting around tables and pretending they're saving the world?' His question is rhetorical. I make no attempt to answer it.

He's in a heightened state. I recognise the signs immediately. His childhood meltdowns come to mind. I blame myself for them: all that unresolved sorrow he must have absorbed in my womb.

'Does your father know you're here?' I ask.

'I haven't spoken to him since he called to tell me you were in hospital and could not be contacted. I can't believe he was so dismissive of your injuries. Tell me how it happened.'

'I slammed on the brakes—'

'Mum, no lies. You're one of the safest drivers I know.' He drums his fingers against the side of the chair. 'Did something happen with Dad?'

'No, of course not. I lost concentration and was forced to brake suddenly.'

He shrugs, probably unconvinced, and lets it drop. 'Douglas says you're rejoining the campaign as soon as you're discharged. You don't look in any condition to join that circus out there. You need time to recuperate.'

'The election will be over in two weeks. Then life will return to normal.' Another lie, smooth as honey, slides between us. I've tried to keep the truth from my sons. Nothing will be served by increasing the tension between them and Aloysius, but Jonathan's expression reveals an awareness of the true nature of his parents' marriage.

'*Normal?*' He tosses the word back at me. I'm affected by his jumpiness. Something else is wrong. Unlike Douglas with his urbane front, I always recognise the signs when Jonathan is burdened.

'What's bothering you? Apart from me being in hospital.'

'I'm worried about the foundation.' He comes straight to the point. 'Have you gone over your accounts recently?'

'As it happens, I did so on the day of my accident.' The foundation is the last thing I'd expected him to mention. 'Why are you asking?

'Are they in order?'

'What's this about, Jonathan? You've never been interested in the foundation before now.'

'*Are* they, Mum? Did you notice any discrepancies?' His insistence has a purpose.

I force my mind back to the day I discovered Aloysius's fraudulent accounting. The realisation that he was aware of Gaby's past, and mine, has pushed everything else into the background.

'Yes.' I nod slowly. 'Tell me what you've discovered.'

'Nothing, as yet. But I met Roy Doran in a bar soon after I moved to New York. He said he was over there to meet with doners to Dad's campaign. He was drunk, so it was hard to separate the verbiage from the facts.'

'What did Roy say?' I'm alert now, the haziness that had taken over my mind dissipating.

'He said something about your foundation being the biggest donor to his campaign, and the most untraceable one. Is everything okay with Isabelle's Quest? If not, as chair of the board, you'll be responsible for not exercising due diligence.'

Aloysius's arrivals are always unannounced. I've no time to waste or try and figure out what Roy was doing in New York. I haven't seen him for months now. Aloysius shrugs when I ask and says he's taking a break from the campaign. Something to do with his mother being ill or maybe it's his father. The idea of him being a link between Aloysius's well-heeled American doners is ridiculous. That is Niels Van Lingen's responsibility. A smooth professional with a financial background, Niels uses his charm to separate doners from their cash; unlike Roy, who would be more likely to use a cosh.

'Check the pockets in my trousers and see if you can find a flash drive.'

I point towards the hospital room's wardrobe where my clothes hang. It's possible I'm imagining the action I took in Aloysius's office. There is only one way to find out.

Jonathan does as I ask.

'No questions,' I say when he removes the flash drive. 'Take it with you and study it. Aloysius mustn't know it exists.'

'This is connected to your injury?' His glance rakes over my face and he nods, as if I've already confirmed his suspicions.

'I'm not prepared to talk about it now, Jonathan. I just need you to do as I say. Douglas says you've been in contact with Gaby Grace.'

'Gaby?' He sounds surprised. 'I was in her neighbourhood and dropped in to say hello.'

'I want you to meet her again. Give her a message from me. Tell her Aloysius is no longer in the dark.'

'What's that supposed to mean?' he asks. 'It sounds like a warning.'

'She'll understand.'

'Is she in some kind of trouble?'

'Jonathan, I'm asking you to trust me. Now leave before Aloysius discovers you're here.'

'You've always been a mystery to me.' He looks at me, his hands shoved deeply into his pockets. I can see his confusion and the struggle he's having with himself not to question me further. 'Okay, I'll do as you ask. I'm going back to New York tomorrow. This is just a flying visit, literally. I needed to see with my own eyes how you're doing.' He kisses my cheek and hurries from the ward.

*Aloysius is no longer in the dark.* Will she understand Jonathan's cryptic message? Will it alert her to the fact that the secret we share is hanging by the thread of tolerance, and the filaments are unravelling?

When they finally come apart, I've absolutely no idea what my husband will do. My only certainty is that his revenge on those who have deceived him will be merciless.

# FORTY-SIX

## GABRIELLE

Once again, Jonathan's arrival is unexpected. Not so late this time, he climbs the stairs to my apartment as twilight is falling. I unhook chains, slide the locks across, and allow him to carry the chill of a winter's evening into my self-imposed prison.

He's back from Ireland, a flying visit, literally an overnighter, he says. He was worried about Maria and needed to see for himself that she was okay.

''How is she?' I ask.

'She seemed fine.'

'*Seemed*?'

'I guess.' He shrugs, oblivious of my eagerness for detail, any detail, no matter how small. 'Hard to tell with her. Big smile, you know. Covers a multitude. Have you seen those ridiculous conspiracy theories about her accident?'

'Yes. They're appalling.'

'We live in a crazy world, Gaby.'

'Tell me about it. How much longer will she be in hospital?'

'A few more days and then she'll be campaigning again. *Madness*. My father's getting his own way, as usual.'

'She's strong, Jonathan. She'll cope.'

'I'm not so sure... ' He pauses, his expression uncertain. 'When you were working on those podcasts you must have got to know him fairly well. What did you think of him?'

I'm surprised by his directness. 'Jonathan, I can't answer that question with any accuracy.'

'But you must have formed an opinion,' he says. 'I'd like to hear it.'

'He's ambitious—'

'But is he honest?'

'Why do you ask?'

'It's something Roy Doran said a while back when I bumped into him in the Brazen Molly—'

'The pub on Fourth Avenue?' I'm surprised to discover that Roy has been in New York.

'That's the one.' Jonathan nods. 'He said stuff that bothered me about my father's campaign donations. When I mentioned that to Mum, she gave me a flash drive. She never explained why she had it with her in the hospital, but it contains financial information that will hang her out to dry if my father loses the election.' He scowls every time he mentions Aloysius. 'What Roy said is true.'

'What exactly did he say?'

'He was drunk so not a lot of it made sense. It only came back to me when Mum had her accident. Something about my father robbing Peter to pay Paul and she'd go ballistic if she discovered the truth.'

'Do you know what he meant?'

'Not then. Now that I've examined the flash drive, I understand what my father's been doing. Will you work with me on a podcast and expose the truth?'

'Do you realise what you're saying?' I'm shocked by his reckless disregard for his family's reputation.

'Yes.' His reply is unambiguous.

'Your father would be in serious trouble?' I know my

warning will fall on deaf ears, but I feel obliged to make him aware of what he'll unleash. 'He'd lose the election and probably go to prison.'

'That's my hope.' He sounds defiant and determined.

'Do you hate him that much?'

'And more,' he replies. 'You can't possibly understand—'

'Oh, but I do, Jonathan.' Interrupting him, I feel a barely controllable fury as I think of my own father.

He stops what he's about to say and observes me. 'I know I rubbished those podcasts you did with him. But you're good at what you do.'

'What would Maria think if she knew what you plan to do with that information?' I ask him.

'Why else would she hand it over to me?' He answers my question with another.

'You can't assume—' I begin before he speaks over me.

'She also asked me to pass on a message to you. What's this she said now?' He taps his forehead before he continues. 'Something about my father no longer being in darkness... no... in the dark. Yes, that's it. She said he's no longer in the dark. Does that make any sense to you?' He sounds bemused by the message he's just delivered. 'She was still in a state of shock after her surgery so I'm not sure if she was fully cognisant.'

Oh, yes, she was. Maria knew exactly what she was saying. A warning. Don't ignore it. Aloysius has discovered my identity. How has that happened? How has he reacted? I can't bear to think about it. I link my fingers and flex my hands so that they are rock steady when I ask the next question.

'Is Roy Doran still in New York?'

'Far as I know. Douglas said my father has a new security guard.'

'When did you meet Roy?'

'Sometime before Christmas... no, it was earlier. Probably

mid-November.' He hesitates before continuing. 'Are you okay? Did I say something to upset you?'

'I'm fine, Jonathan. Just under pressure at work.' I grapple with an incredulous suspicion. I dismiss it instinctively yet immediately circle back to it.

'Don't overdo it, Gaby,' warns Jonathan. 'This city can hack the insides out of you if you're not careful.'

I fight the urge to hold on to him. My adopted city has not hacked out my insides. It took an intruder with silent footsteps to do so.

'Will you work with me on the podcast?' Jonathan asks.

'I'll work with you but not on a podcast. I want you to contact Killian Ormond.'

'The *Bayview* journalist?'

'Political editor. He has clout.'

'What makes you think he'd give my mother favourable coverage?'

'I'll be with him every step of the way. You have my word for it.' The ground is shifting under me and resettling on a solid foundation.

He nods. 'Your word is good enough.' He ignores my outstretched hand when he's leaving and hugs me. 'I'll be back in touch after I've spoken to Killian.'

When I'm alone again, the locks secure, I open my wallet and take out the newspaper clipping. I haven't looked at it since Clognua. I was delirious that night, consumed with thoughts of Maria. Now, looking back, I recall the sudden stab of fear I felt when Aloysius returned my wallet. Later, I'd checked the side flap to see if the newspaper clipping was still there. Why had I felt the need to do that? Was it an unconscious dread I've never acknowledged until now?

I've examined the clipping so often that the paper has thinned on the folds. It has been refolded in a different way and there is a slight tear on one of the seams. Someone else has handled it.

Only one name comes to mind.

*Aloysius is no longer in the dark.*

My father is a shadow in that photograph. A smudge that Aloysius would have long forgotten under different circumstances. The clipping trembles in my hand. I hear a creak on the stairs and collapse to my knees.

It's Zac, home from his show with gossip and doughnuts. I rise slowly, too frightened to feel foolish, and unlock my door.

I've been in the Brazen Molly on several occasions. An Irish pub, it has the usual congenial atmosphere, the fake bric-a-brac that reflects an Ireland long vanished, good food and Guinness.

It's late afternoon and the pub is quiet as it waits for the offices to empty.

'The calm before the storm,' says Justin, the only barman on duty.

I order a sparkling water and ask him to add three ice cubes and a slice of lime. Cassie will always remain just a tap away from my shoulder. In time, I hope that tap will become kinder, gentler.

Justin is Irish. County Clare, he says as he shakes my hand. Ten years in the Big Apple and still searching for the great American dream.

I show him a group photograph I took on my phone when I was making the *Red Tape Unreeled* podcasts. I enlarge Roy's image. Unlike the rest of us, he isn't smiling, the line of his clenched lips in keeping with his cantankerous expression. His sleeves are rolled up, even though it was a cold morning. Freckled, muscular arms folded over his chest.

'Can't say I recognise him,' says Justin. 'I only started here a month ago. But I wouldn't like to bump into him on a dark night. Sorry if I'm insulting a friend of yours.'

'He's no friend of mine. But I'm anxious to trace him.'

'Are you a cop?' He leans his elbows on the bar and cups his chin in his hands.

'No. I work in radio. I'm interested in interviewing him for NY Eyz.'

'Thought I recognised your name. You're *the* Gaby Grace.'

'Guilty, as charged.' I allow myself to smile, even though small talk is the last thing on my mind.

'You've a right mouth on you but I like what you do.' He grins and nods approvingly. 'Tell you what. I'll give you my cell number and you send me that photo. I'll check with the other bar staff. See if they remember him. He's got a mug on him they're not likely to forget.'

I remember Roy standing outside the hospital on the night I visited Maria. Shadowing Aloysius, he blended into the darkness, and, later, in the hotel bar, he bid us goodnight in order to get his 'beauty sleep'. An unusual joke from a man with such a taciturn personality.

His accent – I hear it again. Only this time he's not joking when he shouts at Wayne to call off his 'fuckin' animal'.

The echo of his words shivers along my spine and prickles my skin in goosebumps. Is it possible to take a gigantic leap from one boulder to another without slipping, especially when my head is spinning? Such a ferocious leap is bound to make it spin, particularly the notion that it was Roy Doran who had his hands around my neck. When that was not enough to end my life, he came to my apartment to finish the job.

My breathing is fast and shallow, as it was on the night he pressed a pillow to my face.

. . .

Justin rings in the evening. He checked the files on the security cameras. Roy Doran spent five successive nights in November drinking in the Brazen Molly. Two of the dates coincide with my attacks.

'Thanks, Justin.' Strange to be able to speak so casually when I can still feel Roy Doran's fingers clogging my throat with dread.

# FORTY-SEVEN

## GABRIELLE

An interesting fact about the twins is that they have distinct handwriting. Susanne's slants to the left and Jessica's scrawl tends to the right. I can't remember either of them ever writing to me. Texts and WhatsApp's are our usual means of communication. I'm surprised find an airmail envelope with Susanne's handwriting in my mailbox when I return from my morning show.

Her letter is brief.

*Hi Gaby,*

*Jessica and I are finally sorting out Mum's stuff. We found this enclosed letter in the wash bag she used whenever she stayed at the Ashford Clinic. It's from Dad and is unopened, despite being stamped – it was never sent to you, for whatever reason. I hope it won't upset you, but I know you'd want to have it.*

*Visit soon. We saw too little of you at Christmas, though Jessica and I both agree that your time in Trabawn was well spent... Ha ha and nudge nudge, wink wink...*

*Love and hugs and kisses from us all,*

*Susanne xxx*

An enclosed airmail envelope had been stamped, ready to be posted. Why was it never sent to my apartment? I tear the envelope open.

The letter consists of eight pages, all numbered. According to the date, it was written three weeks before my father's death. His handwriting was shaky but still legible.

I read it to the end before replacing it carefully back in the envelope.

I never used to cry. Pride and defiance prevented me from doing so when I was a teenager. When I believed Lucas had broken my heart and was unaware that fractures heal, I refused to shed a tear. My father's confession and Cassie's haunted past have undone me. Nowadays, tears are never far away. I shed them with the same fierceness as I did on the night Maria explained to me the dangers that would follow the owning of our relationship.

I dry my eyes and wash my face. Anger rushes through my grief. I allow it to ignite and flare. In this instant, I understand the urge that causes people to commit murder.

I don't ring Freida – the nurse who looked after my father in his final weeks – until the afternoon, when I've had time to cool down. I leave a message on her voice mail. An hour later, she returns my call. She speaks quietly, a hushed tone that suggests she's on night duty.

'I can't talk for long,' she says. 'I'd have left it until tomorrow to contact you but you sounded distressed. What's wrong?'

'I'm having a bad day, Freida, and am feeling very emotional about my father.'

'That's not surprising, Gaby. You've had a difficult time. How can I help you?'

'He wrote to me a few weeks before he died. Do you remember him doing so?'

'Let me think.' She pauses. Back home, night has fallen. Music is playing in the background, a gentle rhythm that might be easing another patient along their final path. 'Yes, now that you mention it, I recall having it stamped in Trabawn post office and posting it,' she says. 'Why do you ask?'

'I'd like to thank you for obliging him. The letter was important and meant a lot to me.'

'To Dominick, also. He was anxious that you receive it as soon as possible.'

'You were so kind to him. We can never thank you enough. I know you're with a patient, so I won't delay you any longer.'

After finishing the call, I read his letter again. The words are familiar to me by now, yet they still wrench my heart. Cassie must have called into the post office and stopped it. No other explanation is possible.

Aoife Shine, who shared a desk with me in primary school, runs the post office in Trabawn. Too late to ring her now. I'll contact her as soon as my show ends tomorrow morning.

'I heard you were home for Christmas,' Aoife says, when I ring her from the Lucky Black Cat. 'And that you and Killian Osborne have got it together at last.'

'The Trabawn drumbeat must be as active as ever.' I fall into the familiar cadences of my Kerry accent.

'Rat-a-tat... rat-a-tat! You and Killian got the drum solo.' She laughs and excuses herself to serve a customer. I hear them talking in the background. It's raining in Trabawn and there's a traffic snarl-up on Burly's Head.

'Sorry for keeping you.' Aoife is back again. 'What can I help you with?'

'I'm ringing on the off chance that you might remember a letter my father wrote to me shortly before he died. He gave it to Freida Williams. She went to school with us—'

'Yes, I remember Freida. She's with the hospice now.'

'That's right. She looked after my father and promised to post his letter. It was never sent, even though it was airmail stamped.'

'It must be the one Cassie took back.' Aoife sounds thoughtful. 'She was lucky as Billy was just emptying the post box when she arrived. She needed to add something to it. Are you telling me you never received it?'

'No, I didn't. But the twins found it among Cassie's possessions. I guess she forgot to post it.'

'Poor Cassie. It's hard to believe she's also gone from us.'

'Thanks, Aoife. And thanks also for your help.'

It's snowing outside. A blizzard riding on the wind and tossing the trees. How fitting that the elements are in tune with my fury. So much is clear now. No more missing pieces.

And then, as if to contradict this assertion, Justin phones me from the Brazen Molly.

# FORTY-EIGHT

## MARIA

Killian Osmond's arrival into my hospital room takes place just before the evening visits end. He must know that Aloysius is spending the night in Cork and Douglas is working late in the *Dail*. Otherwise, he would not be here, smiling as if it was the most natural thing to visit me. He must intend to check my condition and report it to the nation.

Unlike me, he seems relaxed in a slim-fitting dark blue suit and an open-necked white shirt. Sunglasses are shoved into his wheat-blond hair and his disarming smile reminds me to be on my guard. I've always been suspicious of him. All I ever saw was a man intent on harming my family. What a fool I was not to accept that the harm came from within.

'Gaby sent me,' he says before I can speak. 'She received your message and asked me to make contact with you.'

I try to speak but the words won't come.

'Can you pretend that I'm doing an interview with you if a nurse comes in?' he asks.

I nod. 'Is everything all right with... with my... with Gaby?'

He places a recording device on the trolley beside the bed but makes no effort to switch it on.

'You're a remarkable woman, Mrs Russell—' His voice drops a notch as he sits down and leans towards me.

'Maria, please. And there's nothing remarkable about me.'

'I beg to differ. You're every bit as remarkable as your daughter.'

I allow the significance of what he said to sink in. Lurid headlines swim before my eyes. The splash they will make, the judgements and condemnations that will follow. They will also spell the ruination of Aloysius's presidential hopes. This thought brings little comfort. My husband's ambitions are insignificant compared to the impact this information and its revelation will have on my sons.

'Did Gaby tell you?' I don't have the will or the desire to deny what he said.

'She confided in me, yes.'

I take comfort from the word 'confide' but perceptions die hard. Even now, knowing that he has become the keeper of our secret, I'm afraid of his power to expose me.

'How well do you know Gaby?' I ask.

'Well enough to marry her if she agrees,' he replies. 'Will I have to ask your permission first?'

So, there it is. I know so little about her life and even less about his, apart from the fact that Shauna Ross was in love with him until recently. She understood from the beginning that becoming involved with a political journalist was risky, but she was upfront with Douglas when she and Killian moved in together. We never worried that she would cross the line and mix politics with pleasure. She was professional but also ambitious, as she made clear when she decided to run as a candidate in the next council election. That decision ended her relationship with Killian, or so she told us. I'd always suspected there was a deeper reason. That reason is sitting in front of me now, his composure marred by a rush of colour to his cheeks.

'Gaby and I go back a long way,' he says. 'We were engaged

when we were teenagers. Then circumstances changed and sent us in different directions.'

I've a lifetime of information to discover about my daughter, but now my only concern is to find out why she revealed our secret to one of the most meticulous journalists in the media.

'Your son Jonathan has been in touch with me,' he says. 'On Gaby's advice, he passed on some interesting information that you'd gathered about your husband's campaign funds.'

I nod at him to continue when he pauses, as if waiting for me to elaborate on the reasons why I don't trust my husband.

'I've enough information to destroy him with an exposé.' He states this with conviction. 'Would you be prepared to work with me on making that a reality?'

'Aloysius would have you in court for defamation before you could draw breath.' I dismiss his suggestion, knowing how capable my husband is of pulling powerful strings. 'And I desperately need to contact Gaby. He knows the truth about her.'

I can still feel the force of his blows, his watchfulness, even when he's away from me.

Killian checks his laptop bag and removes an envelope. 'Gaby understood the message you sent with Jonathan.' His head is close to mine as he hands the envelope to me. 'She has a more important story to tell. She asked me to place it in your hands.'

He waits until I open the envelope and remove what looks like photocopied sheets of paper stapled together.

'She has the original letter,' he says. 'Dominick wrote it shortly before his death. It was never sent and only came into her possession recently.'

I turn the pages. The handwriting, though quavery and faint, is instantly recognisable. Killian uses the name 'Dominick' with easy familiarity but he will always be Cormac to me. He wrote to me once after he was refused permission to visit Beech Park again. I was surprised by the quality of his handwriting. In an institution where kindness was a forgotten cause, someone had taken time to teach him good penmanship.

Eight pages are filled with his words. I'm weakened by the betrayal that he laid out in such stark terms.

What am I to do with this knowledge of an act so cruel that it is impossible for me to comprehend the mind who planned it, then carried it out with such meticulous care?

Killian Osmond leaves as quietly as he arrived. I fold the letter and slide it under my pillow. Am I imagining its heat penetrating the cushioned depths or is it my own anger that ignites the room and makes it almost impossible to breathe? A nurse enters with a phone and hands it to me. Aloysius finally has a moment to spare. He will be with me tomorrow as soon as he returns to Dublin.

He arrives this afternoon with a box of chocolates for the nurses, and a photographer he's hired to show the nation that I'll soon be ready to return to the campaign trail.

His arm has the unyielding pressure of iron when he lands it across my shoulders. We smile at the camera... *Easy peasy...*

Today, we're dining with business groups. Later, we'll tour a factory and visit a hospital. Pain killers help. Aloysius insisted that a walking stick would signify an infirmity and I must leave it at home. With only a week to go before the election, the pace is frenetic. Aloysius has no difficulty keeping up with it. This is his world, one that demands stamina, ruthlessness, and a bag of dirty tricks. Roy's absence has made him even more on edge than usual. Like-minded, the rough and the smooth, they operated a discreet war of attrition on those who dared to stand in their way. Roy's decision to drop out of the campaign remains as mysterious as his sudden disappearance.

The other candidates have not fared well during this final stage. Caroline Slone has been heavily criticised for supporting the annexing of an empty business premises in her student days and turning it into a homeless shelter. Jack Blake has gained an equal amount of odium and support for his critical stance on immigration. Edward Kinsella is reputed to have a mistress hidden in a mews. All efforts to find her have come to naught, but that hasn't stopped the speculation on social media.

In a hospital, where Aloysius is visiting the sick in a recently revamped ward, I'm served tea and sandwiches by an efficient woman with a food trolley and the name *Trudy* embroidered on the pocket of her uniform. She says she will vote for Aloysius. The slogan '*Reclaim our Right to Traditional Family Values*' carries a strong message, she believes. When I ask her to use one word to describe what it means to her, she says, 'Security.'

How comforting that sounds. I'd like to tell her that the security she seeks does not exist when it's promised by a man with feet of clay. If Aloysius wins this election, he'll imprison me in grandeur and silence me with his fists.

Snatches of Cormac's letter have created an echo. One that replicates his voice when it was soft with love for me.

> *If I'd succeeded in falling out of love with Maria, then, maybe, I could go to my grave content to remain silent. Ignorance is bliss or so we're told, yet we're also expected to believe that the truth can set us free. Forgive me, Gaby, but I must tell you that my real name is Cormac Gallagher and Maria Russell is your mother. Oh, my darling child, I feel your shock. It will be*

*followed by anger and outrage but please... please read on and try to understand the decision I made.*

By sending me this letter, my daughter has pulled the pin on a bomb that has been primed for twenty-nine years. As yet, neither of us can tell where the shrapnel will land.

# FORTY-NINE

## GABRIELLE

I stand between two police officers in a morgue. Frozen in death, Roy Doran looks as menacing as he did in life. I picture him stumbling from my apartment, dazed and disoriented in unfamiliar surroundings. He'd walked as far as a vacant site designated for renewal and still waiting for work to begin. He must have stepped into the path of an oncoming car and, dressed as he was in black, he would have been difficult to see in a badly lit area of wasteland.

Justin had mentioned my visit to Melanie, the owner of the Brazen Molly. She was on holidays for two weeks in November during which time Roy would have been in her bar. In the hope that someone would identify the victim, the police had released an artist's impression of his face to the hospitality sector. When Justin showed her Roy's photograph, she'd contacted the police after noticing similarities between it and the artist's impression.

'Time is running out for him,' one of the officers tells me. 'If you don't recognise him, he'll have to go unnamed into the ground.'

Under ordinary circumstances, this unidentified man would have been buried in Potters' Field on Hart Island. But a search is still ongoing for the hit and run driver. The officers believe the driver stopped to rob him of his phone and any other form of ID, or else an opportunistic passerby did so.

All that was left in his pockets was a ski mask.

In the weeks that followed his second attack, I'd waited for him to strike again. Third time lucky. The reason it didn't take place lies before me now. Those sleepless nights and panicked days, waiting for footsteps behind me, an arm around my neck, had left their mark on me. Invisible, admittedly, unlike the blow to the side of Roy's face. It disfigured his cheek, and his blackened eyelid added to the damage Zac inflicted on him with his baseball bat. An action that saved my life but could easily implicate Zac if the police decided that a crime of grievous bodily harm resulting in Roy's accidental death had been committed.

I shake my head when the officers ask if I can name him. Let him lie in an unidentified grave, as Paddy Murdock does. I'm not going to involve Zac in the unfolding mystery of my existence.

Does his disappearance haunt Aloysius Russell as the campaign draws to a close? Do the secrets they shared plague him? Does he fear that one day Roy will sell them to the highest bidder? Has he hired another killer, one tasked with the responsibility of silencing me? My friends wrapped me in a blanket of security. Their vigilance kept me safe. Now, the time has come to venture into the open again and confront the truth.

Esther from Flatbush rings when I announce that this is my last *Gaby's Good Morning Wake-up*. She praises me for my integrity, humour, empathy and radio presence. The word 'leprechaun' is never mentioned.

Sophy from Bed-Stuy comes on to wish me well and insist that I call into the Lucky Black Cat for a final serving of delicious pancakes with bacon and maple syrup. I allow her the free advertising space. She deserves it.

Emily has finally accepted my resignation. She argued that I was still suffering from post-traumatic stress and was not in a fit state to make important decisions.

'I fully appreciate the impact the attacker has had on your mental state,' she said. 'NY Eyz would be more than willing to cover your treatment. You're going places here. It would be a shame to give up your career without looking at the options available to help you.'

'It's not PTS,' I assure her. 'It's a family matter that needs sorting out.'

'We can give you a leave of absence to do so.'

'Thank you, but no. Apart from my family, long-distance relationships are too difficult.'

'All relationships are difficult,' she replied. 'You try relating to three teenagers who believe I've colonised their home and brain-washed their father. Honestly, Gaby, I can never see us becoming a family. We're not shaped for it.'

'Families don't come in standardised shapes,' I replied. 'It'll work out if you give it a chance. I'm sure it will.'

In fact, I'm not sure of anything. Except that I need to talk to my mother.

This time when we meet there is no hesitation. Killian has provided cover for us by way of a secluded meeting room in *Bayview Dispatch*, and we can hold each other for as long as it takes.

Maria is thin and fragile. Pain has etched deeper lines on her face. I see them beneath the make-up that is applied each morning and afternoon by a skilled beautician. Outwardly, she sparkles; inwardly, she burns. I feel her heat, savour it, share it.

Maria and I accept that DNA tests are unnecessary, but

those we love will need that assurance when we reveal the truth. This time there is no agonising wait for the results. We are in no doubt about the bond that binds us and when the affirmation arrives, we know the hour is drawing nigh.

I take a flight from Dublin into Kerry airport, where Jessica picks me up. Like Emily, she's astonished that I've quit my job... *again*.

'Did Killian force you to choose?' she asks, in a charged tone. 'That's not something I'd stand for.'

Susanne told me on the quiet that Nicholas wants another baby and a full-time wife at home. That a sea-faring man needs his comforts when he comes ashore. Trouble in the love nest, apparently.

'This has nothing to do with Killian,' I reply. 'It concerns us, as a family.'

'*Really*. What's up?'

'It's something that's very important to me but I want to wait 'til Susanne is with us.'

'Okay, then.' She smiles and casts a covert look at my stomach as she presses harder on the accelerator.

My nephews are sleeping. A text from Susanne warns Jessica not to ring the doorbell. We enter quietly through the back door.

'Gaby has news for us.' Jessica switches on the kettle and nods at her twin. They communicate by their usual telepathic powers and Susanne's gaze settles immediately on my stomach. I ache for them. If only I *was* telling them that they would soon become aunts. Instead, I'm about to detonate everything they took for granted about their parents.

My nephews sleep through this agonising revelation. Their

mothers' faces are ashen, and taut with the same disbelief I first experienced when I discovered my true identity. They interrupt me constantly, incredulity turning to outrage, denial and agonised questions. I don't add to their shock by telling them about Paddy Murdock. Let Cassie rest in peace. I owe her that much.

Bit by bit, they quieten down. I see them joining dots as they begin to understand their mother's anger and anxieties, her need to drink, the arguments she picked with me, the rage she displayed when our father upset her, and, tragically, her reaction to the photograph that led to her death. I show them the DNA results and, finally, my father's letter.

No longer able to deny the evidence therein, they are in tears by the end of it. We come together then, united in grief. A circle of sisters who share a bristling secret that has the power to destroy or redeem us.

Josh is the first to cry and is closely followed by Michael. My sisters hold their sons a little closer. I can tell from their expressions that they are imagining the void that would await them should they awaken from dreams to find an empty cot.

# FIFTY

## MARIA

Tonight is the last debate and the most important one. With only three days to go before the election, Aloysius's campaign team is cautiously optimistic. The polls have turned in favour of him. To his surprise, the reaction to Douglas after his appearance on *Hunter's Hour* has been mainly positive. Our son has been praised for his openness and integrity. The efforts of journalists to report on a schism between father and son has failed to gain traction and Aloysius, holding his finger to the wind as usual, takes every opportunity to be photographed beside Douglas. Seeing them together, relaxed and smiling to the outward eye, it's difficult to believe they haven't spoken civilly to each other since Christmas Day.

The debate, chaired by Gemma Hunter, begins. The audience has been vetted in advance. No chance of a sudden interruption.

Each candidate has three minutes for a personal presentation before the debate becomes a battleground. Aloysius is at his finest, confident and knowledgeable, able to answer each point made. He makes his audience laugh, while the others are too intent on giving the right answer, rather than the true one, to relax.

My nails make indents in my skin. Yesterday, Jonathan returned from New York at my behest. I gathered my sons around me and showed them a photocopy of the letter Cormac attempted to send to Gaby, their half-sister.

I wished they were still children, and I could rock away their distress. As it was, I could only watch their changing expressions as they read the pages that Cormac Gallagher had painfully filled with his distinctive flourishes.

'This can't possibly be true.' Jonathan was the first to speak when he finished the last page. 'Tell me this is some kind of *obscene* joke?'

Douglas, who was holding the letter, folded it carefully before laying it on the table and resting his hands on it. 'How long have you known?' he asked. If he was shocked by what he'd read he showed no signs of it, apart from a nerve twitching on his temple. The same genetic tic as his father, but his face seemed cast in stone as he waited for my answer.

'Since Clognua,' I replied. 'Do you remember when I collapsed...?' I struggled to think my way through the questions they would ask. 'Gaby was sitting beside you, Jonathan, and you looked so alike. The thought that Gaby could be Belle... that she could be your sister... it came at me like a blast, and I collapsed from its force. I'd no memory of that instant when I recovered consciousness.'

I had to stop to control my breath. Jonathan filled a glass with water and handed it to me. Neither of them spoke as I described the unbelievable night in Clognua hospital when I realised that I had become whole again.

'How could *anyone* inflict such pain on another person...?' Jonathan stopped, as if lost for words. His face was drawn tight with shock, each feature finely defined. Once again, I could see those essential similarities between him and Gaby. 'I can't take it in... I simply *can't*... I wish her father was still alive and I could tell him how I feel.' He was close to tears, but it was anger that glittered in his eyes.

'Do you believe his letter is genuine?' I asked Douglas.

'Yes, I do.' Douglas nodded and slid it into an inside pocket in his jacket. 'It explains why I was drawn to Gaby from the beginning. She filled something that was missing within me. There's no other way I can explain it. When I talked to Oisín about her, he almost got it right – he called her my "soul sister".'

'Jonathan, what do you think?' I asked my youngest son.

'I believed she was a ghost when I was child,' he replied. 'A ghost who was determined to overshadow me, no matter what I did to please you.' He struggled to elaborate on his initial reaction to Gaby. 'I had that same crazy sensation when I met her first. Call it jealousy, resentment, whatever. It makes sense now in a weird way. What happened to her and to us was not just criminal, it was *evil*.'

'Are you ready for the reaction if this letter goes public?' I ask them. 'The media will be all over it.'

Douglas nods. No doubting his determination. He is used to the scourge of publicity, but I'm not so sure Jonathan will be able to handle it.

But Jonathan's reply is as firm as his brother's response. 'We don't have any other option. Belle never was a ghost. It's time I allowed her to breathe.'

The debate is nearing its conclusion. On the podiums, the fixed smiles on the candidates' faces hide the relief they must be feeling that no one has stumbled irrevocably into a trap. Gemma Hunter has conducted the debate impartially. She was quick to rein in anyone who spoke for too long or insisted on shouting their opinions.

This release of tension is not being experienced by the studio audience. The stir they make is barely perceptible at first, yet the vibration of an undercurrent running through them is beginning to strengthen.

The couple sitting in front of me have already taken out their mobile phones. Their screens light up. Everyone was ordered to either switch off or mute their phones before the debate started. Undaunted by this expressed wish from the producer, the ripple effect is spreading. I feel the tingling in my fingertips and along the length of my arms. My breath shortens and my sons, sitting on either side of me, must be equally transfixed by this unfolding drama.

Heads are bent, screens flashing. No one appears to be paying attention to Gemma, who is asking each candidate about the first decision they will make if elected. She signals to Edward Kinsella, who's outlining the many successful decisions he made as president, to be quiet, and touches her earpiece. The candidates look puzzled, aware that they have lost their studio audience, and that Gemma is being fed information from her producer.

'This is a news flash,' she announces. 'We've just received incredible information that we have verified and found to be correct.' She speaks urgently, aware that she needs to draw her audience away from their phones and back to her. 'Isabelle Russell has been found.'

Two red spots have appeared on her cheeks. She must know that the information she's delivered to the audience, and to the nation, could turn out to be a hoax – or the most earth-shattering revelation she will ever make.

Aloysius is captured in the glare of a camera. No time for masking. His full-on expression is transfixed with... what? Fear, certainly; shock and rage, the blood in his face mounting as he struggles to stay on top of the unfolding story.

'When did you receive this amazing news?' Gemma asks

him. She has recovered her poise and is concentrating on his response.

'Someone is playing a cruel and deliberate trick to distract from this important debate.' His skin glistens. A red sheen that a camera highlights with merciless clarity. 'It's not the first time my family has been targeted in this outrageous way.' His voice rasps as he struggles to continue. His mouth must be dry and bereft of words that sound convincing.

The atmosphere in the studio sharpens even further as more phones are taken out of pockets and handbags. Most of the audience are reading their screens. Gemma must still be receiving information from the control desk if her alert stance, and the way she touches her earpiece is any indication.

My sons sit rigid on either side of me as a second camera zooms in on us. We're calm, locked in our determination to see this scenario through to the end. A woman seated near the front begins to cry. Her tears are immediately caught on camera.

'If that's the truth, then why have I received information that your daughter is in the audience?' Gemma asks.

Aloysius's eyes swivel sideways. That's all that's needed to reveal his panic. No amount of make-up can disguise his colour, or the twitches in his cheek and temple.

'It's not true.' He speaks too loudly, his harshness emphasising his frustration. 'Fake news has been the ugliest element of this campaign. What you're doing now is giving credence to a disgraceful hoax.'

'If that's the case, would the woman who claims to be Isabelle Russell please make herself known to us?' says Gemma.

Gaby rises from her seat in the back row. The audience turn from their screens to gaze at her as she descends the steps towards the debate arena. Their awed expressions suggest they are in the presence of an apparition. As if testing this possibility, a woman reaches out to touch her.

To me, Gaby has never looked more beautiful or more

dangerous. In this stunned atmosphere it seems as if her feet barely touch the ground. I stand and draw her to me. We glide across the space that separates decades of deceit from the truth and, together, we stand before Aloysius.

I know the words of Cormac's letter to our daughter off by heart. Diving into his words, I've lost myself briefly in his arms and in the strength of his resolve to love me until his dying day.

Is love enough to forgive him for keeping his secret until seconds before his death? How many times was he tempted to reveal the truth to me? I'll never know the answer. That's the way of it, sometimes. Not every question has an answer, and graves are filled with those that remained unspoken. Do I forgive him in this moment as his truth is rolled out for public consumption?

How can I not? His reason makes sense, even though it sliced like a blade through my heart.

# FIFTY-ONE

## CORMAC

*My dearest daughter,*

*Please come home. I'm nearing the end of my life. I need to talk to you. I tried to do so in New York. I lacked the courage to speak then, but Death now has me by the ankles and is determined to succeed.*

*I want to leave this world with a clear conscience. I've destroyed the life of a woman I've always loved with a deep and abiding passion. Her name is Maria. I met her when I was a boy. A skinny, neglected child with no family and no hope of a future.*

*I've told you very little about St Alexis, the orphanage where I grew up. Named after the patron saint of pilgrims and beggars, it was to the latter that we lads belonged and we were never allowed to forget it. The only time I felt like a pilgrim was when I visited Beech Park.*

*You can't imagine what it was like to go from the atmosphere of fear and hatred at St Alexis to Beech Park. It was as if I'd travelled from hell to heaven when I walked from one set of gates through another. Light and warmth, good food and Maria.*

*I loved her beyond reason and was still crazed from it when I met Cassie. She was my salvation but what I felt for her in those early years of our marriage was gratitude. In time, I discovered that love can grow from the most fragile stalk – always remember that Gaby – and I was content... or as content as a man can be with the burden I was forced to carry.*

*I need to get to the point of my letter. I can only write a few lines at a time. Cassie comes in and out, and her concern overpowers me, as does guilt. By contacting you am I betraying her? I must trust you. Make sure that whatever decision you make does not harm her... or Maria.*

*If I'd succeeded in falling out of love with Maria, then, maybe, I could go to my grave content to remain silent. Ignorance is bliss or so we're told yet we're also expected to believe that the truth can set us free.*

*Forgive me, Gaby, but I must tell you that that my real name is Cormac Gallagher and Maria Russell is your mother. Oh, my darling child, I feel your shock. It will be followed by anger and outrage but please... please read on and try to understand the decision I made.*

*Maria's father was a politician. One of the few good ones. Maria was his only child. We played with her occasionally during summer holidays and always on a day after Christmas. By us, I mean myself and Paddy Murdock, who slept in the next bed to mine at St Alexis.*

*Her mother had died young, so this loss helped her to understand the hollowness of our lives without parents. She adored her father. I watched them together and saw what my life could be like if my father had chosen to stay rather than running away.*

*George made it possible for me to join the Garda Síochána. Being a policeman gave me a sense of belonging to something that mattered. I studied hard and was assigned to the Special Detective Unit, the security force responsible for protecting politicians. When I saw Maria again, she was married to Aloysius Russell and George was dead.*

*I'd seen her wedding photo in the papers and always believed she'd replaced George with another father figure. But Aloysius was not like her father. I'd heard stories about him from the detectives who provided his security. Rude, arrogant, and unscrupulous, they said. It didn't take long to verify those facts when I was assigned to protect him.*

*Heart-stopping, that's what it was when I saw Maria again. Even now, thinking about her, I'm transported back to that moment. She pretended not to recognise me. I took my cue from her and did the same. Later, I would discover that her husband was jealous to the point of insanity, not from love or passion, but from the need to possess.*

*We took such risks. Secret meetings. We were in love, dizzy from the force of it. She had a son. She would lose him if she left. We spent one night together when Aloysius was abroad. He'd been assigned another garda detective to replace me. That was the night you were conceived.*

*I never provided protection for Aloysius again. Instead, I was accused of having links with a drug dealer and fired from the force. I was unable to find other work. Eventually, I became homeless. It doesn't take long, Gaby. It's a domino effect. I won't go into details but if you can imagine those dominoes collapsing one after another, then that was how it happened.*

*I coped. St Alexis had given me the mental stamina to deal with the meaningless abuse that is meted out to the homeless. I lived in a tent on the derelict site of a demolished factory. I blamed fate for my changed circumstances and only discovered how my career had been ruined when Aloysius Russell stopped one night at the tent where I was sleeping and urinated on me.*

*He'd hired a detective to spy on Maria. Ironic that I, trained in detection, failed to notice him. Truth is, I was blinded by love.*

*One night together. That was all the evidence Aloysius needed to understand the reason for Maria's resistance to his advances and why, a month later, knowing she was pregnant with my child, she returned to his bed.*

*He'd organised everything. His car was parked nearby. You were swaddled in a blanket and asleep on the back seat. Next to you was a bundle containing forged passports with new identities, a birth certificate, and tickets for a ferry to take us to England in the dead of night.*

*He told me that Maria had given birth to you. His exact words were, 'She delivered a bastard, just as your own whore mother did. And just like your whore mother, I won't raise a bastard.'*

*He handed you over to me, along with a backpack containing three feeds, nappies, and an envelope with one hundred pounds. Was that an act of kindness? No. A starving baby and a homeless man could easily be traced. He gave us just enough to survive until we reached England and could merge into the throng.*

*If the truth was exposed, he'd make certain that anyone close to me, any children yet to be born, a wife I'd yet to meet, would be killed. As for me, with my ruined reputation, I'd be accused of stealing you. Who were the gardaí likely to believe? We both knew the answer.*

*I can't remember much of what he said after that. All I heard was his threat to kill Maria if I ever went to the police. He described how he would do it. An overdose. The verdict: suicide by grief.*

*I never doubted his determination. He had no humanity and would not hesitate to carry out his threat.*

*Twenty-eight years have gone by since then. I discarded the identity he gave me as soon as I'd the means to do so. I've seen how he thrived on your disappearance, milking sympathy votes, and money, from the public. I can't go to my grave and leave him free... but what am I to do? I'm tormented.*

*Cassie was drawn into my story through no fault of her own. I was forced to tell her how you came into our lives. But not the full truth. She believes I stole you as an act of revenge when Maria turned her back on me. It was easier that way. She doesn't know how dangerous Aloysius is. The strings he would pull if she reported him to the guards. She had her own reasons for staying silent, but I couldn't take that risk.*

*One night of passion, and the price Maria has paid is incalculable. So, also, is the burden Cassie was forced to bear. I'll be dead soon. I welcome the release it will bring but I can't carry this secret to my grave. I must think about your rights. A child conceived in love and reared on deception. Should you be protected from the truth or be made aware of who you are?*

*I stole you, not by deed, but by my silence. I should have found the courage to confront Aloysius Russell. Was it fear that prevented me from exposing him? Yes. The risk was too high. He'd pulled powerful strings to ruin my career. What if he used the same tactics again and carried out his threats to destroy everyone I love? It was easy to find reasons for not acting, but the time has come to ask myself this question.*

*Was it love, rather than fear, that tied my hands? Love that kept me silent? That love for you, my daughter, was it the reason that overrode every decision I made to reveal the truth? All that death will do is release me from the burden of having to answer such a question.*

*Another day has passed, Gaby. I can't hesitate any longer. I must give this letter to Freida? She has agreed to post it for me. Come to my side as soon as you read it and we can decide how to take Aloysius Russell down.*

*He made one mistake that night. His fingerprints were all over those passports. My years in the force were not wasted. They gave me the skills to record and copy every whorl on his deceitful fingers. You'll find the passports and the copies of his fingerprints in a safe deposit box in my bank. My bank manager has the key and instructions to hand them over to you. I pray that you'll have the resolve to bring him to justice.*

*Come quickly.*

*I love you, Gaby.*

*Dad*

# FIFTY-TWO

## GABRIELLE

One year later

I sit between my husband and my mother as we wait in the courtroom for the jury to deliver their verdict. My half-sisters and half-brothers are also with us, all of us together and united, as we have been since the beginning of this trial. Maria's eyes are downcast, her fingers entwined with mine. Fingers are important. Those whorls, loops and arches that print our unique identity is the reason we're here today. Forensics at its finest made it possible to bring Aloysius to trial.

His defence team argued that trial by social media had already taken place with the online publication of my father's letter during the presidential debate. The judge decided otherwise, which means that the courtroom is packed with media and spectators.

When Maria decided to release the letter my father wrote to me, the presidential debate was the only platform she considered. She understood the risk of being consumed in the inferno that would follow. My father's admission of their forbidden love affair and all that stemmed from its force could have destroyed her. She stood her ground and refused to express shame or regret that she once loved wildly, and wilfully.

Aloysius, unable to cope with the scandal, immediately withdrew from the campaign. Killian, corralled by guidelines that forbid the publication of information that cannot be verified, had to stand on the sidelines as an exposé that would have enhanced his reputation trended internationally on social media.

Trabawn was besieged. The house where I was reared became a shrine to curiosity until the new owners took out an injunction that forbade anyone from trampling over their garden with their cameras and microphones.

Had Cassie been able to foretell what would happen if the facts of my abduction became public? Like Cassandra, her namesake, had she suffered the despair of knowing she would never be believed until it was too late?

The jury has returned. Expressions sphinx-like, they file into their seats and wait for the chairperson to announce their verdict. Guilty on a charge of kidnapping.

The judge interrupts the excited buzz that has broken out in court. He speaks directly to Aloysius. 'I'm obliged under current sentencing guidelines to limit your term of imprisonment on the kidnapping charge of Isabelle Russell to seven years. This sentence does not reflect the seriousness of your crime or the cruelty with which you carried it out. You held a position of authority in government for decades and were actively engaged in a campaign to become Ireland's head of state with the knowledge that you'd caused the greatest unhappiness to the woman you claimed to love. You argued in your defence that the child in question, Isabelle Russell, who was three weeks old when she was removed by you from her cradle, was not your legitimate daughter. You also claimed to have serious issues with anger management and jealously. I've refused to take such issues into consideration. You, Mr Aloysius Russell, come across as a man without compassion and lacking in humanity. You lived a lie for twenty-nine years by repeatedly deceiving your wife and the public. The Garda Síochána was forced to waste valuable police resources in a search that was instigated by your actions. The file on Isabelle's disappearance remained open until you were brought to justice. I hope that your imprisonment will allow you time to reflect on your crimes.'

He sentences Aloysius to a custodial sentence of seven years for my kidnapping. On a second charge of perjury, he's sentenced to a further ten years imprisonment, which he will serve consecutively.

Aloysius remains impassive as he listens to the judge delivering a judgement that will place him behind bars for seventeen years. Lying under oath has consequences.

I take a last look at him before he's led away. This brutal man with his impressive bearing still stands tall. There is venom in his gaze as he takes in the court and all who came to see justice done. The evidence on which he was convicted was slender, yet it withstood everything his defence team brought against it. He'll appeal, of course. Maybe he'll succeed in reducing his sentence. Whatever he decides to do no longer matters. He's lost what he treasures most: the power to govern was his aphrodisiac, and the weapon that finally brought him down.

We stand outside the court, two families conjoined, and face the waiting media. Maria reads a joint statement that thanks all who supported us in the months leading to the trial and throughout the long hours in court. She holds her head high, as she did when Aloysius's defence team savaged her reputation and demanded intimate details of her short-lived affair with my father. Now, it is over and all she wants to do is continue to work with her foundation and look forward to becoming a grandmother.

In three months, I'll give birth to a daughter. Killian will be with me as our child forges her way into the world. I'll call her Cassandra and never abbreviate her beautiful name. It's a forlorn attempt to seek forgiveness from the woman who gave me love until the evilness of Aloysius Russell opened her own path to hellish guilt.

On difficult days, when her ghost sits too heavily on my shoulders, I wonder what direction my life would have taken had I chosen to believe my father's fevered confession was nothing more than a slip of the tongue. What if all I heard was a whispered endearment. '*I love you*'?

Instead, I allowed his dying words to become a roar that silenced everything in its path except the truth.

# EPILOGUE

## GABRIELLE

His roar has become a lullaby that I hum to my daughter when she awakens in the small hours. That's when the stars are at their brightest and the new day is but a sliver on the horizon. My hold on Cassandra is at its closest, then. I think about fortified walls and armoured guards, a Rapunzel tower that no one dare climb.

Are such fears normal? Do they come with the mantle of motherhood or am I re-experiencing the moment Aloysius Russell lifted me from my cradle with nothing on his mind except revenge?

Sometimes, my phone bleeps and my mother's name is visible on the screen. I read her comforting texts and know that she is also awake and remembering.

My fears are banished when morning breaks and Cassandra lies between us, her downy head resting against Killian's chest. Our little prophetess, her mouth a pucker of contentment. Our future happiness written wide in the searching gaze of her dark-green eyes.

# A LETTER FROM LAURA

Dear Reader,

Thank you for reading *Not Their Daughter*. If you enjoyed it and want to keep up to date with all my latest releases, just sign up at the following link. Your email address will never be shared and you can unsubscribe at any time.

*www.bookouture.com/laura-elliot*

Thank you for following the trail of discovery that began with three words. *I stole you*.

I clearly remember the instant they came to me. I was driving my two young grandchildren home to their parents and they, in the spirit of rivalry, were attempting to out-sing each other's versions of *The Wheels on the Bus*. Despite the noise from the back seat, those three words echoed clearly in my head. They came unaccompanied. No free-flowing stream of consciousness. Nor did they trigger an idea that would fit perfectly in a concise outline for my next book.

The words continued to buzz like a repetitive and obsessive bee around my head over the next few weeks. I'd already written one book about a child who had been stolen at birth (titled, unsurprisingly, *Stolen Child*) and had not intended returning to that theme.

Now, faced with the task of writing a new book, it seemed as if my Muse had decided otherwise. I wrote down my three words and left them to mellow. Finally, they began to talk to me. Under what circumstances could those words be uttered? Who would utter them? Who would hear them? What would they unleash?

Like ghosts arriving on a midnight train, my characters came into view. Gabrielle Grace emerged, followed by her father. Then Cassie and the twins, Maria, and her family.... and Aloysius. As the story progressed, I realised it was as much about the power Aloysius wielded as it was about Gabrielle's search for her true identity.

I'm fascinated by politics and how those in thrall to its hubris can corrupt, deceive, control, and manipulate the truth. And how they can fall to earth with shattering suddenness.

The character, Aloysius Russell, is entirely fictitious, as are all my characters. However, I've witnessed enough such campaigns to know how tumultuous they can be. As the bravest go forward, the media sharpens its knives, knowing how a well-oiled political machine can suddenly come undone during the campaign.

I enjoyed setting the action within such a fertile battle-ground yet often paused over those months of writing to reflect on how those three words *I Stole You* had brought me on such an intriguing journey.

I hope you enjoyed reading *Not Their Daughter* as much as I enjoyed writing it. If you did so, and would like to leave a review on Amazon, I'd appreciate it very much.

Warmest wishes,

Laura Elliot

# KEEP IN TOUCH WITH LAURA

www.lauraelliotauthor.com

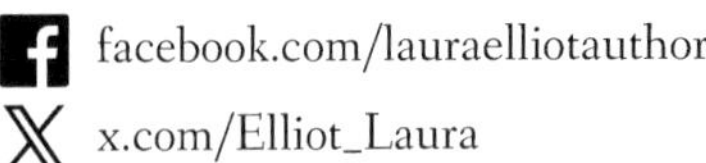

facebook.com/lauraelliotauthor

x.com/Elliot_Laura

## ACKNOWLEDGEMENTS

Once again, at the conclusion of another book, I find myself emerging from an imaginary world into one that keeps a steady hand on my real life and welcomes me back each time.

I'd like to express my thanks to those who supported me throughout the time I was writing *Not Their Daughter*. First, as always, is my husband, Seán Considine, who never falters in his belief that I'll bring each book to its conclusion and is able to drown out my belief to the contrary during those dark, doubtful moments.

To my family, Tony, Ciara and Michelle, my sons-in-law, Roddy and Harry, and my daughter-in-law, Louise. Each in their own unique way form an arch of love and support. A special shout out to the even younger generation, my grand-children, Romy, Ava, Nina and Seán, who fill my life with joy and laughter.

Thank you to my editor, Natasha Harding. Her encouragement and keen-eyed analysis of my story added to the pleasure of writing *Not Their Daughter*. She was ably assisted by my copyeditor, Belinda Jones, and my proofreader, Claire Rushbrook. Their diligence was much appreciated, as was the support I received from Jen Shannon, managing editorial executive. A word of thanks also to PR and media manager Noelle Holten for the exciting publicity opportunities she created around the publication of *Not Their Daughter*. The cover is a delight and was designed by Lisa Brewster. I love it. Thank you.

To my dear friends who know when to call and coax me

from my writing cave with wine and good food, you are a special part of my life. I thank you for your friendships. Long may our leisurely lunches last.

And you, my reader, where would I be without you? Thank you for buying my books, for reviewing them, and personally contacting me. Your letters are always a delight to read.

# PUBLISHING TEAM

**Turning a manuscript into a book requires the efforts of many people. The publishing team at Bookouture would like to acknowledge everyone who contributed to this publication.**

**Audio**
Alba Proko
Sinead O'Connor
Melissa Tran

**Commercial**
Lauren Morrissette
Hannah Richmond
Imogen Allport

**Cover design**
The Brewster Project

**Data and analysis**
Mark Alder
Mohamed Bussuri

**Editorial**
Natasha Harding
Lizzie Brien

**Copyeditor**
Belinda Jones

**Proofreader**
Claire Rushbrook

**Marketing**
Alex Crow
Melanie Price
Occy Carr
Cíara Rosney
Martyna Młynarska

**Operations and distribution**
Marina Valles
Stephanie Straub

**Production**
Hannah Snetsinger
Mandy Kullar
Jen Shannon
Ria Clare

**Publicity**
Kim Nash
Noelle Holten
Jess Readett
Sarah Hardy

**Rights and contracts**
Peta Nightingale
Richard King
Saidah Graham